Where the Campaign Ends

A Novel

by

J.P. Dalton

This is a work of fiction. Names, characters, businesses, places, events, locales, and incidents are either the products of the author's imagination or used in a fictitious manner. Any resemblance to actual persons, living or dead, or actual events is purely coincidental.

WHERE THE CAMPAIGN ENDS

Copyright © 2018 J.P. Dalton

Editing by Stephanie Parent

To Kathie, without whom I would never

have seen Del Mar

CHAPTER ONE

"You feeling okay, Boss? You look like hell."

Riley Evans stood next to her longtime employer Ryan Williams in the wings of the Alys Stephens Performing Arts Center in Birmingham, Alabama. Outside, furious storms rolled through north-central Alabama, and the pair could feel more than hear the muffled thunder rumbling through the building.

Williams had spent the past two decades working as a political consultant, but this night and the months preceding had been well outside his normal experience. He surveyed the scene unfolding around him at the Republican Party's election results watch party with a mix of dismay and resignation. Across the stage, a jazz band attempted to infuse energy into the cavernous room with a series of old standards. Two big-screen televisions flanked the ballroom, currently showing welcome messages but ready to tune to local television as soon as polls closed and results started to come in. Candidates for offices big and small, from the hopeful future Senator Merrick Comstock to incumbent County Commissioner Gloria Castille, sat with well-wishers in various green rooms throughout the facility. And high above it all, tucked safely in netting in the rafters, red, white and blue balloons were waiting to be released in a deluge when Comstock's victory had been assured. Dozens of well-dressed men and women mingled throughout the hall, drinking flutes of champagne and snacking on hors d'oeuvres delivered by waiters in faux black-tie attire. Husbands and wives, mothers and fathers, sons and daughters, all had gathered together for what they hoped to be a traditional celebration in what had been the most non-traditional of years.

For all the people there, it was the lack of attendance that most caught Ryan's attention. Only a few hundred people had braved the thunderstorms pummeling Jefferson County to come to the party, rather than the 1,300 the center normally held. At least, Ryan hoped the droves stayed away because of the rain and not the equally stormy campaign the state had endured for the past few months. The air felt heavy from the humidity outside and tasted stale as it was circulated through the building's heating system.

Ryan let Riley's question sit and turned toward his assistant, who was more partner than employee after years working together. "We've never had anything like this," he said.

"Rain happens."

He glanced over his left shoulder and smirked. "I'm not talking about the rain. What in the hell are we doing here?"

Riley's brows rose in surprise. This was the closest to an admission of error she had heard from the ever-confident Ryan since they'd met. "Are you feeling okay? You're not really getting introspective on me after all these years, are you?" Riley put a hand on Ryan's arm and turned him to face her. "You know the rules. Hell, Boss, you wrote the rules. We come in, we do the job. Win or lose, we do the best we can with what we have and that's that. No emotions, no regrets."

Ryan smiled thinly. "Did I really make you that cynical?"

"I'm really not, not like you," she said. "If I was I wouldn't have Nick waiting for me when this is done."

"You're really choosing this moment to harp on me again for not settling down with someone?"

"Not at all. But sometimes having a better half keeps a person from making a stupid decision, like coming across the country to get the wrong candidate elected."

"That's what I have you for," he grunted.

Ryan turned back toward the half-empty auditorium, Riley following suit. "The rain's going to screw with our numbers."

"It happens."

Riley took a look at the man standing beside her. He looked as he always did on Election Night. A tailored black suit accenting his trim 6-foot-2 frame, pinpoint white button-down shirt and, on this evening, a violet paisley tie. *Power comes from the man*, he always told her, *not the tie*. Straight brown hair suspended with product and combed up and to the right. Not the slightest hint of a five o'clock shadow appearing on his square jawline.

But, despite his usual outward appearance, something was different. This was the fourth election cycle they had worked together, and it was the first time she had seen Ryan melancholy as they awaited results. Even with defeat certain, he always had been able to draw energy from the end of the campaign, like a high-schooler on the last day of school. As she watched him, a single, unexpected bead of sweat rolled from his forehead, down his nose and dripped onto his tie.

"Ryan."

He lifted his chin slightly in response.

"Seriously, are you feeling okay?"

"I'm just tired, Riley," he said. "I'm very, very tired."

***

Several hundred feet away in an auxiliary building, Merrick Ogden Comstock IV was holding court to a select group of advisers, friends and general hangers-on.

"The first thing I'm gonna do in the Senate is ban this shit," Comstock said, lifting his champagne glass and smashing it to the floor. He reached into a jacket pocket for his once-full flask of whiskey, took a long pull and passed it to the handful of men standing close to him.

"A man deserves a decent drink," one said with a smile.

"Goddamn right," Comstock agreed. "Especially after a pooch-screwing like this."

Comstock traced his family's roots in Alabama back three decades before the Civil War. He himself had already served four terms in the Alabama Legislature, three in the House and one in the Senate, before deciding it was his time to move into the big leagues, the United States Senate. There were four things that Merrick Ogden Comstock the IV loved above all others—bourbon, women, Crimson Tide football and the sound of his own voice. Only the latter would prove to be a significant barrier to victory.

Three months earlier, the candidate had been speaking to a crowd on a sweltering day in Montgomery when a man near the back of the group held aloft a tattered Confederate flag. Ryan spoke into his Apple watch and security slowly made their way over to the man, asking him to lower the stars and bars. Comstock, seeing the movement in the crowd, stopped in the middle of his stump speech on Washington gridlock and pointed.

"Hey there, leave him be," the candidate said. The two security guards stopped, and Ryan's heart felt like it did as well. "Sir, my great-great-great-great-great-granddaddy fought under Hood and Lee for Alabama, and I couldn't be prouder of it. Don't ever let anyone tell you that our heritage is something to be afraid of. You hold that flag high and wave it proud."

Ryan blanched. The Civil War and the lost cause certainly weren't among his talking points for Comstock. Within two days, that nine-point lead was down to five.

Ryan, Comstock and Comstock's chief adviser, Marianne Jewell, met that night and reached an agreement that the candidate would stick to his script no matter what. No one had sent that message to his supporters. At Comstock's next stop, a half-dozen stars-and-bars were waving at different places in the crowd. At the next, more than a dozen. While his numbers among the so-called Independents were sliding into oblivion, his overall percentage started to stabilize. Not a politician for nothing, Comstock abandoned his script entirely and started ad-libbing about "our heritage" being under attack, and crowds that had started to become far less diverse ate up every word of it. Soon his speeches devolved into rhetoric that would have been expected in the early 1960s.

Amazingly, only Ryan and Riley seemed to be concerned about the direction the campaign had taken, not to mention the political toxicity that would attach itself to anyone who had been part of it.

"If he doesn't cut this shit out, I'm outta here," he would tell Jewell.

"There's the fucking door, carpetbagger," she replied, knowing full well it was too late for Ryan to pull the abort handle. All he could do was go invisible as much as possible. No television appearances in defense of his candidate, no newspaper interviews either on or off the record. Work quietly to distance himself and his firm with comments on deep background from well-disguised sources, never from himself or Riley. And most importantly, get his own talking points straight for when this train wreck came into the station, whether it was successful or on fire.

Jewell, naturally, shared none of Ryan's concerns as she looked at Comstock on this long-awaited election night and smiled proudly. He was a true son of the South, carrier of a proud heritage that was slowly being stripped in a new age of political correctness. If people didn't understand that, the hell with them. And that could go double for Ryan, the carpetbagger from somewhere out West who hadn't set foot in the state until his first check cashed.

"Word is the turnout wasn't that great because of the storms," one of Comstock's cronies said.

"Doesn't matter," Comstock said with a wave of the flask. "These people know me. Hell, they'd cross a flooding Tallapoosa to make sure I'm in DC protecting them from all those crooks."

Jewell walked over to where Comstock stood, took the flask out of his hand and took a quick sip. "We know they did, Merrick. The tallies will show it soon."

***

In truth, Ryan was feeling much more than tired. Walking the fifty feet from the side of the stage to the small room he had commandeered as his office, he became short of breath. Ryan sat in one of the well-worn blue recliners and put his hand to his chest, his heart racing as he consciously tried to take a series of deep breaths to bring his body back under control, Riley close on his heels.

"I swear," he said quietly, "I'm not going to let this bastard be the death of me." *He just might*, a small voice said inside his head.

Stress was part and parcel of his job. Long nights ended with a quick drink of whatever was handy and a sleeping pill or two to battle the ever-running dialogs and to-do lists running through his head. Mornings began with several cups of coffee to shake off the hangover from the sleeping pills. An accelerated heartbeat was less a cause for concern than just another Monday.

But this? It felt as if one of the elephants in the Republican motif in the auditorium had come to life and sat squarely on his chest.

Imagine the headlines if you keel over right here, the voice said. Hotshot carpetbagging campaigner dead at 48.

Shit.

"Riley," he said between gulps of air. "Find me a doctor. Quickly."

***

When Riley and the doctor came into the room, Ryan was sitting on the floor, his back against the wall and legs straight out in front of him. He had loosened his tie and unfastened the top two buttons of his shirt. His suit jacket was folded neatly on a nearby chair.

"Ryan!" she shouted, crossing the room in three strides and kneeling down beside him, the EMT close behind.

"It's just fatigue," he said unconvincingly. A loud crack of thunder boomed through the building, causing all three to jump and drawing a mix of gasps and cheers Ryan could hear through the wall.

"Did you fall, sir?" the EMT asked.

Ryan shook his head and looked toward Riley. "We lose anyone yet?"

"Not yet," she said. "I think they feel safer in here than out on the roads right now."

"How bad is it?"

"A couple of inches of rain. I'm told that's a drizzle around these parts."

Ryan smiled and started a laugh which turned into a cough. "I don't suppose we can send Comstock out for sandwiches."

Riley took his hand and laughed.

The EMT stared at his watch as he took Ryan's pulse, then reached into a medical kit for a blood pressure cuff.

"How does it look?"

11

"Just breathe normally, sir."

"Like I haven't been trying to do that for the last twenty minutes."

Riley placed a finger on his lips. "For once, shut up."

The EMT wrote down the numbers and started asking Ryan a series of questions—did his left side hurt, was there any numbness in his fingers or toes, was he dizzy, did he feel nauseated. As Ryan was answering no repeatedly, Riley's phone rang. She stood quickly and moved to the far side of the small room. The first results, Ryan thought. He half listened to the EMT talk about his pulse of ninety-something and his blood pressure of 150 some-odd over some other number also over 100 as he watched Riley's expression turn grim. "Text what you have," she said quietly and walked back to Ryan's side.

"The rain keep our people home?"

Riley forced a smile she didn't feel. "It's not important," she said, "it's still early."

"Sir, I think we need to get you to the hospital."

Ryan shook his head with effort. "Not a chance. We're not done here yet."

"Ryan..." Riley said.

"I said we're not done." He looked the EMT in the eyes. "Is it a heart attack?"

"I can't be certain."

"Guess."

"I don't guess, sir."

"Then I'll guess for you and say no," Ryan said, slowly rising to his feet and shuffling to the recliner. "I don't care what we need to do, but I'm not leaving this building with one percent of the precincts in and an auditorium full of people."

"Half full," Riley corrected him.

Ryan shot her a pained glance. "Remind me to fire you before I die."

***

Nearly 300 miles to the south, Ronny Rounds was wishing he had the opportunity to fire someone. Rounds was a fishing magnate from Bayou La Batre, hard against the Gulf of Mexico, and traditionally one of the largest donors to the Republican Party in the state. Merrick Ogden Comstock IV was his own pet project, an old-fashioned water carrier who would head to Washington, enjoy the perks of being a senator and never forget the man who got him there when a favor might be needed.

It was Rounds who had personally hired Ryan based on his reputation within Republican campaign circles, flying him to Alabama on his private jet. Rounds knew Ryan had never worked west of the Continental Divide but, after all, politics was politics.

"What do you know about Alabama, Ryan?" Rounds had asked at that first meeting.

"They tend to win a lot of football games, Ronny." Ryan had never met the man but, at this stage of his career, he was well past the days of using words like mister and sir, especially when the caller flied him cross-country just to talk.

"That they do. Now tell me what you really know."

"Honestly, Ronny, just what I read in the papers and hear on the coconut telegraph. It's on the wrong side of the Mississippi."

"I see." Rounds leaned over his desk, the blue waters of the Gulf fading into a gray horizon behind him. "What exactly would it take for you to cross the river?"

As the early reports from around the state came in, Rounds was ready to send Ryan back across the Mississippi as fast as possible. A local, he fumed, would have handled the whole stars-and-bars thing without a blink. It was their history, for Christ's sake. And when Comstock decided to pretend he was George Wallace and paraphrase the state's most famous politician-slash-segregationist?

"Let us ride to the call of freedom-loving blood that is in us and send our answer to the tyranny that clanks its chains upon the South," Comstock said at a rally in Huntsville ten days before the election. "In the name of the greatest people that have ever trod this earth, I draw a line on the dust and toss the gauntlet before the feet of tyranny and say... Alabamans first now, Alabamans first tomorrow and Alabamans first forever. God bless you and God bless the great state of Alabama."

Rounds wished he had thought of it himself. Sure, Wallace had distanced himself from that line and others before he passed into the great beyond, but hell, Rounds's own daddy had made a point of teaching him this little bit of state history. "Never forget the pride that is being an Alabaman," he told Ronny.

Ryan Williams? He had wanted to "walk it back," whatever the hell that meant, explain that Comstock was just pledging to take care of his own back home, like these yokels from Dixie didn't already understand Comstock's point.

Yes, Comstock fell in the polls, but that was what happened when you tried to apologize for being a proud son of Alabama, Rounds thought.

Proof of the damage done by Ryan was being delivered to Rounds with each update showing Comstock trailing by one to two percentage points, not just in the baby blue, less than purely conservative stripe of counties across the state's middle. Even down here on the Gulf, where Comstock vowed to help the shrimping and fishing industries once he got to office, the margins were either thinly in favor of Comstock or moving in the wrong direction.

It was time, Rounds thought, to find someone's ass to chew.

CHAPTER TWO

The building shook as a deafening crack of thunder rolled through the auditorium. A barely audible sizzling sound followed, and the lights dimmed. Ryan felt the hair on his arms stand on end as the air was filled with the nearly palatable taste of electricity. Children cried and parents gasped at the ferocity of the storm.

Not that any of this mattered to Rounds.

"What in the hell was that?" he yelled into the phone.

"Divine retribution," Ryan answered quietly, nodding toward the door for Riley to see what was happening in the main room.

"What did you say, boy?" Rounds screamed even louder.

Ryan took as deep a breath as he could. "It was a lightning strike, Ronny. Felt like it was right on top of us."

"Lightning strike?"

"Yeah, Ronny, the kind that comes with the thunderstorms that were in your neck of the woods this morning."

"I didn't call for a fucking weather report, Williams."

I don't need the aggravation right now. "Look, Ronny. I get that you're not happy with the early returns. Give it some time. But

I've got to get some sort of crowd control going before people disappear into this mess." Another peal of thunder boomed overhead, albeit quieter than the last. The storms were slowly moving away.

"I paid you to win this thing," Rounds said.

"And it still may be money well spent. I've got work to do," Ryan said, abruptly ending the call. Somewhere in a side theater, Comstock was feeling neglected and Jewell was texting every few minutes demanding to know where Ryan was. Outside, the maelstrom continued delivering drenching rain and howling wind. Then there was the small matter of the panic-inducing lightning strike.

Ryan took another too-shallow deep breath, pushed himself out of the recliner with his hands and turned toward the dressing-room mirror. Dark circles had formed under his eyes and his normally ruddy complexion was pasty from the pain. Doesn't matter, he thought. Ryan stretched to his full height, reached up to tighten and straighten his tie and took another breath. He then walked slowly out the door to the main hallway, nearly colliding with Riley in the process.

"What are you doing?" she said, grabbing Ryan by the forearm.

"Someone needs to say something."

"So you think death personified strolling on stage is going to be reassuring?"

Ryan smiled through teeth gritted against the weight bearing down on his chest. "Seriously, remind me again to fire you."

He continued down the hallway, gathered himself on the edge of the stage and walked purposefully to the podium. *This should be worth a Golden Globe*, he thought as he took hold of both sides of the podium in a white-knuckled grip.

"Ladies and gentlemen," he started before becoming less formal. "Folks, do me a favor and come into the hall and away from those windows."

As he waited, he glanced over his shoulder and noticed the television screens were dark. The satellite signal had disappeared when the storm started to move through the area.

"Folks, as you may have noticed there's one heck of a storm going on out there," he said, earning some nervous laughter. "So let's do this. Go ahead, bring your food and drinks on in and hang out in here and listen to the band." He nodded toward the jazz band, offstage taking a break. "I know the signs say not to bring that stuff in, but we'll worry about the mess later." *That should have been the campaign slogan.* "We'll get the TVs back on the results as soon as we can, but I can tell you that, weather aside, things are looking pretty good so far." *As long as you don't fact-check me with your smartphones.* "But with the weather, let the little ones curl up in your lap and take a nap because y'all are better off in here for now. So, really, thanks for coming out and be patient with us while we work everything out. Sound good?"

The band came back on stage as Ryan left to light applause, walking with a confident stride he didn't at all feel. As he came offstage, he took Riley by the wrist, walked her out of view and dropped heavily to a knee, gasping. The EMT emerged from the shadows, picked Ryan up by his elbow and helped him back into the dressing room.

"Sir, I have to insist..."

"The hospital's not an option."

"Look, Ryan," Riley said. "The damn thing is two blocks away. You've got to go. I can handle this side of things."

Ryan shook his head again. "The last thing I need is to have video of an ambulance rolling out of here showing on CNN."

"Seriously, that's your concern?" Riley asked in exasperation. She took her purse off the desk and took out her keys. "Jesus, we can drive you in my car, isn't that right?" She turned toward the EMT with a sharp look that indicated argument would be unwelcome.

"Um, ma'am..."

She turned back to Ryan triumphantly. "See? That's settled. There's a stage door in the back where he can meet you, get you over to the emergency room and get you checked out."

"And what are you going to do here?"

Riley smiled and bent into a shallow curtsy. "Playing the role of Edith Wilson this evening, Riley Evans." Edith was President Woodrow Wilson's second wife who, after his husband's serious stroke, worked tirelessly and successfully to mask the true severity of his incapacity.

If he had felt better, Ryan would have laughed, but doing so now would take too much effort.

"Let's do it," he said, cringing. "Quietly."

***

The cold downpour felt refreshing on Ryan's pain-tightened face. He closed his eyes and turned his head upward into the falling rain for a few seconds before sliding into the passenger seat of Riley's car. Water coated the roadways, but the hospital was only two blocks and a pair of right turns away from the Stephens Center. Ryan tried to step out of the car when they arrived at the emergency room but was gently pushed back into his seat by Riley, who would be returning as soon as he was checked in.

"Wait for him," she said as the EMT jogged through the sliding glass doors and called for help. A moment later he returned with an attendant pushing a wheelchair in front of her.

"I'm not being pushed in that goddamn thing," he said, trying again to stand.

"It's policy, sir," the EMT said. "They're taking you straight back."

"There's no wait?"

"Not when it's a cardiac case." He looked up at Riley. "Did you want to come back, miss?"

Riley looked down at Ryan, who shook his head. "Get back there—I'm not going anywhere."

18

She leaned over and kissed his forehead as tears welled in her eyes.

"Christ," he said, "I'm not dying."

"I know." She started walking back to the driver's side door when Ryan called out to her.

"Maybe I won't fire you after all," he said.

"I'll just quit instead," she answered, ducking into the car and disappearing into the rain.

The attendant watched Riley's red hair disappear into the car and gave Ryan an approving look. "Is she..." he asked, his voice trailing off.

Ryan looked at the attendant and then glanced at the retreating taillights. "Riley?" he said with a chuckle. "Hell, she's far too smart for that."

***

Riley returned to the Stephens Center, stopping first at Comstock's holding room and apologizing for the delay in answering Jewell's dozen texts. She explained that Ryan was busy checking exit polling results from the northern part of the state. Two things were readily apparent—Comstock was well into his cups, and neither Jewell nor Comstock was happy with a lead that was hovering just under one percent more than four hours after the polls had closed.

"I'm supposed to have a mandate from the people," Comstock slurred, "not this couple thousand vote shit."

"A win is a win," Riley said patiently.

"I told that boss of yours that keeping Merrick to script was a mistake," Jewell added.

Not as big a mistake as letting him speak at all, Riley thought. "Maybe so," she said diplomatically, "but we both believe the victory we've been working for will come."

"Would be nice if he could be bothered to come in and say that," Jewell said with a sneer.

"I'm sure Ryan would rather be here with you all, too."

"Fuck it," Comstock said. "When do I give my acceptance speech?"

Riley looked down and took a deep breath. What in the world had caused Ryan to agree to work for this buffoon? "We probably want to wait until there's enough of a lead with enough precincts reporting that we can be sure of the win."

"When will that be?"

Opening her phone and glancing at the latest results, Riley shrugged. "I'd say you've got time to take a catnap, Mr. Comstock."

Jewell threw up her hands in frustration and marched over to a sagging Comstock as Riley quietly slipped back out the door.

***

Ryan shuddered at the chalky aftertaste in his mouth. Non-chewable aspirin, he decided, should never be chewed, at least not by someone with taste buds.

A blood-pressure cuff was wrapped around his left forearm, and a white plastic clip on his right index finger provided details on his pulse rate and his body's oxygen levels.

"Looks like you're having trouble breathing," the triage nurse said, glancing at the monitor now showing Ryan's oxygenation at 83 percent.

"No kidding," Ryan said, his strained voice dripping with sarcasm. "That little thing can tell you that?"

"It's always good to confirm," the nurse said without humor. "Are you able to unbutton your shirt so we can take an EKG?"

Ryan unfastened the first two buttons below the already open button and stopped. "It's a little harder than I remember."

"I've got it," the nurse said, releasing the remainder of the buttons. He helped Ryan sit forward, taking off his shirt and T-shirt, and picking up a stack of EKG lead sensors. One by one he removed the protective backing and placed the sticky underside against Ryan's skin. One each on his right and left

20

collarbones. One just to the right side of his sternum near the middle of his ribs. An arc of five starting opposite the one on the right and stretching across the bottom outline of his left breast. Two more, one on each side of his abdomen. Then he took the leads themselves and connected them to the metal tops of each sensor before asking Ryan to lean back and breathe as normally as possible.

"What do you do?" the nurse asked.

"When I'm not trying to pass out? I'm a campaign consultant."

The nurse nodded reflexively. "Yesterday was election day, wasn't it." Ryan realized it was now after midnight and nodded. "How did your person do?"

"The jury's still out."

After double-checking the connections, the nurse pressed a button on the EKG machine itself, and the needles started to move across the paper as they emitted a soft buzzing sound. The noise reminded Ryan of his old daisy-wheel printer circa 1990, only quieter. The nurse furrowed his brow as he watched the wave patterns print across the page.

"What is it?" Ryan asked.

"You say you don't have any pain in your chest?"

"No."

"Left side or left arm?"

"No."

"Any headache or stiffness in your neck."

Ryan shook his head. "Maybe a little stiffness, but it's been a long day."

The nurse nodded, stood quickly and poked his head around the curtain, motioning with his arm for someone to come into the room.

"What have you had to eat and when was the last time you ate?"

"A couple of tacos before the polls closed," Ryan said, his muscles stiffening as one of the on-duty doctors strode into the room. "What the hell's going on, Doc?"

The doctor nodded at the nurse, who started unfastening leads as quickly as possible. "Mr. Williams, you're in the middle of a cardiac episode," the doctor said. "We need to get you back to surgery."

Ryan stared, disbelieving. "Slow down. What do you mean by episode? A heart attack?"

"It's possible, if not today than in the past. But you've got some sort of blockage we need to get cleared like yesterday. Do you have a medical power of attorney?"

"What? No."

The nurse picked up the phone from the wall mount and pressed a button. An instant later, a ringing like a doorbell sounded from the intercom system, followed by a robotic voice. "Code blue, Triage three. Code blue, Triage three."

Ryan's eyes widened. "Code blue? Doesn't that mean I'm dying?"

"Not always," the doctor said. "It's a catchall."

"Meaning?"

The nurse smiled grimly. "Get the hell into that room as fast as you can." He removed the blood-pressure cuff from Ryan's arm and the oxygen monitor from his finger. Ryan's already fuzzy brain was spinning from the medical tag team. "We can take care of a medical POA in minutes. Is there family you want to list just in case?"

"No," Ryan said tersely.

"Okay," the nurse answered. "Is there anyone you need to call?"

Ryan thought of Riley but hesitated. "You're thinking I'm walking out of here?"

"I can't promise anything but the prognosis," the doctor started.

"Skip the jargon, Doc," Ryan interrupted.

"The sooner we move, the better things will look."

Ryan nodded as additional attendants arrived to wheel him through the emergency room, down a long hallway to pre-op. "I'm good," he said. A quick text would do.

***

Riley glanced at her phone as it buzzed in her hand.

"DOCS WANT TO RUN MORE TESTS," the text from Ryan read. "ANY NEWS?"

"RACE TOO CLOSE TO CALL," she responded. "COMSTOCK TOO DRUNK TO STAND."

Even on his way toward emergency surgery, Ryan couldn't help but smile. "SEND EVERYONE HOME. GET SOME SLEEP."

He turned off his phone and handed it to an attendant who was putting Ryan's jewelry and other personal items in a plastic bag with a drawstring across the top.

"Are they coming here?"

"Nah," Ryan said with confidence he didn't feel. "Let them get some sleep. I'll catch them up in the morning." *I hope.*

CHAPTER THREE

Ryan shivered against the cold of the operating room.

Why do they keep it so cold? he wondered. *And if I'm shivering, how is the doctor supposed to keep his hands steady? Shouldn't we be doing this on a beach?*

"My hands aren't going to shake because I'm not dressed in a gown and lying on a metal table, Mr. Williams."

Oh shit. Can this guy read minds, too?

The doctor's eyes crinkled, betraying a smile underneath his surgical mask. "No, Ryan, you're babbling out loud."

Much better. Wait, did I also say what I was thinking about the nurse or was that only in my mind?

"That one was private," she said. "Until now. Care to share?"

"I'm good now, thanks."

A few minutes earlier, the surgeon's attractive assistant had rubbed Ryan's inner right thigh with a numbing agent, which meant that the prick of the needle inserted in search of an artery merely stung rather than hurt like hell. Even that sting was eased by the drugs pumped into Ryan's system through the IV tube in his left elbow. Rather than general anesthesia, Ryan was given sedatives that would create a so-called "twilight" effect.

He'd be somewhat awake, more or less aware and at some moments less than coherent depending on what medicine caused which synapse to misfire.

The surgeon fed a thin guide wire and following catheter through Ryan's thigh, into his artery and then up to his heart akin to a plumber's snake searching for a hairball. Ryan felt a persistent pressure and a slight sense of discomfort which his brain told him would be pain if not for the really good shit the anesthesiologist was providing.

"Do you need me for this part?" he asked as the surgeon inserted a small amount of dye into Ryan's veins to help illuminate the blockage on angiograms to come.

"Are you planning on going somewhere?" the nurse asked.

"Metaphysically. I've got something to figure out."

She smiled. Nothing proved as entertaining as patients when the anesthesia hit. "And what would that be?"

"The meaning of life. Oh, and why I'm having a conversation with a zebra on such a serious occasion."

And with that, Ryan silently said goodbye to the zebra/nurse, closed his eyes and drifted into that hazy realm between waking and sleep where people can focus on long-ago memories, albeit with some oft creative alterations.

***

Ryan stood behind a folding table at the Chicago Days festival in Mesa, the city in which he had grown up. Once upon a time, this had been the Mesa Days festival—one of those salute-the-founders events that take place almost everywhere there's a high school marching band and Boy and Girl Scouts to march. That was before the Mesa City Council realized their largely imported population had more affection for Chicago than Mesa and was far more likely to drop considerable money celebrating everything from back home in weather fifty degrees warmer.

Next to Ryan was Charles Baxter—Charlie, or Doc—who was halfway through medical school after graduating with Ryan at nearby Arizona State University in Tempe. They had known each other since elementary school, a rarity given the imported population's near-constant mobility. Once people had uprooted themselves to come to the Phoenix area, they seemed less interested in creating roots than always moving in search of that bigger house in that seemingly nicer school district, the constant pursuit of greener grass on the other side of the proverbial fence.

Off to their right, the zebra walked free down Center Street, a red balloon on a string clutched in his teeth.

Now that I think of it, who ordered the zebra? Ryan scrunched his eyebrows together and the zebra reluctantly took his leave from the memory.

Ryan and Charlie, but not the zebra, were gathering signatures for Ryan's first campaign as an adult—his own self-run effort to earn a seat on the Mesa City Council. He had moved to the southwest corner of the city with his parents in the late 1970s, an area that was supposedly the next big thing for a city otherwise still centered around the Mormon Temple near the city center. The problem, at least in the mind of subsequently elected councils, was that Ryan's neighborhood was on the city's landlocked western edge and the new big thing was the swath of empty land annexed far to the northeast. The Ranch, which had been so excited to get a library branch and a fire station of its own, was seeing its time in the spotlight usurped by the unlimited vistas twenty miles distant.

Ryan was determined to change that plan. Overconfident in his own knowledge after two years working at a public relations firm that specialized in political campaigns, he decided to run for his own seat on his city council. Never mind that he was only in his twenties, about half the age of the rest of the council members, or that he wasn't Mormon which, while not a requirement, certainly didn't hurt one's chances of getting elected in Mesa well into the late 1990s. After seeing how little most politicians seemed to know independent of what their staff told them, he was certain he had intelligence in spades to serve well.

But there was a small problem when he started to gather the necessary signatures at the festival. Standing just off the sidewalk on the southern edge of once family friendly Pioneer Park, Ryan started to panic. Charlie and a couple other friends were moving out from the safety of the table and asking passersby for a quick signature but Ryan, the candidate, was paralyzed with fear at the idea of starting a conversation with random strangers going about their day.

"What the hell, dude?" Charlie asked after an hour of watching Ryan do next to nothing but smile uncomfortably when someone approached.

"I can't do this," Ryan said.

"What do you mean you can't? You walk up, introduce yourself, shake a hand, get them to sign. Then on to the next one. Simple."

Ryan knew it was anything but simple, as did the zebra, who now sauntered into the picture with two gazelles and a grinning bear, and Ryan's thoughts turned to the bare necessities. *Wait. Damn it! Get the hell out of here! This isn't a Disney pic!*

Smirking animals dismissed, Ryan went back to his conversation. "I can't, Doc. I mean, I try and come around the table, take one step, maybe a second and then this overwhelming fear takes over, there's a 500-pound lead weight on my chest and I can't move."

Charlie shook his head. "Let me get this straight. I can drop you on a microphone at Dobson High and you can announce the game in front of a few thousand people." Ryan nodded. "I can take you to Sun Devil Stadium and before the game's over you'll have butted into a half-dozen conversations and, rather than the people being annoyed, they leave feeling like your new best friend." Ryan nodded again. "But here, when all you have to do is smile and shake a hand, you can't move?"

"That's pretty much it."

"Well, that's pretty much it for your campaign, Ry. I mean, it's going to be hard serving a constituency when you're a mute."

"Maybe not." The zebra made another attempt to enter the frame, and this time Ryan let him stay. Who could stay mad at a zebra, after all?

"Mr. Williams," the zebra said. Ryan just stared in disbelief.

"Ryan!" he heard again, and with some effort he opened his eyes. It was the surgeon who, to Ryan's relief, had two hands, no hooves and no stripes.

"Yeah," he said softly.

"We found the blockage. Actually, blockages. Good news is we should be able to get them open, which will relieve the pressure you're feeling on your chest. Bad news is it's going to take a little time."

"That's fine. Send the zebra over if you need me," he said before closing his eyes and drifting back.

Where was I?

"You were going to make Charlie run for office," the zebra said.

Cool, thanks.

"You're going to run instead of me."

"Me? Bullshit!"

"No, Charlie, seriously. It's not like we're on different pages. We put you out front, I'll manage the campaign and once you win we're golden."

Charlie shook his head. "I've got school, a job, residencies eventually. And I might even want to go out with a woman once in a while. I mean, what if I don't want to do this?"

29

Ryan clasped a hand on his friend's shoulder and smiled. "Trust me, buddy. You're going to enjoy victory."

And so they dispensed with the signatures already gathered, put Charles Baxter's name down as the candidate on some blank signature sheets, and Charlie went back to stopping strangers while Ryan stood smiling behind the table, sharing a candied apple with the zebra, who had traded his balloon to Ryan for a bite. Within an hour, the pressure Ryan had felt on his chest at the idea talking to strangers was lifted.

"We're done, Ryan," the doctor said. "How do you feel?"

"Groovy. But I could use some real sleep."

"We've got you covered once you get to post-op. Sit tight."

***

He closed his eyes again and found himself in a Arizona House committee room fronted by a U-shape dais. *What committee meeting do I have today?* he thought as he tried to decide which of several nearly identical first-floor committee this might be. None of the committees had permanent rooms, so determining who was meeting where was anyone's guess unless someone read the posted agenda.

He was sitting in the front row of public seating near the left wall. Directly in front of him was a walnut-shaded podium with a microphone from which those either called to testify or simply wanting to be heard could address the committee members. Between the public seating and the dais was one large, square table with six seats, three on each side. Here was where staff would sit, with the majority party having twice as many staff members in attendance as the minority. Power games.

Ryan glanced over his shoulder to view an otherwise empty room but, when he turned back, the committee and staff seats all were filled. That's when he noticed Riley sitting at the front right corner of the staff table. Her bright red hair fell just below her shoulders with neatly trimmed bangs framing her face. Trim, alabaster legs emerged from the bottom of a black skirt.

Why are you sitting up there? he wanted to ask before realizing the committee meeting was already in progress. He glanced up at the dais and saw George Flannery, chairman of the House judiciary committee, speaking, though he couldn't make out the words.

George? You're in Congress now. What gives?

Suddenly that realization one has when they know they're in the middle of a dream came to Ryan. He looked down and realized he was dressed in a light green dress shirt with a multihued tie of lions resting upon the African savanna, assuming the savanna was largely constructed of ridiculously bright amber and gold waves of scrub grass. *Jesus, it's 1997. Do I really have to watch Arizona win the NCAA title again? Once was bad enough.*

Except it couldn't have been 1997. Ryan had poached Riley—saved was the word he preferred—from the House's Republican staff, but not until after he had directed Flannery's successful campaign for Congress in 2002.

Flannery looked at the public seating area and called Ryan's name.

"Me?"

"Yes, Mr. Williams. And today, please. I'm supposed to be in Washington right now."

Ryan blinked, and he was at the podium without actually rising. "So what are you doing here, Geo—Mr. Chairman?"

Flannery stared at Ryan over the top of his reading glasses. "Do you remember why I brought you here?"

Of course Ryan remembered. Shortly after helping Charlie Baxter get elected to the city council, Ryan received a call from Flannery, who even then was working his way up the ladder in the House's Republican hierarchy. In that same election, the Republicans had expected to enhance their already

31

commanding majority in both Arizona chambers. Instead, they lost four seats to Democrats riding the incumbent president's re-election coattails.

A week after the campaign, Flannery called Baxter and asked for Ryan's number. That night, when he got home from work, there was a message asking if he might be free for lunch to discuss the just-completed election and to talk about what was to come in two years' time. Ryan didn't remember much about the conversation he had that evening, other than two beautiful words—"paying gig."

The interview, as it turned out to be, took place at a local restaurant. Ryan talked about his worn shoe leather and even pulled out a pair of near-pristine letters, one from John McCain—congressman, senator and presidential runner-up—and the other from the great Ronald Reagan's mimeograph machine thanking him for his service in the 1984 campaign, when Ryan helped The Great Communicator win by peeling address labels and affixing them to hundreds of envelopes.

"What," Flannery asked, "do you think we're going to see next time out?"

"For the city or your district?"

"The entire state."

Ryan's breath caught, and he blanched ever so briefly at the unexpected question. He had paid minimal attention to the other races his firm was involved with and had sat through a pair of post-mortems following the election, but had not really analyzed anything.

"Don't worry about it, kid," Flannery said, reveling in eliciting the reaction he'd hoped for. "I've already got people telling me what they think, which sounds too much like what they think I want to hear. What I want you to do is go home, then come down to my office on Monday and tell me what your opinion is. There's no right answer except for the one I want. And do you know what answer I want from you?"

"The right one?" Ryan stammered.

"No," Flannery said, laying a couple of twenties on the table for the tab. "The honest one."

Two days later, Ryan was hired as an assistant campaign analyst for the state Republican committee with specific duties advising Flannery and the committee chairmen on legislative issues. He was twenty-six years old.

Six years later, Flannery decided to leave the state legislature after sixteen years and run for Congress. The first person he told was his wife. The second was Ryan. The challenge wouldn't come in the primary election, where the Republicans weren't about to dilute their slight chances by having a legitimate candidate waste money on a primary battle, but in the general. Flannery was going to enter the race against the incumbent, a seven-term Republican, Steve Chesterfield.

Ryan came along for one simple reason—he knew that such tenure in Congress ironically left Chesterfield vulnerable back home in Arizona, where he had spent increasingly less time through the years. The race was winnable and, with him at the helm, he felt even a coin flip would fall his and Flannery's way. It did, which made Flannery's sitting in a committee chamber in Phoenix more than a little disconcerting.

"I have only one question for you," Flannery said as he took off his glasses entirely. "What are you doing here?"

"In this chamber?"

Riley turned to her right and faced her future boss. "No, Ryan. He wants to know what you are doing in Alabama."

"I was hired."

Flannery shook his head. "No shit, Ryan. But what are you doing here? Why the hell did you take this campaign?"

Ryan paused, looked at Riley, who was still looking back at him expectantly, and then back toward the dais. "What answer do you want me to give you?"

Flannery had morphed into the same zebra. *He must be getting paid by the scene.* "The honest one, Mr. Williams."

Ryan didn't answer but instead found himself reviewing his bank account balance on his iPhone. That was answer enough.

"What are you doing here, Ryan?" he heard Riley ask.

"The money was too good," he murmured before realizing he had spoken out loud. He slowly opened his eyes, took a deep breath and inhaled the faint scent of a familiar perfume. Riley was sitting next to the left side of his bed, iPhone in hand as she reviewed more election returns and a series of texts from Rounds, reporters and even the national committee. She had shed the gunmetal gray dress she had worn to the election party the night before in favor of black slacks and a dark gray sweater adorned with dozens of sparkling sequins. She looked up and broke into a wide smile as Ryan reached for her hand.

"You're awake," she said, taking his left hand in hers.

"You're supposed to be asleep."

"And you're supposed to be just having tests run."

Ryan smirked. "Technically, they did run some tests."

"Not funny," she said. "Why didn't you tell me what was happening? You could have died."

"It was unlikely," he said. "And you had your hands full with our wonderful candidate. Speaking of which ..."

"Still too close to call," she said. "But I suggest not watching CNN later."

"How bad is it?"

"Only Comstock missing the bottom stair at the auditorium and falling ass over teakettle into a puddle on the grass to the right of the steps."

Ryan started laughing but immediately felt tired. "I guess it's too late to cost him any votes."

They both fell quiet for a few moments, Ryan picturing a dripping Comstock and Riley actively ignoring her phone.

"So what happens from here?" Riley asked.

"That's a hell of a good question. For you, you're going back to your apartment and getting some sleep."

"Ryan—"

"That's an order. They're keeping me at least through the day just to make sure. When the doctor tells me the next steps, I'll text you. In the meantime, help me out and start getting my stuff packed."

"We're leaving?"

"As soon as I'm medically clear. Our part in this shit show is over."

CHAPTER FOUR

R yan and Riley's part in the election was concluding, but the election itself wasn't quite ending.

Merrick Ogden Comstock glowered from behind the rostrum in a ballroom at the Sheraton Birmingham Hotel. Three days after votes were cast, ballots from remote precincts most affected by the Election Day thunderstorms had been tallied and Comstock, the apparent shoo-in to serve Alabama in the US Senate, trailed by just under 9,000 votes. Ryan had delivered the news earlier in the day on a conference call with Rounds and Comstock, setting off the latter into a fury of incriminations and curses and vows to battle the results all the way to the by-God Supreme Court if necessary. Rounds, having exhausted his desire to yell at Ryan the morning after the election—Ryan had not told him of the hospital trip and felt no obligation to do so—simply asked what options existed.

"Realistically, Ronny, the best chance would be recounts," Ryan said.

"You're goddamn right we're recounting!" Comstock screamed. "We shouldn't even be—"

"Shut up, Merrick," Rounds interjected, frustration pitching his voice a half-octave higher. "I'm sorry, Ryan. Continue."

"Thank you, Ronny," Ryan said, grinning as he imagined Comstock's face turning various shades of crimson in anger and, now, embarrassment. "If you do it, it's got to be county by county or, better yet, precinct by precinct where the margins are close. Going statewide would take too long and, frankly, you don't want to have the elections folks playing with ballots in precincts you've already won."

"Where do we start?"

"I've got my folks verifying numbers so they have an accurate map to work with. I'm also going to have Nicholas, an attorney I have on staff, out here by tonight so he can start working with your attorneys to get the paperwork filed."

"How long will this take?"

"Hard to say. Minnesota had one recount that took about nine months to settle, but that was only a few hundred vote margin. And they weren't dealing with votes on paper ballots marked in permanent marker. I'd think we'll be done one way or the other within a handful of weeks."

"What do I do in the meantime," Comstock asked, "sit on my ass?"

"Well, Merrick, since you seem absolutely incapable of shutting up for more than twenty consecutive seconds, you're going to address your supporters in about two hours," Rounds said bitterly. "Be humble, be confident and for Christ's sake, stick to what we write for once. Then go home and let the grown-ups work."

"Ronny..." Comstock started pleadingly.

"Don't Ronny me, Merrick. Take the speech, read it and hightail it out of there."

"Riley will be there to meet with you a half hour before you go on stage. We'll make sure you sound good," Ryan added.

"You better."

The speech itself was entirely unmemorable, aside from Comstock's inability to feign anything resembling a smile. He thanked his family, his supporters in the room and the good people of Alabama who had turned out through terrible weather to play their part in the democratic process. Comstock hated the last part. "Half of those stupid bastards voted for the wrong fucking guy," he fumed backstage. Now, he said to the small gathering in front of him, he would continue to allow that process to move forward to make sure every vote was counted, because every vote counts.

Ryan glanced over at Riley, taking twisted pleasure in adding the Democratic Party's mantra from the 2000 election to Comstock's speech. It was a brief glimmer of humor to cap what had been three months of misery.

***

In truth, the loss had repercussions extending well outside the state of Alabama. Sixteen Senate seats had been contested on Election Day and, when all was said and done, the Democrats had picked up four seats, two more than the GOP expected even given the usual slump the party in charge experiences every mid-term. And Alabama's loss was one more than the party could afford. A Comstock loss in a state that was as red as a fire engine was not part of anyone's calculus, even with all his self-inflicted wounds along the way. If the recount efforts failed as expected, Ryan was reminded in an afternoon phone call with Flannery, the Democrats would leave the country's upper chamber in a fifty-fifty deadlock. And that would put a serious crimp into the leadership's legislative planning, given the near impossibility of getting the Senate Republican caucus on the same page for anything more serious than a breakfast menu.

Ryan could do little more than grunt in the affirmative as the call continued with Flannery, speaking now as a member of the Republican National Committee and not Ryan's benefactor.

Explaining Comstock's unsuitability was pointless. Ryan's job was to make sure his candidate won, and he hadn't done that. After forty largely unproductive minutes, he walked to the taxi stand in front of the hotel to go a mile southeast to Birmingham's Loft District. Riley was already standing in front of the Rogue Tavern, a restaurant housed at the end of a line of single-story shops inside a building trimmed in distressed, whitewashed brick. Large windows lined the front and the entrance, two-thirds of the way down on the east side, was a pair of wood doors accented with intersecting, decorative iron.

Riley and Ryan walked in and continued on to the restaurant's outdoor patio. Round wood tables were flanked by steel and wicker chairs in a patio enclosed by the same distressed brick. Overhead, strands of white lights were wrapped around the trio of beams with the open sky beyond. Birmingham's ever-fickle weather now provided a comfortable sixty degrees without a cloud to be seen.

"They do realize he was a buffoon, right?" Riley asked after they claimed a table near an unlit propane heat lamp.

"Of course they do. But we both know how much that matters right now."

Ryan glanced up as the server approached and ordered a pair of Trim Tab Rescue Ships, a pale ale brewed locally.

Riley looked across the table and arched her eyebrow. "Are you really supposed to be doing that?"

Ryan shrugged. "What the doctor doesn't know won't hurt him."

Her look lingered for an extra few moments before she shook it off. "So what happens now?"

"What happens now is we hope for a miracle with the recounts."

"Which won't happen."

"Which won't happen, but we still can hope. After that, we hope that the national folks are in a forgiving mood and our phone keeps ringing."

"And if it doesn't?"

"If it doesn't, dear Riley, we content ourselves with working the great state of Arizona. And maybe I'll try and get on the panel at CNN. Last time I checked they only had a dozen people yelling at each other."

Riley laughed as the beers arrived. "You wouldn't dare."

"Anything for a paycheck," Ryan said, raising a glass.

"What are we toasting?" Nicholas Sartini, the firm's legal adviser and Riley's longtime boyfriend, stood behind Riley's chair, earning a squeal of greeting as she quickly rose, threw her arms around his neck and gave him a warm kiss.

"Only the end of our careers, but don't sweat it," Ryan said, half rising from his chair to shake Nicholas's hand after he and Riley untangled. Nicholas took the chair in front of him, holding tightly to Riley's hand. "You'd think you two hadn't seen each other in months."

"My boss doesn't let me fly home during a campaign," Riley said.

"And mine keeps me busy keeping an eye on a half-dozen legislatures and Congress," Nicholas added.

"He sounds like a total dick," Ryan said.

"I wouldn't say total," Riley said dryly, earning a small smile from Ryan.

Nicholas called the server over and ordered a beer of his own.

"Speaking of my boss," Nicholas said, "how are you feeling?"

"Never better."

Nicholas looked at Riley. "How is he feeling?"

"The man says he's fine."

"I said I'm fine. When the guy who signs the checks says he's fine, move to the next topic."

"No problem," Nicholas said, taking a pull off Riley's beer. "So let's start the next topic."

The trio spent the next hour discussing recount strategy over two additional rounds of beers and a round of Rogue Burgers and fries. Riley glanced over at Ryan more than once, watching with some concern as he polished off the red meat and alcohol only three days removed from having an artery reopened with a balloon. If Ryan caught her staring, he gave no outward sign. When they were done, they walked outside and took a taxi back to the extended-stay executive suites in which they'd both been living.

"Use the company card to get a room," Ryan said when they arrived at the hotel, earning a giggle from Riley. "Oh, yeah. Sorry. You two go, well, whatever you two do. Just make sure he's ready to go in the morning."

"I'm ready to go right now," Nicholas said, slurring his words slightly.

Ryan started to respond but thought better of it. He clapped Nicholas on the shoulder, walked unsteadily to the elevator and went up to his room.

"You sure he's okay?" Nicholas asked, his forehead crinkled in concern.

Riley shook her head slowly. "I honestly have no idea."

***

Ryan stepped into the entryway of his room and kicked his shoes across the room, where they thudded against the far wall. As he walked along the same path, he unbuttoned his golf shirt, untucked it from his black denim jeans and removed his belt. His body drained of adrenaline but filled with the city's excellent micro-brewed offerings, Ryan saw the bed beckoning from his suite's second room. For a moment he paused, thinking it would be nice to have someone to wind down with himself, but dismissed the thought. Relationships were entanglements, obstacles to the ultimate goal.

He sank heavily into the recliner in the living-room area and picked up the tablet computer sitting on the oval accent table next to the chair. He opened a browser and took a quick look at first CNN and then *Politico* to see what was written about Comstock, but thought better of it. Instead, he leaned his head back, unbuttoned his pants, opened the recliner to full extension and closed his eyes.

Within minutes he was asleep. Ryan found himself back in that same committee room in the Arizona Legislature, and Flannery was back in the chair's central seat—but the voice questioning Ryan wasn't Flannery's.

"Mr. Williams, do you know why we called you back in today?" Riley asked. Ryan glanced up from the lectern in front of him and saw her sitting where Flannery had been, red hair pulled back into a ponytail and straight bangs hanging just above the black-framed glasses she was wearing in lieu of her contacts.

Christ, she's beautiful.

"Mr. Williams?"

"Sorry, Ri—I mean, Madam Chairperson. I'm not exactly sure what this is about." He noticed Flannery had shifted two seats to the right, where he was reading the *Arizona Republic*. On the other side of the dais, the zebra had returned and was slurping coffee from a mug sitting on the desk. "No fingers," Ryan said, drawing a stern look from the animal. "Must make it tough."

"Let's focus on the question at hand, Mr. Williams." Riley removed her glasses for effect and shook her hair from the ponytail in slow motion like she was starring in a conditioner commercial. "Why did we come to Alabama?"

This sounds familiar. "As I told George, the money was too good to pass up."

43

"I see. Had you ever stepped foot in Alabama before accepting this job?"

"No, ma'am."

"Don't pull the folksy routine on me. Madam Chairperson or, if you must, Riley will suffice." She shuffled a few papers before continuing. "Had you ever given any thought to anything about the state of Alabama other than how the football team gets too many great recruits?"

"Can we investigate that?"

"No, because Saban is a genius and we all know it. You will kindly answer the question."

"No, Riley, I'd never given things much thought."

"But you took the job anyway."

"As I said, the money was too good to pass up."

Riley stared quietly for a moment, then started shuffling papers.

"Mr. Williams," the zebra said, his coffee forgotten for the moment, "how many times would you say you've taken a campaign just for the money?"

"The zebra gets to ask questions?" Ryan asked incredulously.

"The witness will answer the zebra's question," Riley said, still shuffling through what now appeared to be two reams of paperwork.

"Until now, probably never."

"Then why now?" Riley asked.

"It wasn't just the money," Ryan said. "This also was a Senate campaign. As in, one step below a presidential campaign."

Riley's glasses were back on, and she stared at Ryan over the top of them. "If Merrick Comstock were running for president, would you take that campaign on?"

"Hell no."

"But you felt he was good enough for the people of Alabama."

"I didn't know better."

"Shouldn't you have?"

Ryan raised his hands outward from his body in a show of surrender. *I can't even win an argument with her in my own dreams.*

"Moving to other topics, you had a cardiac procedure two days ago."

"Yes, Madam Chairperson." Ryan suddenly realized he was sitting down at the staff table.

"And the doctor's recommendations included greasy burgers and beer?"

"I'd like to think there's a grace period in play here."

"Is that because you were given a clean bill of health? Or because you don't want to think about what he said about your valve."

"How do you know about that?"

"I don't know," Riley said pointedly. "You, however, do, and this is your dream. Tell us about the valve."

Ryan sighed. "He said there was a slight leak in my mitral valve. I don't remember the exact term."

"It's prolapsed, possibly from a silent heart attack somewhere in your past."

"That's it. Anyway, the only way to repair it is open-heart surgery, and it's not worth the risk for such a slight leak."

"But..."

Isn't it time to wake up from this? Anyone?

"Mr. Williams..."

"Next topic."

Riley and the zebra shook their heads in unison. Flannery switched to the sports section.

"Fine, Ryan, final topic. Why don't you like Nicholas?"

Where was this going? "I like him just fine, otherwise I wouldn't have hired him."

"You don't like him now as much as you did then."

Ryan started to ask how she knew then remembered, this was his subconscious show. *This suuuuuuuucks.*

45

"Is it apparent?"

"Only to me and only because I know your looks too well after all these years."

"And what look am I giving him?"

"Like a lesser stag is trying to claim your territory."

"Territory?"

The room suddenly was empty, and Riley was leaning against the table in front of Ryan. She wore a spaghetti-strapped black cocktail dress that ended just above mid-thigh and matching three-inch heels.

"We both know you love me."

Oh shit. "May I plead the Fifth Amendment here?"

"If you need to."

"Do you know that for sure?"

Riley tilted her head to the side. "Do you mean, does the real Riley know that?"

Ryan nodded.

"I'm sure she knows you care about her. But she probably sees it more as the way a father would care about his daughter."

"Which is what it is."

"Except for when it isn't," she said, leaning down and kissing him softly on the lips. Somewhere in the background he could hear a zebra braying.

Ryan jolted awake in the recliner and looked around anxiously before realizing he was back in his hotel room. Alone. He stood up, walked to the bedroom, took off his shirt and pants and lay down in hopes of a dreamless sleep.

***

The next morning Ryan sat in a booth at Over Easy, a breakfast place not far from the hotel, when Riley and Nicholas walked in. They were holding hands and she was visibly giddy, her smile and stride exuding happiness and excitement. It was when they sat and placed their joined hands on the table that Ryan noticed the diamond ring on Riley's left hand.

"...and when I woke up," she said, "there was a stuffed zebra next to me with this ring tied with a string around its neck."

That damn zebra is everywhere.

Ryan's insides suddenly felt hollow and his senses numb. It wasn't that he had any claim on her other than professionally but the idea of a married Riley still was a surprise. He stood and feigned a smile as he congratulated them both, but his mind was empty except for one simple thought. It was time to get the hell out of Alabama for good.

CHAPTER FIVE

Highway 93 cuts a diagonal path across western Arizona, beginning in the one-time mining town of Wickenburg an hour northwest of Phoenix and running northwest across Maricopa, Yavapai and Mohave Counties until it reaches Interstate 40 just east of Kingman, which itself is an hour southeast of the Nevada border. Take the first right out of the traffic circle entering Wickenburg proper, just past the McDonald's and Subway and Tastee-Freez, and drive away from the few remaining streets in town and past landscapes that constitute most people's idea of Arizona—a desolate vista of scrub brush, endless desert and tall saguaro cactus reaching their arms toward the sky.

Except, only a few miles outside of town, Joshua trees begin to appear, not actual trees but tall yucca plants, growing from a single trunk several feet above the ground before exploding into multiple branches, each an individual collage of green, spiny leaves. At first they are scattered, a few on either side of the road. Suddenly there are thousands crowding the desert floor, nearly obscuring the horizon and mountains beyond and giving the Joshua Tree Parkway its eponymous name. Then the

Joshua trees are gone as well, giving way to rounded, granite boulders stacked one atop the next like a children's tower of blocks. Eons of exposure to wind and rain caused minor fissures within the granite to grow into full-fledged cracks, chunks of granite calving off the main formation like icebergs off a glacier, eventually rounding at the whim of the elements.

Soon the boulders also disappear and the road moves out of the Sonoran Desert and into the Mohave, turning westward before reaching the Coconino Plateau between the Grand Canyon and I-40 and running through Kingman, which still boasts a portion of the old Route 66. Northwest of Kingman the road forks. To the north were the majesty of Hoover Dam and Lake Mead and the glittering lights of Las Vegas. To the west, the road moved across flat landscape until reaching small, jagged mountain peaks similarly carved by millennia of wind and water. Then comes a pass that spills more than 3,000 feet of elevation in the span of a dozen miles and opens onto Bullhead City, Laughlin and the lower Colorado River valley.

There was a time when Ryan would have taken notice of the scenery, though the admonitions that this was the nation's deadliest highway posted repeatedly in the 1980s and early '90s—along with the dozens of stark white crosses lining the shoulders of the asphalt—tended to discourage much sightseeing. But having already made this trip scores of times, he took no more notice than he would driving down his home street. Instead, he sped along the highway in his salsa red Jaguar F-TYPE convertible, oblivious to the world around him. The fabric top was up in deference to the cool temperatures on this first Saturday after Thanksgiving, and a mix of Johnny Cash and Jimmy Buffett blared through his Meridian sound system connected to satellite radio. Life was too short for mediocre music and commercials, he believed.

He had spent Thanksgiving at the Talking Stick Casino and Resort just outside the Scottsdale limits on the Salt River Indian

Reservation, turning down invitations from Charlie and Riley to join their families for the day and instead dining alone in the Wandering Horse Buffet. Charlie, who doubled not only as Ryan's best friend but also his doctor, would undoubtedly want to spend time talking about his heart procedure—his office had been calling every three days since Ryan came back, trying to get him to schedule an appointment. Riley would be with her parents and Nicholas, who had returned earlier in the week once Comstock's defeat was made official. Normally this wouldn't be an issue, but Ryan had found himself trying to avoid Riley since Nicholas had proposed. It was utterly ridiculous to have such mixed feelings on the matter, he realized, but given his recent brush with mortality, rationality was not always carrying the day.

The holidays had been difficult for Ryan for the more than a decade since his parents had passed away. His father had been certain he wouldn't live past forty-nine because his own father had died then of a heart attack. He made it past that milestone with two decades to spare before suddenly collapsing at a warehouse store. An undetected blood clot had worked its way to his brain, and he was gone before he finished falling to the floor. Ryan's mother spent the next five years becoming ever more reclusive before also passing of natural causes in her sleep. His brother was more than a dozen years older, and they had never been particularly close because of the age gap. Ryan had no spouse, current or former, no girlfriend and few close friends. All were willingly sacrificed in favor of a laser focus on his career. Combined with that ever-present anxiety when he wasn't fully in control of a situation, he was more than comfortable keeping most people at Facebook distance where he could care or not care, like or not like at his leisure.

That didn't mean loneliness didn't set in, which was why Ryan spent considerable time at casinos. It wasn't the gambling itself that drew him but the ability to be alone within a crowd, feeding off the energy of those around him even if he wanted next to nothing to do with the bulk of them. He could anonymously begin conversations in the sports book with those around him no matter what the circumstance, such as the time a group of Liverpool fans, who had spent the entirety of a Champions League match screaming at their high-priced German forward, invited him to join them for several rounds of beer. It was an afternoon to remember, especially since all were vacationing Brits who had passing interest at most about American politics. But he also could withdraw within himself at a craps table, ignoring the shenanigans around him and instead thinking only of the odds and the tumbling dice.

Ryan arrived at the eastern shore of the Colorado River and made the left turn onto the bridge into Laughlin. The Colorado River, while diminished from full strength due to Hoover and Davis Dams, was flowing strongly even at this late date, though within a couple of weeks the levels would drop precipitously for the winter. Across the river was Casino Drive, a much smaller version of its Las Vegas cousin with a fraction of the neon and a tiny percentage of the crowds. On the left was Don Laughlin's Riverside, followed by the Aquarius and the somewhat newer Edgewater. Soon he drove past the smiling cowboy of the Pioneer and the Colorado Belle, which boasted a faux-riverboat facade. The one-time Ramada Express, one-time home of Ryan's beloved double-deck blackjack but long since branded the Tropicana, was the lone casino on the right side of the road, and visitors scurried across the crosswalk with only minimal interest in the traffic signals. He continued driving south until he reached Harrah's, located down a hill and well beyond Laughlin's other resorts. Between Harrah's Ak-Chin Casino in Maricopa, forty-five minutes south of Phoenix, and the company's multiple properties in Vegas, Ryan had accumulated enough comped nights to book a full-week vacation, which was exactly what he'd done. Assisting the company with local legislation in Arizona had earned him invitation-only rewards status to boot.

He drove down the incline into the parking lot and stopped at the valet entrance. Ryan flashed his card at the valet along with a ten-dollar bill and watched as his luggage quickly was unloaded and rolled to the bell desk. He entered the casino through glass doors, turned right once inside and walked to the registration desk, player's club card again in hand.

"Welcome back, Mr. Williams," the clerk said reflexively. Unlike the manager and some of the pit bosses Ryan had known for some time, the young man in front of him was relatively new. "How long are you going to be staying with us?"

"For the week," he said. Ryan handed over a credit card along with the reward card and watched as his luggage was rolled near the desk. "Have them take that upstairs for me," he said, also asking for a reservation at the casino's steakhouse.

"My pleasure, sir." The clerk shouted a room number over his shoulder, slid a paper across to Ryan for a quick signature, and then Ryan went looking for a blackjack table.

Harrah's gaming floor was a large oval connected in the front registration area and near the back of the casino. On the left side was a small, sparsely-populated gaming section. On the right was the main casino, which extended across the bulk of the ground floor. Ryan's room was on the east side of the North Tower and overlooked the Colorado River, Bullhead City and the mountains beyond. Ryan walked toward the gaming tables until he saw a familiar face wearing an immaculate thousand-dollar suit.

"Bob," he said, smiling and extending his hand toward the gaming supervisor, "how are we doing, my friend?"

"Excellent, Mr. Williams," Bob replied, taking Ryan's hand with a firm grip. "I hope you had a good Thanksgiving."

"It was better for me than the turkey," Ryan said, drawing a laugh even though he'd told Bob the same joke several years in a row.

"What's your pleasure tonight, Mr. Williams?"

"Honestly, Bob, I think I'd like to play solo for a while."

"Consider it done." Bob gestured toward a dealer waiting to enter the evening rotation and instructed her to set up one of the closed blackjack tables in the row. It would soon be open but only for Ryan, who would be playing three hands at once. Invitation-only status, Ryan thought, came with its privileges.

***

Ryan walked deliberately from the blackjack table to the steakhouse, head down less from the sting of losing a few hundred dollars than from the effect of multiple glasses of rum and coke. He was seated at a table near the right-hand wall and sat facing the entrance. His server soon approached the table for his drink order, followed by a familiar but unexpected face.

"Two bourbons and one more menu," Charlie Baxter said as he sat down across from Ryan, who rolled his eyes with a mix of surprise and annoyance. "And then he'll be drinking water the rest of the evening."

The server looked at Ryan, who nodded in agreement.

"I didn't think you made house calls," Ryan said after a few moments.

"Call it a special circumstance."

"The circumstance being?"

"A particularly difficult, stubborn and idiotic patient who doesn't understand that when his doctor's office calls every other day, maybe a return call is in order."

"I thought it was a fundraising call for the doctors' annual holiday gala," Ryan said, earning a brief laugh. "So you drove all the way up here just to see me?"

"Flew, actually. What's the point of a pilot's license if you don't take advantage of it?"

The server returned with their drinks, took their orders and retreated.

"Time for business," Charlie said. "How are you feeling?"

"I'm good. How about you?"

Charlie shook his head and took a sip of bourbon. Ryan responded by finishing half his glass in one long pull.

"I'm not sure you're appreciating how serious your situation is, Ryan."

"Serious? My odometer's been rolled back, Doc. Arteries clear, heart pumping, blood flowing, all is good."

"If only."

"Charlie, have I ever told you the underlying concept of every Jewish holiday?"

"Probably."

"They tried to kill us, we lived, let's eat. Same thing here. My heart tried to kill me, I lived, let's eat."

"It's not quite that simple," Charlie said. "First, technically speaking you were killing your heart with your lifestyle, so put the blame where it belongs. Second, your heart's not in perfect working order. That mitral valve issue is concerning."

Ryan shook his head. "The doctor in Alabama said it was minor."

"It is minor, Ryan, unless it's not. You may feel nothing. You may feel palpitations, almost like your heart skips a beat. And if you don't do something about the way you're living your life, there's a more than decent chance we're going to be installing a new valve somewhere down the line."

"What's more than decent?"

"Probably fifty-fifty within the next ten to fifteen years."

Ryan finished his bourbon and chased it with a sip of water as their steaks arrived.

"There's no low-pressure version of what I do, Doc."

"Then maybe it's time to start stepping away from the day-to-day."

Ryan laughed indignantly. "And who's going to take my place?"

"Riley's been ready for two years and you know it."

"She's getting married," Ryan said quietly.

"What does that have to do with the business?"

"You wouldn't understand."

Charlie reached across the table and grabbed Ryan's wrist. "Look, Ry. Just because you decided the only way to do this was to make it the center of your life, doesn't mean that's the only way to succeed. Most people understand that before their heart goes on strike."

Ryan said nothing, instead focusing on the rib eye on his plate.

"You've got walk-away money, right?"

Ryan looked up at his friend and nodded.

"Maybe it's just time to walk away."

"And do what?"

Charlie let go of Ryan's arm and leaned back in his chair. "That's easy, Ry. Live."

CHAPTER SIX

Ryan woke early the next morning, opened the curtains and watched the first pink and orange fingers of dawn over the riverside houses of Bullhead City, the river below still cast in dark shadow. He was desperately thirsty after drinking the night before and, after a quick shower, grabbed his tablet and took the elevator down to the twenty-four-hour café for breakfast. The restaurant was designed like a Mexican beach café, assuming the café had been approved through multiple focus groups and also housed a keno parlor. He sat a table near the hotel lobby and ordered the first of a series of coffees. In front of him, a middle-aged woman was playing a *Love Boat* slot machine—the same small portion of the show's theme song playing repeatedly with each spin. Was the game really exciting and new? he thought snarkily. At the table next door were two couples of senior citizens, discussing the latest shenanigans of the country's deeply unpopular president and blaming the unfair news media for his troubles. Ryan shook his head. Everyone seemed to think that the yearly trip to the ballot box gave them some insight into how the game really was played. Even the most connected reporters only knew one-tenth of the story, and they had contacts, while the general public relied on Facebook and Twitter for their reality.

To that point, as he ate his avocado and bacon omelet and downed copious amounts of coffee and water, he scanned through a half-dozen websites to catch up on whatever political news he might have missed. Even if was only the slightest slice of what was taking place.

That, he thought, was part of the problem. Much of Charlie's advice had been straightforward—cut the alcohol to a relative minimum, exercise a little more to lose the extra 20 pounds Ryan carried in the middle of his otherwise lean frame, shift the diet away from steaks and potatoes to chicken and fish, stay away from white foods like flour, rice and bread—all the same things Ryan could have learned by watching Dr. Oz. But stepping away from the business he had built from the ground up was a different story. It was more than just a career. Ryan lived and breathed politics the way other men studied baseball box scores, absorbing as much information as possible from around the country even though, his ill-fated Alabama adventure aside, his territory encompassed only the Four Corners states and Nevada. Reading the *Washington Post*, *New York Times*, *Arizona Capitol Times* and *Politico* was as reflexive as brushing his teeth.

Politics would continue to exist and he could continue to watch the show from the sidelines but, Ryan thought, if there were no opportunity to take action on everything he had learned, then what was the point? Knowledge was currency in his world, and in this respect Ryan was incredibly wealthy. From the day he first walked into the Arizona Legislature, Ryan had read as many political biographies and histories as he could get his hands on. His personal library at home held several hundred such books, purchased through the years at local secondhand bookstores, not because of the reduced price but for the sheer thrill of the hunt. Though he carried his tablet everywhere, he never tired of the feel of physically turning a page.

Two decades of study had given Ryan a long-range perspective others, particularly politicians looking only as far as the next election, lacked. If history teaches us anything, he had told his staff countless times, it's that almost nothing happens that hasn't happened before. It was his own guard against overreaction in a world where false sea changes seemingly occurred on every turn of the twenty-four-hour news cycle. And that perspective had made him a valuable commodity within this enclosed universe in which he lived and worked. The question now was how to broadcast that he was as valuable as ever even with the recent challenges.

Breakfast over, his stomach full and a coffee to-go in a Styrofoam cup in hand, Ryan walked across the casino floor to the building's far eastern side. Harrah's was situated on a bluff two stories above the Colorado River itself, and the only way to get to the river was by taking an elevator down two levels and then walking down an inclined concrete walkway that led both to the hotel's beach and a floating dock where a river taxi soon would arrive. He stood along the railing of the dock, jacket closed against the winds gusting through the river channel, and watched as the deep-blue Colorado River flowed strongly southward. To his left, a lone brave soul rode a jet ski in defiance of the cold and current.

When the taxi arrived, Ryan paid the fare and moved to the back of the boat. He leaned back and placed his left arm on the railing behind him as a half-dozen other passengers boarded, voices muted in testament to their own hangovers. More came and went as he rode the boat to the top end of its run at the Riverside Hotel on the far north end of Casino Drive. He exited the dock and turned right onto Laughlin's riverwalk, a wide sidewalk situated between the casinos and the water that ran from the Riverside down to the Pioneer and Colorado Belle.

After ducking into the Starbucks at the Aquarius to buy a fresh hot coffee less the various add-ons offered, he settled onto a bench just outside the casino and pulled out his tablet. He needed to think things through.

***

When Ryan started his firm, its only focus was consulting on campaigns. Over time, however, the candidates he helped get elected also wanted additional guidance on many of the issues they confronted once in office. Legislative staff was always available but, ultimately, that staff answered to the state house speaker and senate president. Three-quarters of those elected to the legislature were content with that arrangement. For the other 25 percent, they turned to Ryan for help. Adding Riley, with her staff experience, helped, and over the next several years Ryan hired a handful of law school graduates straight out of the university and created a legislative division.

He also had added a third aspect to the business, acting as lobbyists for school districts who otherwise would rely on their own staff members, who had far too many other duties to devote their time to lobbying. The money wasn't anything spectacular, especially with a state legislature driven to reduce education funding at every turn, but Ryan had a soft spot for the school districts thanks to a handful of teachers who had stirred his interest in history and civics.

To avoid conflicts between the lobbying and campaign arms, Ryan at first was selective about the candidates with which he worked. Put simply, if a candidate was full-bore behind school vouchers and other ideas designed to further weaken an already feeble education system, they never were invited through the front door of his firm. In time, he sequestered himself within the campaign consulting branch and left the lobbying arm to operate freely, having already had their path set forth for them, which allowed Ryan to expand his scope of work exponentially.

Which is how you ended up working for Merrick Ogden Comstock, the familiar voice said.

Ryan grimaced at the mere thought of Comstock's name as he opened a text document on the tablet.

He listed the three divisions—campaigns, legislation and lobbying—then added additional lines with one-off jobs he and his firm had performed, such as setting up the occasional out-of-season fundraiser to help longtime clients. Then he started adding names of staff under each of the divisions. Much of the information already was sitting on his company's website, but he found it easier to think if he did the work longhand.

The lobbying division was the easiest issue to solve, as he already had walked away. Nicholas had emerged as both the most knowledgeable and innovating of his legal staff, uncovering loopholes and sensing unintended consequences well before anyone else on either Ryan's or the legislative staff. If working for the legislature paid anything, Ryan thought, he would have lost him to the government long ago.

Legislative also would be a relatively easy fix. The work had started with Riley, and she had developed almost as deep a network of contacts as Ryan and had been ready to take over for more than a year. In truth, Ryan had slowly drifted away from this area as well, even if he never formally ceded the reins.

That left campaign consulting, which would be the biggest obstacle at all.

Ryan learned early that guiding a campaign was far more about psychology than strategy. There are only so many ways to skin a cat, his father often said, and that held true for campaigns. The trappings may change, the scenery may differ, the stakes might vary greatly, but the basics were the basics. Build name recognition, create a brand people trust, uncover issues on which voters will connect, rinse and repeat. That was the easy part.

What separated Ryan was his ability to anticipate his candidate's fears and anxieties, their uncertainties and their bouts with self-doubt. Political candidates are used to a certain level of adulation which generally allows them to edge away from the pack in smaller settings.

"Think of the people who ran for student council in high school," Flannery told Ryan during one late-night drinking foray while both were still in the Arizona house.

"High school's a popularity contest, George."

"All elections are. And when they're at home the night before the election, every one of those candidates is shitting bricks wondering if people really like them or not. All but one of them's going to find out they didn't."

Knowing you can't please everyone sounds great on a theoretical level. It's when you're presented with concrete evidence of their dislike—speeches by opponents, endorsements, newspaper and television stories—that even the most outwardly self-confident person stares long and hard in the mirror.

Most of Ryan's time was spent crafting the narrative his candidates thought of when they looked in the mirror. He wasn't Bundini Brown, mindlessly following behind Muhammad Ali and yelling, "You're the champ, Champ. Ain't no one else gonna be the champ because you're the champ, Champ." Flannery even had told Ryan in that same alcohol-fueled conversation that he was "too fucking honest for your own good." The idea was to present the truth, but not in an unvarnished manner. No matter what happened, no matter how deep the hole into which a campaign was sinking, Ryan needed to make sure his people knew there was a path out of the muck, if only they kept putting one step in front of the other and moving forward.

Even when the candidate was a self-absorbed imbecile running for a Senate seat from Alabama.

Did Riley have that capability? She had spent the summer with Ryan in Alabama working for Comstock and for the past eight years, she had been at his side for every campaign.

Ever since he realized that he loved her.

"That had nothing to with it. I was training her."

Then that means that she's ready to take over.

"I can't see her going solo. She's too young."

You were younger.

"I started earlier. She still needs my help."

You need to be with her so you can pretend you're not alone.

"Fuck me," Ryan blurted out, causing a pair of co-eds to shift to the far side of the walkway to avoid the lunatic on the bench cursing for no reason. He drained the last of his coffee, shut off the tablet, stood up and started walking south toward the Colorado Belle.

Looking back, Ryan had hired Riley because she was beautiful and brilliant and could put up with his sarcasm. As time went on, 80 percent of his affection for her was paternal. He was her mentor and, with proper guidance and a little luck, he would help her reach heights he hadn't imagined. But the other 20 percent left him thinking that if only he were twenty years younger and not nearly as single-minded, something might have been there. And if he was really honest with himself, which he chose not to be very often, he only thought of the age difference to salve his own ego, since Riley had never hinted at the slightest romantic notion where he was involved in the many years they had worked together.

An idealized manifestation distracting from one's own internal career-versus-love conflict - that was how a high-priced therapist had summed up the situation once upon a time.

Logistically, he could find a way to step away from the business. Letting go of that pipe dream, however, would require a level of introspection and reality he wasn't certain he was ready to handle. No matter how self-confident the person, there were chinks in the armor. He was no different.

Having enough money could help a man walk away from anything except his own inner demons, he thought as he started walking down toward the river taxi stand. Those damn things will follow you anywhere.

Ryan's self-destructive reverie was interrupted by the vibration of his phone. He pulled it from his pocket and took a quick glance. His stomach flipped and his heart started to race. An escape from purgatory appeared near at hand.

For the first time since Ryan left Alabama, Flannery was calling.

***

"He didn't give you any details?" Charlie asked Ryan. They were sitting at a table in El Burro Boracho, Guy Fieri's branded Mexican restaurant inside Harrah's. A painting of Fieri's tattoo of his sister was illuminated overhead.

Ryan took a drink and shook his head. "You know what George is like, always wants to play things close to the vest. He just said to be in San Diego Tuesday night for dinner."

"So when he says jump."

"Don't be an asshole, Charlie. You know damn well—"

"—that without the work he threw your way, you wouldn't be where you are. Yeah, I know."

Charlie always believed Ryan to be far too deferential when it came to Flannery. Helping Flannery win his congressional seat was the feat that moved Ryan and his firm onto the radar screen outside of Arizona. A kind word or two from Flannery no doubt helped guarantee others called Ryan first but, ultimately, it was the work itself that spoke to people. That and Ryan's unparalleled ability to charm even the most jaded politicians.

"It's a free trip to San Diego, Doc. It's hard to find fault in that."

"If you know what you're walking into, maybe."

Ryan paused as his oversized queso casero enchiladas and Charlie's pork chile verde burrito was delivered. "What's the worst thing that's going to happen, they ask me about what happened in Alabama? The guy was an asshole. End of story."

Charlie chewed thoughtfully on a forkful of pork chile. "We talked about you taking a break."

"You talked about me taking a break. I said I would consider it, and I will continue considering it after dinner," Ryan said. "Look, Doc, the reality is I still have a business to run. I can't up and walk away from it on a dime any more than you could decide to duck out on the surgeries you have scheduled the next two months."

"That's different."

"In importance to life and the universe, yes. In strictly business terms, not so much. Honestly, it's a dinner meeting and I'm drinking on George's tab."

"In extreme moderation," Charlie interjected.

"In moderation," Ryan said with a sigh. "It's only dinner, Mom. Lighten up."

CHAPTER SEVEN

Flannery, Ryan admitted to himself as he pulled up to the restaurant, had pretty good taste. C-Level was located on the southeastern tip of Harbor Island on the north side of San Diego Harbor. Half the restaurant was on the island itself, the remainder on a platform above the water supported by numerous wooden supports. Ryan handed his keys to a valet, walked in and was escorted to a table on the patio. A heat lamp set in the wood frame of the patio's roof helped offset the cold night air flowing off the water. In the distance, Ryan could see the lights of the San Diego skyline and, further south, Coronado Island.

Moments later, Flannery walked outside with a pair of fresh drinks from the bar and handed one to his longtime friend. "It's good to see you, Ryan."

"Good to be seen, George," Ryan said, extending his hand briefly before Flannery sat down across from him. "That's one hell of a view."

Flannery looked over his shoulder with practiced indifference. "Almost as good as the view I'm shooting for."

"Never one to waste time on small talk, right?" Ryan settled back in his chair with a wry smile. "What's the news?"

Flannery glanced up as a server approached to take Ryan's drink order, then leaned conspiratorially over the table. "I'm going to make the run."

Ryan tilted his head briefly to the side before the meaning of the words registered, but couldn't come up with anything more clever to say than, "Really."

Flannery leaned back. "I had expected a little more excitement."

"It's not that, George. It's not that at all. I just wasn't expecting to hear it." Ryan raised his glass of water toward the center of the table in a toast. "*Mazel tov.*" Flannery nodded and tapped his tumbler of scotch against Ryan's glass. "When are you making it official?"

"There's paperwork to file and groundwork to be laid."

"Which is why I'm here."

Flannery shrugged before continuing. "I'm thinking I'll make the announcement in the next couple of months."

"We just finished mid-terms, George. You've got plenty of time before the actual election."

"Not as much as you might think, at least when it comes to fundraising and putting together a ground game. President's different than the Senate, to say the least."

"But you can get a lot of that going without the formal announcement."

Flannery pulled his eyebrows together into a scowl. "Why are you so hung up on the timing? You know that it's got to be before spring."

Ryan took a short sip of his drink before leaning over his arms on the table. "Do you remember last time? Before all was said and done, more than a dozen people saying they were running when only a handful of them had even the slightest chance?"

"I'd like to think I'm at the head of that group."

"Maybe you will be. But there's a fine line between recognition and exposure." Ryan paused. Adrenaline started to surge through his veins and his thoughts became more focused, all doubt eliminated. This was the rush he craved. Diagnosing a problem, crafting a solution and presenting it for maximum effect. "CNN and Fox, with those horseshit debates months before anyone goes to the poll for even a primary, candidates like monkeys yowling to be heard over each other and to get a few seconds of camera time, trying desperately to create a memorable sound bite but unable to stand out because everything blends into a cacophony of white noise. And that doesn't even take into account the poor bastards relegated to the pre-debate debate, which may as well air on the Food Network for as much as anyone cares."

He glanced at Flannery and saw the look of recognition in his eyes. Flannery could argue with Ryan but not his analysis. The congressman unconsciously had formed his hands into fists and his face had flushed. "No one would be shoving me into the undercard."

"Almost certainly not," Ryan said, leaning back casually, reveling in Flannery's discomfort. Nothing was accomplished when a candidate was comfortable. "But no one who was stuck there ever thought they would be either."

This time, Flannery turned purposefully toward the water and blew out a long breath to regain his composure. Thirty seconds passed in silence, then a minute. Finally, Flannery took in a deep breath and blew it out audibly. "What is your suggestion, Ryan?" he asked without turning back toward the table.

"Set up the exploratory committee. Play it coy for a while. Make sure the people that know, know, and let the bulk of the talking heads spend their time speculating about it. With your resume, you can loom large over the field without having to be a part of it, at least until the late summer. Don't let this recent rush to enter the race dictate your play. Let the other idiots bash each other's heads in while you stay outside the fray, watch and collect a list of everyone's weaknesses, then come riding in as the party's savior and play off the cards everyone played."

Flannery nodded but said nothing. Ryan gazed absently at the skyline, running through the work that would need to be done to position Flannery properly for a White House run. In truth, he had been building strategy for just such a campaign ever since George first was elected to the House. Ryan had read the hackneyed memoirs from both the winning and losing sides, searched for articles where the managers were interviewed. He had spent days studying what had worked in the past and what hadn't, what to focus on and what to set aside, how to utilize so-called "big data" and when to rely on one's own instinct. And above all else, how to always look like everything was going according to plan.

And maybe, just maybe, when the election was done and Flannery was in the White House, Ryan would find himself rewarded with some staff position within the White House. He'd have to step away from his firm during that period but when he returned, his one-time western political outpost would be a national brand and he would write his own memoirs, complete with an obscene advance from the publisher, and spend the remainder of his days deigning this group or that with his presence for a high-paid speech. But he'd do so out of desire not need, because he would have reached the pinnacle. Wasn't that ultimately the point of everything, to win until there were no more victories to be won?

Ryan's reverie was interrupted only by the server returning to the table. "Senator Flannery," he said, "the rest of your party is waiting inside."

The rest of what? What the hell?

***

70

Flannery and Ryan walked past a central bar and into Island Prime, C Level's sister restaurant occupying the west side of the building. The nearly dozen tables atop the enclosed pier were filled with men in dark suits and dazzling solid power ties and women in severe business dresses and sensible, professional heels. Ryan recognized only two initially—Jorge Fuente, one of California's two senators, and Barbara O'Hanlon, Flannery's chief-in-staff back in Washington.

"Quite an exciting night," O'Hanlon said with a broad smile.

"Quite." Ryan was simultaneously trying to hold eye contact while taking stock of the remainder of the room. No wonder he didn't want to be questioned on timing, Ryan thought. That decision clearly already had been made.

O'Hanlon said something else but Ryan didn't hear it. Instead, he found himself staring as someone strode purposefully toward him. Tall, dark hair graying at the temples and swept back dramatically from a prominent forehead, two-thousand-dollar navy suit cut just so, light blue Oxford shirt and a bold paisley tie with swirling blues, blacks and grays, an air of confidence strong enough to hold lesser beings at a two-foot distance on aura alone. Ryan, usually no slouch sartorially, felt himself wilting.

"Mr. Williams," Seth Afolayan said, "how are things in the desert? Must be a relief to be back after that whole Alabama thing." Afolayan already had two presidential campaigns under his belt, the first unsuccessful but the latter resulting in a four-percent victory, a veritable landslide in modern terms. *And he's here at Flannery's request.*

The pissing contest had begun. "Going well," Ryan said with a smile he didn't feel. "How are things in the swamp?"

"Not a problem when you're the biggest gator there." Afolayan grinned broadly, perfect white teeth set in a smile that radiated no warmth, eyes focused like a predator bearing down on its dinner. "I hear you're going to be helping us out in this part of the world."

Helping us? Ryan's face fell, and he knew from the change in Afolayan's stare that it was visible. "We were just talking about that, actually."

"Good, good," Afolayan said quickly, and Ryan knew he hadn't been listening to the response. "Well, get yourself some food and make sure they keep your drinks fresh for you. We've got a lot of work to do after tonight." With that Afolayan was gone, leaving a wake of overpriced cologne.

Ryan stood still, unable to move nor process what had just taken place. *Helping us out.* There only was one possible meaning, but Ryan's mind wasn't prepared to accept the idea of taking a backseat to anyone, much less a pampered prick like Seth Afolayan. He looked at Flannery, who caught his eyes for just a moment before pointedly turning back to the latest victim of his constant charm offensive. *It's got to be a competition*, Ryan thought. That was the only thing that made sense. Didn't Flannery owe his congressional career to Ryan's efforts? *Fuck Afolayan. This is my candidate.*

He took one step toward Flannery when he felt it, an intense pressure suddenly squeezing the air out of his chest. Ryan took a deep breath and another step, but the weight on his sternum only intensified. His abdomen, his legs, even his feet felt suddenly warm, and perspiration was released from every pore in one mad rush. He shuffled toward a nearby table, grabbed a cocktail napkin and dabbed at his forehead and the back of his neck, but the paper was quickly saturated.

Not fucking again.

A server hurriedly approached. "Sir, are you okay?" Ryan stared back mutely. The pressure on his chest eased, but he was unable to take more than a half-full breath. "Sir?"

Ryan fumbled in his pocket for his valet slip and a five-dollar bill. "Have them get my car, would you? The quicker the better."

***

It took Ryan fifteen minutes to drive from the restaurant to the UC San Diego Medical Center. He had left the restaurant quickly, not stopping to say goodbye to anyone, especially Flannery, Afolayan or O'Hanlon. The drive itself was a blur of headlights and taillights, intermittent traffic and endless stoplights determined to turn red every time he approached, none of which helped the tightness in his chest and head. He finally caught a break when he entered the emergency room parking lot, finding a parking spot close to the automatic sliding front doors. He paused twice in the 150 feet from his parking spot to the entrance, trying without success to catch his breath. At the front desk, he explained that he was less than a month from angioplasty and the previously laconic nurse suddenly burst into motion, spinning in her chair and calling out to someone behind her. Ryan was ushered quickly into triage, settled into a wheelchair without complaint, and offered his left arm for the blood-pressure cuff and a finger for the white and gray pulse and oxygen clip. Ryan closed his eyes and leaned back in his chair, sweat pouring down the sides of his face and the back of his neck in spite of the cool temperatures outside. His damp shirt and pants were plastered to his body. Yet another new, unwelcome experience.

"Blood pressure 121 over 76," the triage nurse said, "not too bad."

Not too bad?

"Pulse 83, a little high..."

Only a little?

"Oxygen 99...98 percent. Excellent, Mr. Williams."

"Then why," he said, pausing for a series of shallow breaths, "can't I get any air?"

"Do me a favor, Mr. Williams, and hold your breath for me."
Ryan shook his head frantically. "Can't do that."

"It won't be for long," the nurse said patiently, "just for ten seconds or so. Just try, okay?"

Ryan nodded and the nurse counted backward from three. "Now," she said.

After only three seconds Ryan felt himself desperately yearning to breathe, to open as wide as possible, arch his back and suck in as much air as he could. And maybe they would give him an oxygen mask to help rather than playing silly games to see if he would turn blue.

"...and time," the nurse said.

Ryan opened his eyes and gave the nurse a dubious look. "That was ten seconds?"

"Actually closer to fifteen," the nurse said. "Let's do that again."

Another countdown, another purposeful inhale and Ryan held his breath again.

"Let it out slowly as I count back from five," the nurse said and Ryan nodded, letting the last air rush out of him as the count reached one.

"Was that fifteen seconds again?"

"Closer to thirty that time. How does your chest feel?"

Ryan had been so busy listening to the nurse's count that he failed to notice his breathing deepening and his heartbeat fading into the background once again.

"How did that happen?" he asked.

"Call it magic. Let's get you back to a room."

Unlike his hospital trip in Birmingham, there was comparatively little activity after he was wheeled from triage to one of the small patient rooms in the emergency room. The room was cold enough to comfortably hang sides of meat, and Ryan was grateful when a nurse made an appearance and offered a warm blanket. Less enjoyable was the doctor's insistence that he be kept without food or water until blood work results came back. He was given an EKG and an echo-cardiogram, neither of which revealed anything different than the prior month's test.

The doctors in the emergency room decided they wanted him kept overnight for observation, so Ryan stepped from the bed to a gurney, declining the helping hands offered, and was taken upstairs to discover he would not have a private room. Another man was in the bed closest to the door, and the thin curtain between beds did nothing to muffle either his roommate's deep, hacking cough or his muttering in what Ryan assumed to be his native tongue while waiting for the floor staff to find a translator to assist. Ryan turned on the television and spent an hour watching basketball highlights on ESPN before he was taken back downstairs for a nuclear stress test. This wasn't the stress test most people imagine, where the patient is ordered to run on a treadmill at increasingly higher speeds and steeper inclines for the duration of the test. Instead, the nuclear stress test was induced chemically while the patient lay still on a gurney. Given Ryan's respiratory issues earlier in what was now the prior evening, the doctors opted for a test they could end at the first sign of distress.

A chemical isotope was injected into Ryan's bloodstream and the discomfort was immediate. True to the on-staff cardiologist's word, the test didn't hurt. Rather, it felt like all of Ryan's arteries and veins had been hooked up to a fire hose which then was turned on full blast.

"In case you're wondering," the cardiologist said, "this is what a heart attack feels like. Or so I've been told."

"That's bloody wonderful, Doc," Ryan answered through gritted teeth.

Once the test was done he was taken back upstairs and given the impossible instruction to get some rest, a difficulty in any hospital, much less when quartered with a bronchial Kumeyaay.

Or Barona Mission. Or whatever the hell the suffering bastard was, Ryan thought impatiently.

In spite of the noise, he managed to fall asleep for what actually was ninety minutes but felt like ten before he was awoken by the same cardiologist who had performed the nuclear stress test.

"I have some good news, Mr. Williams," he said through a thick East Indian accent. "It appears that your heart is doing well, aside from the damage from your past heart episode last month."

"So what was the problem?"

The doctor paused as if searching for the right words to say. "That's a little more complicated. Were you doing anything strenuous before you came in, like exercising or something else?"

"I came in wearing a shirt and tie, Doc. So no, I wasn't exercising. I was at a dinner meeting."

"Were you drinking during the meeting?"

Ryan could feel frustration building, fueled as much by exhaustion as anything else, but pushed it back down. "Nothing of note. We went through all of this when I first checked in."

"I understand," the doctor said patiently. "I'm just ruling out the obvious. So no exercise, no excessive alcohol. You were sitting down, presumably eating during a dinner meeting."

"I didn't make it past the appetizer."

"Understood. But you came into the hospital drenched, presumably in sweat unless a rain shower rolled through," the doctor said with an attempt at humor.

"So?"

"So, that's a little unusual when it's only sixty degrees out. You also said that all of a sudden you had trouble breathing."

Ryan nodded. "We were talking, then I felt some tightness in my chest and then I found myself gasping for air. Or I would have been gasping, but I didn't want the people I was with to know what was happening."

"And why was that?"

Because one cardiac episode elicits sympathy. A second elicits undesired health questions. "I wasn't up for being the main dinner entertainment when the ambulance showed up," he lied.

"I see. And were there any other symptoms you noticed?"

"No," Ryan said, but then paused. "Actually, I guess it felt a little bit like someone was squeezing my head, compressing everything and making my head feel tight, too, if that makes sense."

"It does," the doctor said, pulling a chair close to the bed and sitting down. "Here's what my diagnosis is, Mr. Williams. You had a panic attack."

"That's not possible," Ryan said forcefully. "I've never had anything like that."

"In fact, you had one in Alabama, if the records that were sent over were correct. At least, you had some symptoms that were more appropriate to a panic attack than an actual heart attack. It's my belief that they were put on the back burner, as it were, because of the arterial blockage."

"But the tightness in my chest this time was the same as it was then."

"It might have felt similar physically. But physiologically, these were two different events."

"I couldn't breathe," Ryan said, his voice dropping.

"Whatever the initial trigger," the doctor said, "you started hyperventilating. It wasn't that you weren't getting enough air when you came into the ER. You were getting too much."

Ryan shook his head slowly. "This makes no sense."

"You know, Mr. Williams, this is good news. Another cardiac episode so soon after the first would have been troubling."

"So what you're saying is the problem's in my head."

The doctor tilted his head to the left and right as he debated a response. "That's not necessarily how I would put it. What I would say is your body reacted strongly to what could have been an unusual or stressful situation. Were there any such moments at your meeting?"

Only from the moment Flannery and I walked into the banquet room. "There were a handful."

"There you go," the doctor said, patting Ryan swiftly on the right knee. "Now, I want you go get some rest."

"Um, Doc, the other guy—"

"I've found you a single room. Apparently your incredibly audible sighing was as grating to him as his coughing was to you. We'll get you something to help you sleep, feed you in the morning and see how tomorrow morning plays out just to make sure there's nothing we missed. In the meantime, I want you to focus on your breath. Deep breath in through your nose, out through your mouth. And imagine you're anywhere but here. It helps. Good night, Mr. Williams."

Ryan nodded a goodbye, first to the doctor and then to the floor nurse when he said he'd be back to get Ryan moved in a few minutes. He leaned back heavily into his pillow, closed his eyes and tried to breathe deeply through clenched teeth as he saw his entire career unspooling like the paper in the EKG machine. If his body couldn't handle the stress of the job, what chance did he have to continue?

CHAPTER EIGHT

F reed from the hospital for the second time in less than a month, Ryan exited the parking lot and soon was on Interstate 8 heading toward the ocean. A low-pressure system had moved in while he was in captivity and leaden skies unleashed heavy rain showers in fat, cold drops. He turned north when he reached the 5, Sea World appearing to the left of the freeway, exited on Garnet and drove until he reached the Pacific Coast Highway. One block south was World Famous, his favorite restaurant in the city. He pulled up in front of the valet—parking at the Promenade center in front of the restaurant was notoriously difficult to find—and walked inside.

The ceilings and walls of the main part of the restaurant were covered in dark wood paneling. To the left of the entrance, through a narrow dining area, was an exposed patio hard against the ironically named concrete Pacific Beach boardwalk. Though the windows lining the patio were glass, the only protection from the elements above was gray screens, and runoff poured off the main building onto the patio's tile floors as the biting wind coming off the ocean chilled the main dining area as well.

A smarter person would have opted for a table near the bar on the north side of the property but, after another day spent enduring an antiseptic, fluorescent-lit atmosphere punctuated with assorted beeping and other aural assaults, he was more than happy to zip up his sweatshirt and revel in the semi-muffled roar of the ocean. The hostess politely disguised her surprise at his choice and hurried quickly back to the relative warmth of her station at the front of the restaurant. Ryan took a seat facing the ocean, ordered an iced tea and shrimp tacos and turned his attention to the rolling waves. The water reflected the sky's gray mood. Whitecaps were visible well beyond the surf line, and wind-driven breakers crashed hard against the shore. Off to his left, a pair of surfers with more bravery than common sense endured the sea's lashings in search of a curling wave beckoning them to dog-paddle forward and take a chance.

Where some people viewed hospitals as places to be healed, Ryan viewed them as steel and glass towers of death. For every person being treated and recovering, another was passing out of this world while their loved ones watched and waited. Assuming they had loved ones to know of their passing in the first place. The impression had been with him ever since he was eight and his neighbor's mother, an administrator at a local hospital, offered to take him and her daughter to a movie. But first, she needed to stop at the office to pick up some paperwork and she left the two of them in the large, central atrium. All Ryan could feel was the paralyzing sensation of being surrounded by unseen illness. His discomfort wasn't as granular as germaphobia, but rather an aversion to the entire scene.

Now he had spent nearly a week of the past month inside different hospital rooms as nurses stuck him with needles, some to take copious amounts of blood and others to inflict the joy of a burning heparin shot in his abdomen. He winced at the bruising on the crook of his arm from the intravenous fluids and unconsciously reached down and rubbed his abdomen over the dull itch of the injection sites. More galling than the discomfort was knowing this latest trip was caused not by his suddenly balky heart, but his own fraying nervous system. Feeling like damaged goods was painful enough, but it was far worse knowing that everyone in the room at C-Level also knew it, seeing the pity in their expressions as they eyed him as one would a wounded thoroughbred while they waited for the veterinarian to give the final injection to put him out of his misery. And that was before he had hurried out the door with his chest constricted.

It's not your fault, he thought, his decades in politics automatically leading him to deflection. *If you hadn't been surrounded by imbeciles in Alabama. If Flannery had been honest up front instead of foisting Afolayan on you out of the blue.*

His embarrassment and frustration started to turn into righteous indignation. This had nothing to do with his tight-wire walk of a lifestyle and the constant demands upon his faculties. All that he had worked for was being undone, and not by a stranger, but by the person who had groomed him for such work in the first place. How dare Flannery think of Ryan as less than ready, as irrevocably damaged? Who the fuck did he think he was, treating Ryan like an afterthought and shoving him aside for the Washington snake in a suit when they were on the verge of the pinnacle? "I'm Ryan fucking Williams," he muttered.

Ryan, entirely lost in thought and oblivious to the maelstrom outside, startled as a strong gust of wind blew water off the main restaurant's solid roof and onto the patio a few feet to his right. Wind bent the runoff flowing off the roof on an arc closer to his table, and his pant leg was dotted with a handful of deflected drops. Common sense would lead someone to find a more sheltered table, but when his food came he told the server to leave a pitcher of iced tea behind along with the check to save her from coming to his table in this abandoned corner of the restaurant. He ate his tacos quickly lest the weather turn them cold, then leaned back and flipped on his tablet. Browser tabs opened and closed—the holy trinity of the *Times*, *Post* and *Politico*—and he glanced through until he saw a headline on the latter site's Playbook section that sent chills down his arms that the weather had failed to do.

SOURCE: FLANNERY EXPLORING PRESIDENTIAL OPTIONS

"That motherfucker," he said quietly, opening the link. The story itself was only a half-dozen paragraphs long and had little to no detail about the dinner at C-Level. The only people mentioned by name were Flannery, Afolayan and "Ryan Williams, late of Merrick Comstock's failed Senate run in Alabama."

Ryan's face flushed and his left hand squeezed into a fist. When he was at the Arizona Legislature, leadership dreaded the thrice-weekly arrival of the subscription newsletter known as the *Yellow Sheet* because there was no telling what otherwise secret news would appear. Playbook was the modern equivalent, a combination of news leaked directly or picked clean from the tumult of Twitter and acquiring a life of its own.

But that was the lesser part of Ryan's frustration. For all he knew, Flannery told a friendly reporter the barest sketch of the meeting as an additional trial balloon to see what, if any, reaction followed. Rather, it was the nine-word epitaph following his own name that left him livid. That, he knew was Afolayan's work, a kick to the kidneys to make sure Ryan stayed down on the mat.

This can't stand, he thought moments before his heart palpitated and his head began to throb, angering him all the more. A vision of Lyndon Baines Johnson addressing a civil-rights symposium at his presidential library and popping nitro pills like Pez candy entered Ryan's mind unbidden, and he shook it off. He had been given his daily dose of his new high-blood-pressure medicine at the hospital, which meant this was his nerves acting up again. "Fuck," he said quietly, closing his eyes and forcing himself to take deeper breaths until the sudden discomfort started to fade.

***

Ryan closed his tablet then found his server near the warmer bar area, handing her a fifty-dollar bill to cover a twenty-dollar tab in hopes of reversing his current deficit of karma. While he waited for the valet to retrieve his car, he walked away from the protection of the awning and stood along the seawall on the ocean side of the boardwalk to watch the ocean. Rain lashed against him, soaking his clothes in seconds. The heat in his face dissipated so quickly that he found himself chuckling, imagining steam hissing and rising off his skin as the frigid raindrops met anger-fueled crimson skin.

The smile faded once he left the parking lot. California, along with his native Arizona, was a place where raindrops induced panic among drivers. Through most of the country, nothing short of a hurricane or blizzard would cause consternation. But drop a little precipitation on the roadways in Southern California or Phoenix, and most drivers were as lost as ants whose pheromone trails had been disrupted. That was the one thing for which he could give the people of Alabama credit. They knew how to drive in shitty weather.

He drove east on Garnet through slow, confused traffic until the street morphed into a freeway on-ramp. He reluctantly turned onto the interstate rather than attempt a foray onto surface streets covered to varying degrees with flowing runoff, and immediately found himself in the middle of a virtual six-lane parking lot. Traffic lifted where another freeway took commuters east toward Scripps Ranch and other inland neighborhoods but, thanks to an inevitable accident blocking two lanes just past the interchange, Ryan still spent nearly an hour trying to travel the handful of miles back to his hotel in the Gaslamp District. He had experienced both all that he loved and hated about San Diego in the span of an hour, moving from the open vista of the Pacific to the claustrophobic reality of traffic so thick it would be quicker to hop from roof to roof along the cars rather than continue driving.

Unfortunately, the extended drive gave Ryan considerable time to think, and with each beat of his windshield wipers his mood darkened. Like a hurricane feeding off warm tropical waters, his own anger drew from his frustration, his irritation, his pain, corkscrewing inside of him and twisting his thoughts in upon themselves faster and faster, becoming increasingly chaotic until his mind was but a black vortex of negative emotions impenetrable to any other thoughts. Cars passing in a faster lane of traffic, a missed traffic light coming off the expressway, the splash of water from another car's rooster tail through a puddle, all became mortal sins in his mind, and even still his mood descended farther until he knew there was no chance he could break the mood itself. All he could do was wait until the pressure became so great and the anger so profound that it ran out of emotional fuel on which to feed. Then the spell would end and the dark clouds surrounding his head would open, if not into some sort of sunlight, then at least into a lesser shade of gray.

Finally arriving at the hotel, he handed his car off to another valet and, upon reaching his room, stripped off his still damp clothes and stepped into a hot shower, hoping the events of the past few days would follow the water down the drain. Ryan leaned against the shower's side walls, closed his eyes and finally the darkness began to lift, rising off of him with the steam billowing over the glass enclosure.

Exiting the bathroom wearing one of the hotel's bathrobes, Ryan glanced at his phone and saw a message waiting from Charlie.

DEL MAR RACETRACK TOMORROW. 2 P.M. POST. CHECK OUT - HOTEL ROOM RESERVED FOR YOU. SEE YOU THERE.

Ryan started to turn on his tablet to see where the hell Del Mar was but changed his mind. He'd had enough for the day. He reached into the bottom drawer of his nightstand, pulled out a bottle of Maker's Mark and took a sip straight from the neck.

***

The following day, after a fitful but blessedly dreamless sleep, Ryan was back on Interstate 5 heading north past La Jolla and Torrey Pines until the Del Mar Thoroughbred Club and Del Mar fairgrounds appeared to his left. When the track opened in 1937, it was but one small feature at a property that was to give the then-intermittent San Diego County Fair a permanent home, but the dirt oval itself soon became the primary attraction. Seabiscuit had raced there in a match race broadcast coast-to-coast in 1938, and Hollywood luminaries soon made the ninety-minute drive south to play and be seen. Bing Crosby, who greeted the first visitors to the track in 1937, soon was joined by W.C. Fields, Don Ameche, Ava Gardner and more Hollywood royalty, at least until racing was suspended for World War II. With a little imagination, one could still imagine them leaning on the rails of the paddock, dressed in their Southern California finery.

In the early 1990s the original grandstand was demolished and replaced by the towering, six-story building that Ryan saw as he pulled into the parking lot. Beige stucco walls were accented by brick-red clay tiles with an elevated center cupola. The primary entrance was flanked by a pair of towers, each topped with a weather vane featuring a thoroughbred standing at rest.

Following additional directions sent by Charlie, Ryan picked up his ticket at will call and made his way to one of several viewing boxes on the third level of the grandstand. As the host walked him to his seat, he ordered a double whiskey and Coke to help keep his nerves on an even keel. His heart, after all, wasn't the problem right now. He was searching for his box when he saw her, red hair peeking out from a floppy gray straw hat, and he pulled up short. The only thing missing was the ray of sunshine and sappy, soaring soundtrack from *The Natural* when Glenn Close stood up in St. Louis. *Nice trick, Charlie.*

"You're looking better than normal, Doc," he said as he walked into the box.

"I would certainly hope so," Riley said, rising to give Ryan a long hug and a kiss on the cheek before they both sat down.

"Whose idea was this, may I ask?"

"A combined effort, actually. I wanted to check in with you after the latest episode and Charlie knew you'd ignore what he told you, so I became the new messenger."

"Why would I listen to you if I won't listen to my own doctor?"

"Because, Boss, you are crazy but not stupid. But you're also a man, which makes you incapable of admitting weakness in front of another male lest you be seen as something other than the alpha."

Ryan reached into his satchel for his tablet. "It's actually good that you're here, Riley. We've got some work to get done." A few taps on the screen recalled a map of the United States covered in shades of red and blue, not unlike the maps the news networks use on the air each election cycle. Ryan was gesturing at different states, different counties, laying out the groundwork of a plan that could insert him more forcefully into Flannery's campaign, and only after a couple minutes of speaking and gesticulating did he notice that Riley was staring out at the track and likely hadn't heard a word.

"Hey," he said with rising frustration. "What gives?"

Riley turned toward him, her eyes ice cold. "This is what they asked you to do?"

"Not exactly," he said with a half shrug, "but that's not a problem. We just need to let Afolayan know who we are."

"What exactly did he ask you to do?"

"He talked about our work in the Four Corners but, like I said, that's only temporary."

"Not Afolayan," she said, shaking her head tightly. "What did George say that he wanted you to do?"

Ryan started to answer and stopped. He had replayed the conversation by the water multiple times in his head but only now was realizing how little Flannery had said. "He asked me my advice about timing."

"And he's going to follow it."

"As far as I know."

"But did he say so, Ryan?"

"Not in those exact words, Riley, but I know the man. He just didn't want to piss all over Afolayan in public. It's fine."

She shook her head again and looked back at the track, where the horses running in the first race were being guided into the starting gates. Those sitting around them moved toward the edge of their seats in anticipation, but Ryan and Riley were oblivious to their environment. "I didn't come out here for this," she said softly.

"Excuse me?"

Riley turned back, eyes blazing and jaw set in anger. "I said that I didn't come out here for this."

"Come out here for what?"

"For this," she yelled, reaching out and pulling the tablet out of his hands, turning it off and dropping it in her oversize purse in one smooth motion. A hostess arrived with Ryan's drink but

Riley, face now fully flushed, yelled at her to take it back and return with ice water. Ryan gave a quick nod of assent before turning on his assistant.

"What the hell are you doing?" he screamed.

"What the hell am I doing? Jesus, Ryan. Are you really this goddamn stupid?"

"Watch it," he said, pointing a finger at her only to have her slap it away.

"No, Ryan, you watch it. I just flew 400 miles at your doctor's request to try and drill the slightest bit of reason into that thick skull of yours, and all you want to do is describe your grand plan for expanding your role in a campaign in which Flannery is including you only as a favor."

"Bullshit," he said, turning away as the crowd alternately groaned and cheered as the horses crossed the finish line.

"Bullshit?" She took hold of his left arm and pulled until he looked back at her. "What was that blurb in *Politico* yesterday, then? Was that following your advice? And when was the last time the Four Corner states mattered in the slightest in a presidential election, Ryan?"

"Colorado and Arizona in 2016..."

" ...were inventions of the media," she interrupted. "The action was back East and through the Midwest. That's it."

"So we work our way that direction."

Riley threw her hands up in frustration. "You don't think he already has people working on that?" She looked and saw the pained expression on his face and softened her tone. "This isn't a job offer, Ryan. It's fucking charity. And you're better than that."

"You're wrong," he said, his voice little more than a whisper.

"Really? How long did it take before someone mentioned Alabama. One minute? Two?" Ryan ground his jaws together but said nothing. "Are you going to sit there and tell me that little dig Afolayan planted wasn't intentional? God, Ryan, how many times have you done shit like that yourself?"

"You saw that?"

"Of course I saw that. Everyone saw that. You're walking wounded, and that's not even taking into account your recent health episodes."

"And what does that make you?" he said coldly.

"Me? I'm second in command to a former golden child, which sucks. Not because I'm not here for you but because you...we...deserve better than to be judged on the basis of one racist fuck who couldn't get out of his own way. The difference is I realize it and I'm accepting it."

"I'm not ready to do that," Ryan said. "He owes me this campaign."

"Except he doesn't, Boss," she spat out. Regaining her composure, she reached out to Ryan, touching his forearm gently. "On top of that, your doctor is telling you to take a step back. Your body is telling you to take a step back. And this," she said, showing him the *Politico* article on her phone, "is telling you it's time to take a step back."

"Or maybe that it's time to prove myself."

"You've done that, Ryan, over and over again. But right now, it doesn't matter. Flannery doesn't want to leave you behind, so he's offering you a token."

"Can't you see? I can turn that into so much more."

"But they won't let you." Riley turned in her seat to face him more fully. "Look, I came out here because I care about you and I'm worried about you, not to sit here and watch you try and kill yourself tilting at windmills."

"Is that what you think this is?"

"If you're more concerned with gaining territory in a nonexistent campaign than taking care of yourself, then yeah, I do."

"You don't understand, Riley."

"No, I don't. More to the point, I don't want to." She stood quickly, reached into her purse and handed him back the tablet along with a slip of paper. "This is where you have your hotel reservation for tonight and tomorrow. Charlie figured that would be about as long as you'd be willing to stay put."

"Where are you going?"

Riley sighed heavily and looked out to the west, toward Del Mar's dog beach and the ocean. "I'm going to go find a bar with a view of the water and have a drink."

"You want company?"

"I do," she said with a grim smile, "but not yours. Not tonight. I'll probably end up saying something that will get me fired."

"I haven't fired you yet," he said with a mirthless chuckle.

"At the rate you're going," she said sadly, "you won't need to."

"Would it help at all if I told you I'm in love with you?" He cringed as soon as the words left his mouth. *Trying to fool yourself again, cover a gaping emotional hole with a band-aid?*

She stopped and dropped her head in resignation before continuing on to the exit. Fortunately, she knew him well enough to ignore his momentary insanity.

CHAPTER NINE

R yan drove along Highway 101 until it merged with Camino Del Mar, the city's main street, then turned right into the sprawling L'Auberge Del Mar resort. Like the race track, L'Auberge's history reached back to pre-World War II days. The resort stood on the site of the original Hotel Del Mar—the destination for Hollywood types to retire to when the day at the track ended. Little of the property could be seen from street level. The beauty of the resort instead was revealed gradually as visitors travelled along the main driveway leading to a wide circle with greenery in the center. The tall peaked gable over the entryway, the large windows extending either direction and the gas fireplace to the left of the main doors gave the resort the feel of a Swiss chalet. Inside, the rustic motif disappeared. A wide lobby suffused with natural light from nearly a dozen floor-to-ceiling windows held dozens of comfortable chairs and housed a pair of bars.

Ryan pulled up and handed over his keys and luggage to the valet and noticed a large, holly-flecked wreath on the wall above the fireplace, a nod to the fast-approaching holiday season. But his appreciation was brief. He walked briskly inside, checked in while saying as little as possible, and went up to his room to shower and change. His mind still churned from his conversation with Riley. Who was she to tell him what his future held? He had built his career from the ground up, moving on to bigger and better challenges whenever the opportunity arose. He wasn't about to have his legacy defined by a few months in Alabama and directed by a pompous prick like Seth Afolayan. His destiny remained his own. He stepped out of the shower, changed into one of the provided robes, picked up his tablet and sat at the table and chair in his room overlooking the pool. He could see the tips of the waves off in the distance to his left, but forced his gaze back to the screen in front of him.

There were two distinct parts of Ryan's job. The first was providing direction and messaging to a campaign and, in truth, it was the easier of the two. Having some sense of language helped, but given that sometimes simple was best, a couple quick turns of phrase fed to a candidate and plastered on a website and bumper stickers would in many cases suffice. But where he really earned his keep was crisis management, the ability to avoid as many pitfalls as possible along the way, but then to paper over problems as they arose and keep forward momentum moving. The mechanics were simple enough—identify the issue, determine the extent of the damage, be aware of the worst possible outcome and build a strategy to acknowledge, respond and move on. Translate a situation from an unknown to a known based on past experience and execute accordingly. No emotions. No panic. Simply business.

That was the skill needed now, because Ryan was facing not one crisis but two—the albatross that was Merrick Ogden Comstock, and his health issues. Opening a new document on his tablet, he started working on the first. The issue wasn't that Ryan's candidate lost. It was that a candidate that couldn't conceivably lose still did so, and took down his party's control of the chamber at the same time. Ryan struck through the latter words as soon as he typed them and added a note in italics. *This was only one seat of several—not my doing.* His responsibility started and ended with Comstock, and what crushed his Senate campaign was going off script. End of story.

"DAMAGE," he typed, then looked up from his tablet and stared out the window. He already was seeing the beginnings of it, the tarnish on his own hard-earned brand courtesy of Afolayan. Worse, he wasn't the only one whispering—he was just the only one Ryan knew about. That was the nature of the beast. Inevitably, others in the political community were compounding the damage in ways big and small, subtle and overt. Ryan knew he needed to get ahead of the issue. The only question was how. He watched servers and waitstaff moving between tables downstairs at the Coastline restaurant, and a smile slowly crept over his face. The answer began with the source of his latest problem. He picked up his phone and typed a quick text to a friendly reporter at an online political website, offering the story of the Comstock campaign as dictated by himself. It was a move he should have made some time ago had his health and subsequent anger not gotten in the way.

"Keep the emotions out," he muttered to himself, shaking his head at his own error.

With burgeoning confidence, he closed the document and opened a new one. "HEALTH," he typed, pausing before adding "CARDIAC EPISODE." He looked at the words, the first time he had written or spoken them, and scoffed at his own hesitation to use the phrase. He was still on the right side of the grass, so why fear admitting what really had happened? *But that's not all of it*, he thought. Ryan shook his head quickly. "I liked you better when you were a zebra," he said to that small voice. No, there would be no need to go any further on the health front. This was his narrative to mold as he chose. The second trip to the hospital? Nothing more than a justifiable knee-jerk reaction to symptoms uncomfortably close to a second episode that turned out to be nothing at all. An excess of caution born of an initial situation. End of story.

His phone buzzed and he glanced down to see a return text asking about his availability for an interview. "Like Pavlov's dog," he said to no one as he smiled widely, leaned back in his chair and started running down the questions in his own mind. Done correctly, he thought, he could work his heart issues into the story but do so in such a manner that he became an object of sympathy, not pity. He wouldn't be the consultant who couldn't control a candidate or, in the end, his own stress. He would be the man who invested so much into trying to spit shine the turd that was Merrick Comstock that he damn near killed himself in the effort. It was a matter of semantics, he knew, but on such things empires had been built.

For the first time in what felt like forever, Ryan felt full confidence rushing through him. Then he stood and glanced at the mirror over the dresser, and the small voice returned. *You can lie to them, Ryan, but you can't lie to me.* "Fuck you," he said bitterly, turning to the closet to find something to wear downstairs to the bar.

***

Ten minutes later he walked into the lobby, home to the Living Room bar. True to its name, there was a fully stocked bar on the right side of the room. Toward the back was living-room furniture and decor pulled straight from *Better Homes.* Through the high glass doors to Ryan's right was the Coastline, which featured views of the ocean several blocks away, and beyond that the pool and Blue Bar. One lonely couple huddled at a round table with a white linen tablecloth next to a flaming heat lamp at Coastline, while everyone else remained inside on this unseasonably cool evening.

Ryan moved to the far side of the bar and took one of the two chairs, providing him a view of the majority of the room and the ocean beyond. He had left his ubiquitous tablet upstairs, content for the moment in the groundwork he had already laid. The pent-up anger of the past few days transformed into focused determination. Ryan ordered a whiskey and coke from the bartender and eased back contently onto his bar chair. He would worry about his alcohol intake tomorrow.

A short while later, two women walked into the lobby and sat at the long side of the bar closest to the windows and ordered drinks. Ryan took brief notice of them as he sipped his whiskey and ordered some calamari. He was so intent on how he would turn the next day's interview into a triumph that he didn't notice when one of the two women left and the other, a tall brunette in a classic black cocktail dress, sat down in the corner chair next to him. She wore green eyeshadow that helped give her dark brown eyes a lighter, almost amber, cast. Light pink gloss highlighted the fullness of her lips. Ryan didn't know what fragrance she wore, only that it could have been marketed under the name enchantress. Straight black hair, curling toward her chin at the bottom, and sleek bangs framed her face and when she smiled, the slightest of creases appeared in the outside of her eyes.

The woman looked at Ryan's appetizer plate, delicately lifted a piece of calamari, dipped it into the small accompanying bowl of marinara and popped it into her mouth.

"By all means help yourself," he said with a bemused smile.

"I usually do," she said, her eyes twinkling.

He extended his hand in introduction, but she instead placed a finger on his lips. "Let's not do the whole name thing. What brings you here, business or pleasure?"

"Business."

"Hmmm, what kind?"

"You don't want my name, but you want to know what I do for a living?"

"Surprise me," she said.

"Okay," he said, taking a sip of his drink and ordering refills for both of them. "I'm a shepherd. We're having a convention in town."

She smiled and leaned in closer. "And where would this convention be?"

"Well, that's the problem. Bo Peep was organizing the whole thing and, well, you can imagine how that turned out." She broke out laughing and raised a hand toward her mouth. "Sufficiently surprised?"

"Definitely so. So what should I call you, Mr. Shepherd?"

What would a good name for a shepherd be? Ryan wondered. The only two shepherds he could think of were Moses and Ralph the dog from the coyote cartoons. "Seamus will do," he said finally.

"Nice to meet you, Seamus. You may call me Scarlet."

"I supposed you're here because somebody burned down your plantation," he said with a grin.

A momentary sadness passed across her face, like a single gray cloud obscuring the sun, and it passed nearly as quickly. "Let's say there were more visitors to Tara than I had imagined, so a few days by the water seemed grand."

"Why Del Mar?"

Scarlet leaned back, her eyes opening a touch wider in surprise. "Have you not walked around this place yet?"

Ryan shook his head.

"This is like Fantasyland for grown-ups, right down to the too-expensive appetizers. Oh, and you don't have to stand in line for hours with cranky, tired three-year-olds who don't really want to go on the Peter Pan ride after all. If you can't suspend reality for a little while here with the ocean visible almost everywhere you go and just settle into the vibe, there may be no hope for you."

"That sounds ominous."

"Not really, Seamus. You're already here, after all."

"That I am," he conceded. "Though," he continued, his expression hardening, "I must say I'm not entirely certain I am the right man for whatever this may be."

"Oh, Seamus," she said with an exaggerated pout, "let's not ruin the fun. I am neither an escort nor the police, if that is your concern."

"I didn't meant to imply—"

Scarlet sighed and flashed a sad smile. "It's fine," Scarlet said, reaching to cover Ryan's hand. Warmth pulsated from the back of his hand through his wrist and down his arm. "I have been anything but subtle. I just thought I'd seen a fellow traveler who might benefit from the presence of a partner for a spell.

"I certainly could," she added quietly.

The bartender delivered the drinks and Ryan raised his newly arrived glass, clinking it against Scarlet's in a toast. "To weary fellow travelers."

"*Salud*," she said before taking a long pull off her cosmopolitan.

"By the way. Where did your friend go?"

Scarlet shrugged. "I imagine she went off on her own hunting expedition after I called dibs."

"Dibs? Oh, please tell me I became the subject of a friendly competition between the two of you."

"Sorry, champ," she said. "You really weren't her type anyway."

"We can't please everyone."

Their conversation continued in a similar vein for another twenty minutes, during which time Ryan determined that Scarlet, whatever her actual name, had taken a severe dislike to men after finding her boyfriend visiting neighboring plantations, and that her solution was to plow a new field of her own to exact cosmic revenge.

"Speaking of which," she said, leaning in conspiratorially, "I have a question to ask you."

"It's not about that bitch Bo Peep, is it?"

"Not at all," she said, laughing before turning serious. "Have you ever made love in a genie bottle?"

"Not since I watched Jeannie reruns when I was a teenager."?

She turned her head to the side quizzically. ""As in I dream of or the cartoon with Babu?"

"Cartoons," he replied. "But did I mention I was a teenager?"

"Excellent point," she said. "Maybe you should try it in reality."

"That would be one hell of a trick."

She reached into her clutch and pulled out a small plastic bag of gummy bears. "Have you been trick-or-treating?" he asked.

Scarlet arched her eyebrows. "No tricks, lover," she said. She was about to open the bag when Ryan reached across and took it from her, turning it over in his hands to make sure it was hermetically sealed. "So suspicious, Seamus."

"Mom told me to always check the candy wrappers," Ryan said as he handed the bag back. "What can I say?"

"How responsible of you." Scarlet opened the bag with exaggerated motions, showing empty hands like a magician for effect. Once open, she reached in and pulled out one blue and one red candy. "Choose."

"Is this where I learn the secret of the Matrix?"

Scarlet grinned mischievously. "Follow the white rabbit, Seamus." He reached over for the red bear and eyed it skeptically while Scarlet took the other, popped it in her mouth and started to chew it slowly. He held it up to his nose and could smell the faintest hint of marijuana attached to the gelatin. She leaned close and kissed him gently on the lips. "Don't you want to come with me...Seamus?" she purred, reaching out and running her index finger along his right arm as she did so.

"One more for luck," he said, kissing her in return before putting the gummy bear on his tongue and swallowing it whole.

"Such a hurry for a man who spends his days on a mountainside."

"I wonder what my sheep will say when I wake up without a kidney tomorrow morning."

"Oh, wow," she said. "You've figured out my motive. In fact, my partner is filling a bathtub with ice as we speak." He looked blankly at her before she continued. "Just relax, baby, and tell me more about the demanding life of a shepherd."

It was just over a half hour later when Ryan felt his mind beginning to cloud, that slightly buzzed feeling akin to that one extra drink that takes you from mere enjoyment into a deep relaxation. "Ah, Seamus," Scarlet said, "I see we're about to go down the rabbit hole."

"You too?"

She leaned over to kiss him. "I've been waiting for you to arrive."

They moved from the bar onto a love seat situated nearby, and Scarlet asked a server for a pair of iced teas. "You'll never feel the caffeine," she said in answer to Ryan's questioning look. "So you were telling me about your flock."

"Ummm..."

"Seamus, don't offer a girl a thorough flock and then don't deliver," she said with a mischievous look. "Continue."

Ryan continued the story briefly but discovered his thoughts were getting more muddled, his peripheral vision cloudier. Suddenly he was unable to perform more than one act at a time. Wherever his eyes fell, his full attention was centered on that one place to the exclusion of all others. Scarlet burst into another giggling fit next to him.

"What did I miss?" he asked.

"The last half of your sentence," she said. "You just stopped halfway through."

"Really?" Ryan tried to remember what he had been saying but the words were gone. His memory was reduced to a handful of snippets, most arriving on a thirty-second delay from the time he actually had uttered or heard the words. "What was I talking about?"

"I don't have any idea," she said, and they both started to laugh, the room and people around them melting into nothingness.

***

Time seemingly disappeared, or at least split into parallel paths of decidedly different speeds. Ryan felt like he was watching the still camera during the high-speed musical montage from some cheesy '80s movie, or from the traffic scenes where the camera holds still while headlights and taillights stream quickly past. Words, sentences, thoughts all elongated in his mind like multicolored strings of yarn favored by cat-owners for their pets' amusement, and he found himself trying to pull the threads together and knit them into coherence. Single thoughts lasted minutes; sentences took a half hour to form. As he attempted to string together a handful of words, Scarlet picked up the happy hour menu and was walking her index and middle fingers across its surface.

He glanced down at his watch. Two minutes had passed since they'd ordered drinks, yet it felt they had been on the love seat for hours.

"I think...," he started when the server brought the glasses to them.

"I think so too," she said, asking the waitress to close their tab. "You're looking a little bit out of it."

"Me? What about you?"

"I've just spent the last five minutes climbing up the menu, Seamus."

"You mean reading."

"No," she said adamantly. "I mean climbing. Like, looking for letters with descenders to use as handholds so I could pull myself up to the words above."

The waitress returned with the check, and Ryan thought for a moment or two before remembering his room number, as well as his real name. He stood, a little unsteady, and reached out his hand to help Scarlet off the love seat before offering her his elbow. "Well," he said, "let's see if we can find you some other places for your hands to hold on to."

"We're going to miss the sunset," she said. "You're supposed to kiss the person you're with when the sun hits the water."

"Good thing I have a room with windows," he answered, leading her to the elevator.

***

Scarlet disappeared into the bathroom to freshen up after they went upstairs, giving Ryan time to tuck his wallet and tablet into the safe in his room. He stood in front of the safe for an extra moment, amazed that enough synapses had fired in the right order to allow him to do so. She emerged a moment later and he turned to face her. In his mind, they locked into a passionate embrace, mouths and tongues exploring each other as his hands ran down her back and across her hips. He realized she was not wearing panties, though it seemed to take several minutes for the message to reach his brain from his fingertips.

In reality, they awkwardly collided to the side of the bed, kisses lingering as they became so focused on that single act that the passage of time meant nothing. Ryan made a move to try and lift Scarlet into the bed but managed to lift only one leg before she fell backward onto the bed, dissolving into laughter. He followed, bouncing away from where she lay and spending what seemed like hours trying to locate her again on the king-size mattress. Clothes were removed in awkward stages and with no shortage of giggling and, once naked, both lay back on

101

the bed for a moment to catch their breath. They came back together in the middle, Ryan lazily tracing a circle around her nipple for an hour, or a day, or a week, Scarlet moaning and reaching for him, trying to push him just far enough away to have access to his waist without causing him to wobble and fall back onto his ass. Finally she took a firm hold, eased him onto his back purposefully, and guided him inside her.

Ryan's lower half was on autopilot as he struggled to figure out where to focus. When he looked at her breasts swaying in front of him, he lost track of her hips grinding against him. When he concentrated on that, her face became fuzzy and he had to actively remember to lean up now and again and kiss her.

They continued on like this as minutes stretched into hours in his mind when, out of nowhere, Scarlet arched her back and called out to God and then fell heavily back on top of him. He needed only a few extra moments until he finished as well, and his hands fell onto her back as he pulled her close. "Holy shit," he whispered.

"I so needed that, Seamus."

"Scarlet, my dear, I wholeheartedly agree," he said as they panted in rhythm. "Though performing while the name Seamus was being called out was a little disconcerting."

She placed a hand on his chest and pulled herself up. "You seemed to manage just fine, my shepherd," she said with a smile.

She straddled him countless minutes before she shifted and slid down his body, resting her head on his chest as her fingers traced circles in his chest hair. "A small nap might be in order," she said.

"No objections from me." Ryan pulled an additional pillow underneath his head and shoulders and reflexively glanced at the clock on the nightstand. They'd been upstairs for all of fifteen minutes.

CHAPTER TEN

R yan awoke the following morning to the sound of running
water and off-tune humming. He rolled toward the sound,
feeling the cotton sheets rubbing against his entirely bare skin.
Narrow rays of sunshine streamed through a tiny gap in his
hotel room's blackout curtains, and pieces of the prior evening
emerged slowly from the lingering medicinal fog. *Medicinal*...
Ryan lurched toward the nightstand, sat up, turned on the
reading lamp to look for his wallet before remembering that he
had locked it away in the safe the night before. He padded
quietly to the closet and opened the safe, just to be certain. The
sudden tension eased and some of the fog rolled away when he
saw all his credit cards and cash were accounted for. He took a
deep breath, walked to the wide windows and opened the heavy
drapes wide, leaving the gauzy white curtain closest to the glass
closed to keep from flashing the other hotel guests. In the
distance to the left he could see the Pacific, the sun reflecting
off the rippling waves in an array of sparkling gems.

He suddenly realized how dry his mouth felt and went to the
bathroom sink to swig a glass of water. The water still was
running and, with a mischievous grin, he reached for the

bathroom door handle only to find it was locked. His building excitement waned and he wandered back across the room, pulled on his boxer briefs, settled into one of the twin chairs near the window and started flipping through websites on his phone.

Scarlet emerged from the bathroom moments later, a bath towel wrapped around her torso, dripping dark hair plastered against her scalp and back. She turned toward the windows, hesitated ever so briefly and then smiled. "I didn't mean to wake you," she said.

"I didn't mind being awoken," Ryan answered.

"Last night was..."

"Interesting," he finished. Ryan glanced at her shapely legs emerging from the bottom of the towel and started to feel his interest building anew. "It looks like they're serving breakfast on the patio downstairs if you'd like."

She walked across the room, stood next to his chair and leaned over to look at the restaurant below, the towel rising high on her upper thigh as she did so. Ryan impulsively reached out and ran his hand along her leg, starting near the back of her knee and slowly rising higher. Scarlet turned toward him and smiled coyly. "I imagine they'll still have bacon a little later."

"I would imagine so."

Without a word, she untucked her towel and let it fall to the floor. He watched it fall, then slowly, deliberately tracked his eyes back up from her toes to her face. Scarlet reached out a hand and led Ryan back to the bed, thoughts of bacon and eggs temporarily set aside.

An hour later, both their second round and breakfast both complete, Scarlet rose from the table and kissed Ryan on the cheek. "Thank you for a lovely time, Seamus."

"Don't you think it's safe to drop the aliases, Scarlet?"

He saw the same twinkle in her eye as the prior evening, along with the slightest hint of passing sadness, masked nearly as quickly as it appeared. "Meet me for sunset tonight at Poseidon, my shepherd," she said. "We can discuss names then."

"Until sunset," he said, taking her hand and brushing his lips across her fingers before watching her walk back into the lobby, the black dress hugging her body as perfectly as the night before. Taking the early hour at least somewhat into account, he ordered a rum with pineapple juice and turned his attention to the interview coming up later in the day.

***

That evening, Ryan sat in one of the high chairs at the L-shaped bar inside Poseidon, an upscale restaurant located a few yards off the water on Del Mar Beach. Couples gathered at the tables on the outdoor patio, vying for the seat closest to the several space heaters warming the cold air as the ocean rushed upon the shore and retreated back upon itself. It was still relatively early but the winter sun was low on the horizon, bathing the restaurant and the beach in golden rays. Ryan nursed a whiskey and Coke, glancing every now again toward the restaurant's entrance to his left before turning the other direction to watch the water.

"What time was she supposed to be here?"

Ryan turned back to see one of the two bartenders standing in front of him, a questioning look on his face. "Excuse me?"

"The woman you're waiting for. What time did she say she'll be here?"

Ryan looked down at his watch. "That would be about twenty minutes ago," he said with a grimace.

"Ah. Sorry about that, boss. At least you've still got the view."

"The view wasn't bad last night either," Ryan said with a wink, and the bartender answered with a knowing smile. "But really, it's not that big of a deal... Scott," Ryan added with a glance at the man's nametag. The bartender nodded with practiced nonchalance, tapped the bar with the flat of his hand and moved off to check on other patrons.

Ryan realized he should feel disappointed but didn't. Not after the half hour he had spent on the phone with the reporter.

He rehashed everything that had taken place during the campaign almost by rote, the result of spending several weeks reviewing every detail and crafting the story of what had happened and why Comstock had doomed himself to lose. The reporter asked clarifying questions now and then but, for the most part, the conversation was less interview than thirty-minute soliloquy about how he, Ryan Williams, had done everything possible to save an obstinate, crass, backward candidate from himself.

"Hell, Bob," Ryan said, "I damn near died in the effort. Tell me how many other consultants can say that?"

"I thought you said your arteries were blocked."

"Let's not ruin a good story with the details," Ryan said with a laugh.

"How about a question off the record, Ryan?"

"Shoot."

"How are you really feeling? I mean, that whole thing had to have scared the shit out of you."

"Entirely off the record?"

"You know me."

"Honestly," he said, pausing for dramatic effect, "I'm feeling better than I have in a long, long time." He could hear the reporter groan in disappointment on the other side of the phone. "Really, Bob. I've got more energy than I ever have and one of the best people I know is running for president. How does it get better than this? Hell, you can even put that on the record."

The reporter's voice perked up noticeably. "About Flannery running?"

"No, no," Ryan said, smiling widely. "Only about how fucking awesome I feel these days. Sorry, buddy."

Ryan drained the remainder of his drink, waved the empty glass toward the bartender for a refill and turned back toward the beach. It seemed the population on the sand had doubled over the last few minutes as sunset approached, all standing in mute admiration as the sun approached the water's edge. Surfers and paddleboarders alike sat on their boards, ignoring the passing waves in silent salute to the majesty of nature. Patrons at the bar wandered onto the patio to take a quick picture of the sky, now a mix of brilliant yellow, flaming orange and deep reds, and the din of chatter ebbed as the sun's lowest edge kissed the top of the ocean.

The bartender returned with Ryan's refill and himself stopped to watch the scene.

"Is it always like this?" Ryan asked, his voice low given the quiet around him.

"Pretty much, unless it's raining. But can you blame them?"

"I'm from Arizona," he said with a half shrug. "Dusty air. We have sunsets like you wouldn't believe most nights."

"But it's different when it's the ocean."

"I'll give you that," Ryan said, raising his glass as if in salute. "That's hard to duplicate."

He took a sip and gazed at the tableau in front of him, noticing for the first time a slender woman standing calf deep in the surf. Where everyone else in the water wore a wetsuit, she was dressed in a tight black tank top and matching black yoga pants, the bottom edges of which were soaked in salt water. Her dark hair was pulled back in a ponytail that reached below her shoulder blades. She stood erect yet somehow relaxed, chest and face thrust forward toward the half-set sun, arms at shallow angles by her side. She stood in profile, revealing an oval face with high cheekbones, tapering to an angled jawline punctuated with a pronounced, rounded chin.

She appeared both fully in sync with the sunset and entirely separate from the soft buzz around her, serenely aware of everything and focused enough to see nothing at all. Ryan watched, entranced, as she moved deliberately from one position to the next, silhouetted against the setting sun.

"Hey, Scott," Ryan said, glancing at the bartender and nodding toward the water. "What can you tell me about the lady in the water? You ever seen her before?"

Scott tilted his head to the left for a better look and the corner of his lip curled up in a grin. "Oh," he said. "You're looking at Maggie. You have good taste, boss."

"So she lives here, I take it."

"She does. She's got a yoga studio up on the main drive. Great lady. But I can tell you, it ain't gonna happen."

As Ryan turned fully back to the bar, applause broke out as the last of the sun's disc slipped below the horizon, leaving only the shimmering rays in its wake. "What's not going to happen?"

"More or less whatever you're thinking."

"She have a husband? Boyfriend? Girlfriend?"

Scott chuckled. "None that I know of. Let's suffice it to say many suitors have performed reconnaissance from afar, but no one I know of has actually gained entrance to the fortress."

"Sounds like a challenge."

"Do with it what you will," Scott said, tapping the bar again out of habit as a pair of newcomers sat a few seats to Ryan's right.

***

Maggie Roberson kicked off her flip-flops and walked into the surf until the water covered her calves. She shivered against the bracing sea washing around her but smiled at the feeling of refreshment. Her body came to life as the fading sun shone on her face and every skin cell reacted to the touch of the ocean. She placed her feet a few inches apart and held her arms down by her sides at a slight angle. *Tadasana.* After a handful of deep

108

breaths she closed her eyes, inhaled and spread her arms out wide, then moved them up and pressed her hands together over her head before lowering her arms with a long exhale until her hands were in front of her chest. *Urdhva hastasana.* On dry land this would be followed by additional yoga poses but here, in the rolling white surf, she instead moved her hands back to her sides in *tadasana*, the mountain pose, and focused on the water around her.

The cold kiss of the Pacific Ocean was bracing where it first made contact with her skin. Water splashed higher at random intervals, rolling onto the beach. Then gravity would take hold and the water would run back off of the sand, seeking its natural level, sucking the gritty mud out from underneath her feet as it retreated. She moved her awareness to the soles of her feet and felt each individual grain of sand pulling away, rushing across the silt already deposited from countless waves before and partially burying her sinking feet. She unconsciously shifted her weight until her feet emerged from the mud and she was back in balance.

Even as she did that, though, she could hear the gurgling as the retreating water met the incoming tide, the returning water moving out to sea underneath the broken wave heading toward shore, a portion of that wave moving counterclockwise as it was drawn with the water being pulled back into the ocean, the otherwise blue water turning tan from the circulating sand. The seemingly eternal sound lasted but a few seconds before the momentum of the wave won, sending water back up the beach and around her legs to start the process again. Except the process never was repeated identically, odd waves crashing hard and splashing water up her abdomen and across her chest, others barely reaching her feet before withdrawing. Every now and again, she would hear the loud crash of a particularly large wave cresting and breaking a couple dozen feet offshore to signify the end of a set, and then she'd count the seconds until the fast-moving water reached her.

The ocean, she thought, was both oblivious to her presence and fully aware, moving around her as if she were no more than a pebble while simultaneously pulling at her, enticing her to become part of the system. She slowly became aware of the rhythm of her own heartbeat, consistent as the waves yet predictable in a way the water never could be.

Soon the sixty-degree water would take its toll and strip her feet of feeling. Soon the muscles of her legs, though soothed by the cool water, would ask her to shift her weight rather than remain still against the odds. Once the sunset had released everyone from its spell, the sounds of activity around her, the breathing of beach walkers and the jingle of dog collars and leashes and even the faint conversation from the restaurants behind her, would compete for her attention with the ocean and the inner stillness she had created.

But not now. Not yet.

Another wave rolled in and she took another cleansing breath, allowing the briny aroma to sink deep into her lungs as a slight smile crossed her face in the sun's final rays.

***

Someone laughed loudly inside the bar, and Ryan reflexively turned to look. A man who looked like something out of a 1980s movie—short stature, oddly combed hair and a too-wispy mustache—was entertaining a trio of women, all of whom acted as if they'd never seen anyone more handsome or heard anyone more funny. It must be the size of his wallet, Ryan thought with a catty smirk. He watched for another few seconds before turning back to the water to take another look at Maggie, but she'd already disappeared into the quickening darkness. He got up and quickly went out the restaurant's entrance, but she was nowhere to be seen. His shoulders sagged as disappointment swept through. Catching himself, he chuckled at the absurdity of his petulance. If it was another one-nighter he was looking for, he could find a suitable target within minutes just as he had the night before. And, frankly, what else should he be looking for while staying in a pricey hotel hundreds of miles from home?

Ryan chuckled again and turned back toward the restaurant, but swiveled back to the walkway from the beach after just a few steps. What exactly was it that he had seen, and why did it seem to matter?

Ego, he thought. It had to be ego. Another chance to distance himself from the man in the hospital and prove once again that he was as impervious as before. He closed his eyes, rocked his neck from side to side as if to work out a kink, and sighed. *You're going to need to do a lot more than get laid a few times to feel like you used to, dummy.* "Fuck," he muttered. He dropped his head and pinched the bridge of his nose, pushing that last thought back into the recesses of his subconscious, at least temporarily, and forced a small, determined smile. "Then again," he said quietly, "a little challenge never hurt anyone." Ryan bobbed his head a couple of times in affirmation, tapped one of the wooden posts in the restaurant's entryway, and went back to his barstool for another round.

***

Maggie walked along the water's edge in a deep purple sundress, flip-flops in hand as her feet left imprints upon the damp sand. Though the sun shone bright in the sky, she was alone on the beach. None of the usual collection of tourists, dog walkers and joggers. No surfers in the water. No one at any of the lifeguard stations. She glanced over her shoulder toward Poseidon and the patio was empty there as well, as if no one else existed. Suddenly a fog started to build on the horizon and roll toward the beach. Clouds that were nowhere to be seen moments ago scudded across the sky, muting the landscape with gray light. The fog poured onshore, visibility dropped, but she kept walking. Then a shadow appeared in front of her, causing her to stop moving and her heart to race in alarm. She felt more than heard the voice coming from the person now in front of her, shrouded in the mist.

Relax, it said. *It's me.*

Even sound asleep, her subconscious recognized the recurring dream. Her imagined self took a deep breath, knowing in advance how everything would play out. She took a step forward and saw the facial features she once had known so well, but which now had turned indistinct. "Bruce," she said as tears built reflexively in her eyes at the sight of her long-deceased husband.

"Why do you always cry when you see me?"

"For the same reason you always ask the question," she said, stepping forward again and reaching out in vain to take the shadow's hand. "I'm afraid I'm beginning to forget what you look like."

"You won't," Bruce said, "not entirely. You know that."

"I miss you terribly." Tears streamed down her cheeks. She thought of moving forward but knew from past dreams that he always would be just out of reach. These dreams followed a set pattern, and she could sense her subconscious guiding her from one part, one sentence to the next.

"I miss you, too." Then the unexpected happened. Bruce leaned forward and took her hand in his, and suddenly she felt the rush of memory. Dream or no, she was certain she could feel the pressure of his touch in her palm and smell the scent of his cologne floating lightly on the breeze. She looked down at their entwined hands, eyes wide in surprise. "How?" she stammered.

Bruce took another step and the mist cleared a little more. She noticed for the first time that there was a golden haze surrounding them as the sun fought through the fog and clouds. "It's time, Maggie."

"Time for what?" This was an unfamiliar thread, a script she had not seen before. But as he flashed a familiar smile, the right corner of his lip tugged upward, she realized she knew the answer to her own question. She shook her head against the idea, fought against the notion that she was ready to find someone and try to build a real relationship versus the short-term flings with which she had staved off loneliness without committing her heart. *It's been five years.* His voice entered her thoughts unbidden, and the resistance she was feeling started to melt at the edges.

A question formed in her mind but was answered almost immediately. "He's looking for you," Bruce said. "He doesn't know it yet, but he is. He's lost at the moment." He glanced over his shoulder where a second figure appeared, dark and indistinct, shrouded in shadows. Maggie squinted, strained her eyes, searching for any identifying features without success. She was filled with a sense of uncertainty, of sadness. And of curiosity.

"How will I know him?"

Bruce smiled, withdrew his hand and moved back into the again-gathering mists. "An open mind and an open heart. The universe will take care of the rest."

He was disappearing quickly, and Maggie had the sudden sense she would not be seeing him again. "Wait!" she yelled, but her voice was muted by the clinging fog. As suddenly as he had appeared, he was gone. The fog withdrew but not the clouds, and once again she was alone on the gray-filtered beach. Then she woke up, and the details faded almost immediately from memory.

Gathering a robe around her, she walked onto the deck extending from her bedroom. Her house was on the Del Mar Heights themselves, two blocks north of Camino del Mar and only a few blocks more away from her studio space. Like her studio, her house had been purchased with money won in a settlement following the auto accident that had claimed Bruce's life—money and a home and a studio she gladly would have traded to have Bruce back. Even though, from the message she'd just received from the universe, maybe the time had come for her to move on.

"An open mind and an open heart," she said, echoing Bruce's last statement and knowing those words were plucked from the conclusion of the yoga classes she taught daily. "If only it were always that easy."

CHAPTER ELEVEN

Ryan drove down the hill from L'Auberge to Coast Boulevard and the beach shortly after sunrise the following morning. He parked in the public lot between Poseidon and the Del Mar Motel on the beach, joining surfers who stood behind the trunks of their cars changing into wetsuits as they prepared to search for suitable waves in the cold waters of the Pacific. Ryan walked past the 17th Street lifeguard station and took a few steps to his left in search of breakfast. He was standing just beyond Poseidon's open patio, which was followed by the enclosed patio at Jake's, another restaurant that only opened in the mornings for Sunday brunch. Beyond Jake's the land next to the ocean began to rise into tall, chiseled rock bluffs, on top of which was Powerhouse Park.

He turned back to the north and had to adjust his path almost immediately. The surf was at high tide and licked the edges of tall mounds of sand along the east side of the beach, forcing Ryan to the beach's far right-hand edge. He watched the first rays of sunlight playing across the rough face of the North Bluff Preserve along the northern side of Del Mar's famous Dog Beach. Beyond the bluffs in the distance to the left was Cardiff State Beach, and shrouded in shadow even further beyond were the hulking purple peaks of the Santa Ana Mountains between San Diego and Orange Counties. He paused now and again to watch surfers riding across the sun-tipped tops of the incoming waves. Here and there people jogged singly and in groups of two and residents walked their dogs, all six of their legs dancing away from the water when a particularly large wave swept up the beach.

The vibe on the beach here was entirely different than the more familiar Pacific Beach, with bicyclists and roller skaters dodging in and out of pedestrians along the boardwalk, which itself was fronted by multiple hotels and restaurants in addition to World Famous. Here, there were only a pair of restaurants and an aging two-story motel. After that, there was nothing but a long line of homes elevated from the beach atop a six-foot high concrete seawall. The point of Del Mar Beach, Ryan slowly realized, was the beach itself. Which was terrific, unless one was looking for scrambled eggs, bacon and a patio on which to sit and read the morning news which, if all went well, would include oneself.

After walking a half mile up the beach, Ryan turned back south toward the parking lot. Normally he would already have glanced through the usual websites, but he intentionally waited. It wasn't a comeback. It had been far too short a time. This, he thought, was a reassertion of his position in the political world, a reminder to Flannery and Afolayan and anyone else who might think he couldn't continue in the game that he still was someone to be reckoned with. He wanted to savor the moment, to sit beaming at those around him, sitting tall as he sipped on a Bloody Mary. Even if they had no idea who he was or why he was so damned happy, they would feel the power of his presence.

Except there was no restaurant, forcing him to return back up 15th Street to find a place to eat.

As he walked past the motel and turned to the parking lot, he saw movement out of the corner of his eye and stopped short. She was there, the woman from the night before, standing on a mat on the wood-plank patio of the motel, screened from the wind by large panes of Plexiglas along the patio's outer edge. She was balanced on her hands and toes as if ready to start doing push-ups, then leapt forward gracefully as a gazelle unto her feet were between her hands. Her balance newly centered, she rose to a standing position, eyes closed, arms at her sides. Then she raised them above her head, pressing the palms together and pulling them down to her chest. Every move was perfectly choreographed to convey serenity. She took a deep breath, smiled and opened eyes that sparkled a deep, crystalline blue. Only then did she glance to her left to see Ryan, standing motionless at the side of the patio railing.

"You look lost," she said mildly.

Ryan cocked his head to the side before shaking it, bringing himself back to life. "I, um," he started, then regained his rhetorical footing. "I was looking for breakfast, actually."

"Then you definitely are lost," she said. "First time in town?"

"Obviously so." Ryan stepped around the wood railing and sat down in one of the wood chairs on the patio. "Are you staying here?" he asked, gesturing toward the hotel with a tilt of his head.

"No, no," she said, laughing briefly. "I just borrow the patio from time to time."

"The owners don't mind that you're using the place as a yoga studio?"

"This is not my studio," she said. "I simply prefer to practice my personal yoga in sight of mother ocean when the universe so allows. The owners have an understanding of her ways, and we have an understanding regarding the patio."

"Her ways?"

Maggie stepped off her mat and walked to the patio's edge by the glass. "Where I end up depends entirely on her," Maggie said patiently. "If the tide allows, I'll take a spot on the sand. But on days the tide decides to run as high as it does today, I come here."

Ryan stood up and moved next to her. "Isn't the tide a function of the moon and gravity?"

"So they say." Ryan looked at her quizzically, and she couldn't help but laugh. "I'm fully aware of the science," she said quickly. "The moon in its orbit determines high tides and low tides. But as for how high or how low any given wave breaks upon the sand, scientific explanation doesn't do the process justice. It lacks lyricism."

"I'll grant you that." He extended his right hand toward her. "My name is Ryan, incidentally, though I'm not sure if it's sufficiently lyrical."

She smiled anew as she took his hand, a dimple creasing her right cheek but not the left. "It will suffice," she said. "Maggie."

Ryan turned toward the water, feigning a casualness he didn't feel. "Where, if I might ask, is your real studio?"

Maggie stared at him for a moment or two, then shook her head. "It is where I need to be shortly lest I disappoint my students," she said, seeing sadness flash across Ryan's face at her deflection. "If you're still feeling hungry, there's a wonderful place up on Camino del Mar that features crepes."

"More lyrical than simple eggs and bacon, I suppose?" He turned back in her direction, but she had stepped back across the patio and was rolling up her mat. His gaze lingered for a moment, then he sighed to himself. "It was nice meeting you, Maggie," he said, faking a smile as he started to walk back toward the parking lot. Ryan clenched his jaw. The voice he had banished the night before when he lost sight of her was pushing its way to the front of his mind, and he was in no mood. He was between the patio and the lifeguard station when she called out to him.

"How long are you here for, Ryan?"

"To be determined," he said. "Why?"

She walked to him and touched him lightly on the left elbow. "Enjoy your breakfast," she said with a smile and walked the opposite direction. He stood watching until she disappeared around the corner of the hotel, only then retreating to his car to find some food.

***

Maggie eased into her car, pushed a button on her dashboard to start the engine and leaned deeply into the driver's seat. She closed her eyes, pressed her palms against her cheeks and rubbed her temples as warm air from the heater started to fill the interior. Dropping her hands, she opened her eyes and saw Ryan getting into his own car a row over and closer to the street. There had been no reason to ask how long he was staying and absolutely no reason to go back to him after she walked away, except...except she already was in the process of doing both before she realized she had done so. He definitely was handsome and carried himself with a certain confident air, both common traits along the coast. Maybe it was as simple as him not being native to the area and not possessing the usual coastal vibe. Maggie looked down at her dashboard and saw she suddenly was running late, even with her studio barely a mile away. Only after she turned right onto Coast Boulevard did she realize she was smiling.

***

The reason so many people in Del Mar spent time out walking, Ryan mused as he drove down Camino del Mar, was the utter lack of available public parking. After leaving the parking lot at L'Auberge, he spent ten minutes driving in circles looking for a parking spot on the street before eventually retreating back to where he started on 15th Street and walking

119

south along Camino del Mar. The several shops and restaurants he passed all were labeled with old-fashioned, shingle-style wooden signs. He continued walking for nearly a block before finding Crepes and Corks, not coincidentally known for crepes both sweet and savory and a decent wine list. Inside was a large, flat griddle akin to what one would find at a Mongolian barbecue restaurant with seats along the left side of the cooking area and tables to the right. The outdoor patio to the right of the front door was half-filled with diners, many of whom had brought their dogs along for breakfast.

Once seated, Ryan pulled out his tablet and opened a browser to check a couple of websites, but the story about himself he had hoped to see wasn't there. Odds are the reporter still was trying to get comments from Comstock and his handlers. He then went through a few other websites as he waited for his chorizo-filled crepe before closing the tablet and relaxing back into his chair. The sun was warm on his face, offset by the ever-present cool breeze blowing down the avenue. As on the beach, the sidewalks were home to people decked out in athletic wear and windbreakers walking their dogs. Del Mar, as Ryan learned from the bartender at Poseidon the night before, claimed to be the most dog-friendly city in the United States, and he had seen nothing to dispute the assertion.

His breakfast arrived and Ryan ate slowly as he decided what his next steps should be. His one-day trip to San Diego had lasted nearly a week, and he was due to check out of his hotel later that day. He could return to Phoenix but there was no real work to be done until after Christmas, when he was scheduled to meet with the half-dozen freshman legislators whose campaigns his firm had handled to help them prepare for the legislature's opening session just after New Year's. Going back also would mean having to resolve the situation with Riley. She was angry. He was angry, too, but not at her. That anger was reserved for the unwanted changes in his life the past several weeks.

When it came to Riley, he was embarrassed. There never had been a question of affection between the two, but his position as her boss left the intimacy of their relationship at a father-daughter level. He never dared breach that boundary because, though Ryan was the boss, he also knew how indispensable she was to his business after all these years. The problem, he thought, was she knew it as well. So he would apologize and she would accept and they would patch things up as they always had. He just wasn't in a hurry this time.

At the same time, there was no reason to stay in California either. He had no business here, no connections...no purpose. The ocean beckoned, but watching the ocean wasn't going to help him put his career, his life, back on track.

The food was finished and the check waiting on the table. Ryan was leaning back in his chair when he saw a woman walking across the street. Unlike everyone else in windbreakers and sweaters, she had stepped from her car waring forest green yoga pants and a matching, midriff-baring Lycra tank top. She stopped at a storefront on the opposite side of Camino del Mar, four doors down from where Ryan was sitting. He smiled to himself, tossed a twenty-dollar bill into the leather receipt holder, left the restaurant and jogged through gaps in traffic across the road. To his right was a simple wood shingle with "Namaste" written in flowery script. He had heard the word countless times and knew it had something to with yoga and Zen. Maybe it meant hello. No matter.

He walked over and looked through windows that revealed only a small check-in area with a counter and three leather-covered chairs. There was a wooden door in the wall opposite the window which he assumed led to the studio itself. He went to open the front door but stopped, his hand inches away from the wood and metal handle. What was he going to do, barge into a yoga class inside a studio which was probably but not definitely Maggie's?

Instead, he looked further down the block and saw another sidewalk café two storefronts down, walked in, ordered an iced tea and went back to watching the world go by, or at least the portion of the world moving past the yoga studio's narrow storefront. His patience was rewarded an hour later when a small group of men and women emerged from the front door at the conclusion of their class. He paid the bill, walked quickly to the yoga studio and opened the door. Maggie was leaning on the front counter talking to the woman in the forest green outfit Ryan had seen before. Maggie glanced past her student to see Ryan standing there and nodded before returning to her conversation already in progress. He waited, wondering at the nervousness he felt in his stomach like some bashful freshman about to ask a pretty girl to the homecoming dance.

Who in the hell are you, man? A career, a life built on imperturbability, and he was unnerved by an attractive stranger in yoga pants. More specifically, one who looked absolutely incredible in yoga pants.

Maggie gave the woman a quick hug and a warm smile, walked her to the door and then turned to Ryan.

"Are you here to sign up for classes?"

"What? No. I was across the street," he said, gesturing vaguely toward the road.

"Oh yes," she said, "the crepes. So you figured you would just stop by since you were in the neighborhood?"

"You're making the entire thing sound far more cliché than it really is. I was just curious."

"About?"

Ryan paused. "About what your real studio looked like, among other things."

Maggie crooked an eyebrow. "Do you usually tour yoga studios when on vacation?"

"This," he said with a chagrined look, "would be the first time."

"Well then," she said with a nod, "let me give you the grand tour." She walked to the door separating the atrium and back area. "It may not be the fanciest place in the world, but it's mine."

Through the door was a long hallway with two doors separated by a drinking fountain on the left wall and a glass door on the right. "We have locker rooms over on that side," she said with a vague wave of her left hand, "and the practice area is here. You'll need to kick your shoes off if you don't mind."

Floor-to-ceiling mirrors lined the front of the room and the other three walls were painted hunter green. He stepped onto the bamboo flooring and felt the slightest hint of padding beneath the hard wood.

"Do you do hot yoga here?"

"Not per se, but I try and keep it a little warmer than normal to help the muscles stretch a little bit.

"Have you ever tried yoga?"

"Me?" he said with a chuckle. "Uh, no. Not my cup of tea."

She placed a hand on her hip and tilted her head to the side. "How so?"

"It's just," he stammered. "It all seems a little..."

"Feminine?"

"I wasn't going to say that."

"You didn't need to. Your expression was saying it for you."

"Sorry," he mumbled.

"You should be," she said as he cast his glance downward. "But I'll let it go this time. I have several students who are men, and I know of dozens of pro athletes who also practice."

"You're kidding me."

"Why would I do that? Look, eighty percent of what I teach is how to breathe. Without breath, without focus, the rest doesn't matter a great deal. And, frankly, it takes more effort than you apparently believe." She walked behind him and reached up to take hold of the top of his shoulders. He leaned back into her touch, and she could feel the bunched tightness of his muscles extending across from the sides of his neck. A sense of familiarity washed over her as she noticed the radiating warmth of his skin beneath her fingers, and the feeling disappeared as quickly. She shook her head to rid it of the feeling, took a quiet, controlling breath and continued. "Try and roll your shoulders back."

"Excuse me?"

"Lift your shoulders up and roll them back toward me," she said, gently pulling his shoulders up through the resistance of his tension and then toward her. "That's it. Now close your eyes."

"This feels silly."

"Then stop thinking so hard. Just inhale long and slow through your nose, hold it at the top and then exhale through your mouth."

"Now tell me," she said after a couple of breaths, "what were you thinking about?"

"My luggage waiting at the bell desk at the hotel."

She moved around Ryan and looked at him more intently than she'd intended. "You're leaving today?"

He gave a small shrug. "Theoretically. I mean, I don't have to be anywhere but my reservation at the hotel is over."

"So if you don't need to be anywhere, why go?"

"Why does it matter if I stay?"

They looked at each other for a long moment as sweat began to bead on Ryan's forehead from the dull heat of the room.

"How would you like a real yoga lesson on the house?" The words were out of her mouth before she knew it, and she fought to keep her face impassive. There's no harm, she told herself. He'll be departing soon enough.

"I'm not sure," he started, stopping when she took his left hand in her right and placed her left hand alongside his cheek. That same sense of déjà vu returned, and she searched her memory without success to determine the cause. She surrendered, assuming his tense energy was seeping into her own, and took another cleansing breath. "Whatever it is you have circulating in that brain of yours," she said, "I can help you come to peace with it. Or at least closer than you are now."

Ryan took a half step back as his brow lowered in confusion. "How could you know?" he asked quietly.

"I don't," Maggie said. "Not specifically. But I can feel this jumbled, frustrated energy radiating off you in waves."

"Would you," he said, finding his voice anew, "would you have dinner with me tonight?"

Maggie smiled as she lowered her hand from his face. Something pulled at the corner of her mind, telling her to accept the invitation, but she forcibly pushed the idea aside. "Be here tomorrow at ten a.m. We can talk more then."

"Don't you have a class tomorrow at ten?"

"Be here," she said, pulling him gently out the door and back into the hallway. He shivered unconsciously as the cooler air struck his damp skin. "Yoga pants and skintight stretchable tops are required."

He nodded absently, then realized what she said. "Wait..."

"I'm messing with you, Ryan. T-shirt and workout shorts will do. No shoes in the studio, obviously. Do you have a mat? Of course you don't have a mat. We have spares here." Stop the nervous rambling, she told herself. "Deal?"

He nodded, the fog that suddenly had invaded his brain not lifting until he found himself on the sidewalk with the door closing behind him. Ryan turned toward the door as if to say something, but simply stood for an extra moment or two before heading back toward his car. Still unsure of what had just happened, his thoughts congealed into one. He needed to find a place to stay the night.

"Deal," he said to no one in particular.

***

"Please tell me you're not taking in another stray," Maggie's friend Liz said as they sat a table at the Del Mar Tasting Room.

"Well, not when you put it that way," Maggie said, taking a sip of merlot.

"Let me guess. He's tall, handsome and troubled in some way."

"Not every man I talk to is troubled."

"True," Liz said with a slight nod, "but the vast majority seem to be. What's his deal? Daddy issues? Still trying to find himself? Wife doesn't understand him?"

"Liz!"

"What was that one's name, Rodney?"

"Roderick," Maggie said, "and that was a long time ago when I was far less, um, centered than I am now."

Liz picked up the half-empty bottle and refilled both their glasses. "I know there's a flaw with him, Mags, so just tell me."

Maggie stared across the table for a moment and sighed in resignation. "Outwardly he seems to have everything together."

"But?"

"But," Maggie said with an exaggerated pause, "there's a quiver behind the usual alpha male bravado."

"And?"

"And his aura's sort of a chaotic, turbulent mess."

"Of course it is," Liz said in exasperation. "And you're the one who's going to calm it down?"

Maggie shook her head and took another drink. "He's only in town for another day or two, so no."

"Then why even spend the time meeting with him tomorrow morning?"

Maggie stared thoughtfully into at her wineglass, slowly swirling the remnants of the deep-burgundy merlot around the bottom. She had spent much of her day trying to unravel the feelings she'd had when she had touched Ryan's shoulders. It was like a nagging itch deep in her consciousness that, no matter how hard she tried, she couldn't relieve. She had seen him only twice. and yet...

"Maggie?"

She looked up, unaware of how long she had been staring blankly into the glass. How could she answer Liz's question, how could she explain that something about Ryan felt not just right but necessary for reasons unknown, when she couldn't figure it out for herself? For the sake of ending the silence and Liz's interrogating glaze, Maggie gave her friend an enigmatic smile. "Did I mention he was attractive?" Banal, she thought, but safe.

"Because that's in such short supply here."

"True. But this one's different."

Liz lifted her eyebrow skeptically in response. "He's tall. Trim but not thin. Seems like he would look sexy as hell in a suit but looks equally comfortable in shorts and flip-flops. Hair that looks good even when ruffled by the wind."

"He needs product, then."

"That's my point. He doesn't. Beach-blown hair works for him. But it's not just his looks, Liz. It's the way he carries himself."

"You said his aura was jumbled mess."

"I only could tell it was a jumbled mess because there is something underneath made of granite. He has the deep, soulful brown eyes and, when he looks at you, he almost is looking through you, trying to unlock your innermost secrets. Not so he can use them against you but so he can encourage you to embrace them."

Liz shook her head skeptically. "You got all of this out of a chance meeting on the beach and a five-minute talk in your studio?"

"You can spend years with someone and not have a sense of who they truly are," Maggie answered patiently. "Or you can know someone in an instant, if the universe so desires."

"Fine. He's not just another project. But he's still leaving town."

"Liz," she said, her feet seeking and finding familiar ground, "if I can somehow make his day or his week or his month or, hell, his life just a little better, why wouldn't I?"

Liz leaned back and shook her head. "You're too damned good for your own good sometimes, you know that?"

Maggie smiled widely. "Let's not make me sound like Mother Teresa here," she said, raising her glass mostly in relief that Liz had not pushed her any harder. "I did say he was cute."

CHAPTER TWELVE

Ryan settled into a wooden deck chair on the upstairs balcony of the motel where he had seen Maggie the day before. The sun was struggling to burn through early morning overcast from the last vestiges of the previous day's rains, and the stream of dog walkers already moved along the edge of the water as it approached high tide. He took a sip of coffee before opening a browser on his tablet, and his morning immediately took a turn for the worse.

The first blow struck when Ryan saw the headline in the *Post*, declaring Flannery's creation of an exploratory committee for the presidential run discussed only a few days earlier. He opened a second tab only to find the same headline waiting in the *Times*. "That arrogant bastard," he muttered to himself, trying to funnel disappointment into anger. The campaign he had been building toward his entire career was going on without him. Worse was what was waiting on the website where he had hoped to plant the story of his recovery. Instead, under the headline "How the Senate Was Lost," was an in-depth written by the same reporter he'd spoken to two days earlier. Scanning quickly through the text, he realized the article was both factual, which was fine, but also objective, which hadn't been his design. He was quoted extensively, but there were also quotes from Marianne Jewell, damning his ignorance of the ways of politics outside his own sphere. "He came in here thinking he had all the answers and never once thought to ask what had worked here before. You can't expect some carpetbagging outsider to waltz in here and know the people of Alabama."

Her view was, he thought, utter bullshit. She clearly had no better idea what the voters wanted than he had, else she would have found a better candidate to back. But he was supposed to have been the campaign whisperer. Bullshit or not, it was now in print for anyone to read.

Still, those stories didn't sting nearly as much as the final punch to the stomach, the text message from Riley urging him to call and their subsequent conversation.

"This still is my fucking firm, Riley!" A couple walking their beagle along the beach turned at the outburst and scurried away, heads shaking.

"And it will remain your firm, Ryan," she replied evenly. "I'm not telling you to abandon it. I can't do that and I wouldn't. What I'm telling you is that for the sake of everything you have built, everything I have stood by your side and helped you build, you take a break."

"You're putting your own boss out on administrative leave."

"No. I'm asking my boss to take a sabbatical. And if my boss were thinking correctly, he'd realize it's a damn good idea."

"Why now? Legislative sessions are starting in a couple of weeks. There's far too much work to be done, far too many people I need to meet with between now and then." No response came, the silence stretching quickly into discomfort. "What is it you aren't telling me?" he asked, voice dropping but losing none of the anger. "What am I missing?"

"Christ," she said softly. "Leadership has started scheduling meetings, Ryan. But they're asking that you not be part of them."

Ryan's face flushed and he quickly stood up from his chair. "Who the fuck are they to request that?"

"They, Ryan, are our clients."

As quickly as the adrenaline had surged through his veins it subsided, leaving him exhausted. "Most of them wouldn't even be there if not for what we've done for them," he said plaintively.

"That may be true," Riley answered. "But they're the ones who hire us. You know that."

Ryan said nothing, settling heavily back into the chair and staring blankly at the incoming waves.

"Look, Boss. We've been fighting a storm since Election Day, first literally and then everything that's come after. It has grown and grown and the harder you have fought against it the worse it's gotten."

"It's not right," he said, his voice little more than a whisper.

"Of course it's not right. But it's the reality. So you have two choices right now. You can lash yourself to the wheel and stubbornly continue steering through the heart of the storm with all sails flying, at the risk of losing everything you have created, or you can give in to the gale, pick a spot on the horizon, steer that direction and live to fight another day."

Ryan chuckled. "Nautical references?"

"I've been reading Aubrey. It seemed apropos."

He stared out at the distant horizon, where the gray sea merged with the steel-gray clouds filling the sky, a darkness matched only by his own mood. If this was exile, he thought bitterly, at least it was better than Elba. "Boss?" He continued watching until he saw the outline of a ship making its way well beyond the coast, to a destination he could only imagine. "Ryan, you there?"

131

"I need time," he said finally.

"That's what I've been trying to tell you."

"No," he said, "I need time to think. And I'm also going to need some clothes."

"Clothes?"

Ryan stood again, took a step forward and leaned heavily on the railing overlooking the patio and beach beyond, his pulse hammering through his temples. "If I've been banished, I'd rather do my thinking here."

This time it was Riley who fell quiet. "For how long?"

"That's one hell of a good question, Riley," he said, disconnecting the call. He knew Riley was right. He had been spiraling for more than a month. He could feel the pull of his defeat and his body's betrayal, smothering him like a wet, thick cloth, dragging him further into his own anger and leaving him few options but to futilely attempt to fight back. A career spent turning situations around for others, and he had no idea how to turn around his own. Rage boiled inside of him and Ryan felt a need to lash out physically, to kick a trash can or punch a wall or abuse any other inanimate object as punishment for his own failures. His phone buzzed with a silly alert for Words with Friends, which was all the provocation Ryan needed. He took a final glance at his phone in his hand, then flung it like a Frisbee toward the sand below, listening as it landed on the damp beach with a satisfying, wet splat. The red at the edge of his vision subsided and his pulse began to calm as he watched the tide continue its march up the beach, waves licking at the phone, its black case stark against the sand. Satisfaction turned to abashment as water crested over the phone, pulling it further into the surf.

"Fuck, that was stupid," he muttered to himself before hurrying down the stairs and onto the beach to recover it.

He ran his fingerprint over the home button and discovered, to his surprise, the phone was still functional. He took a step toward the hotel, then glanced north at the long row of houses lining the beach and decided to take a walk. Two blocks down the sand, he found what he hadn't known he needed until that moment.

In front of him stood a two-story home covered in dark brown shingles white trim. Both the dining area below and bedroom above featured wide windows opening onto a patio that led to the sand and providing ample ambient light. Outside the bedroom was a white-trimmed observation deck set atop the flat one-story, perfect for watching the waves roll in.

Most importantly, there was a small sign hanging on the seawall just off the patio—AVAILABLE.

He strode up the half-dozen wood steps, stepped over the locked wooden half-gate set within the seawall itself and peered in the windows. Comfortable furnishings were arranged with the windows and beckoning ocean the centerpiece of the décor.

Ryan paused, took a deep breath, and smiled for the first time that day. "Yes, I'm calling about the house you have on Del Mar Beach. What are you asking? ... Do the furnishings I see through the windows stay? ... Good. How quickly can you get down here with the lease? I'd like to be in by tonight.

"Credit check? I understand. By the way, I'll be paying the month's rent and deposits in cash. Does that help?"

***

Maggie stood in the entry room of her studio, welcoming the nearly dozen students coming to her morning class but constantly looking past them to the street beyond. She took a quick look at the clock on the wall. It was just a minute or two before ten, and it wouldn't do for her to show disrespect for her clients by not starting on time. She opened the front door, walked to the sidewalk and glanced in either direction, but there was no sign of Ryan. With an inward sigh she went back inside, kicked off her shoes and walked into the studio with a wide smile.

"Namaste."

***

That evening, rent paid and keys having been delivered earlier that afternoon, Ryan stepped into the deck of his home for the next month in newly purchased sweatpants and hoodie. He sat in one of the deck lounges and looked up toward the dark skies filled with hundreds and hundreds of stars. Reflexively he looked for familiar celestial landmarks such as Orion and the Big Dipper before gazing toward the horizon just as Venus, itself low on the western horizon, was swallowed by a blank dark mass that only could be the edge of the next storm system heading toward the California coast.

He had brought his tablet to the deck with him out of habit and picked it up off a side table before thinking twice and setting it back down. Given his current position adrift in the political world, there was nothing he needed to see urgently. Instead, he took a long pull off a bottle of Corona from the six-pack at his side and, leaning more heavily into the chair with a sigh, he started counting stars.

***

Ryan stood on a broad sidewalk under hazy, overcast skies. Trees had been planted in blank spots in the concrete at regular intervals, the precious dirt protected by rust-colored metal grating, and the leaves swayed gently in a soft breeze. All around him people were moving purposefully this way and that, on their way to a particular location for reasons unknown and unknowable. He glanced around to get his own bearings, realizing he wasn't certain of his own destination other than that it was forward. Which was problematic because he was frozen in place.

He concentrated on his right leg, focusing on the muscles within, urging them to take a step forward. After several seconds his foot lifted off the ground. His leg felt unfathomably heavy, his lower back trembling as it attempted to support the weight of his leg, hamstrings and quadriceps aching with effort, but it swung forward and took the smallest of steps. Moving his left leg took less concentration, but the agony of the weight was just as great. After shuffling a handful of steps forward, Ryan paused, his brow kneaded tightly and his lungs gasping for air. He had walked all of a yard. He looked again at the road ahead, searching for the causes of his struggle, a steep incline or perhaps howling winds. But the road was flat, the air movement not enough to lift the smallest of kites. People kept streaming past him in both directions, unhindered by whatever was rendering him nearly immobile. Looking ahead, he realized there was a particular building that he was trying to reach, though he couldn't recall why.

His mind reached back to physical therapy sessions he had endured after severely spraining his ankle and the ease with which he could push a rolling chair backward with his legs compared to pulling it forward. Inspired, he turned around to start moving backward up the sidewalk. Suddenly he was making progress, though it was all he could do not to bump into people who were blocking his path in increasing numbers. After a couple of minutes he stopped and turned around only to see the building he was trying to reach was further away than it had been before. He tried to ask passersby what was happening, but words wouldn't form, and they all seemed to look through him anyway. Frustration and anger built within him until all he could do was look up at the heavens and unleash an agonized howl...

He woke with a start, still in the lounge on the deck with the morning dew heavy upon the blankets he had wrapped himself in the night before. Empty beer bottles surrounded him, with the one remaining untouched bottle standing mockingly in the steel bucket now filled with cold water. His joints ached from sleeping outside in the cold in an upright lounge, and he panicked. The line between dream and reality had blurred to where he wasn't sure if his near-paralysis was real. He stood gingerly and took a few small, tentative steps, feeling the aches from the night before but none of the overwhelming heaviness. But he wasn't satisfied. Hurrying downstairs, he paused only long enough to chug one bottle of water and grab a second, then went out the front door to take a walk and banish the dream back to his subconscious mind.

***

Ryan paused at the street in front of the house. The street rose to the south in a slight incline, falling off to the north in equal measure. His mind went back to the stress in his dream of seemingly surmounting a steep incline on an otherwise flat street, and he wanted no part of any elevation change. Instead he went back through the house to the beachfront patio and, carefully descending the half-dozen steps, walked onto the sand and headed south. The clouds Ryan had seen the night before on the western horizon now were overhead. Rain squalls could be seen over the ocean while a strong wind blew cold off the water, but he didn't care. He strode confidently at the edge of the surf, occasional waves washing over his ankles as he swung his arms with feeling and breathed in the crisp, salty ocean air. With each step, the dream moved further to the periphery of his thoughts and a small, satisfied smile broke across his face.

As he walked past the motel he slowed to look for Maggie on the patio and the sand in front, but she wasn't there. He kept moving past Poseidon and was approaching the volleyball net in front of Jake's just beyond when the first rain began to fall. The wind-whipped drops were biting on his exposed face, hands and legs, but he continued walking until he reached bluffs upon which Powerhouse Park sat well above him. He leaned against the exposed rock and dirt, a mix of increasing rain and spray off the water whipping into his face. Runoff started to flow down the side of the bluffs, quickly soaking the back of his sweatshirt and shorts. Ryan took a step forward,

136

leaned his head back and opened his mouth wide, just as a kindergartener would. Water streamed down his face and raindrops landed heavily on his tongue. With each drop, the lingering darkness from the dream faded. It was cathartic.

Only the sound of thunder rolling ominously across the waves ended Ryan's reverie and, suddenly, he became aware of just how cold and wet he was. He rose slowly, a playful bounce in his step despite the deteriorating weather, and turned to return to his rental. The rising tide pushed him closer to the high mounds of sand in front of the seawall. Next to the lifeguard station, the runoff from the parking lot and sidewalk had combined with the incoming waves to create a deepening channel in the sand. Ryan stepped carefully down one side and, after a wave rushed in up to his knees, climbed clumsily up the loose, saturated sand on the far side. He paused at the top of the channel to take off his shoes and socks, which were soaked with seawater.

"You're still here after all," a voice called.

He turned to his right and smiled at the sight of Maggie on her mat. She stood easily on her left leg, her right foot resting on her left thigh with the rest of the leg angling away, her palms pressed together in front of her sternum. "I'm still here."

Effortlessly she lowered her right leg, raised her left and assumed the same pose on the opposite side. "Most people have the sense to stay out of the rain."

Sensing an unspoken invitation, Ryan exited the beach and moved to the relative dryness under the motel's second-story deck. "When you live in Phoenix, rain is a delicacy."

"Maybe true. But pneumonia doesn't generally care where you live."

"I owe you an apology," he said, taking a step forward.

"Not at all," she said, still facing the water as she moved purposefully through other poses. "It simply was an invitation."

"I needed to find a place to stay, happened across a vacation rental and time got away from me."

"You owe me no explanation, Ryan. As I said, I thought you had gone back home. I'm glad to see you're still here."

"You are?"

She picked up the towel on top of her equipment bag, turned and faced him. "I'm always happy when someone takes steps they believe will lead to their happiness."

"I'm not entirely certain that's the case," he said.

"If it wasn't, you wouldn't have done it. We all are smarter than we seem when we stop thinking so much and simply let ourselves be."

"So is there another class at ten a.m. today?"

"There is but it's full," she said with a small shake of her head.

"Later then?"

"Not today, actually." Ryan's gaze dropped to her mat. Seeing his face fall, she quickly added, "but we might be able to continue our conversations at lunch, if you are so inclined."

His countenance brightened. "That would be nice."

"Good," she said as she packed away her towel, slid on her shoes and started to roll her mat. "Let's say twelve thirty then at the Pillbox Tavern, Solana Beach."

She was at the edge of the patio when Ryan asked, "Where is that, by the way?"

She looked over her right shoulder and smiled. "I'm sure you have Google on that tablet of yours. Use it."

CHAPTER THIRTEEN

"Good to see Google still works," Maggie said with a smile.

"I wouldn't have found it if it didn't," he said.

The Pillbox Tavern sat in the middle of a strip center a few blocks north of the ocean, the lone two-story structure among the four stores. There was a wide, roll-down window set within the periwinkle walls to the right of white French doors inlaid with glass. Normally open, it was closed today to protect diners from the rain and wind. An old-fashioned iron weather vane was perched atop the building.

Ryan walked in and saw Maggie sitting directly in front of him on a bench seat. She waved, as if the room wasn't small enough that he hadn't immediately seen her, and gestured to the wooden bar chair across the table from her.

A waitress appeared and took their drink orders, iced tea for Maggie and a locally-brewed Hefeweizen for Ryan. Any thought of going with the non-alcoholic beverage his heart required disappeared with a new wave of nervousness.

"So, Ryan," she said, "why are you still here?"

Ryan half snorted as he put his glass down. "You make it sound as if I should have had a police escort to the Imperial County line."

"What I meant was, I thought you were only visiting from out of town for a few days."

The server returned with their drinks and they ordered their food. Ryan decided to take a chance on a grilled mahi sandwich, while Maggie ordered the cheeseburger and fries.

"A burger? Really?"

She tilted her head to the side. "Does that surprise you for some reason?"

"I guess I had assumed..."

"You assumed that because I own a yoga studio, I'm some sort of California yoga hippie who only eats tofu and organic bean sprouts?"

Ryan's face flushed, and he looked down at the table. "I don't think I would have put it quite like that."

"At least you have the decency to feel properly chagrined." Ryan looked up to see Maggie smiling broadly at his discomfort. "I will, however, concede that I do not eat a great deal of red meat. But, frankly, sometimes a girl wants a burger and a beer."

He lifted his beer glass in a toast. "To burgers and beer," he said, clinking his glass to hers.

"Indeed," she answered before both took a drink.

They say quietly for a moment before Maggie spoke again. "You didn't answer my question."

"Which question was that?"

"Why you decided to stay?"

Because I'm pursuing a beautiful woman who makes me feel like I'm seventeen. Oh, and I have nowhere else to be. "My, uh, work circumstances shifted in a direction where I found myself with additional time on my hands."

Maggie crinkled her brow in concern. "You were let go?"

"I certainly hope not, considering it's my name on the building."

Now it was time for Maggie to look surprised. "What exactly is it that you do?"

This will be good. "I'm a political consultant."

"Oh," she said quietly, her eyes moving away from his toward the television on the wall.

"Wow," he said. "Now who is being judgmental?"

Her gaze returned quickly. "I'm not being judgmental. It's just, you know...politics."

"It's politics," he said in a mocking voice. "I'll have you know it's not what you see on the news, Maggie. It's more...intimate...than that."

"Intimate?" She placed an elbow on the table and cradled her chin in her hand. "Oh, do tell."

Their food arrived and both tucked in to their meals.

"My entire job," Ryan said after washing down a couple bites of sandwich with the beer, "is about building connections, establishing relationships. It's about creating emotional intimacy in its most basic form, a basis on which you can earn people's support and respect at best, or, at a minimum, their vote. Most people who run for office have good intentions when they begin. It's just they don't necessarily have any idea how to sell their value to the public and, if elected, how to get done what they wish to accomplish."

"And you help them with that."

"My firm does, yes."

"For a fee."

"I don't see you leading free yoga classes on the beach, Maggie."

Her face tightened and her muscles tensed as she took another drink, and Ryan tried to retreat. "What I mean is, everyone needs a way to make a living. Most of us would like to think that we're making a difference. This is the way I'm doing that."

"Are you, though?"

Ryan started to answer but checked himself as visions of the recent campaign raced through his head. "More often than not," he said. "But the intent is there."

"And how does all of this translate to you being here?"

"You invited me," he said as their plates arrived.

"Sarcasm," she said with a roll of her eyes, "how lovely."

"It's a gift. But to answer the question, I decided I could use some time away from the real world and thought life by the ocean would be a nice place to start."

"A cure for a restless soul?"

"What makes you say restless?"

Maggie thoughtfully chewed the bite she had taken as she looked at Ryan. "It's the energy you're giving off."

"You mentioned that the other day, too."

"I did. And, to be honest, it seems even more intense now than then."

"I'm not sure why. I feel just fine."

"Perhaps for the moment but..."

"But?"

She put down the French fry she had just picked up and leaned in closer to the table. "There is a frustration in you that's palpable. Confusion. Sadness. Almost as if you are trying your best to force a mood you're not entirely feeling."

"Don't tell me," he said. "You see all of this in my appearance?"

"I do," she said quietly. "But it's also in your eyes. Your face is smiling but your eyes aren't following. You're looking for something."

"What would that be?" he said.

"I have no idea." She shifted back in her chair and shook herself, as if exiting a trance. "Neither do you, I think."

"That's infuriatingly vague."

"The universe often is," she said with a wry smile.

***

The rain had stopped by the time Ryan returned to his house after a quick stop at the grocery store to fill the empty refrigerator. He pulled out a bottle of Corona, sliced a lime and sat down at the kitchen table adjacent to one of the high windows facing the water. Maggie's last words repeated themselves in his head. He didn't question their accuracy—he had felt adrift for some time. But he hadn't realized that his malaise was on public display, and he had absolutely no idea how to relieve the confusion.

One of the main advantages of his career had been that he had remained busy. Moments of introspection were few and far between because of the sheer pace of the work and, with a long string of successful campaigns under his belt, there rarely was a need to examine what had taken place in any depth. But the events of the past several months had been different, not so much in the outcome—his candidates had lost before—but in his inability to convince a candidate to follow his lead. Or perhaps it was his own inability to adjust to circumstances well beyond his comfort zone in order to create a successful outcome. He had managed to reach this particular place in life without metaphorically looking at himself in the mirror. But since he looked in the reflecting glass in Birmingham the night of his cardiac episode, it had felt like the man in the mirror was taunting him, mocking him, calling him out as a fraud.

He watched as an intrepid couple and their less than happy golden retriever fought through driving gusts whipped off the ocean, determined to get in their walk on the beach no matter what, and his mind went back to the dream from the night before, his own inability to move forward despite an utter lack of encumbrance. Ryan reminded himself that it had only been a dream. But did that mean that the dream itself was without meaning? Or was he simply overthinking everything now that he had an excess of time on his hands? He briefly considered taking to the beach for another walk, but he saw a squall making its way ever closer to shore and thought better of another soaking.

Ryan was, in a word, trapped. Trapped in a house hundreds of miles away from home, trapped within the echoing doubts of his own mind. Becoming more manic by the moment, he stood up and paced between the kitchen table and the great room, logging thoughtless steps without any clear purpose. When that failed to clear his mood, he leaned heavily against the wall, put his hands on top of his head and closed his eyes.

A vision entered his mind unbidden. It was Maggie, captured in the silhouette of sunset when he first saw her on the beach a few days earlier. This time, however, she stopped mid-flow, turned to him sitting at the bar and flashed a welcoming smile. "Breathe, Ryan," she said. He tilted his head to the side, trying to figure out how her voice had carried to him where he sat, but as he did so she shook her head and beckoned to him with her right hand. "Stop thinking," she said softly. "Breathe."

Ryan walked back to the table, powered up his tablet and looked through the app store until he found what he was looking for—meditations and guided breathing exercises. Something Riley had mentioned she used when the stress became too great. If someone had looked in his kitchen window at this moment, they likely would have thought he'd lost his mind. He frantically pulled off his sweatshirt and T-shirt, then unzipped his pants and kicked them aside until he stood alone in the great room of his rental wearing nothing but navy boxer shorts and a pair of black athletic socks, breathing heavily as he started the app.

"This is a sixty-three point guided meditation," the female voice intoned softly.

Sixty-three, he thought. *What a bizarre number. Why not just sixty? Wait. I'm defeating the purpose of a relaxation tape.*

"Follow if you wish, or do you as choose," the voice continued. "Close your eyes or, if you so desire, keep them open. It doesn't matter what you choose as long as you choose and breathe..."

At first, he actively tried to focus on each separate area named, tensing with the effort as he envisioned this finger and then that illuminated. Within a minute, however, lulled by the soft, measured voice on the application, he let his thoughts wander until they were spaced apart like the waves outside, one coming every few seconds only to pass quickly out of view. Soon those disappeared as well and Ryan, nearly naked on an area rug on top of a cold hardwood floor, fell fast asleep.

***

Ryan stared at the ballot inside his voting booth which, in Arizona, consisted of a waist-high blue plastic table divided into separate areas by two-foot-tall corrugated plastic walls. He started to mark his vote with the black felt-tip marker, but the pen wouldn't work. He tested the tip on the back of his right hand, leaving a satisfying black dot but, when the pen touched the paper again, it wouldn't write. Ryan stared at the pen, shook it a few times to try and get the ink flowing, and left another test dot on his palm. But when he turned back to the paper this time, the candidate he wanted to vote for was no longer on the ballot. He looked around, trying to figure out who had changed his ballot, then looked back down and saw the name again but under the wrong office. *This makes no sense*, he thought as he started to mark the ballot, only to discover the pen was broken again. Frustrated, he threw the balky pen across the room, leaned into the booth next to him and took another pen. Taking no chances, he scribbled on the wall of his voting partition and turned back to his ballot, but the name was missing again.

"Sir," he heard someone say. "You need to hurry up, we're closed." He looked around and realized the only people left in the polling place were the volunteers, all looking exhausted and, frankly, pissed.

"The pen's not working."

"Don't be silly, sir. Just cast your vote so we can all go home."

His mind churned as he looked at the paper, which now was entirely blank. "There aren't any names."

The volunteer walked over and picked up the ballot out of the booth. "Really, sir?" he said, holding up a once-again full ballot. "Do you need assistance with this?"

Ryan shook his head mutely, took back the paper and started to cast his vote, but the name he was looking for was gone again. When he turned around, he was alone in the room. He walked out the front door of the polling place to find the volunteers loading the balloting equipment into a plain white van and preparing to leave. "But I haven't voted yet!" he shouted, but no one took notice. Placing the paper against the side of the building, he found the name he was looking for and marked the ballot, only to see the red glow of brake lights reflecting off the building's wall.

"Wait!" he shouted, jogging after the van as it pulled away. He stopped in a greenspace, hunched over and panting, and the sprinklers came on. He looked down at the ballot, which now was dripping running ink onto the lawn.

Then he was awake, his eyes opening slowly as he turned to see heavy rains lashing against the windows. *Why didn't the pen work?* he thought pointlessly as he rolled onto all fours and stood stiffly, arching his back until he heard a pair of satisfying pops.

He walked into the kitchen, filled a glass of water and drank it quickly to eliminate the aftertaste of the afternoon's beer. Surveying the situation outside, he called a local pizza place and flipped on the television to see the local station's coverage of the storm: Is it raining in San Diego? Yep. Scripps Ranch? Yep. Imperial Beach? Affirmative, there is water falling from the sky.

Rain confirmed, his mind drifted. Two stress-inducing dreams in two nights. On the one hand, he couldn't recall the last time he'd had even one such dream. On the other hand, he didn't usually pay much attention. *It's only as much of an issue as you make it.*

Remembering for the first time that he still was wearing only the boxers and socks, he hurriedly dressed and awaited the arrival of dinner. Nothing was so bad that a couple of slices of pepperoni pizza couldn't serve as cure.

CHAPTER FOURTEEN

"The idea here isn't to have your mind go blank," Maggie said to the half-dozen students in her morning yoga class as they lay on their backs on the floor, one knee pulled high and draped over the other in a lower-back stretch. "Thinking of nothing can take as much effort as to think of any particular topic. The idea is to focus your thoughts on your breathing. Through your breathing you will ground yourself in the moment. What happened yesterday or earlier today is over, so acknowledge those thoughts and move on. The guy who cut you off in traffic has forgotten you, so don't continue thinking of him. Acknowledge and move on. What's to come this afternoon hasn't been written and won't be until it happens, so acknowledge those concerns for the future and move on. Create an inner bubble of calm, and know that calm can be impenetrable if only you resist fighting outside thoughts, and instead acknowledge them and do what?"

"Move on," Ryan muttered through tight lips as he stretched in the back left corner of the room. His right leg, shoulders and upper back were flat on the floor, his left hip elevated and rotated so that his bent left leg dangled to the right of his borrowed yoga mat. There was less an intense pain than a persistent pulling in his lower back, which Maggie described as bunched muscle fibers tearing and separating in order to grow back stronger than before. The calm of which Maggie was speaking was nowhere to be found as Ryan's full energy was devoted to trying to contort sparingly used core muscles into the position she desired. He stole a glance at the clock, and his heart sank when he discovered the class was only five minutes old.

Maggie passed out nylon and cloth straps and her students began a deep stretching of their legs, wrapping the straps around the bottoms of their feet and pulling their legs back toward their foreheads with their hands. Ryan's leg reached a sixty-degree, then seventy-degree angle and stopped. As the seconds wore on, he felt his hamstring seemingly lengthen before his leg began shaking with the effort of remaining in the air.

"When you exhale," Maggie said as she walked amongst her students, "pull the strap a little more and bring your leg a little closer past vertical. Your slow, confident, controlled exhale tells the brain to relax, which allows you to move deeper into your stretch."

Ryan heard the words, but they held no meaning. His leg shook more with every passing moment, his forearms were beginning to weaken and his breath came in hisses and gasps past clenched teeth. His eyes were squeezed shut and the left side of his upper lip curled into a weary snarl. He wanted nothing so much as for class to end.

"Now lower your leg and drop it to the side so that it's at a right angle to your other leg," she said.

His right leg burned as he lowered it and rearranged the strap before swinging it to the right, vaguely perpendicular to the rest of his prone form. His mind drifted to Jack Aubrey and other fictional naval adventurers, and he envisioned his leg as a massive spar swinging from one side of a ship to the other, complete with little men climbing the stays and shifting sail to hold momentum and course. Ryan choked out a brief laugh, but then the shaking came on again and he begin to notice an uncomfortable warmth in his left hip as his snarl intensified.

Then from nowhere he felt a hand lay flat upon his forehead and another wrap around his right hand as it held the strap. "Take a deep breath," Maggie whispered.

"Easier said than done," he gasped.

"Shhhhhh. Breathe in through your mouth, starting in three, two, one..." Her voice drifted off as Ryan pulled in as much air as he could manage. "Now let it go slowly through your nose," she said, and he followed. As he did so, she gently pulled back on the strap, pulling his leg closer to a ninety-degree angle. "Again," she said, and again he inhaled deeply and exhaled slowly, and she pulled the strap back another half inch. At the same time, the shaking subsided and the painful heat flaring in his hip receded to a low, comfortable warmth. "You're doing fantastic," she purred, removing her hand from his and placing both of her palms against his temples for just a moment before slowly pulling away, fingers tracing soft lines from the edge of his eyebrow to his hairline.

Ryan and the others switched legs and he continued to work through legs wobbling in midair despite the steadying strap, along with a growing stiffness in his lower back. After a series of stretches that mirrored the prior set, Maggie asked her students to stand at the front of their mats. Ryan rolled to his side and then struggled to his knees, his leg muscles fatigued to a numb warmth. He ordered his right leg off the mat and placed his foot in front of him but, when he tried to push off, nothing happened. He tried again to push up off the foot and the toes of his left leg, but the strength wasn't there. Around him, the others were starting a flow of movement: standing, stretching upward, bending, shifting down to the mat and then back up again, but he was stuck in neutral, resting on one knee. Maggie glanced over, smiled warmly, and silently waved her hand forward, gesturing for Ryan to return to his back, which he gratefully did, legs bent at the knee. After a moment, he grabbed the towel on the floor next to him and draped it over his eyes. Part of his mind wanted to chastise him for not completing the class, but his exhaustion was such that it took but a moment to acknowledge the self-flagellation and return to thoughts of nothing but breathing. His tailbone and shoulder blades sank heavily into the mat and, for the first time in what felt like forever, Ryan's mind went still.

***

Maggie taught another three ninety-minute sessions that day, covering for her studio's other instructor, who had called out with a cold. One class blended into the next, both the flows and the verbal instruction almost identical from one to the next. She normally prided herself in providing a varied experience for her students, as opposed to some of the larger, national studio chains where each class was a clone of the one before. Some valued precision through repetition, while she favored variety for both the body and spirit, lest the yoga become more mechanical than spiritual. When the day called for multiple classes in succession, however, practicality won out.

Ryan, at the conclusion of the first class, had shuffled slowly out of the studio and waited respectfully while she said goodbye to her other students. He had asked her to join him for lunch but, with a full schedule ahead, she had declined. At least, that was the reason she gave. In truth, Liz's words from dinner a couple of nights earlier had been on her mind since. Maggie did have a weakness for men who, if not broken, were in need of some sort of repair. Seemingly curing them of whatever ailments of the spirit afflicted them validated her in a way she craved, even if she knew the feeling to be both fleeting and somewhat false. Because more often than not, the ultimate

152

problem with these gentlemen was an inability to express or even maintain the mature feelings expected of a grown adult—which meant, ultimately, what they claimed as the cure for their issues was a night spent in Maggie's bed. Not that knowing that truth had saved her from waking up after making the same mistake on more than one occasion over the prior few years.

At least with Ryan, resistance was somewhat easier to come by. He was on vacation, nothing more, and sometime over the next month or so would be returning to, what was it? Arizona. All she knew of Arizona was cactus and dry heat and dust and more dry heat and the silicone-laden streets of Scottsdale and even more heat. As she walked to her bicycle chained to a tree in front of the studio, the sea breeze tinged with salt blowing gently on her face and through her hair, she could think of nothing less alluring than scorching heat far from the embrace of the ocean. The ocean, which had been her sustenance since the accident which nearly had taken her life.

After a brief stop at a street taco shop, she rode up the hill leading to home. A dozen whitewashed steps led to the front door of her home, which was elevated above both the street front and the lot itself. She locked her bike on the wrought-iron railing to the right of the door, took a quick glance over her shoulder and smiled at the sight of the sun reflecting off the Pacific as it lowered in the western sky. Walking quickly through the family room, she grabbed a plate from her kitchen cabinets onto which she dropped her carne asada tacos and took a coconut water from the refrigerator before heading to the back of the house. Her bedroom was above the garage, which was at street level on the southern edge of the home. French doors opened onto a rectangular deck, trimmed in redwood-stained pine, just large enough for a pair of wooden Adirondack chairs and an accent table. She put down the plate and drink, picked up a long butane lighter and brought the round citronella candle on the table to life before settling deeply into her favorite right-hand chair. Then she took a sip of her water and nibbled on her dinner while she watched the sun set.

Maggie lingered on the deck after the sun was below the horizon, watching the orange rays above the water morph to red and then violet. Deep purple and eventually black would follow, but by that point she already had gone back inside to grab a windbreaker against the sudden chill, driven by the ever-present breezes, that washed over the area once the sun had disappeared. She rinsed her plate before putting it in the dishwasher and poured herself a glass of merlot from a bottle sitting on the counter. Next to the bottle was her book of the week, a story of one yoga devotee's efforts to find peace through the nearly impossible act of wall walking—standing a foot or so away from a wall, bending backward and walking one's fingers down the wall until the wall walker was standing in an inverted letter u, hands and feet on the ground at the same time facing opposite directions. She had tried wall walking once, long ago, and decided that one attempt was sufficient.

She took the wine and book and walked out the kitchen door to her waiting backyard. As the sky darkened, her backyard came to life. There were solar-powered accent lights at the base of a pineapple palm, two banana plants and a multitude of aloe and birds of paradise. Small white lights wrapped around the mulberry tree in the middle of the grassy area and, off to the right, two iron posts that at one point held a laundry line now were adorned with a string of circular, translucent white bulbs. Behind the yard was another home situated even higher on the heights, but a long stand of bamboo, hibiscus and oleanders along her back wall eliminated most of the house from view. Her friends always assumed she had purchased the home for the view of the ocean out front, but it was this backyard, her own peaceful, verdant cocoon to share or not share with the world as she saw fit, which called to her spirit and it was here she retreated most evenings, sometimes even sitting through light drizzles just to inhale the sea-tinged air.

Half-reclining on a chaise lounge, Maggie started to open her book but stopped when she saw the gibbous moon beginning to rise over the roof line of her neighbors' home, glowing a bright white in the otherwise inky black sky. She put the book back down on the table, picked up a remote control and turned on a small, cylinder-shaped wireless speaker which paired quickly to her phone. Maggie sifted through her music, tapped on her screen and the Counting Crows started to play softly.

She got up, unplugged her white string lights, and went inside to grab the remainder of the bottle of wine before returning to her lounge. Leaning back, with a deep sigh, she watched the lonely moon inch incrementally higher in the sky, surrounded by stars yet not one of them.

CHAPTER FIFTEEN

Breathe.

The small inspiration poster, a copse of trees surrounded by a black border and text in bright white letters, seemed a cruel joke to Ryan as he stared at it hanging on the right wall of the yoga studio. Maggie also was urging her students to breathe, which Ryan viewed as equally mocking if not impossible. He had returned two days after his first yoga adventure, once most of the soreness had subsided and he once again was able to move more or less freely. This time, he had started strong. In fact, the lower back stretches at the start of class ached than his last attempt, and he basked in the pleasant warmth in his muscles as they stretched themselves once again. Such was their nature, tearing microscopically in order to reform stronger than before. He was fine when he was on his hands and knees, alternating between arching his back into cat pose and dropping his back and thrusting his chest forward in cow pose, though if asked he would not be able to name a single time he saw a cow with its chest thrust out proudly. Next came a controlled twist, exhaling as he lifted his right hand off the mat and rotating his head upward.

Then Maggie said it was time to thread the needle. Ryan was still on his knees but his left hand was now positioned to the right of his torso to provide leverage, and his right arm was thrust far enough beneath his body to cause his right shoulder to rest on the mat. His head was propped alternately on his right temple or right ear, depending on which position was least uncomfortable at the given second. And, despite the exhortations from Maggie and the poster both, breath was difficult to come by.

"We're only going to stay here another fifteen to twenty seconds," she said calmly, and Ryan began contemplating why fifteen to twenty seconds in the world of yoga felt longer than it did when performing nearly any other activity, including hopping on one foot. Or sex.

He chuckled softly to himself at the inanity of that last thought and, almost miraculously, the distraction from his otherwise painful contortions allowed him to take in a controlled breath. It wasn't deep, but it also wasn't rushed through gritted teeth. He paused as his lungs filled as much as they could given their current alignment, then let the breath out slowly, and as he did so, the discomfort in his right shoulder and his head faded into the background in favor of that same warmth he had experienced at the beginning of class. He smiled with satisfaction as Maggie instructed to come back to their hands and knees and shake out their right arms and shoulders before switching to the left side. When Ryan drove his left arm under his torso and rested his head near the top of his left ear, he did so with a satisfied smile because, suddenly, he understood, at least on a basic level, what it was to breathe.

***

"Two down," Maggie said. She and Ryan were sitting on the enclosed patio of Iris, a comfort-food restaurant a few blocks east of the ocean and across a two-lane road from the Los Penaquitos Lagoon and Torrey Pines State Reserve. Hints of water could be seen here and there through reeds and other marsh grasses across flat land, which eventually rose into the tree-lined hills of the reserve itself across a two-lane road. Low gray clouds scudded across the sky above those hills, and the grasses bent to the ocean breezes still strong a few miles away from the coast itself. The duo sat near a window set in a pine-treated wall while a canvas roof protected them from the deteriorating elements.

"Is there a countdown I should be aware of?" Ryan asked after taking a sip of iced tea.

"Not per se," Maggie said, "though after another class or two I'll need to formally enroll you and get payment other than in food. Assuming..." Her voice trailed off knowingly.

"Assuming I want to continue coming to class."

"Most people come into their first class with some preconceived notion of what to expect based on what they've seen on television or in movies," Maggie said. "Suffice it to say, they quickly discover that it's not what they thought it might be."

"Which turns some people off."

"Not as much as you might think. Some will abandon the practice immediately, though the majority seem to find some one thing that causes them to come back a second time, even if it's the momentary quiet they found in savasana."

"The one good shot theory of golf?"

Maggie canted her head to the side. "I've never played the game."

"You're fortunate," Ryan said with a laugh. "The theory is no matter how terrible a golfer you are, you will at some point during a round hit that one perfect shot, and you will feel it translate up through your club and into your arms and shoulders and eventually your brain, and the ball will fly true and soar seemingly for hours and you become convinced that you, at that moment, have sensed the divine. And the pursuit of that feeling will bring you back to the course, even though the other 134 times you swung the club should have convinced you to throw your bag in the lake."

"So 135 shots is a lot?"

Ryan looked disbelievingly at Maggie, who looked back at him earnestly. "Yeah, Maggie. That's a lot." The waiter came and placed a plate of duck pot stickers on the table between them. "I'm sorry," Ryan said after he left. "Please, continue."

"It's actually an apt comparison," she said as she dipped a pot sticker in the house dipping sauce, a tangy combination of soy, sweet chili and lemongrass which seemed to have been grown fifty feet beyond the patio windows. "Sometimes people become too anxious to find that feeling in other parts of the class and lack the patience to understand that proficiency comes in one's own time. Maybe their frustration at not being able to perform this or that pose stays with them and, instead of clearing their minds at the end of class, they focus not on what they could do but what they could not. Or maybe the idea of feeling otherwise dormant muscles cry out for relief after class is too much for them, because they don't understand that the pain is necessary to continue growing. And that is why the third class usually tells me whether someone is committed enough to the growth to keep coming."

Ryan nodded and leaned back in his chair. "So what do you think about me?"

"In what context?"

"Do you see me as someone who will be back for that ever-important third class and the journey beyond?"

"That," she said, pointing at him with a new pot sticker, "is an unfair question."

He leaned forward and rested his forearms on the tablecloth. "How so?"

"Ryan, if I say I don't expect you to come back, then it's likely your competitive nature will take over and you'll appear simply to prove me wrong. If I tell you that I think you had that divine moment today, as you put it, then you will spend your time replaying the class in your head and trying to deconstruct the feeling rather than just acknowledging the moment."

"You think I had that moment?"

"Does it really matter what I think?"

"You're the expert."

"It's your body, your mind. Why would you need affirmation?"

Ryan raised his eyebrows in surrender and leaned back against in the chair. "For a few seconds, maybe a minute, I realized I wasn't trying to hold a pose as much as I was trying to make sure I kept breathing rather than gritting my teeth."

"And how did that work out?"

"It became easier to stay in the pose."

The waiter returned and took their orders, a seafood salad for Maggie and the ahi sandwich for Ryan. "You sound surprised," Maggie said after their teas were filled and the server withdrew once again.

"That's not the right word, I don't think."

"Tell me a better word."

Ryan took a long drink from his glass and watched the reeds bend to the wind. "I would say contented."

"That is a better word. You win."

Ryan smiled broadly. "A nod to my competitive nature, conceding a victory to me?"

"Not at all," she said. "Consider it a well-deserved affirmation. But, as you continue on this journey, you need to find those compliments within yourself."

He sighed softly as the smile faded, and his gaze into the distance became less focused.

She leaned across and laid her arm on the table palm up, motioning him to lean forward. "Hey," she said, "where did you just go?"

Ryan remained reclining in his chair, turned to Maggie and smiled wanly. "To do what I do for a living, you need to have the utmost conviction that every action you take is correct. Even if it turns out not to be right, you find a way to convince yourself that the action was correct but that some unforeseen outside chance stepped in to screw up what was otherwise a brilliant, flawless strategy. Without that conviction, that certainty of being right, you never will get a client facing their own uncertainties to push them aside and follow you."

"What you're describing is an impossibility. No one is right 100 percent of the time."

"Oh," he said quickly, "I know. That reality is what strikes you when the lights are turned down and you look in the mirror to wash your face and brush your teeth before bed. It's what echoes in your head as you close your eyes and try to think of something—anything—that will let you fall asleep. Those are the times when you discover that all your work to convince yourself you're bulletproof is pointless, and those are the times when the false affirmations you tell yourself simply to get through the day ring hollow."

Maggie took a long look at Ryan and saw, for an instant, a vulnerability that hadn't been present when they walked into the restaurant. "The practice isn't about lying to yourself, Ryan," she said softly. "It's about finding within yourself the ability to recognize and accept yourself for who and what you are."

The expression she saw disappeared almost instantly in favor of the previous bravado. "Of course it is," he said. "And I do recognize who I am." Maggie noticed that the second part of the equation, acceptance, was missing but, as she debated whether to say something, their lunch arrived and they quietly tucked into their food.

***

162

Liz settled into one of the lounges on Maggie's patio, a glass of merlot in her hand. "So this is now two dates with this guy."

Maggie shot Liz a wounded look. "I hardly consider lunch after class a date."

"Forgive me. I forgot that it's part of your normal routine to have someone cover your afternoon class while you go get lunch with a student," Liz answered mockingly.

Maggie smiled shyly. "He's not a student if he's not formally enrolled."

"Look at you, finding loopholes to justify adjusted philosophy. I'm so proud of you."

"Do I really need to mention—"

"No," Liz said, cutting her off. "First off, always do what I say and ignore what I do. Secondly, this conversation is about you."

The two fell quiet as the low moan of the Surfliner carried across the air, followed a minute later by the rattling of its wheels on the tracks on the heights above the beach to the west.

"Is this still about his aura?" Liz asked when the quiet returned, save the sound of crickets chirping in the bushes.

"He's an interesting person and I enjoy talking to him. Shouldn't that suffice?"

"It does, if that's the extent of your interest. Where was it you said he lived?"

"Phoenix."

"And he's here for how long?"

"Just under a month." Maggie sighed, knowing where this line of questions was going to lead. "I'm not building a future around him, Liz. Like I said, he's fun to talk to. He has a way of keeping a person on their toes." She flinched internally at the white lie in the statement, but she wasn't about to tell Liz about the dream. Not yet.

"How so?"

"He's...funny isn't the right word. He's clever. Sometimes amusing, but generally in a way where you need to actively think to keep up with his train of thought."

"A man with a brain? I thought that species had gone extinct a decade or so ago."

"That's because you're only searching for them at wine bar happy hours."

Now it was Liz's turn to feign being wounded. "Such shade, girl. And I'll have you know I'm not only looking during happy hour."

Maggie grinned and clinked her half-empty wineglass against Liz's. "Forgive me."

The quiet enveloped them again. To their right, the photovoltaic sensor turned on the small white globe lights as the sky evolved from a hazy blue to deeper shades of violet.

"Promise me you're not going to let yourself get hurt when he inevitably leaves," Liz said quietly.

"I won't."

Liz turned to her right to face Maggie. "You won't promise or you won't get hurt?" Maggie said nothing, instead smiling and raising her eyebrows. Liz shook her head, downed her wine in one gulp and held her glass out for another refill.

***

Ryan rushed down Camino del Mar toward Maggie's studio. As per usual, the closest parking spot he could find was nearly a block away and, while entering her morning class late would not be the end of the world, he was too respectful of her to want to be a mid-session distraction.

After their lunch, Ryan had returned to his rental and spent time sitting on the patio, thinking about what she had said. Recognition and acceptance. He'd often heard stories of baseball pitchers who, as they aged and their fastball wasn't as fast as it once was, were faced with a tough decision. They could fight reality and continue trying to be who they once were, usually with little success, or they could accept the changes, adapt and extend their careers.

What is it you want to do?

He thought of that singular moment from class, contorted like a pretzel, when all he was focused on was the rise and fall of his own chest with each breath. So simple yet so poignant, his entire world distilled into one simple action. Such a moment of peace was not part of his being before but, now that he had discovered it, he could choose either to continue exploring that path, or to ignore it in favor of what he always had been.

It was, he realized, no choice at all. Which was why, early this morning, he had walked into Walmart and bought a yoga mat and why, now, he was hurrying along the sidewalk to enroll formally in Maggie's class, his new mat suspended by a strap slung across his shoulder.

He opened the front door just as Maggie was following the last student into the studio proper. She glanced over her shoulder at the new arrival, then turned fully and smiled when she realized it was Ryan walking across the entryway. Her smile widened when she saw him slip the mat off his shoulder.

"Sorry I'm late," he said between heavy breaths.

"You're just in time," she answered. She nodded toward the rolled mat in his hand. "I see you've been shopping."

"Like I said, it's like that one good shot in golf. I've got to see if I can do it again."

She reached out and touched his elbow, guiding him toward the studio door. "Then let's see what we can do."

CHAPTER SIXTEEN

Riley leaned her back against a wall near the bar, right leg extended and left leg bent at an angle with her heel pressed against the painted concrete blocks. She took a sip of her rum and Coke and glanced to her left at the entrance to the patio at Switch, a locally owned restaurant in Phoenix's central corridor downtown. Ryan had chosen the restaurant as the site of his company's holiday party a half-dozen years earlier and here they returned faithfully every year, as regularly as the swallows returning to Capistrano. Except, the lead swallow had yet to make an appearance. She looked down at her watch and turned again toward the wrought-iron gate at the end of the long, narrow patio and shook her head.

Nicholas dutifully stood next to his fiancée, watching her pretend to smile. at the firm's other employees even as she fidgeted and kept a near-constant eye on the gate. She glanced up at Nicholas and her features softened. He felt himself catch his breath as the bulbs above alternated from red to white to green in a sequence used only for Christmas and Cinco de Mayo parties. She wore little makeup, just a touch of blush and a light dusting of eyeshadow, but as the lights moved from green to white, in those instants before the colors shifted again, he felt as if we were looking at an angel descended from on high. Which was why he was okay knowing that, even when they were husband and wife, she never would be his entirely.

Everyone had been concerned since Ryan had nearly collapsed in Alabama but, for Riley, the worry was far deeper. Whatever Ryan had built, Riley had been there for every step, every growing pain. She loved Ryan and Nicholas knew it, even if she wouldn't admit it. Not the kind of love that led to marriage and children and the like, but the deep affection that comes when two people know each other intimately, if not physically. This was part of what loving Riley meant—accepting that there always would be a part of her that belonged to her career, to the firm...to Ryan.

"Looking for him every five minutes isn't going to make him appear," he said finally.

"The watched pot theory," she asked, still watching the gate and the parking lot beyond. "Physics dictates that whether you're watching the water or not, eventually it's going to boil if the heat is applied."

Nicholas reached out, gently cupped her chin in his hand and turned her face toward his. "The only law that applies to Ryan is he will appear if he wishes to appear."

Riley sighed and started to twist her head again, but Nicholas gently held it in place. "Riley," he said softly, "you're running the show right now. Time to stop worrying about Ryan and mingle with the employees who are looking to you for leadership."

At that she smiled, placed her right palm flat against his face and pushed herself off the wall with her left foot. "You're annoying when you're right."

"Good thing it doesn't happen often, eh?"

And he was right, she thought. She had sent the invitation to Ryan a week ago, more reminder than formal invite as the date had been set at the beginning of the year. But he never responded, not to the e-mail nor the two text messages she had sent as follow-ups in the days since. They hadn't spoken since the day she'd told him to take some time off, and their lone communication was a handful of four-word responses from him when she e-mailed him for his opinion on the rare matter that only he could handle. She didn't know if he had come back to Phoenix or if he still was in San Diego in his somewhat self-imposed exile. The more she thought about it, the more she hoped he was sitting somewhere on the beach, breathing in the salt air and watching the waves lap onto the sand.

Riley took one more look at the parking lot and thought she saw a shadow in the darkness, but couldn't be certain with the lights overhead affecting her vision. So she contented herself with the image of Ryan at the beach, reached back to take Nicholas's hand, and started making the rounds.

***

Ryan was not, in fact, sitting and watching the waves roll in.

Instead, he was seated on a stool at the bar of the restaurant next door to Switch, Durant's. It was a low-lit steakhouse from another era, one in which the biggest decisions facing the Arizona government were settled in quiet booths where the scotch and the cigars flowed freely. The cigars had become unwelcome but the scotch still flowed, and Ryan leaned heavily on his elbows propped on the dark walnut bar and stared into his third glass of the evening as he debated what to do next. He had arrived some time earlier and parked in the common lot, looking in on the party already in progress. All of his dozen employees and their spouses or plus-ones appeared to be in attendance which, for Ryan, was a mixed blessing. The more people there, the more times he would have to answer questions about the equally unpalatable subjects of his health and his hiatus. He would like to believe the questions would be borne of genuine concern—he wasn't the type of boss who expected obsequiousness from his employees, blatant or otherwise. But even the idea of repeating "I'm doing fine, thanks" more than twice left his palms sweating and his heart knocking uncomfortably against his rib cage.

He had returned to the Valley the day before, catching an early-morning flight and renting a car since his still was in California. It had been a snap decision. He hadn't even mentioned to Maggie that he would miss class the next few days. He drove to his loft in the Biltmore area, down the block from the historic Arizona Biltmore resort and across the street from the Ritz-Carlton. Ryan parked in the underground lot and took the elevator to his fourteenth-floor loft, which was exactly as he had left it before meeting with Flannery in San Diego. It had been only a couple of weeks but felt like months, a feeling augmented by the mustiness of the stale air inside the loft. He went from room to room opening windows, finishing with the arcadia door that opened to a balcony overlooking the Ritz and, four miles further to the east, the head and hump of the appropriately named Camelback Mountain. There was an accumulation of mail on the kitchen counter, presumably brought upstairs by Riley in his absence. He flipped through the envelopes quickly before dumping the four-inch-high pile into a trash can. If it was important, he thought, they would get back to him. He applied the same theory to his old-fashioned answering machine, deleting the two dozen messages without listening to a single word.

With the basic housekeeping out of the way, Ryan took a look around the great room of his loft and sighed. He was home and he had absolutely no idea what to do next. He had considered going into the office and even drove past the front of the building before thinking better of it. Voluntary or forced, he was on hiatus and didn't want to either deal with any questions or interrupt the work already in progress. Truthfully, he only knew what his employees were doing in the broadest of strokes. December was a busy month, at least on the legislative side of the business, as House and Senate veterans and freshmen alike started putting together outlines of bills for the coming session. Most would have a life expectancy just this side of the common housefly, receiving a first reading before disappearing onto a committee calendar never to be seen again, but nearly all could benefit from some guidance. That was where Nicholas and his two assistants came into play. They worked with legislative staff to help turn their clients' dreams into some sort of coherent bill, while Ryan or Riley would suggest the best way of helping the bill escape the opening-day morass.

Riley, he thought with a grim smile. There was no doubt she was keeping the operation moving forward smoothly in his absence. He had been grooming her to be, if not his successor, then his partner from the time he hired her away from the state house, and it was because of his confidence in her that he had grudgingly accepted his Southern California sabbatical.

Would she smile or yell when he walked through the front door of the office? Ryan's face flushed at the mere idea that he cared. This was his company after all, built from the ground up and successful long before he recruited her. The idea that he needed someone's permission to return...

Except it wasn't permission he was seeking as much as affirmation. One advantage of turning her into an adversary through all of this was he could project his own conscience on her, turn her into a personal Jiminy Cricket, spouting boring directions while Pinocchio wanted only to be an actor and carouse on Pleasure Island regardless of the impact on his own health. Ryan knew all along the boring course was what his nerves, his mind, his heart required. But admitting that would require also admitting that he was both getting older and, even more painfully, merely mortal. Ryan knew it wasn't fair to put her in that position. What she had deserved was for Ryan to step away cleanly, voluntarily, without the arguments. All he needed to say was that he needed her help while he recovered and that he trusted her, because he did and he did. But he also knew that without the work...there only was so much yoga a person could do to try and fill sixteen or so waking hours a day.

What would she say about yoga? he'd thought earlier that evening as he stood by his rental car and looked in at Switch's narrow patio. Then the crowds working their way between the buffet and the open bar parted and he saw her, red hair even more red as the lights overhead passed from one color to the next, with Nicholas by her side. She was leaning against a wall but soon laughed at something her fiancé said.

He couldn't go in, strolling through the gate and instantly becoming the center of attention. But what would everyone think if he skipped the gathering altogether? All Ryan knew for certain was he needed a drink. So, instead of walking forward into Switch, he went instead to the right and stepped into Durant's through the entrance that led through the kitchen, then made an immediate right and settled into his stool in search of courage in liquid form.

After draining what remained of his whiskey and Coke, signaled for another refill, then pulled out his phone and sent a quick text to Riley. "HOW GOES IT?"

"ALL FULL, HAPPY AND GETTING DRUNK. ALL SAY HI AND THANKS."

The message faded, he saw his own reflection on the glass screen of the phone and felt foolish. One incident had stripped away his confident facade, revealing the always worried man below and, try as Ryan might, he couldn't regain control from the man in the mirror. But he had to at least try.

"THEY CAN TELL ME IN PERSON." He stood slowly, just to make sure his legs were fully under him, downed the last two fingers of scotch in one gulp, threw a hundred on the bar top and headed next door.

***

Two hours later, Ryan, Riley and Nicholas sat at a square table on the otherwise-deserted patio, sipping whiskey poured from the dregs of a bottle they had started sharing earlier. Ryan realized soon after walking over from Durant's that Riley must have told everyone to go easy when he arrived, as questions about his health and recent whereabouts were infrequent at most. "Good to see you" and "thanks for the booze" constituted the bulk of the comments made his direction which, at a different time and a more-sober frame of mind, he would have found off-putting. But at the moment, he considered the dearth of small talk a blessing.

Ryan leaned back in his cushioned steel-frame chair and looked at the glass bulbs above, which now were shining a muted white, a mini-universe of stars hanging between himself and the actual dark sky above.

"We weren't sure you were going to come," Riley said.

"I wasn't sure I was going to come, either."

"People were happy to see you."

Ryan smiled wanly. "I was happy to be seen."

Riley turned toward Nicholas in frustration. She'd been trying to draw Ryan into conversation for some time without success. He was friendly and polite but his words were guarded, as if he had spent the past couple of weeks erecting a wall between himself and those who knew him best. Riley raised her eyebrows, silently imploring Nicholas to help try and draw Ryan out. Nicholas's shoulders slumped and he downed the remainder of his whiskey in one gulp.

"So, Ryan," he started tentatively, "what plans do you have from here?"

"Undetermined," Ryan said, still turned toward the lights but closing his eyes for brief periods in elongated blinks.

Nicholas changed tack and went for the direct approach. "That's not like you."

Ryan closed his eyes, clenched his jaw and took a deep breath before leveling his gaze at Nicholas. "What I mean is," Nicholas stammered, "you generally have everything planned out seven steps ahead."

Ryan stared at the two of them, his protege and her fiancé, and debated what to say as a series of angry retorts ran through his mind. *Of course I don't have a plan,* he thought, *I'm on a forced hiatus. What is the point of planning when there's nothing to be done?* Adrenaline flowed through his system, overpowering the alcohol, and he could feel his heart beating harder in his chest. Slowly, deliberately, he tilted his head back against the top of his chair and looked again at the lights, taking a pair of deep, calming breaths. Nicholas started to say something, but Riley placed her hand on his knee and he fell silent.

"I am trying," Ryan said slowly, "to surrender to the working of the universe." Riley's brow furrowed and she glanced quickly at Nicholas, who shrugged. "I would like to think...no, I have to think that there was some particular reason that everything happened at once—my heart, Flannery fucking me and choosing that prick Afolayan, you all but kicking me out the front door of my own firm."

"Ryan—" Riley started.

"It's fine," Ryan said quickly, slowly lowering his gaze once again. "Actually, it's not fine. Not by a long shot. But—" he said as Riley made to interrupt in defense as second time. "But, it likely was the right decision on your part, unwelcome as it was on mine."

He refilled his glass with the final finger left in the bottle, took a sip and leaned back in his chair, his eyes unfocused as he looked at the wooden beams covering the short, covered portion of Switch's patio. "Nearly every day, at least when it hasn't been raining, I've watched the sun set into the waves. Have you ever done that?"

"It's been a while," Nicholas said.

Ryan nodded. In his mind's eye he could see the sun's golden globe slowly sinking below the horizon as the once-blue sky erupted in hues of yellow, orange and red. "If one is inclined to think about things, the enormity of the ocean stretching out as far as you can see, the immensity of the sun millions and millions of miles in the distance, it's not difficult to determine that what we do here doesn't mean much of a damn. That we're just the slightest motes of dust living out our infinitesimally paltry number of years as best we can and that time given to anger, to frustration, to regret, is just so many wasted minutes and hours."

"I never knew bourbon made you so introspective," Riley said with a chuckle.

Ryan smiled and shook his head. "It's not the alcohol," he said softly, his mind wandering for a few moments before he returned his focus to the patio. "At least," he added, "not only the alcohol."

"And in answer to your question," he said, picking up his glass and gesturing toward Nicholas, "I'm going to spend tomorrow sleeping off what I expect to be an epic hangover and then, on Monday, take a trip to the Capitol."

"The Capitol?" Riley asked.

"Don't worry," Ryan said, raising his hands palms outward. "I'm not going to get in the way of what I assume you're already doing. I just thought it might be beneficial if the Speaker sees that I am, in fact, still alive. For future purposes."

"That's not a bad idea," Nicholas said. He raised his glass and held it in Ryan's direction in mute salute.

Riley looked at Nicholas and then back at Ryan as the two men clinked their glasses together. "Should I let staff know you're coming in?"

"Red," he said, "the day I can't walk into the Arizona House and stroll into the Speaker's office is the day I retire once and for all." Seeing her stare incredulously at him, he smirked and

175

quickly added, "Besides, I'll text him tomorrow and offer him lunch."

***

Early the next morning, Riley made a quick phone call. "Representative Stephens," she said, "this is Riley Evans. Yes, Ryan Williams' assistant. Listen, I need your help with something."

CHAPTER SEVENTEEN

Ryan sat contentedly on the right side of a bench, green slats upon a tempered steel frame. In front of the sidewalk at his feet was a wide street, except there were no cars, just pedestrians walking this way and that. Two metal tracks ran down the middle of the street, tracks for some sort of conveyance. Beyond the street was another sidewalk and then, separated by fabricated steel posts and chains finished in faux burnished bronze, was a pond surrounded by greenery with a single tree emerging from the center of the pond. Ducks swam in lazy circles until they sensed someone approaching the chains at the edge of the pond with popcorn, or maybe a mouse-eared pretzel.

"Yes," Ryan heard someone say to his left, "you're at the happiest place on earth, or so the brochures say." He turned and the purple zebra was sitting on the left side of the bench, upright against the wood backing, lower legs crossed wide.

"Seriously, man, we need to have a conversation about this stalking thing you're doing."

"How can I be stalking you," the zebra said, still facing forward, "if I'm trapped in your head and carted around everywhere you go?"

"Such unassailable logic from such a creature," Ryan said dismissively.

"Creature? Is that what you think of me?" the zebra asked, turning toward Ryan with what posed as an indignant look, his voice wounded. "All I do is try and help you and this is how you repay me?"

"Help me?" Ryan yelled, the crowds on the sidewalk stopping to watch the argument. "When the hell have you helped me? All you do is come in here and go all meta on me when all I want to do is sleep."

"Perhaps this is the only time you're truly willing to listen. And knowing this, your brain releases me in this manifestation so that you'll listen to all the logic you're currently ignoring."

"Fine," Ryan spat, "what is it that I'm ignoring?"

"Where are we, Ryan, right now..."

"We're sitting near Walt's statue, across from Frontierland."

"No, Ryan," the zebra said. The scenery around them changed, the tree in the center of the pond evolving into a lifeguard's station, the greenery surrounding the pond dissolving into bright blue skies over endless seas, the street and sidewalks morphing into a brilliant, white-gray sand beach. "We're in San Diego."

"Del Mar, actually," Ryan muttered.

"Do you want to know the one thing both places have in common?"

"If I say no, will you go away?"

The zebra stood and walked onto the beach, his hooves leaving impressions as grains of sand were pushed into the air with each step before swirling in the wind and blowing toward Ryan's now bare feet. "The one thing is neither place is real."

Ryan barked a sarcastic laugh. "That's because this is a dream," he said, turning to his right, looking for affirmation from a pair of beagles suddenly sitting next to him.

"God, you're a stubborn prick."

"Get on with your point."

The zebra lifted his front right leg as if he were modeling in front of a game-show studio's worth of prizes. "Look around you, Ryan. Both places are make-believe come to life. Except, neither really exists."

"Of course they exist," Ryan said, suddenly standing calf deep in the surf. "The bench, the pond, the sidewalks all were real. This water cascading around me, this is real. None of this is my imagination."

"The things are real, but the sense of comfort they give you isn't." Ryan waved the zebra off with his hand and turned toward the horizon. "This isn't your home, Ryan. You have nothing tethering you here. You're walking through this place like a tourist in Anaheim, taking in the sights, participating in the local rituals whether it be the corn dog cart there or Maggie's yoga classes here. But in the end, your presence is superficial at best. At some point you're going to have to walk through that exit, knowing your pass has expired and that you're going back to your own reality. This place—the ocean, the wind, the people and their pets, Maggie—all will go on after you leave just as they did every day before you arrived, and in time, you'll be nothing but a memory—if that. And you'll be back where you were in the hospital in Alabama—broken, damaged and alone."

"Fuck you," Ryan said through clenched teeth, his palms balling into fists as tears came to his eyes and his vision went crimson.

"Yeah, Ryan, fuck me. Fuck both of us. But it doesn't change our current situation."

"Which is?"

"That right now we're not needed anywhere. So whatever we do, it's just not going to matter."

Those last words continued echoing in Ryan's head as he slowly opened his eyes and saw the cherry-wood blades of the ceiling fan circling slowly over his head, while sunshine tried to peak around the vertical wood blinds of his loft. The dreams were becoming more persistent, and he was becoming more determined to ignore them. It wasn't as if that damned purple zebra wasn't telling him what he already knew. He had run away from home, driven by fear of mortality and the certain crumbling of his career, accomplishing nothing and solving none of the problems dogging him. Reality was waiting for him—at his office, at the Capitol, in the quiet, dark corners of his mind that he would prefer not to acknowledge.

Ryan swung his legs out of bed and stood with effort, slowly made his way to the shower and stood under the rush of hot water, letting it run across his head and down his body. He tried to visualize the nervousness and the fear and the uncertainty being washed away and disappearing down the drain, and with the cleansing a return of his former confidence, his swagger. The feeling of invulnerability lost in a span of a few hours in Birmingham. He emerged minutes later and stood in front of his mirror clad only in a towel, stretching to his full height. He took a deep breath and exhaled over and again, standing imperceptibly taller with each repetition. His jaw set and a slight smirk came to his face. All was as it had been...except his eyes, which reflected the doubt he was trying to mask. With that realization he shrank back into himself. The man in the mirror, like that damned purple zebra, wasn't about to be fooled.

"Then again," he said out loud to no one, "I only have to fool everyone else."

He turned toward his walk-in closet and quickly assembled his armor—charcoal gray slacks, a bold red polo, socks displaying strips of bacon and black leather shoes. Not too formal, not too informal. Relaxed. Confident. Self-assured. He looked again in the mirror with an appraising glance and, ignoring the uncertainty in his eyes, nodded in approval.

It was time to announce his return.

***

Ryan stepped into the third-floor gallery overlooking the darkened chamber of the Arizona House of Representatives, walked down a handful of stairs and settled into a chair in the front row, just to the right of the center aisle. For all his years at the legislature, he virtually never had sat in his particular spot. His preferred area was the upper rows, near the entry doors, where he could watch the proceedings without himself being noticed. Other lobbyists looked to remain in the line of vision of various House members; Ryan preferred to be in a place where he could slip out as needed and otherwise blend into the beige-painted walls. Besides, he always thought, if he had done his work correctly, then he didn't need to be watching like a hawk.

The circular chamber opened before him, two stories tall with the turquoise-carpeted floor of the House set on the second floor. Six rows of walnut desks arced from the front third of the room to the back, split by a wide central aisle. The first rows were reserved for the majority leader, majority whip and other committee chairmen, and then the remainder of the members were arrayed behind, with the members from the minority party relegated to the back. Ryan had heard that the main advantage of those seats was the ability to slip into the cloakroom behind for an ice cream sandwich during particularly dull debates.

Ryan had spent countless hours in this room, watching the board to make sure his own whip counts were correct. Which they generally were, which was how he remained in business on the lobbying side. The emergency lights above illuminated the front row and the state seal, emblazoned in full color centered in front of the dais.

Ryan was home.

"I always heard there were ghosts up here in the cheap seats," a deep bass voice rumbled from over Ryan's left shoulder. He had been so deep into his reverie that he hadn't noticed Dominic Stephens walk into the gallery and take a seat one row up and across the aisle to Ryan's left. Ryan craned his neck and upper torso to look at Stephens. Portly, African-American in his early sixties, his scalp bald across the top with close-cut hair showing at the temples and the muscle of his athletic youth long since turned to fluff, the six-foot-four House Minority Leader could fill a room with his presence, even when folded into a small chair as he was now. Even this close to the holidays, with the building inhabited only by skeleton staff, administrative assistants and the Capitol police, Stephens wore a maroon button-down shirt, turquoise-encrusted bola tie and gray slacks held aloft with tailored suspenders.

"I ain't dead yet." Ryan extended his hand, which Stephens gripped in both of his before Ryan withdrew and turned back toward the open chamber, twisting his neck to and fro to relieve a sudden crick. "Dare I ask how you knew I'd be here?"

"Oh, Willy," Stephens said, "you know me. There's always little birds chirping if you only take the time to listen to them." Willy was short for Slick Willy, the nickname Stephens had given him years ago after helping outmaneuver him on an education bill, only to come back and convince the Republican leadership to include one of the other party's amendments.

"Uh-huh," Ryan grunted. "And what else have your birds been telling you?"

"Not much more than what's common knowledge, you traipsing across the country like a damn fool to work for some lunatic and damn near dying in the process."

"I wouldn't say I nearly died, Dom."

Stephens whistled dismissively. "Save it for the peeps who don't have a zipper on their chest."

"Yet here you sit, the picture of golden youth and radiance."

"Fuck you," Stephens said good-naturedly. "How you feelin', Ryan?"

"Never better, of course. Rented a place by the ocean, watching the seagulls float by."

"Willy, I've had more bypasses than I-17 under construction. How you really doin'?"

Ryan's head dropped and he sighed. "It's been like walking in an earthquake, Dom. I can't seem to get my feet under me without feeling like the ground's going to shift all over again."

"They have support groups for us cardiac kids, you know."

"Please," Ryan said, glancing over his shoulder. "This coming from the man who wouldn't be caught dead within 10 miles of a group like that."

Stephens raised his hands, palms out in surrender. "Just sayin', Willy, just sayin'." They fell silent for a moment, both staring out over the darkened chamber. The air in the gallery was heavy, and Ryan thought for a minute that maybe there really were ghosts present.

"So what's the grand plan for this session, Dom?"

"Oh, so you can run and tell your buddy the Speaker when you meet him for lunch later?"

"Fucking birds."

"I didn't need birds for that, Willy. That's just plain common sense."

"How so?"

"You've been a ghost for the last six weeks, and now you show up here? No way you're not going to be paying your respects to Mister Speaker."

"I was going to come by your office, too."

"Don't bother with that. I ain't got any feelings for you to hurt. This place ripped them out of me a decade ago."

Stephens paused, laughed softly to himself and shook his head as he mentally calculated just how long he'd been serving his district. Long enough that the other members of his caucus, even the less-tenured but older employees, referred to him as Gramps. "Riley tell you about the crazy shit coming down the pike from the newbies?"

"Not really," Ryan said, shaking his head. "I'm assuming secession with a side helping of nullification just in case the great Republic of Arizona doesn't break away from the United States this time around."

"Shit, Willy, I wish it was that harmless. Them G-O-people, some of whom you helped get here—thanks for that, by the way—are determined to tear down the gub'mint that they have been elected to serve in. They don't want anyone to tell them what they can and can't do, but..."

"They're in a hurry to tell the rest of us what we can and can't," Ryan interrupted. "You know damn well the big man's not going to let three-quarters of that even get a committee hearing."

"Probably not," Stephens conceded, "but the other quarter's enough to turn a man white." Ryan looked over his shoulder and arched an eyebrow. "Besides," Stephens continued, "he's got more and more people on the fringes who are pressuring him to do what they want him to do."

"Not enough to challenge him, though."

"Unless someone else gets ambitious. But hey, this ain't your problem, Willy. You're just a ghost. Speaking of which."

Ryan glanced at his watch. "Not bad, Dom. Took you only six minutes to get to the question."

"So tell me then," Stephens said. "Why in the hell did you work for that guy, whatever his name was...Commie-stock?"

184

"Comstock," Ryan said, spitting out the name like a rotten piece of fruit. He gazed through the darkness and saw the state seal engraved on the walnut panels behind the Speaker's dais, but his mind's eye drifted to the beach, to the roar and force of the ocean crashing against the sand as high tide rolled in. "I was trying to turn the tide," he said finally.

Stephens rose with a groan, stepped down a row and sat heavily on the aisle steps next to Ryan. "Try it without the gibberish."

"No gibberish, Dom," Ryan said, closing his eyes and smelling the salt in the air. "The last few years it's felt like we've been riding a two-spoke centrifuge and everyone in this room, everyone in this country has been spinning further out to the extremes. There still are some exceptions like you and me holding on for dear life back near the middle, but the pull keeps getting stronger. And once you fall into the mewling mob of the extremes, there's no room left for logic or for cooperation. God forbid you talk to someone on the other side, much less actually consider their opinions valid in any way. There's no discourse left, just screaming."

"But Comstock was one of those screamers."

"You don't know the half of it," Ryan said with a dry chuckle.

"So why work for him?"

"I don't know," Ryan said, but even as he did so the reasoning emerged like the sun peeking out from behind the clouds. "Part of it was I figured if I could run a campaign the way I always have, focus on issues and not the bullshit screaming about personalities and ideas that have no chance of ever coming to fruition, that I might be able to get that spinning to slow down. And if I could do that in a different region, maybe I could do the same on a national stage."

"Flannery?"

"Whoever," Ryan said, shaking his head.

"I mean, did Flannery tell you to go?"

"I know he's the one who gave my name to Rounds, but he didn't tell me I had to go."

Stephens stared hard at Ryan. "Have you ever asked yourself why he recommended you to that campaign?"

"I assume because he thought I would succeed."

"Was that a real possibility?"

"Where are you going with this, Dom?"

"Ryan," he said, switching again to his given name, "from everything I've read, everything I've heard about that idiot Comstock, there was nothing there that a campaign consultant could help, no matter how wily they might be. Either he was going to get elected on the force of his crimson neck, or he was going to get crushed by people with common sense. But there wasn't a damn thing anyone could do to move the needle one way or the other, especially when it became clear he couldn't get out of his own way if a train was coming for him."

"Are you seriously trying to tell me that Flannery—George Flannery—hung me out to dry there?" Ryan's face flushed scarlet and his voice rose. "Why would he do that?"

"Settle down, Willy, this ain't good for your heart."

Ryan rose to his feet and stood over Stephens, who looked back, calm but concerned. "Don't give me this 'settle down' shit now, Dom! Tell me why you think he would do that."

"Maybe he didn't intentionally do it," Stephens said evenly. "Maybe he didn't realize how bleak the outlook really was because someone else was doing the recommending and, because he wanted to see you add a line to your resume and because he believed in you, he went along with it not knowing the steaming pile of dog shit he was throwing you into. It's not like you stopped and thought about it much either, right?"

Suddenly, something clicked into place, like that one piece of a jigsaw puzzle which makes the whole picture clear. Ryan felt light-headed as the blood rushed from his face and the anger-fueled adrenaline subsided. He had been set up to fail. But not by Flannery.

"Afolayan," he muttered as he sat back heavily into a chair and stared at the dais in front of him.

"Come again?"

"Seth Afolayan," Ryan repeated. "He's the one who told George to make the call."

"That's the character who's running his campaign?" Ryan nodded. "So he told George to send you to Alabama, knowing you weren't coming out alive?" Ryan darted a quick look at Stephens, who quickly added "no pun intended."

"George and I had talked about him running for a while now. There was never a question about what my role was going to be," Ryan said, his voice trailing off.

"And Afolayan saw a likely horse to hitch his wagon to and a competitor to hold the reins. So off to 'Bama you went."

"How did I not fucking see this?"

Stephens clapped Ryan on the shoulder, then pushed down for leverage as he stood up. "Ego, son," Stephens said. "All of us think we're invincible until the moment it becomes clear that we're not." Ryan looked up then stood slowly, as if he'd aged ten years in the last ten minutes, arching his back to stretch before shaking Stephens' hand once again.

"What's your plan now, Willy?"

"I don't know."

"I'm not talking life, man, I'm talking this afternoon."

"I've got lunch with Mister Speaker now, then ..."

"Worry about that part later, Ryan. Eat some food, get your feet under you and your arms around all this. Then take the next step."

Ryan nodded absentmindedly. "You up for a beer later?"

"Would if I could, but my daughter's bringing the grandkids over."

"Good for you, Dom," Ryan said, his voice strengthening. "I mean that."

"Maybe tomorrow then?"

Ryan turned back toward the gallery and shook his head. "I'm heading back to San Diego tomorrow," he said, surprised by the words even as he spoke them. Where there once had been silence, he now could hear the faint, rhythmic roar of the waves breaking onto the sand and see the silhouette of a woman practicing yoga on a sunset-framed beach He had not yet purchased a return plane ticket but knew he needed to get back, to get away from the capital and everything surrounding it. What had felt like home for so long suddenly seemed cold, unfamiliar.

"As you said, Willy, good for you. And I mean that, too" Stephens walked up the steps to the top of the gallery and turned to find Ryan still at the bottom row. "Don't be a stranger, Ryan, okay?"

Ryan nodded and watched as Stephens' bulky frame filled the doorway before disappearing down the hall to his office. Ryan tapped the gallery railing twice and followed Stephens' path up the steps, turning instead to the left toward the lobby, the elevators and his car.

CHAPTER EIGHTEEN

Maggie watched the wind-whipped rain lash trees, sidewalks and awnings along Camino del Mar through the window of her studio. She had arrived at her usual time, knowing all the while that the rain would keep all but the hardiest of practitioners away, and the weather proved her right. Two people came to her first class and, five minutes before her next, none had appeared. Outside the window, even the traffic seemed sparser than normal, as if all normal life functions ceased in Del Mar when water droplets fell from the sky. Her cell phone rang and, with one last glance outside, she answered on the second ring.

"Tell me you've canceled the rest of the schedule," Liz said immediately.

"Hello to you, too," Maggie said, "and no, not quite yet."

"Why in the world not? Are you now offering classes to amphibians?"

Maggie smiled to herself. "A frog in pigeon pose? How very Doctor Moreau-esque."

"Just send the group text, flip the sign to closed and come down to Poseidon. Monsoons call for cocktails."

"What doesn't call for a cocktail in your world?"

"We can discuss it when you get there. Now move your ass. My Christmas break doesn't last forever," Liz said before abruptly ending the call.

Maggie looked out at the avenue, presumably searching for familiar yet drenched faces sprinting through raindrops to get to her front door, but really looking for only one. After enrolling in classes, Ryan returned Tuesday and Wednesday but hadn't been back since. She had thought nothing of it Thursday and little more Friday. By Saturday she was curious, and by today she had become concerned. He was living alone in his house on the beach, no relatives or friends in the area. Who would even know if something had happened to him, if he'd had some sort of cardiac incident and...

She quickly forced that train of thought from her mind. More likely, he had to go somewhere on business and hadn't mentioned it. Why would he need to, anyway? It wasn't as if they were together in some way. Though it might have come up had she not turned down his lunch invitations all three days after class since he had enrolled. She couched her decision around the idea of not dating a student but, truthfully, she knew from the flutter in her stomach when he was near that she was falling for him. Declining the lunch invitations had been her way of trying to temper her emotions.

Maybe he simply had gone home. Maybe rebuffing him had made him lose interest in the classes, made him lose interest in her, and he had packed his suitcase and gone back to Phoenix. Her emotions tugged down at the corners of her lips at the thought of it. Why should it matter if he did? *It should because it does, silly girl.*

She got up from the lounge near the window and started turning off the lights and locking up the studio. Sitting alone in an empty building was doing nothing for her mood, her thoughts bouncing around in her head a reflection of the drumming of the rain echoing off the inside walls, muted but persistent. One drink wouldn't hurt.

***

Ryan reflexively gripped the armrests on either side of his chair as the plane began to descend through the heavy, dark, low clouds covering San Diego. After lunch, he had returned to his loft to grab his bag, returned his rental car and walked into Phoenix Sky Harbor's Terminal 4 to take the first flight back to the coast. Three hours later, he was on final approach and bracing to land at San Diego International, which involved a last-minute drop as aircraft cleared the buildings at the end of the runway before safely kissing tires to tarmac. He had avoided alcohol, knowing he still had a half-hour drive from the airport north to Del Mar but, once he was back in his rental, a bottle would be opened.

***

Maggie approached Ryan's house from the beach side, or at least what she thought was his house. The rain had stopped but the clouds still hovered close overhead. She had his address from his enrollment earlier in the week but didn't want to walk along the narrow alleys between the houses hard against the beach and those a few dozen feet to the east, not until she knew she was at the right place. She searched for the blue umbrellas on the deck he had described and finally found them, several blocks north of Poseidon and the public parking lot. She walked through the gap in the seawall, double-checked the street number that was mounted on the wall in ceramic tile and rapped on the door but, as she had suspected, there was no answer.

Liz's words echoed in Maggie's head as she stood on the porch. Ryan was, in fact, little more than a visitor, one whose time soon would be up, and then he would be returning to his real life while she remained here. Better to not get involved and instead focus on helping him down a path toward some spiritual peace. *Then*, she thought, *you can go back to searching for your own.*

She walked back through the seawall and up the stairs to his patio, where she tossed the envelope she had been holding on a small wicker table and settled into one of the Adirondack lounges sitting on the wood planking. Before meeting Liz, Maggie had decided to invite him to a small party, an open house of sorts, at her house on Christmas Eve. It was nothing formal, just a place for her to gather with her friends, drink some wine and rue the day all of their parents had told them that Santa didn't really exist. What was that about not getting involved? Liz asked her, and Maggie said she simply was reaching out to someone who probably could use the company. Except she had no real idea if he did or didn't, or if he even would be in town when the holiday hit.

Might not be in town, she reminded herself. Assuming he didn't already leave. She leaned forward with a start, stood quickly and walked to the glass arcadia doors, looking for anything of his. There, on the wood floor in front of his couch, was his newly-purchased yoga mat and she breathed a small sigh of relief. *You're being ridiculous*, she told herself. *He's going to leave at some point. Better to understand that now.* Maggie did understand but did not feel any less empty at the thought.

She picked the envelope up again, exited the patio and started walking north toward Dog Beach.

***

The sun tried to emerge from dark, lingering clouds as it slowly dipped toward the western horizon. Ryan sat in a patio chair, a glass of rum to his left and his phone in his right hand. He had changed into a sweatshirt and jeans once he got back to his house as protection from the cold, poured his drink and went directly to the patio and the ocean beyond. His mind churned like the surf crashing and withdrawing, spinning upon itself in an endless cycle. He wanted physically to lash out, to

192

drive his fist in Afolayan's jaw and see him fly backward like in a karate B movie. Not that it would change anything, but it would be satisfying nevertheless.

He thought of different approaches, any angle he could find to get his footing back and return to life before the Alabama detour, but the bubbling anger made any sustained focus impossible. Or maybe he simply tired of the inevitable answer to every line of thought: this was where he was, and it wasn't going to change anytime soon.

Ryan gulped down the rum, refilled his glass and spent ten minutes picking up the phone, ready to dial, then putting it back down on the small glass-covered table to his side. Finally, he scrolled through his contacts and placed the only call he could safely make.

"Hey there," Riley said. "Where are you?"

"Back at the beach," he said. "If I was overtly rude last night..."

"Not overtly." He could hear the smile in her voice, which only served to darken his mood further.

"Did you know, Riley?"

"Know what?"

Ryan took a deep breath before answering. "I saw Dom Stevens today at the capitol. He suggested the trip to Alabama was some sort of kamikaze mission, doomed to end in failure no matter what we did."

"Do you believe him?"

"I'm so inclined at the moment. And I want to know if you knew."

It was Riley's turn to pause. "There were times when I wondered what in the hell we were doing there, why you had opted for a moron like Comstock. Maybe I had an inkling not everything was adding up, but did I know outright? No, Ryan, I didn't know. I would have run like hell if I did."

"You suspected but you stayed. Why?"

"That's a stupid goddamn question, Boss. I stayed because we had a job to do, as fucked up as it turned out to be." She paused and her voice grew quiet. "I stayed because you were there, Ryan."

"I'm sorry," he said, his voice almost inaudible.

"For what?"

"Dragging you down with me."

"You didn't. You haven't. You're not finished, Ryan, no matter what you're thinking in the midst of your self-loathing. We aren't finished." Ryan's eyes misted at the words of support. Support that, to his mind, he didn't deserve. He pinched the bridge of his nose and shook off the emotions just as quickly as they arose. "Is that why you left so quickly?"

Ryan opened his eyes and saw a familiar figure walking along the beach toward his patio, and he broke into what felt like his first smile in days. His roiling frustration faded just as it had in the capitol gallery with Stephens earlier that afternoon. This was his salvation, at least for one portion of his life.

"Ryan, you still there?" Riley asked.

Maggie lifted a hand and waved and Ryan beckoned her toward the patio. "That was part of the reason I needed to go." The sun emerged as she stepped onto the small flight of steps leading from the sand to the patio.

"When are you coming back?"

Ryan closed his eyes, basked in the sudden amber glow of the sun and took a deep breath. "To be determined. Don't worry about me, Riley," he said, his voice brightening. "I'll be fine."

"You always say that."

"This time I mean it," he said, pressing the red circle on his phone to disconnect the call. Maggie walked up to him and he opened his arms and pulled her into his chest, letting the scent of her hair and the warmth of her touch permeate his senses.

Eyes closed, he felt the strain of the past several days dissipate, and his body relaxed into her.

"You've missed class," she said without lifting her head off his chest.

"I've missed you," he said.

She leaned back and lifted her eyes to his face, searching for something she couldn't define. Her thoughts drifted to the mist-filled landscape of her dream, but the details eluded her. Ryan leaned forward and kissed her gently on the lips. Suddenly the memory of the dreamscape came into sharp focus and when she looked at him again, she didn't see his face in front of her, but emerging from the mist into which her husband had pointed. "*He's looking for you,*" he had said, the words echoing anew. She gasped softly and fought back rising emotion. *This can't be,* she thought, but even then the vision of Ryan in her mind merged into the one leaning closer to kiss her once again. Her own surprised confusion merged with his visible need, a desperate desire, to create a whirl of confused energy and she closed her eyes, trying to separate everything. His lips pressed against hers and she leaned in, kissing him back with equal passion.

The sun slipped back behind a cloud and a cold gust rushed off the water. Ryan pulled away, took her by the hand and led her back into the house, just far enough to lean her against the kitchen counter and wrap his arms around her waist. He lowered his head toward her shoulder then turned inward, kissing her neck behind her ear as Maggie let out a small sigh. Then his lips were on hers again as he pressed insistently against her hips. Nothing mattered to Maggie but desire, need, the urge to strip off both of their clothes, wrap an ankle around his buttocks and guide him into her, and her leg subconsciously started to lift.

"I need you," he whispered. Every ounce of her being wanted to answer him in kind but she couldn't form the words, not because they weren't true, but rather because they were more true than she was prepared to admit. With overwhelming effort, Maggie placed her palm on Ryan's chest and gently pushed herself away, his head trying to follow until she lifted a finger and pressed it against his lips and smiled. "I need to go."

He looked hungrily into her eyes. "Stay," he said, summoning as much magnetism as he could muster only to watch her shake her head.

"Not now," she said. "Not tonight."

Ryan's face sagged almost imperceptibly as guilt and embarrassment washed over him. "I'm sorry, Maggie. I didn't mean..."

"I did," she interrupted, smiling as her hand moved to his cheek. Her own heart broke at the look of pain on his face, but she had no choice. She couldn't stay and she couldn't explain the dream to him. Not yet. Maybe not ever, if the hurt she saw manifested in his expression festered. "It was—it is—wonderful," she continued, imparting as much positive emotion as she could. "But I still need to go."

Ryan's hands dropped to his sides, and she leaned up to kiss him on the cheek. "I'll see you tomorrow?" He nodded once, his thoughts churning and his body numb as the adrenaline on which he'd been running evaporated. Then she was walking away, back down the steps to the beach and into the rain. Ryan stood and watched her go, too confused to speak and too numb to react. Soon she was out of sight. He gazed out over the empty water, the beach deserted with the return of the rain, and felt very much alone.

CHAPTER NINETEEN

Ryan cursed silently at the daylight slipping through the cracks between the vertical blinds in his bedroom. He slowly rolled onto his back and tried to lick his lips and film-covered teeth, but his tongue was thick in his mouth, dry from the alcohol consumed the night before after Maggie's surprise appearance and sudden departure. Ryan's legs felt heavy as he swung them over the side of the bed, rolled onto his stomach and stood uneasily. Strands of thoughts came to him through dense fog. He pulled the blinds apart and saw yet another cluster of dark clouds gathering on the horizon, the brooding purplish-gray masses matching his foul mood. He almost would have chalked up Maggie's arrival and their brief sojourn into passion to a dream, except both the warmth of her lips and the crushing disappointment of her leaving lingered, the latter growing stronger by the moment.

Sympathy, he told himself, *nothing more*. Too polite to flinch or turn away, not so interested that she felt the need to stay any longer. If the moment truly had been as wonderful as she'd said, she would not have left him standing alone so quickly. Then again, were his reasons for kissing her any more noble? There was no question he had enjoyed the time they had spent together and that her perpetually positive nature was surprisingly refreshing. Politics was devoid of such optimism. Ryan had been honest when he'd said he missed her during his trip back to Phoenix. At the same time, given his feelings after talking first to Dom and then Riley, he would have kissed anyone just for the connection, the brief and superficial sense of worth. Except that wasn't all he'd felt when his lips touched hers—and did he really want to discount the rare sensation of the butterflies released in his stomach or the instant stoppage of time, the way the wind stopped blowing and the ocean's ebb and flow paused, the sun suspended unmoving atop the distant waves? How could he dismiss something that felt so real, so right?

Because it's all one-sided, he thought, frustration bubbling to the surface as he dressed slowly. A more confident man, or at least one not moving in a post-tequila haze, might think she'd felt as overwhelmed by the moment as he had been. But he was in no mood for consolatory thoughts, even those that held a hint a truth. He walked downstairs to the kitchen, grabbed the bottle of tequila off his counter and the glass he had used the night before from the sink. Seeing his yoga mat on the floor to his right, he snarled and kicked the mat into a corner of the room, then went out to the patio to watch the foaming white horses rush ahead of the incoming storm, while drowning the building storm within his own head.

***

Three miles away, Maggie sat on her patio and stared blankly at the ocean in the distance, lost in thoughts of her own. She had become accustomed to the smoldering frustration just below the surface of Ryan's expression, though she was at a loss to explain its consistent presence. But the look of sadness she saw the night before when she turned to leave was something entirely different—deeper, more primal, and her heart ached at the thought she'd caused such pain. On top of that was her own reaction to the kiss, as unexpected as it was unwanted.

There were two possible reactions after her accident left her acutely aware of the fleeting nature of life. Either embrace love and allow a man into her life, knowing all the while things could go south at any moment, or hold men at a distance, enjoying their company temporarily while not growing any attachments to someone who could be gone the following day. She ultimately chose the latter, which was why she took notice of Ryan in the first place. He fit her short list of requirements— attractive, not local and mature, albeit somewhat emotionally bruised, therefore theoretically not mentally available for anything serious. Whatever happened, she would be in complete control.

Except for when she kissed Ryan and her stomach flipped and her knees weakened and all she wanted to do was fall into him completely, none of which fit her script. Which was why that look, a look she had seen more than once during her brief flings, resonated for the first time. How could she explain to Ryan that she had to leave at that moment, or else she wouldn't have left at all that night, when she couldn't make sense of the feeling herself? Would he listen? Would he even want to talk to her? And why, she kept asking herself, did it really mean so much?

She suddenly was pulled from her reverie by the insistent vibrating of her smart watch's alarm. Her first class was scheduled to start in a half hour. A half hour to find her own focus so she could help others find theirs, but all she could think of was whether Ryan would come to her studio today and what would happen next.

*****

Light drops of rain spattered onto Ryan's patio but he took little notice. He had left his patio only briefly to relieve himself, then returned to his chair. Surfers had arrived to take advantage of the growing surf then departed, the morning beach walkers already had completed their laps and still he sat, staring forward with unseeing eyes. His phone vibrated again and he jumped, having forgotten that it still was sitting next to him. It was a text from Riley, almost identical to the one that was waiting on his phone when he woke up—"ARE YOU OKAY?" He watched until the message notification faded and then turned back toward the water. Almost as an afterthought, he picked up the phone and put it in his pocket to protect it from the rain.

He reached for the bottle of tequila from the table next to him and poured the dregs into his glass, then downed the meager amount in one swallow. His body felt heavy and his mind muddled, but one thought persisted—*How the hell did I get to this point?*

Through the fog in his brain he tried to separate the different strands, the multiple events that had stacked one upon the next over the past several weeks. The election loss was minor. It was the betrayals he couldn't countenance. Actually, the one major betrayal. If he made the effort, he could understand how Flannery had been seduced by Afolayan and bought into the idea of sending Ryan three-quarters of the way across the country to run a campaign in an area with which Ryan wasn't as familiar. And Ryan's ego was such that he took the bait without thought. That, he thought bitterly, was the lure and the pain of politics.

What was harder to reconcile was the actual pain his body, his heart had endured. That night in Birmingham had exposed weakness, an encumbrance he long ago had relegated to the back acres of his persona. Weakness was a liability to be handled, nothing more. But then he nearly collapsed backstage on election night, was forced to sit in a wheelchair and be pushed the hundred feet from triage back to pre-op. Watching the long, white fluorescent bulbs rush past as he then was rolled into surgery, then eventually up to his room. The physical discomfort from where the stent was inserted through his thigh, and the psychological toll that came from being told not only was he not immortal, but he was on the verge of dying in Ala-fucking-bama if he hadn't arrived at the hospital when he did. That was the moment when the impenetrable facade he had built over decades collapsed, and he had spent nearly every moment since running away from rubble he knew couldn't be reassembled.

Years upon years of always displaying an air of cool confidence, of always having an answer and a ready explanation ready, of always being able to present solutions where others focused only on the problems. Thousands of hours spent counseling others on the need for calm, for clarity in thought and action, to avoid overreaction and emotional decisions. Keeping almost everyone he'd known—everyone except Riley and Charlie—at arm's length lest they get close enough to discover the fear lurking behind the imperturbable mask. Decades of always—always—being in control, sliding away in a matter of minutes and eventually disappearing entirely, leaving behind only the doubts, the self-criticism. Seemingly regaining his footing in the time spent with Maggie only to have that foundation ripped out from under him with her abrupt departure the night before.

And most frustrating, his turning to alcohol to try and cover over the pain and uncertainty. Ignoring the memory of nights spent as a child watching his own father rant at the world around him, his paranoia and dissatisfaction fueled by the one beer after another consumed first at a bar on the way home, and then in his well-worn recliner. Disregarding the advice of Charlie, who had told him anything more than the occasional social drink would hasten his return to the hospital and an eventual date to have his chest cracked open. Surrendering control of his thoughts and emotions all for a state of temporary numbness, only to emerge sober and in the same position he was in before the first drink, except now with the added guilt of knowing that, slowly but surely, he was killing himself.

Anger rose within Ryan even as the rain began to fall more heavily and he lashed out at the bottles on the side table, sending the tequila bottle and the glass shattering on the wood planks. A man and woman walking on the beach in the rain looked toward him at the sound of the noise. "What?" he yelled at the top of his voice, rising on unsteady legs. "Mind your own fucking business!" The duo shook their heads and pulled the hoods of their slickers tighter as they walked on. Not satisfied with the broken glass lying near his feet, Ryan swept his leg back to kick the larger pieces off the patio and onto the sand but almost immediately lost his balance and stumbled to his left, close to the sliding door leading to the family room.

"Fuck it," he muttered. With effort he opened the door, walked into the dining area and great room and pulled his sweatshirt off. He thought momentarily of changing out of his jogging shorts into something both dry and warmer, but decided he didn't care enough to do it. Through the red-tinged fog of alcohol and anger came visions of food, and he realized for the first time that he hadn't had anything to eat since the airport in Phoenix the day before. He walked heavily toward the laundry room, sniffed at a T-shirt at the top of a pile and, satisfied that it was at least clean enough, pulled it over his head before pulling out his phone and tapping out a Lyft request. There were no answers here in the middle of someone else's house, the ocean beyond half-hidden through the now-driving rain. Maybe there were no answers to be found at all. Maybe the only solution was to keep running until he could find a modicum of peace.

"Just eat something," he said to no one in particular before taking a seat near the door to wait for his ride.

***

"I apologize, friends." Maggie sat cross-legged on the floor, hands pulled behind her and shoulders rolled back for a long back stretch at the end of her second class. "My focus wasn't entirely here today, and I fear our practice suffered." Driving rain hammered the roof above them to create a background thrum, adding to her own thoughts to further muddle the energy in her studio.

"It was fine, Maggie," one of her students said with a forgiving smile.

"Thank you, Tanya," she said, smiling back wanly. Even admitting that her focus was missing couldn't serve to break the thoughts spinning in her mind. Ryan had not come to class, and she wasn't sure if it was because he was still upset from the night before. And she couldn't bring herself to admit why it mattered so much. "Reach up to pull the light inside you," she said, remembering lips pressed together in the rain, her stomach twisting anew, "and pull it to your heart with love and forgiveness." Everyone followed and raised their arms over their heads, palms together, then pulled them down in front of their chests. "Thank you so much for sharing your yoga with me and for your patience. Namaste."

She took a deep breath and chatted with her class members as they gathered their mats and towels and, for the foresighted fortunate ones, umbrellas and walked out into the raw weather. Locking the door behind the last to depart, she walked to the counter and checked her phone to see two texts. The first, from Liz, invited her to lunch a half-block down. The second, a simple two words, was from Ryan. "I'M SORRY." She stared for a long moment, starting and deleting a response three separate times as her eyes welled with tears. She wiped a stray tear off her cheek with the back of her hand, shook her head, put her phone in her purse, grabbed her own umbrella from a well-used stand by the door and started walking to meet Liz.

Runoff ran in long streams along the gutters, and the sidewalks were sprayed repeatedly by passing cars driving through the rain puddling on the blacktop. On a normal day, the sidewalks would be populated by tourists looking in the windows of local shops and locals heading to grab a bite to eat either during their lunch hour or between surfing and walking sessions on the beach. But the rain had cleared virtually everyone away, and Maggie walked quickly and very much alone to a small restaurant styled as a new American bistro. She stopped at the doorway, shook out her umbrella, then stepped inside and saw Liz sitting at one of the restaurant's dozen tables, this one next to the wide front window.

"You look terrible," Liz said as Maggie approached.

Maggie stared for a moment and shook her head as she sat down. "It's great seeing you too, hon."

"I'm going to go out on a limb and say you didn't sleep much after we spoke," Liz continued, "and that your friend didn't come to class today." Maggie nodded slowly to both statements. "That leaves me just one question, Mags. Why do you give a shit?"

Maggie turned toward the window and watched as the rooster tail from a car swamped an intrepid bicyclist on the far side of the street, which would have been worse if the rider wasn't already soaked to the bone. "I've asked myself the same thing," she said quietly.

"And?"

Maggie started to answer but paused as the server walked over to take their drink orders. "And the simple answer is I don't really know, except it does." Liz leaned back and crossed her arms across her chest in frustration as Maggie turned toward her. "How do you explain why you like a certain song, or how you knew that the house you bought was the right one for you, or that this is the wave you duck under instead of letting it crash over you, or what car you're supposed to buy or,

I don't know, what ice cream to buy when you're depressed and need the comfort?"

"You don't," Liz said with a sigh. "You just know."

"You just know," Maggie said with a slight smile. "There is something there that I can't wrap my mind around. Something I can't walk away from that keeps me thinking about him and, to be honest, it scares the living hell out of me."

"It's that real?"

"Potentially."

"It has been a while."

"Since the accident." Maggie looked down at her hands on the table.

"That's more than potentially, dear."

Maggie tilted her head to the side in a half shrug. "I know. I mean, I don't know yet. But it just might be."

"Wow," Liz said softly.

"Very much so."

After their drinks arrived and they placed their orders without glancing at the menu, they sat quietly and watched the rain run down the window. A bell jingled as the front door opened, and Liz glanced up to see a man walking in. His hair was plastered against his head, his clothing soaked. He looked pale aside from the dark circles clearly visible beneath his eyes. "Talk about looking like hell," she said. Maggie half turned as the man walked to the bistro's small bar area and sat heavily atop one of the barstools.

"Oh, Ryan," she said softly.

"Oh, shit," Liz added under her breath.

CHAPTER TWENTY

R yan slid awkwardly into a black vinyl barstool and ordered a glass of Malibu on the rocks at what was his third stop of the afternoon. He had directed the driver to take him to a dispensary, returning home with a package of TCH-laced chocolate cookies and a bar of marijuana-infused dark chocolate. He dropped the chocolate bar to the side and opened the cookies' foil container with his teeth. A small chunk of cookie flew out of the container and landed on the floor near the dining-room table. "Come here, you tasty little bastard," he said heavily as he leaned down, picked up the small piece and popped it in his mouth. Reaching inside the foil, Ryan pulled out a larger piece of cookie and slowly ate both.

With a second ride share, he answered his stomach's insistent growl with a plateful of sashimi and answered his throbbing head with three glasses of Sapporo and sake. The dull pain left over from the night before slowly slipped away as the food combined with the alcohol and the marijuana to mute the world around him. All worries faded from relevancy, his muscles discernibly relaxed and he settled more deeply into the haze as if falling into an overstuffed sofa.

Then he stood up to go to the restroom, and the comfort shattered. Ryan saw himself in the third person, standing behind and above himself and looking down on his shoulders. "What the hell," he muttered, the words coming from a distance, disassociated from his body. He walked down a narrow hallway to the bathroom and felt the camera through which he viewed himself panning backward as he stood at the urinal. Leaning his head against the cold tile above the stall grounded him, but only momentarily. As he walked away, his view separated into a split screen, one side providing the perspective from his eyes, the other a trailing camera moving with him.

Ryan takes out his phone and orders another ride drifted across his vision like a news chyron and, so prompted, he did just that, stopping only to throw a couple of twenties on the bar top before heading outside. Whether the drive to the bistro took minutes or hours, he couldn't say. Time had lost meaning, just as it had at L'Auberge with Scarlet, but with a sinister twist. Then, time merely had slowed. Now it seemingly didn't exist. And maybe, he thought, he didn't either. *Shit*, he thought, *that's it! I'm already dead!* He looked out the car's windows, searching for proof that he wasn't actually lying dead on the floor of his beach rental, but failed to find anything that couldn't be chalked up to a dream sequence.

Engage the driver in conversation. "How busy has it been today?" *Good work.* His voice sounded confident if muffled. Nothing to see here. He listened carefully to the driver's response, even managed to laugh appropriately in commiseration, secure in the knowledge no one could tell how fucked up he really was.

Remember The Matrix? *The driver doesn't know because he doesn't really exist.* "Fuck," he exhaled.

"Sir?"

Ah shit. That wasn't internal dialog. "Sorry," he said deliberately. "Remembered something I'd forgotten." New plan. Just shut up until we get to the restaurant.

Once inside, the bartender gave Ryan a long look after watching his struggles with the barstool. Ryan matched the bartender with his best imitation of a steady gaze. Satisfied, the bartender turned toward the back wall for the bottle of rum. And scene. Ryan reached for a menu, undecided on whether to order food. He had a nagging desire to eat but was too numb to know whether that instruction was coming from his stomach or the marijuana. Mozzarella sticks, he thought, never hurt anyone.

He looked over his right shoulder, and there was the cause of his current out-of-body, out-of-mind experience. Maggie, sitting slack-jawed in a window booth across from an equally flabbergasted brunette. Too late he realized that what he thought to be a brief glance had turned into a lengthy stare thanks to his altered time horizon. Before he could avert his eyes, she slid out of the booth and walked his way.

"Be cool," he muttered to himself before raising the corner of his lip into something between a smile and a smirk. "Of all the beach joints in all the world," he said as she eased into the chair next to his. Maggie leaned in and kissed Ryan on the cheek, edging away quickly from breath coated with sake and rum.

"It looks like you've had yourself quite the day," she said, staring into heavily bloodshot eyes.

"And to think it's still only noon."

"It's actually closer to five."

"I was thinking Hawaiian thoughts."

"Ryan, you look—"

"Damp?"

"Pale."

"It's the lighting," he said dismissively. "Nothing at all to see."

Maggie searched his face for a moment, then her features softened and she shook her head slowly. "Oh, Ryan," she said, gently placing her left palm against his cheek. "What have you done?"

Ryan pulled her hand away from his face. "I ordered fried cheese," he said, inwardly congratulating himself on not just maintaining a conversation but injecting sarcasm. "It seemed self-evident."

"Do you really not understand why I left last night?"

"Because you didn't want to be there," Ryan said, his voice filled with hurt. "That's usually how that goes."

She smiled bleakly. "No, Ryan," she said softly. "I had to leave exactly because I absolutely didn't want to."

"That makes zero sense."

"Think about it," she said as she rose from the barstool. "It makes perfect sense, if you try." Maggie gave Ryan one final look, shook her head sadly and returned to her table by the window. Ryan continued staring where she had stood, trying without success to find focus through the fog before giving up and returning to his food. Dizziness struck in a wave as he finished off his drink, and he asked the bartender for a glass of water. The room wasn't spinning so much as he felt untethered, his focus bouncing here and there at random like an electron jumping from one orbital to the next. Ryan finished the water in three gulps, reached for his wallet and left a twenty on the polished wooden bar top and pivoted out of his chair. He almost could feel the oxygen atoms in the air colliding with his skin, causing reflex reactions in hundreds of places at once.

Moving with an awkward Joe Cocker-esque gait, Ryan walked to Maggie's seat and placed a steadying hand on the top of the booth behind her. She looked up into his increasingly pale face lined with sweat, unfocused eyes attempting to hold her gaze in return.

"Ryan, are you okay?"

Not even close, he thought. *In fact, I'm probably going to pass out now.*

Ryan jerked his head back, surprised himself by that thought. "I'm good," he lied. "And I want you to know, I do get it." Now, about that loss of consciousness.

"Maybe you ought to sit down," Maggie said and slid toward the window to make room.

The floor's going to be more comfortable. "Thanks, Maggie, but I ought to...." Ryan's voice trailed off as the warning in his head thundered. I SAID LIE DOWN NOW!

With a last, apologetic glance her direction, Ryan collapsed in a heap at the foot of the booth. He didn't hear the bartender curse and swear he hadn't overserved Ryan, and he didn't hear Maggie's stifled cry as Liz called 911 for an ambulance.

***

Ryan shifted uncomfortably in his hospital bed, searching for a position that would allow him to fall asleep. His room in the telemetry department was dark and, mercifully, he had been given a single room. The only light seeped from under a curtain pulled across a three-quarters shut door. But that didn't make getting comfortable any easier. An IV tube was inserted in the crook of his right arm, and the tape holding it in place pulled at his skin any time he moved. On his chest and abdomen were a dozen telemetry leads. His lone solace was he wouldn't lose any more hair to the leads, as the hair already had been ripped off in his last trip to the emergency room. The plastic combined pulse and oxygenation sensor covered the end of his left index finger, and it seemed every moment caused an alarm to start shrieking as one or another piece of equipment was pushed out of place. He had rung for the nurse earlier and now was awaiting approval from both the generalist and Charlie for

211

something to help him sleep, a long shot given all he had consumed.

When the attending had called Charlie earlier with an update on what had happened, that Ryan had managed to drug and drink his way into unconsciousness, Ryan was certain he could hear his friend's screaming through the phone. He couldn't blame him. He had been absolutely useless as a patient to date.

The first time he walked into the emergency room, back in Birmingham, he had been angry. He had seethed with frustration over his body breaking down, his seeming failure to catapult his candidate to victory and the general course of the previous two months, trying to prop up someone destined for defeat from the beginning. In San Diego, he was maudlin. Flannery's decision to layer Ryan almost entirely out of his White House run, and his surprise over his body's struggles with even the most basic stresses of his job, had left him questioning his own usefulness, the very reasons why he chose to live.

This time? He had been stupid. No more, no less. Maggie's departure from his kitchen had been less the cause than the deflection, the one person and event upon which he could focus his frustration, undeserved as it was. But she wasn't the real reason. Politics was.

He chuckled grimly and turned toward the still-open blinds of his room's small window and the city beyond. "How can someone be that self-absorbed and that clueless at the same time?" he said to no one in particular.

Throughout his life, Ryan had seen one-time colleagues, peers and friends fall by the wayside for one reason or another. This one drank too much, this one couldn't seem to stay faithful to that one, this one needed masses of uppers and downers to get through the day. Some had made ludicrous financial decisions, taken poorly conceived risks or simply had the bad fortune to fall ill, sometimes seriously so. He could point to, as the High Holy Days prayer books said, an alphabetical litany of woe. Some had recovered. Others hadn't. From the time he had leaned his back against the wall and slid to the floor to sit in Birmingham, Ryan had felt like he had hit rock bottom only to find himself merely on an unsteady ledge. He had remembered the faces from his past and wondered if they ever knew when they had reached the absolute low point that led to their eventual renewal, or if they, too, kept believing a positive change was in the offing only to be disappointed again.

Ryan had been wrestling with this idea from the moment he regained consciousness just before the doors of the ambulance closed. One EMT had needed to try two different veins to insert a needle for intravenous fluids. The first, which looked strong when the paramedic tapped the crook of his elbow, wouldn't respond after having been tapped so often so recently. He was handed a pair of aspirin, which turned to chalk as he chewed them before taking a sip of water to wash the bitter paste down his throat. The other paramedic took his vitals but Ryan didn't listen to the numbers, knowing instinctively his blood pressure and pulse were going to be elevated. The only real question was whether he had further damaged his heart.

Anger turned to resignation turned to resolve within minutes as the ambulance covered the six miles to the hospital. The last two episodes could be attributed to excessive stress or fatigue, to external stimuli and responses out of his control. This one, however, was different. This was a self-inflicted wound, one which, with luck, he would survive as he had the first two. But could he survive another? Would he really want to try? And, he thought for the first time, did he want to keep putting those few close individuals through the concern and worry for him they had shown, even as he tried to ignore the situation? Was it fair to Charlie or to Riley? Or to Maggie?

He already had been admitted to the hospital when Maggie arrived. She pulled aside the curtain with shaking hands, her face pale and drawn, sat quietly on a chair next to the bed and took his hand. "I had to tell them I was your fiancée," she said with a wavering smile.

"Just don't make me try and get down on one knee right now," he said. They stared at each other, and Maggie was about to break the silence when the attending doctor walked in and started asking the same questions Ryan had answered twice earlier. Yes, he had some sort of blockage cleared about five weeks earlier. Yes, he had what was chalked up to be a panic attack a couple of weeks after that. Yes, he had spent large portions of the previous day traveling, then drinking and downing some edibles, eating only the sushi in between. The doctor's mien was serious, albeit world weary. This was not a unique story.

Ryan turned toward Maggie and his heart went cold. She was standing, shaking, her hand covering her mouth as tears welled in her eyes. She realized in an instant how little she knew about Ryan. She also realized how much he mattered to her regardless. But here he was, essentially confessing to a doctor that he had been living like he couldn't care less whether he lived or died. Like he didn't know how final death was, at least to those who passed. Like he didn't know how the dead could haunt someone for long after they were gone.

"I'm sorry," she said, her voice barely above a whisper. "I can't be here right now." Ryan called after her as she walked through the curtain, but she didn't stop.

He had thought about sending her a text, going as far as typing the first several words before pressing the delete key. Maggie owed him nothing, just as he owed her nothing. Ryan closed his eyes and still saw her face and hoped he'd have the chance to explain. The nurse knocked softly and stepped into his room, carrying a small paper cup with a single pill inside. "Good news," she said, handing both the paper cup and a plastic cup of water to Ryan. "You're lucky they prescribed it."

He took them, tipped the pill into his mouth and gulped the water in two swallows. "Thank you," he said. Once everything had worn off, he was too wound up to sleep unaided.

"Get some rest," she said, turning toward the curtain and the door.

"Hey, Cindy?" he called after her. "Can I ask you a question?"

"Sure," she said, standing with the edge of the curtain resting on her shoulder.

"When do you think a person hits rock bottom?"

"Why do you ask?"

"I just assume working in this department...I'm guessing there are a lot of reasons people end up here, or even elsewhere in the hospital. You said you worked in the ER once upon a time, right?"

"I did," she said as she took a step back into the room.

"So?"

"So what I would tell you is everyone's different, Ryan. But what seems to be the most true is a person hits rock bottom when they make the conscious decision to start moving forward come hell or high water." She paused for a moment. "Does that make sense?"

He smiled back, feeling as if a weight had been lifted. Maybe the answer he had been searching for was this simple after all. "It does," he said finally. "Very much so. Good night, Cindy."

"Good night, Ryan," she said, pulling the curtain and door closed behind her.

***

He woke up around six a.m., when the first of the specialists started coming into his room. First, a check of his vitals, and then yet another in the endless line of blood draws. Breakfast arrived soon thereafter, and Ryan was sitting in a recliner eating a blueberry pancake and toast when Charlie walked in, shutting the door behind him.

"Have you ever heard of the Keeley cure?" Charlie said.

"Good morning to you, too, Doc," Ryan replied.

"Shove your good morning. The Keeley cure," he said, pausing as Charlie turned toward the window. "No? Think of it as an Old West-style intervention. When some cowboy would repeatedly get drunk too often for their own good, his friends would wait until he passed out and then place him in a coffin. Hands folded across the chest, the whole nine yards. Sometimes they even would stand the coffin up, like the photos of the Clanton gang in Tombstone, so people could walk past and honor the recently passed. When the drunk came to it was like waking up at his own funeral. His friends would be standing around mourning his departure while he slowly came to understand that he was lying in his own casket. It usually worked, unless the guy happened to be the most stupid, obstinate and oblivious human being on the planet."

Ryan turned his head slowly and glared at his friend, and Charlie saw the dark circles under his eyes, accentuated further when he turned from the window. "I'd actually thought about doing that," Charlie continued, "get you a nice comfortable slab down in the morgue, have you wake up and realize you were in one of those long drawers and wonder for a little while whether you'd survived the evening. But it seems there are more concerns about insurance and malpractice than there were back in the 1870s and, frankly, I figure you just may end up on that slab soon enough as it is."

"I thought I already had," Ryan said, smiling grimly at the memory. "I'm pretty sure I asked the EMTs to swing by the rental to see if my body was lying inert on the floor."

"Don't forget asking them over and over again to prove you weren't imagining the whole thing," Charlie said. Ryan chuckled at the absurdity of the situation, but his friend's expression didn't change. "Oh, Ryan," he said. "We are well past the laugh-it-all-off phase. No more of this stuff about the second chance you were given, no more talk about how very fortunate you were to have survived because, quite frankly, it doesn't seem like you care. You're so entirely fucked in your head, you've conflated your career and life until you don't realize the latter goes on with or without the former."

"I'm starting to understand that."

"Are you? Are you *really*? Everyone is in shock when they find out that they've had a heart attack and they realize that, yes, they really are mortal after all. But the vast majority of them are smart enough not to hasten their own death once they make that discovery. To think, my concern was cracking you open down the line to replace a valve. You won't live long enough for me to have to worry about it."

"The whole thing hasn't been that easy, Charlie."

"Of course it hasn't. But it should be," he said, his voice rising. "You got a raw deal from Comstock, from George, even from your heart. No one's disputing that. But why in the world would you let those assholes drive you into a grave? What have they done to earn that power over you?"

"So I need to retire."

"It wouldn't be a bad idea," Charlie said, "but I'm more worried about the immediate. I mean, what the fuck was the thought process there? You've got to stop. You came in here with a blood-alcohol count that would make a rock star blush. And that doesn't even include the weed. It's fucking stupid."

"I know," Ryan said. "The weed was a one-shot deal. I'm just trying to find a way forward."

"Then act like it, Ryan. Look, this isn't a particularly difficult recipe to follow. Lose the liquor. Lose the marijuana, anomaly or not. Cut back on the caffeine. Fried foods, red meat, that sort of stuff isn't great, but we'll get to those. Get active once and for all, even if it's only walking a couple of blocks on the beach. Just get your blood moving and your heart pumping and strengthening."

Tears welled and then spilled out over the corners of Ryan's eyes. Jesus, Ryan. Who are you becoming? Pull it together. "I'm not looking to die, Charlie," he said, shaking away the emotion. "I already decided that."

"You can say it all you want," he said. "But at some point, you've got to prove it. Now tell me I can get you released and trust you not to do something moronic again. There's scarier shit in the hospital than what hit your prima donna ass."

Ryan nodded and extended his hand, which Charlie took and shook before clapping Ryan on the shoulder and turning toward the door.

"Hey, Charlie," Ryan called, and the doctor stopped in the doorway. "I'm going to need a lift back to my beach house."

Charlie smiled thinly. "Not from me, you don't. You've got a beautiful woman waiting to drive you back."

Ryan sat up a little straighter. "Did you bring Riley out with you?"

"Not this time," Charlie said. "This one is an unknown to me."

Ryan smiled for what felt like the first time in days. Maggie had come back to get him. Whatever had overcome her the day before and sent her tearfully running toward the exit had run its course. She was here. For him.

At Charlie's urging, the generalist altered the order of his rounds and cleared Ryan to be released. Ryan, somewhat refreshed after hours of being pumped full of intravenous fluids, dressed quickly, called for the nurse and sat down in the mandatory wheelchair for the ride downstairs. But when they reached the waiting room, the nurse pushed him next to a column and stopped. He looked hopefully for Maggie but instead watched another woman walk over and take hold of the chair's handles.

"You were at lunch—"

"It's okay, Ryan," she interrupted. "My name's Liz. I thought it was time that you and I had a chat."

CHAPTER TWENTY-ONE

They sat at a table near the open front window of the Pillbox Tavern. There had been virtually no conversation in the drive to the restaurant. Ryan contented himself spending the drive watching the glare of the sun reflecting off the top of the waves off to his right. The bartender, recognizing Ryan, automatically offered him a Hefeweizen but Ryan declined, opting instead for an iced tea.

"On the wagon?" Liz asked, raising her eyebrows.

"No wagon to climb aboard," Ryan said. "Simply a matter of choice."

"A better choice than yesterday, from what Maggie told me."

Ryan's features softened and he smiled unconsciously. "How is she doing? She left...rather suddenly."

"She's okay," Liz said. Her brow furrowed as she chose her words carefully. "I honestly never thought I'd see her step foot inside a hospital again unless she was the patient."

"Again?"

Liz let the question hang for a few moments as she gazed past Ryan at the tall pine trees swaying gracefully in the ocean breeze. "It's funny," she started finally. "People always talk about getting to know each other when they first meet. 'I want to know everything about you,' blah blah blah. Then they spend the bulk of their time with the other person thinking about what they're going to say next and how best to reveal only the parts about themselves they want seen. Just one facade talking to another."

"I'm sorry," Ryan said, "I don't follow."

"Clearly you hadn't told her much about what had happened to you, otherwise she wouldn't have left the hospital feeling as stunned as she did."

"It hadn't come up," he said defensively.

"It could have if you had wanted it to, but you didn't. Just like she hadn't ever mentioned her husband to you."

Ryan sat up straight and his head started to buzz. "She's...married?"

Liz turned deliberately and looked him in the eye, enjoying his discomfort to at least a small degree before letting him off the hook. "No," she said, "not anymore."

He relaxed almost immediately. "Lots of people get divorced."

"She didn't divorce him, Ryan," Liz said. "Several years back, she and her husband were driving along the Pacific Coast Highway. A drunk wasn't watching where he was going and slammed into the drivers' side of their car. She miraculously ended up with only a concussion and a few bruises. He was unconscious and had to be cut out of the car and passed away shortly after they got to the hospital."

"Jesus."

Liz nodded before continuing. "She recovered in time, in her own way, but some things linger. If she hears a siren she'll tense up and lose her train of thought until she regains control. And she had yet to step foot in a hospital following her release. There was one time she was as sick as I've ever seen her—a high fever, chills, nausea, the works. She clearly was dehydrated and, if nothing else, could have used some IV fluids. But she wouldn't let me take her to the ER. We've had friends have babies, and she would wait until they came home to visit. Nothing would get her near a hospital. At least, not until yesterday."

Ryan glanced up as their lunch arrived, then promptly ignored the food. "Then why would she go yesterday?"

Liz picked up a French fry, dipped it in ketchup and took a bite. "If you can't figure that part out," she said, pointing at Ryan with the other half of the fry, "then you're not nearly as smart as she says you are."

"Wait," he said. "She said I'm smart?"

Liz shook her head and smiled ruefully. "You men are all just little boys looking for affirmation from girls, aren't you?"

The next few minutes drifted quietly as they ate their food. Ryan was looking toward the televisions on the walls but seeing nothing. He didn't know why it mattered that Maggie so clearly cared for him. He just knew that it did. Every now and again he would catch Liz watching him as he worked through what she had said.

"How long have you known her?" he asked finally.

"Since college. We were sorority sisters."

"San Diego State?"

"USD," she replied as Ryan nodded. "Why do you ask?"

"Curious," he said. "You seem like a very good friend to her."

"It's mutual," she said, features softening. "We've been through a lot together." Seeing Ryan's raised eyebrows, she continued, "Men and merlot mostly. One often caused by the other."

"We're not all that bad," he said and smiled wryly.

"And if you are," she said, "there's always more wine."

"Touché," he said, raising his glass of iced tea toward hers. The server arrived with the bill, which Ryan quickly grabbed and dropped a pair of twenties in the vinyl folio. Liz made no objection, simply thanking him. "It's the least I can do. Besides, I still need a ride home."

They drove in silence the few minutes back to his house, Ryan more than content to listen to the radio and look out the window. When the car pulled in front of his house, Ryan turned to her. "Liz," he said, "I understand I don't necessarily have a right to ask this, but would you tell Maggie that I'd like to meet her for breakfast tomorrow morning?"

Liz glanced at him out of the corner of her eye before looking back at the road. "If I were smart, I'd say no. Then again, she's not smart enough to say no either," she said, then sighed. "She asked me to ask you the same thing. Tomorrow morning at eight thirty, Crepes and Corks. You know where that is?"

Ryan nodded and reached out to shake her hand. "Thank you, Liz. I owe you one."

"Just don't hurt her," she said, "or I'll have to send you back to the emergency room. Got it?"

"Loud and clear," he said. He took a step toward the house, then turned and knocked on the passenger-side window of Liz's car.

"Forget something?" she asked after rolling down the glass.

"When you talk to Maggie, thank her for me?"

Liz smiled and reached for the window control. "Tell her yourself tomorrow, Ryan. Just don't screw it up."

***

The blood-red digital display of the alarm clock taunted Ryan throughout the night as he tossed and turned, searching for sufficient calm to fall asleep. Hours marched by one by one each time he looked at the clock, but he didn't seem to find any rest during the interludes. He thought briefly of the bottles on his counter and dismissed the idea just as quickly. Change was necessary. *What you need is clarity, not more confusion.*

At 2:23 a.m. he finally surrendered. He pulled on a sweatshirt and a pair of jogging shorts, and walked barefoot out through his patio and onto the cool sand of the beach. The rows of houses on either side of him were dark save for the occasional porch light. Even the spotlight that shone from Jake's to the south was off at this hour. Above, the cloudless and moonless sky was filled with twinkling dots of white, blue, red and yellow. Something from memory clicked, and he found himself staring at the bright glow of Jupiter, its surface slightly rounder in form than the pinpricks of the surrounding stars. He walked down to the edge of the surf line, the saturated sand simultaneously more densely packed yet less stable. A larger wave washed ashore and covered his feet and ankles in icy salt water. The cold cut through his sleepiness in an instant, temporarily banishing all other thought.

Water rushed around his shins and he stared at his feet as the wave withdrew, pulling sand out from under him. The ocean was at slack tide, neither charging forward nor hurtling back in retreat. Ryan took one step forward then another, walking toward the frothing surf. The next wave hit at his shins and splashed across his groin but he continued moving, slowly, purposefully. Soon he was in calf-deep water with waves crashing around his waist, and still he went on. His sweatshirt was soaked and billowed around him with the changing directions of the water and eventually, with effort, he pulled it off and held it in his right hand as he went deeper, stopping only when he was shoulder deep and needed to push off the ocean floor to leap into the waves before they swamped him.

Surrounded by sixty-degree water, his mind cleared. Tangled lines of emotion divided into separate, manageable strands as quickly as they appeared. Frustration over Comstock, Flannery and Alabama seeped from his pores and into the flowing water. In their place came a vision of Maggie sitting across the table from him, one knee bent and a bare foot on the edge of a chair

225

as she sipped a glass of orange juice. She was smiling. No, she was laughing for reasons he didn't know. He didn't need to know. The buzzing in his brain, the imagined crushing force of stress around his head, the constant tension in his limbs slid away and he was left with this one wonderful thought. Maybe the key to maintaining that invincible facade was to have someone in his life with whom he could let it fall away completely. He'd not even done so with Riley, who seemed to know his thoughts before they formed.

Growing up, Ryan had heard of the physical and spiritual recuperative powers of the mikvah, a Jewish consecrational bath filled with accumulated rainwater, but he thought himself too smart to believe in what amounted to old wives' tales. But here he was, neck-deep in salt rather than rainwater, floating in a cocoon of peacefulness. Ryan's logical side thought the feelings were due to the numbing cold of the ocean, but he dismissed the idea almost as soon as it entered his mind and turned to the prayer the faithful would say when they were submerged.

"*Shema yisroyal Adonai elohainu Adonai echad,*" he mouthed silently between chattering teeth. *Hear o Israel. The Lord is Your God. The Lord is One.* What an odd thought to have come from nowhere, yet entirely in keeping with the moment. Warmth filled his heart and mind, if not his limbs. He was too old to become religious, but at least there was comfort in the long-dormant ritual. He bobbed on the waves and took in his surroundings, ignoring how stupid it was to swim by himself in the dark. The beach remained dark but, behind the initial row of houses, scattered lights rose into the darkness from the houses set on the Del Mar Heights. Turning, the wide expanse of ocean opened in front of him. For the first time, he became aware of twin glows in the sky, Los Angeles in the deep distance to the northwest, San Diego to the south, beckoning as if either city were merely a short swim away. To his left, he saw the faint amber light of a ship miles offshore, crossing north to destinations unknown, and what hours earlier had seemed like an empty void started to fill with the slightest bit of possibility.

What was it that Charlie had been trying to tell him? Live. *You can be free.* Suddenly, in the cold of the Pacific, freedom truly felt possible for the first time. More thoughts of the past several months came unbidden and were dispensed with just as quickly. The giant ball of anger and frustration and professional impotence that he had been rolling up the Sisyphean hill of his mind continued to unravel until nothing remained. Free of the festering anger, free of the doubt, free of the crushing sense of mortality that had enveloped him since that night in Birmingham, causing him to miss the fortune in his recovery. All that he had viewed as a millstone actually was opportunity. For the first time in two decades, the passing of his days was not dictated by a calendar, by legislative and campaign cycles. If he so desired, he could stop viewing himself solely through the prism of his career and simply live.

All he needed to do was carry this mood with him back to shore and not let anything interfere. Easier said than done, of course. But the trail was marked out for him.

Suddenly, he leaned his head back and laughed and swam out further. With three quick strokes he was beyond the surf break and he swung his legs through the water, extended his arms and floated atop the water as he stared at Jupiter above. "There are possibilities, by Jove," he said as much to the planet above as to himself. Ryan let his legs drop, swam forward until his feet touched the silt below and half walked, half swam back to the waiting warmth of the house.

Safely inside, he went to his crumpled yoga mat and set it back in the middle of the floor where it belonged.

CHAPTER TWENTY-TWO

Ryan sat at the outdoor table of a coffee shop on the east side of Camino del Mar, insulated from the crisp morning air by a newly purchased, touristy "San Diego" sweatshirt as he sipped coffee in hopes of chasing away the lingering chill of the night before. The air was heavy with the scent of the recently passed rain, the gutters still damp with the remains of the runoff from the day before. He gazed across the street at the storefronts perched on top of the lowest level of the heights and marveled at the wide-open sky behind them, as if the buildings were merely false fronts on a movie set placed on a vast, flat plain with nothing but blue sky behind. A pair of curious blackbirds sat on the coffee shop's patio rails, staring intently at the nearly untouched blueberry muffin on a small white plate in the center of the table. Why he had ordered it was a mystery. He was supposed to be having breakfast with Maggie in an hour. Ryan broke off a small piece with his thumb and forefinger, divided it in two and tossed the crumbs toward the sidewalk, causing the birds to abandon their perch instantly to claim their prize. At least the birds would enjoy the food.

Less than a mile away, Maggie sat on the patio outside her bedroom and stared into the distance. Watching Ryan being rolled into the ambulance had frightened her; the explanation of why he was heading to the hospital had left her seething, in part for his wanton stupidity and in part because of the depth of feeling for him she'd developed. The argument had raged through her brain for most of the past day, a conflict between not caring about him if he didn't care about his own life, and wanting to be there to show him just what was in front of his eyes, what possibilities existed. She had known dark moods since Bruce's passing but even in the worst of them, the idea of taking her own life never entered her thinking. Was it weakness that caused such thoughts, or simply crushing despair? How did a person even ask that question, much less respond?

It all would be so much easier if she didn't care about him. She could walk away and wash her hands of the entire mess.

But she did care. And so she couldn't walk away.

***

Maggie was already seated on the patio at Corks and Crepes when Ryan arrived. There were other diners next to the patio gate so he walked through the main doors, past the enormous, stainless-steel griddle top where breakfasts were being made and a chef dressed in white said hello, and right to the patio itself.

"Explain yesterday to me," she said evenly almost before his body settled into the chair.

Ryan wanted to say something about the lack of a proper greeting but immediately rejected the notion. He wasn't here to piss her off even more. Just the opposite. He was here to convince her to stick around a little longer. "Where should I begin?"

"Maybe take things back to the point where you almost died a couple of times previously, and were hoping the third time was the charm."

This time, he couldn't withhold his offense. "That's not what happened."

"It sounded like it to me."

"Because you left midstream," he snapped. "Don't judge me when you've only got half the facts."

Maggie felt her own anger rising and wanted to leave, maybe throw her drink at him as she departed just because it seemed like the thing to do. But then, after the water soaked him, he would be sitting there dripping and she would be gone and that would be the end. If she wanted such an ending, there was no reason for her to have met him in the first place.

She searched within herself for a calming thought, an anchor in her frustration, took a deep breath and exhaled slowly before speaking. "Tell me the full story."

What she heard as calm, Ryan heard as patronizing, and his defensiveness escalated. "Why, Maggie? So you can judge me some more?"

"Look," she barked a moment before the server approached to take their orders, which they provided quickly before settling into an uncomfortable silence. Ryan took a breath to speak but Maggie cut him off. "If all you want is an argument, fine. Argue with your crepes. That's not why I asked Liz to invite you to breakfast."

"Then why did you, Maggie?" he asked plaintively, his anger dissolving to a low boil. "Why does it matter what happened before I came to Del Mar? What difference does it make what I've done or haven't done since I've been here, whether I've taken care of myself or ignored my doctor? You made it clear the other night where the limits lie on you and me. So why does this matter so much to you?"

She stared at him for a long moment, then shook her head. "Jesus, Ryan, you're obtuse," she said softly. "How is it you can help your clients see the lay of the land in front of them and what must be done, yet you're completely blind when it comes to yourself?"

When he didn't respond, she reached out her hand to take his. "It matters because you matter. You have since that first day on the patio. I don't know why. I have no logical explanation for it. In fact, logic says I should run away from all of this as fast as possible. But I can't. I can't run from you. Which means I need to understand.

"You have no idea how I felt hearing about what you'd been through. You hadn't said a word about any of it."

Ryan lifted the side of his mouth in a smirk. "It's not exactly the kind of thing you lead with in conversation," he said finally. "My name is Ryan, I think you're beautiful and, oh by the way, my job damn near killed me six weeks ago. Want to catch a movie?"

"Fair enough," she said.

"And let's be honest," he continued, "you haven't exactly been entirely forthcoming with me."

"Bruce." She looked down at her hands and sighed heavily. "On the one hand, I could spend hours telling you everything that attracted me to him and everything that I lost when he passed away. On the other hand, none of that really translates into what's happening now."

Ryan shook his head with frustration. "Of course it translates, just as much as everything that led me here."

She looked up and tears were forming in the corners of her eyes. "I'm not sure you understand," she said softly. "Only Liz knows the whole story. I've never told anyone else. Not family. Not other men I've met. No one." Ryan held her gaze and his features softened, but he said nothing. "It wasn't only Bruce that I lost that night. I...I was pregnant. I was six months along, and we were T-boned by someone making a turn onto Mission Beach Boulevard and not paying attention. The paramedics and doctors did all they could. They rushed me to the hospital, performed an emergency C-section." She shuddered involuntarily and squeezed his hand harder. "It was too late. That's also when they finally told me my husband hadn't survived."

"Oh, Maggie," he said, "I'm so sorry." He reached toward her but she pulled away.

"It wasn't you driving."

"I know, but..."

"But you get tired of hearing people say sorry," she snapped, then caught herself and shook her head. "I came to peace with it long ago," she continued, "at least as much as one can. But there's no point in dwelling on something that happened so long ago."

He nodded. The waitress refilled their drinks and said their crepes would be ready in a few.

"How do you move forward from something like that?"

"I didn't," she said. "Not for months. I essentially holed myself up in my apartment. I stopped doing yoga, stopped exercising entirely. But it didn't matter because I was barely eating. I emerged only when necessary and generally hoped the world would go away. Sound familiar?"

"A little."

She smiled again. "I couldn't stay in Mission Beach, not where I'd be passing the same intersection and seeing all the same sights I had seen the entire time. So I decided to come up to Del Mar and start over again."

"Just that easy."

"Not even close, Ryan. I can't tell you how many early mornings and twilights and nights I spent walking along the shore, replaying everything in my mind, wondering what might have happened if I'd left my apartment a single minute earlier or later that day. I wondered what it was I could have done wrong for the universe to repay me like that. All these circular thoughts rolling in my head like tennis shoes in a dryer, pounding the sides of my skull until I couldn't take it anymore."

"So what changed?" Ryan asked as their food arrived.

"That, you would never believe."

"Try me."

Maggie took a bite of her egg and bacon crepe and a sip of iced tea. "If you laugh, so help me..."

He sensed the mood lightening. "I'm not going to laugh," he said, testing the water with a small grin.

"Brat," she said. "Anyway, I was walking along the beach just before sunset one night, somewhere between your place and Poseidon. There was a woman there, long dark hair tied in a single ponytail, practicing yoga near the edge of the surf. All the weeks I had spent on that sand and I'd never seen her there. I watched as I walked then she looked over at me, smiled and gestured with her hand for me to join her. So I did."

"Is that what got you started on yoga at the beach?"

"It beats sweating your ass off in a 150-degree room, doesn't it?" she asked as he nodded assent. "Anyway, I followed her flow for about fifteen to twenty minutes, then she put her hands together over her heart, bowed my direction with a smile and walked up the beach."

"Did you two keep practicing yoga after that?"

"That was the weird thing, Ryan," she said. "I'd never seen her there before, and I never saw her there again. But in the moment, it seemed like she always had been in that spot, that this one particular portion of beach was meant for her."

"Are you saying you were doing yoga with a ghost?"

Maggie shook her head softly. "Not exactly," she said. "But I do think she was a message from the universe of some sort."

"Telling you what?"

"That it was okay to let go of my anger, of my regret. After she left that night, I sat and watched the waves for over an hour and as I did, I couldn't shake the thought that everything that happens is but the smallest part of the fabric of the universe. And even though I likely would never understand the reasons I lost my child in that car accident, I could come to accept that it was the way things needed to be."

Ryan nodded slowly and finished his crepe.

"Thus the yoga studio."

She nodded and wiped at the trails of tears on her cheeks. "I'd been practicing for years but after the accident, once I finally found some peace in what happened, I felt like it was my purpose to pass along that possibility of inner peace to others." She reached out her hand, and his met hers halfway across the table.

"Ryan, do you think you're the only man who has come to my studio to hit on me?"

"Of course not."

"What Scottie told you at Poseidon the night before we met," she said, pausing as he looked at her quizzically, "and I know what he tells people, was true to a degree. I'm not in the business of being pursued."

"Of course you didn't," she said. "But the thing is, I'm not much for being pursued unless, of course, I choose to be."

"He told you I saw you that night?"

"Eventually. This is a smaller town than you realize for one, for two he's a sometimes student at the studio, and third, he warns off every man who happens to see me because he's had a crush on me for years."

"But you..."

"Are not in the business of being pursued, especially in that sacred space I've created for myself and my students."

"I'm sorry," he said earnestly. "I didn't know."

"Of course you didn't," she said. "But the larger point is, I'm not in the business of being pursued unless I choose to be pursued."

"Which, apparently, you chose where I was concerned."

235

Maggie suddenly remembered the shadow emerging from the fog of her dream, the features—Ryan's features—slowly coming into focus. "Let's say I was somewhere between intrigued and interested at the time."

"And now?"

Maggie smiled and shook her head. "Now I'm sitting across from you, wondering where we go from here."

Ryan looked into Maggie's eyes and recognized the expression of interest he had seen on his patio except, without the sheen of desperation tinting his view, he was able to see it for what it was: fledgling curiosity, the merest ember hoping to blossom into flame, but equally prepared to disappear in an instant if not given what was needed. The question was whether he had either the patience or the capability to nurse that single coal to life after spending the better part of his lifetime not caring beyond his immediate needs.

Like so many things that had happened over the intervening weeks, what Ryan needed was a fresh start. So create one, he thought, breaking into a smile. "I have an idea, if you'll indulge me," he said, leaving the restaurant through the now accessible patio exit before Maggie could respond. She craned her neck to follow, but Ryan had disappeared down the sidewalk.

The server approached to refill their drinks and looked at Ryan's empty chair. "Did you need a box for his food?"

"Honestly," Maggie said, "I don't have the slightest idea." The server topped off the glasses and left with a shrug. A minute passed, then another before Ryan returned through the main entrance and approached the table, an earnest expression on his face.

"Where—"

"Excuse me, miss," Ryan said. "Would you mind if I joined you?"

"What are you doing?" she asked. Ryan looked pointedly at his chair but didn't reply. "Fine," she said resignedly. "I'll go along with your insanity. Ask me again."

"Thank you," he said, smiling. "Would it be okay if I joined you?"

"Since it seems my date has abandoned me, why not. You're even welcome to eat his crepes."

"Thank you," he said again and quickly sat down. "You were having a date, you said?"

Maggie raised her eyebrows and smirked. "More of a morning conversation."

"I see. Well, if I might say so, only a fool would walk away from someone as beautiful as you."

"Oh, I agree," she said. "He's an absolute ass. Fortunately for him, the universe is somewhat insistent that I give him some time to become less foolish."

"My name is Ryan," he said, extending his hand across the table. "Ryan Williams."

At the sound of his last name, tension flowed out of her and she flashed a genuine smile as she took his hand. "Maggie," she said. "Maggie Roberson."

He gently pulled her hand toward his and brushed his lips across her knuckles before releasing her. "It's a pleasure to meet you, Maggie. Now tell me more about this fool you were having breakfast with."

Maggie shook her head. "Let's consider that conversation over, Ryan. Do you live here in the area?"

"Actually, no," he said. "I had a meeting in town not long ago and, well, you probably don't want to hear the whole story."

"Try me," she said.

So he did, explaining in detail the months spent toiling in Alabama and the heart attack he had suffered in Birmingham. He spoke of his anger and denial, going to Laughlin and being chased down by the cardiologist he had ignored, who also happened to be one of his oldest friends. Then coming to San Diego for what was supposed to be a day trip to meet with Flannery about his nascent presidential run, only to end up back in the emergency room with what was best described as a panic attack. Ryan spoke of fighting against the overwhelming sense of being vulnerable, being flawed in a manner that could not be easily disguised. All led to a moment sitting at a bar hard against the Pacific Ocean at sunset and seeing a silhouette of a woman, a silhouette that would come unbidden to his mind at random moments. Of spending time with the woman to whom the silhouette belonged and discovering his anchor, the antidote to the constant dissolution he had felt.

Finally, Ryan told Maggie of the ocean the night before. The sense of endless space, of untold wonder, of discoveries to be made if only within his own realm, and the calmness that came from recognizing his place as one small person under the vast canopy of the stars above. And as he continued, he felt an additional weight lift, the burden of expectations, as he realized her reaction to what he was saying was infinitely less important than him forming the words.

"That's quite the story," she said finally.

"It is," he said. "But for the first time in a long while, I want to see what the next chapters hold."

Maggie got up from her chair and moved into the one next to Ryan. "What do you think might happen next?"

"Hopefully," he said softly, "I can continue to see that woman, who I've come to discover is beautiful both inside and out, and we can write some chapters together."

Maggie leaned toward him, propped an elbow on the table and rested her chin in her hand. "Do you think she'd be interested in joining your story?"

"I'm sure the universe will let me know." He reached up, cupped the side of her face in his hand and they kissed, softly, tenderly. He inhaled the light floral scent of her perfume and let his hand move to the back of her neck, which he massaged gently. The kiss lasted mere seconds but felt like hours as they pulled apart slowly, both smiling, eyes locked, reveling in the moment.

"Such a way with words. You do realize I'm still somewhat less than thrilled with you, yes?" Maggie asked less than convincingly.

"But you're still here," ,he said, "and since you are there's something I keep forgetting that I need to do."

Her eyebrows furrowed together and she tilted her head to the side questioningly. "What's that?"

"I was wondering," he said, "if you might go out on a date with me sometime?"

Maggie's face softened and she giggled. "Of course, you fool."

"There's just one problem," he said. "I don't know anything to do here outside of the beach and eating."

"Don't worry," she said. "Pick me up at the studio this afternoon and I'll think of something."

Ryan leaned back in surprise. "This afternoon?"

"Too soon?"

He shook his head. "Not at all. If anything, I'd likely say not nearly soon enough," he said, moving forward to kiss her again.

CHAPTER TWENTY-THREE

M aggie was standing outside her studio when Ryan walked up the sidewalk to meet her. Her sky-blue crocheted sundress, ridiculous for December almost anywhere else in the country, fell well off her tanned shoulders and was held in place by spaghetti straps that crossed in the back. Tanned, well-sculpted legs peeked out from the loose hemline. She had pulled her hair into a ponytail topped with a matching crocheted hat that began white at the crown and melted into shades of light blue as it approached the brim. She turned at his approach, and he unconsciously paused midstep.

"Wow," he said.

"Wow?"

"I mean," he stammered, "you look...wow."

She giggled, leaned up and kissed him on the cheek. "And to think I was telling Liz how eloquent you are."

"Stunning," he said finally. "You are absolutely stunning."

"Much better," Maggie said. "I have a gift for you, by the way." She reached into a handled paper shopping bag resting on the ground on her far side and pulled out a cream-colored straw hat circled by an olive-green band with white floral print.

"I'm not sure this matches my outfit," he said, glancing down at a bright orange polo and light khaki slacks.

"It's not about the match," she said, reaching up and placing the hat on his head. "It's about the vibe. Scientists have verified that it is absolutely impossible to feel stressed while wearing such a chapeau."

"Scientists, you say?"

Maggie planted her hands on her hips and feigned being hurt. "Do you doubt me? For your information, they were based in the Bahamas."

Ryan laughed and extended a crooked right elbow to Maggie, who threaded her arm through comfortably, and they walked together to his car parked a half-block away.

Under her direction, they left Del Mar and started down the freeway toward San Diego, chatting as they drove between hills and watched the traffic build on the other side of the highway. They continued toward downtown before exiting near the city's Balboa Park museum and recreation district.

"You're taking me to the zoo?" he asked as they drove past a billboard featuring a panda bear chewing on bamboo.

"Not exactly," she said. "Turn there."

Driving past more than a dozen museums and cultural centers southwest of the zoo, Ryan parked in a large asphalt lot near the southern edge of the park, and they walked hand-in-hand uphill along the sidewalk. They moved right and soon were in the wide concrete rounded rectangle of the Spreckels Organ Pavilion. The south side was framed by a pavilion supported by dozens of Grecian columns and in the center, beneath an ornately decorated arch and behind the protection of a massive steel door, were the brass pipes of the world's largest outdoor pipe organ. Aisles of white benches sat on the main level, with two short tiers behind to help with the acoustics. Maggie and Ryan walked slowly around the pavilion hand-in-hand before climbing the tiers and returning to the sidewalk to the north. In the distance, a 747 extended its landing gear as it approached San Diego International.

"That's where we are going," she said, pointing toward a wood-frame Oriental pagoda marking the entrance to the city's Japanese Friendship Gardens.

They walked under the peaked roof and all the noise from outside the garden seemed to fade away immediately. The handful of people that they saw all spoke in muted voices, even as they purchased their admission. Ryan glanced around and saw greenery all around, from bamboo to bonsai trees to running creeks crossed by wooden bridges leading to dirt and gravel trails.

Maggie held Ryan's hand, leading him along the outer trail and pausing now and again for a picture of one sculpture or another along with the occasional, inevitable selfie.

"You know," she said quietly, stopping near a pond filled with enormous, foot-long koi, "I spent a lot of time here after the accident."

"That must make for some tough memories," Ryan said.

She looked up and smiled. "No, no. It's not that at all. This was where I found the impetus to practice and eventually teach yoga. These gardens were exactly what I needed."

"I don't understand," he said.

She took his hand and they started walking along the path again, a pair of koi shadowing them in the water. "What do you think of when you think San Diego?"

"The beach."

"Fair enough. What about getting around town?"

"Oh," he said, "that's a different story. Too congested, too busy. Makes me long for rush hour on I-17 in Phoenix which, by the way, sucks."

"It's a city, in other words," she said, watching as Ryan nodded agreement. "Now look at where we are. Tell me how much you are aware of the traffic on the 5, or the trolley's bells ringing, or anything else going on right now."

"Not very much," he said, a grin appearing in understanding.

"Exactly," she continued. "This is the calm center in the midst of everything else happening around you."

"Just like when you start class, and you encourage your students to set everything else aside and create an atmosphere of calm around them."

She smiled and squeezed his hand. "There's hope for you yet, Ryan." She paused and looked into the distance. "It's not that I ever forgot what happened, or that it hurt any less. But walking here, I was able to at least clear my mind for a few moments and realize that the beauty of the world still existed. And in that, eventually, I came to find acceptance of what happened."

"There are times," he said, "when the things you went through make what happened to me feel unbelievably insignificant."

She turned to face him, an earnest expression on her face. "We all have our paths, Ryan. Some are steeper than others, but we each need to overcome whatever is in front of us and recognize what it took to do so in all cases."

"It doesn't make me any less sorry for what you went through."

"I know," she said, "but it all led me here."

Ahead of them was a large, rectangular pagoda-shaped pavilion surrounded by wide walkways on all sides with benches set against the walls. Ryan nodded toward the building. "I can use a breather," he said. "Let's sit over there for a few."

They walked over and sat on the nearest bench overlooking a koi pond. Parallel white stones stretched a short distance uphill into the distance, disappearing under a curved wooden bridge. A small waterfall ran under the bridge, spilling water into another, larger pond.

Ryan removed his hat, placed it next to him and wiped the sweat from his forehead with the back of his arm as Maggie looked on with concern. "Are you okay?"

"What?" he said distractedly. "Oh, yeah. I'm fine. I'm just not quite 100 percent right now, especially when it comes to walking on inclines."

"You might have wanted to mention that before we went down to the lower garden."

"I'll be fine, Maggie," he said with a tired smile. "Just give me a few."

They sat quietly as Ryan took a series of deep breaths to bring his pulse under control. He closed his eyes and mentally performed an internal systems check, comparing his fatigue now to his last several incidents and, once satisfied, nodded to himself and opened his eyes.

"May I ask you a question while we're killing time?"

"Go for it," he said.

"For all you told me today, there's still one piece missing. Exactly what is it you're looking for, Ryan?"

He half-heartedly pointed at the sky in front of them. "I was watching that plane approaching the runway."

"You know that's not what I meant."

Ryan glanced at Maggie before turning his gaze to the water in front of them. "What makes you believe I'm looking for anything and not simply going along for the ride right now?"

"Because almost everybody is searching for something," she said. "Some more obviously wear their search on their sleeve. Or in their eyes."

"Okay then," he said, turning back toward her. "What are you looking for?"

A slight smile crossed Maggie's face. "Contentment."

"Is that all?"

"Isn't that enough? Happiness comes and goes day to day, week to week. There's no constancy. But contentment, Ryan?

Find that, and happiness and love and joy and forgiveness, all of those beautiful warm emotions, are yours for the taking."

Ryan nodded and looked back at the greenery in front of him. "So that's not just the way you end your yoga classes."

"It wouldn't have the same impact if I didn't believe it."

A mother walked past them pushing a stroller, two children in tow. Maggie's eyes followed them across the patio while Ryan barely noticed. They sat quietly for several more moments before Ryan inhaled deeply and began. "If you had asked me that question even six months ago, I would have had an answer for you. These days, I'm not so certain."

"What would your answer have been then?"

He smirked and shook his head. "Probably something that now seems meaningless."

"That's still a starting point."

"It's a longer story than that," he said, and began telling Maggie about his early days with Charlie and their first campaign together. "Back then, the only idea I had in mind was to try and a make a difference in people's lives, no matter how small it might be. But then we won and the first phone call came, and another opportunity to do something on a higher level became possible."

Ryan felt his adrenaline begin to pulse, stood and walked to the railing and turned back to Maggie. "All of it was such a rush—figuring out what each candidate's best path to victory might be, the issues they absolutely had to care about and the ones that they wanted, writing the speeches and seeing your words move an audience. All of that built to the election nights. Some were over quickly, on others I'd wait all night, sleepless as the returns came through, in order to be the first to tell my candidate what happened. Then, with the legislature, there was the actual bill writing and watching ideas jotted down as bullet points on a yellow pad become law, and knowing that you had a hand in creating something meaningful."

"That doesn't sound like a bad purpose, Ryan."

"It wasn't. Not by a long shot." He paused for a moment, savoring the memories of those late nights and thinking of the best way to get back into the arena. He saw her tilt her head and noticed for the first time he was leaning forward on the balls of his feet, shoulders thrown back, practically bouncing with excitement. Everything, in short, that had contributed to his downfall. Ryan's smile faded, and with effort he took a deep breath and relaxed his posture, seeing his change in demeanor reflected on Maggie's face. His lips curled into a wan smile and he walked back to the bench, sat down and took Maggie's hand in his.

"It was a tremendous purpose, Maggie," he said. "The problem is over time you drift away from the reason you started in the first place. Soon you're no longer working with candidates because you believe in what they stand for and what they will do as much as because someone asks you to step in and help them get elected. And you do that, because that's what you do, but soon it becomes all that you are doing. You never notice the change and even if you did, you wouldn't stop because ego gets in the way and you want to be known inside those circles as the person who gets people elected. If you do that enough, soon you're no longer just working in a certain city or county or even state, you're a factor on the national scene. A king maker. You can demand any price, you can choose or not choose whom to work with, and the simple fact of your decision can help determine a candidate's credibility."

Ryan paused and shook his head sadly as he recalled the past election cycle. "The problem is all of it can go away in an instant. All of the accolades generated by your work, all of the opportunity, the seemingly impregnable air of infallibility, all of it is built on the flimsiest of foundations. Your power is less tangible than assumed and, no matter how many candidates you have succeeded in getting into office, no matter what legislation you have worked behind the scenes to get enacted, everything that you have built through your career can be obliterated faster than an ocean-front home in a hurricane."

"Alabama."

"Yeah," he said. "Alabama. Throw in the added damage that comes with not surviving election night without a trip to the hospital and emergency surgery, and suddenly you become persona non grata."

"It can't really be that cut and dried."

"Hell, Maggie—I'm one of the people who would help cull the herd when someone else had their weaknesses exposed. It's an unbelievably cutthroat business."

"Yet," she said, nodding toward the split wood railing where he had stood a moment before, "you enjoy it."

"More than that. I thrived in that environment."

"You used the past tense."

He nodded and smiled. "Because that's not where I want to be anymore. Not when I can see where it led me."

She smiled with feigned innocence. "To San Diego?"

Ryan returned the smile. "The hospital over and over. This," he said, lifting her hand to his lips for a kiss, "has been the accidental but happy byproduct of the entire fiasco."

Maggie leaned in and they kissed, each reluctant to break contact until they heard footsteps on the wooden planks of the patio. They watched another couple pause at the railing of the koi pond before continuing down the path into the garden's lower trail.

"You never did answer my question, you know," she said.

"That's because I knew what my answer was, not what my answer is." He reached out and cupped her cheek with the palm of his hand. "All I know is that right now I want to keep waking up to the sound of the ocean and spend as little time as possible in the company of doctors, nurses and needles." He glanced down at his wrist reflexively only to remember he had left his watch back at the house.

"What time is it?"

"About 4:45. Why?"

He nodded and did some quick math. "So, by my reckoning we have zero chance of getting back to Del Mar anytime soon thanks to the traffic. Can I interest you in dinner, or have you had too much of me today?"

"I suppose, Mr. Williams, I'll have to find a way to put up with you for a couple hours longer. Do you need me to choose the restaurant again?"

"Not this time," he said. "I've got just the place where we need to go."

***

They sat at a table along San Diego Harbor, the lights of the city's downtown in the background to their right and to their left, the expanse of the Pacific Ocean waiting just beyond the end of Point Loma. The sun had set, leaving a red-orange tableau and quickly falling temperatures behind. In addition to the heat lamps above, a gas-fed fire pit provided additional warmth to those stubborn souls who chose the water view over the full temperature control of the inside dining room. The low moan of one of the harbor's whale watching cruise boats carried across the chill air as it made the starboard turn around Halsley Field on its way back to the docks.

"As many times as I've seen it," Maggie said reverentially, "this never gets old."

"Liz said you've been in San Diego a while," he said, a question buried in his statement.

"All my life. At least, in and around San Diego. Imperial Beach, Mission Bay, USD, now Del Mar."

"Most people would kill to be able to say that."

She smiled softly. "Life's never perfect, but there are far worse places to be."

"So I've come to discover."

They sipped their newly arrived drinks—merlot for her, sparkling water for him—and watched another ship make its way out of the harbor toward the ocean.

"You said this was someplace we needed to go?"

"Or at least I did," he said. "This was where that meeting I came to was being held, the one that turned my three-hour cruise into a multi-week adventure."

"I see."

"Want to know the saddest part? I was sitting at a table not fifteen feet from here and never noticed the view. At least, I never took the second needed to appreciate it."

"That's a shame," she said earnestly.

"That was the state of things."

Another server arrived and dropped off a basket of bread and butter.

"Off to adventures unknown," he said to himself. "Have you ever thought about it?"

"About what?"

"Sailing off beyond the horizon and leaving it all behind."

"Not really," she said. "After the accident I would watch the lights of the ships on the horizon and wonder who they were, where they were going, whether they were running away or running toward something. But I never envied them."

"Never?"

"Honestly, no," she said, reaching across to take his hand in hers. "I feel grounded here, Ryan. Centered. Whenever I needed an escape from whatever might have been troubling me, I came down to the ocean because I knew I would feel my troubles departing with the tide. They were on their own journey, just as I am on mine."

"It's just that easy," he said doubtfully.

"Of course not," she said. "But once you've trained your mind and your emotions to truly relax when you approach the water, it works wonders. It's probably the only thing that got me through after Bruce died. That and Liz. That was the time that confirmed what I always had known."

"Which was?"

"If you're running away from one thing, you're always going to find yourself running away from everything. Better to run toward something."

He nodded, lifted her hand and brushed his lips against her knuckles. "Or not to run at all."

"If you feel the time is right to stop." Ryan saw sadness flash across her face ever so briefly, a quick flicker on her brow as her features darkened, but it was gone almost as quickly.

"What is it you're not asking me?"

She looked at him earnestly and slowly withdrew her hand from his. "We both acknowledge that there is something happening here, yes?"

"I certainly think so."

She drew a deep breath before continuing. "I'm of an age, Ryan, where I'm tiring of wasting my time on silly games. It's more effort than it's worth, feigning interest in what men are saying, wondering what they might be thinking and hoping they're smart enough to pick up on the subtle hints if I'm interested, worrying about whether they are interested back. It's exhausting, frankly."

"So is being alone," he said tentatively.

"I've had my share of company, dear," she said confidently. Blood rushed to Ryan's cheeks, and he took a quick drink of water. "Oh, let's not pretend that you've been a monk until this point in your life. This isn't the kids' table."

"Point conceded," he said, his voice muted with embarrassment.

"At this point of my life, I'm coming to realize I want something more. I need something more."

"Sounds like a fairly recent discovery," he said.

"It is. But it comes with a major question mark."

"I'm not sure I have the answer you want."

"Don't you?"

He was saved from answering by the arrival of their dinner and Maggie's tucking into the food rather than waiting for a response. But, he knew, it was little more than a temporary reprieve. There was a decision pending, whether or not he was ready—stay by the shore a little longer, or head back to Phoenix and return to the grind.

Or not.

After all that he had gone through the past several weeks, the literal pain and rhetorical suffering, the hospital trips and the stress and the betrayals of those he thought he could trust even in a world where no one was trusted longer than it took to utter a sentence, did he really want to jump back in with both feet? How long would it be before his heart and his body decided enough was enough, and there was not another reprieve waiting around the corner?

His business was in good hands even with him several hundred miles away. It would take care of itself. But was he ready to take care of himself?

Logistically, there was no reason to leave. He could extend his current month-long lease or, if need be, find another rental. Hell, he had enough money in the bank where he could buy a house tomorrow without blinking—no mean feat in a world of seven-figure listing prices. His mind drifted to the sting of the ocean on his skin the night before, the pure clarity of thought as he drifted atop the swell, staring up at the endless canopy of stars. Everything that he had deemed important suddenly seemed irrelevant in the face of the grandeur surrounding him, while his own infinitesimal place in the universe was confirmed.

Go. Stay. Work. Retire. Return to shore. Start swimming and don't stop. Nothing he chose would change the course of the universe, so why continue to make choices that led only to stress and misery?

There also was no reason to stay, other than the view from his patio...and the woman seated across the table from him right now. Yes, there was the major question mark of where he would be in the near future. But it was a small concern next to the larger question of how real the feelings he had for Maggie were, and what they potentially could grow to become.

At the edge of his consciousness he heard Maggie's voice and felt her hand covering his. He glanced down and saw his other hand holding a soup spoon, motionless in his bowl of lobster bisque, and realized he had not tasted a drop that he had eaten.

"Hey," she said, "you still with me?"

"Sorry," he said quickly. "I got a little lost in my thoughts."

"Don't apologize to me. Apologize to the chef whose bisque you're wasting." Ryan nodded distractedly as she continued. "Maybe if we ask the server, they can throw it in the microwave for you to warm it back up."

"Good idea," he mumbled.

"Seriously, Ryan," she said, "where are you right now?"

"Sorry," he said again as his eyes focused and his thoughts sharpened. He pulled up a spoonful of soup and took a quick taste. "It's still warm, actually."

Maggie tilted her head to the side, let go of his hand and leaned back into her chair. "Good to know," she said. "That was my biggest concern."

Ryan reached for a dinner roll, tore it in half and dipped it into the bisque then quickly chewed it. "If it helps at all," he said, "I was thinking about that question mark."

"The one for which you may not have the answer I want," she said. Ryan moved back as if he had been slapped, and she realized she sounded more caustic than she had intended.

"That's the one," he began cautiously, searching for the right words. "It's possible that me being at Poseidon the night I saw you on the beach, the rain the following morning chasing you onto the motel patio, my walking past that same patio in a pointless search for breakfast and seeing you there...heck, my even being in Del Mar rather than flying back home after my last dinner here—"

"And your hospital stay."

"Thank you," he said with a roll of his eyes. "Rather than flying home after my hospital stay and some other business here, I decided to stay in town for an extra day or two. Which is when I saw you. Then I decided to stay here for another few weeks."

"Which ends soon," she said.

"Which does end soon," he conceded, "but only if I want it to end. But the thing is, I'm not certain that I want it to end. Maybe all that has happened so far has been coincidence. But, just maybe, the universe is telling me this is where I am supposed to be, and it's all just that simple."

"Believing in the workings of the universe now?" she said with a small smirk.

"There's this yoga teacher who's been working to get me to believe. I'm thinking maybe I should."

***

They drove back to Del Mar in companionable silence, weaving between the hills of Scripps Ranch before breaking into open land, content to hold each other's hand and listen to Jimmy Buffett on the satellite radio of Ryan's rental car, both lost in thought after an emotionally revealing day and evening. Ryan left the freeway and turned right toward the Del Mar Heights, then onto Camino del Mar to take Maggie back to her studio when she changed the destination.

"Turn right at that street," she said quietly. He glanced her direction and simply nodded. Another turn and he was soon in front of a light-colored home, concrete steps leading to a door topped with a steep, shingle-covered gable. "This is me," she said, and he pulled to the right side of the narrow road and parked, the engine still running.

Maggie's breath shortened as her heart started to pound she tried to stifle the urge to be with him that was building inside her. "I'm fairly tempted to invite you in," she said, the slightest hint of hesitation in her voice.

"I'd be fairly tempted to accept," he said. Ryan took a long look at her expression, equal parts earnestness and nerves. "But maybe," he continued, "we've come far enough for one day. We have time."

"Do we?"

Ryan smiled and leaned closer. "I'll call to get my lease extended."

"Don't do it for my sake," she said sharply.

"I'm not," he said. "It's for me. I want to see this through." Maggie returned the smile, leaned in and kissed him, her lips lingering on his as his hand came up, gently grasped the back of her neck and pulled her closer. "I'll see you tomorrow?"

"I've got classes and then Liz and I are having a few friends over tomorrow night," she said. "I've been meaning to invite you since you came back from Arizona."

"I'm not sure I want to get in the way."

"Ryan," she said, "it's Christmas Eve. Nothing will be open. And no one should spend it alone."

Confusion clouded his features as he realized weeks had slipped by without him realizing it had happened. "Christmas Eve already?"

She looked at him and placed the flat of her palm on his cheek. "You poor dear," she said kindly, "you really have had one hell of a month." She gave him one last kiss, opened the door and walked up the steps to her house.

Yes, I have. But it's getting better.

J.P. Dalton

She gave a quick wave as she opened her front door and went inside, then Ryan started his car and went back to his empty rental on the beach.

CHAPTER TWENTY-FOUR

D rop Ryan in a room of possible donors at a fundraiser and he would mingle effortlessly. Balancing just the right amount of charm and implied if not sincere gratitude, he moved from table to table, guest to guest in a never-ending sequence of glad-handing.

But place him in a simple social setting such as this, a room filled with strangers from which he neither wanted nor needed anything, where there was no undercurrent in the conversations, where banalities were just that rather than part of the intricate dance, and he felt trapped. He poured himself a glass of eggnog from a large punch bowl in the kitchen and spent much of the rest of his time working his way around the fringes of the crowd, trying to make himself as small and invisible as possible lest he have to endure question after question about why he was there, who he knew, what he did for a living and other excruciatingly painful chatter. Small talk was best done as part of a larger dance, he thought, not a two-step of its own.

Now and then he would see Maggie across the room and raise an eyebrow and a glass. She would smile back and start moving his direction only to be pulled aside by yet another party guest. Rather than be cornered himself, Ryan kept moving first inside, then outside and eventually working his way upstairs away from everyone.

After searching all over for Ryan, Maggie went to her bedroom and found him sitting on the deck outside, looking out over the houses toward the beach, a bottled water in hand. He half turned as he heard her approach. "Pardon my presumption in entering your bedroom unannounced," he said with a small smile.

"Forgiven...this one time." She moved behind him and placed her hands lightly on his shoulders. "I'm sorry about tonight," she continued. "I didn't stop and think how overwhelming this might be."

"It's fine, Maggie. I just haven't worked a room for anything other than campaign donations or votes in a very long time. It takes a little bit to remember how to be a normal human being again."

She stepped out from behind the chair, sat on his folded legs and wrapped her arms around his neck. His skin was cold even through the fabric of her sweater, and she realized he had been outside for some time. "You're selling yourself a little short." Ryan looked back into her eyes, his hands running the length of her back, and he felt a stirring deep within. "Maybe so," he muttered before pulling her toward him for a slow, passionate kiss. The stirring grew and he found himself regretting going home the night before. This wasn't merely a man's normal reaction at the possibility of sex, but a need to feel the connection with her, the touch of her skin against his, the mingling of their breath, the warmth of her body surrounding him.

She eased away, a sly smile playing along her lips as she glanced down between them, and he realized with embarrassment that she had felt his urgency. His expression fell but she reacted almost instantly, moving her hand to his cheek and whispering "it's okay" before kissing him again, pressing her body against his as her own need grew. The sound of music and conversation from downstairs, the distant roar of the ocean, the general murmur of the night all fell away from their consciousness. Nothing mattered except for this moment, the all-consuming feeling of two souls embracing each other.

The night air was cut by the low moan of a train whistle as the Surfliner turned to the northeast near Seagrove Park off to their left, ending the moment but not their longing. She rested her forehead against his as both worked to catch their breath and cool their uncovered needs. "Wow," he said at last. Maggie laughed and shook her head without breaking the contact between them. "Not the most loquacious summary," she said with a sigh. "But entirely accurate nonetheless." As the sounds of the party returned to her mind, Maggie could hear one voice above the others and knew she had to go.

"Liz is looking for me." She pulled away and made to stand up, but Ryan pulled her back down.

"It's not that large of a house, Maggie," he said with a smirk. "She'll figure it out."

"And that alone might be the issue, unless I want to spend the rest of the evening playing twenty questions."

A mischievous light gleamed in his eyes. "What would you rather spend the evening doing?" She said nothing, but the smoldering look in her eyes provided the answer. He nodded to himself and took his hands from her waist. "Go," he said reluctantly.

"What about you?"

"I'll subtly follow in a few, then probably head home." She started to protest and he placed a finger on her lips. "I'm not sure I have the willpower needed if I see you again downstairs, and your guests didn't come for that show."

She smiled again and rose to leave the balcony before stopping by the door.

"Are you scared by all of this?"

He stood and leaned against the balcony railing. "Absolutely petrified."

"Good," she said, then disappeared into her bedroom, shutting the door behind her.

He turned back toward the ocean and dropped his head. "Wow."

Ryan waited outside for another ten minutes as promised, then quietly went downstairs and left by the back patio door, where his recent whereabouts would be less apparent. His eyes met Maggie's across the room and her face flushed, causing her to make a quick excuse and head his direction. "Thanks for inviting me," he said a touch too loudly, drawing a curious glance from Liz. "I've really enjoyed myself." Maggie stifled a giggle as Liz raised an eyebrow in their direction before turning back to her own conversation.

"That wasn't at all obvious," she said quietly.

"You're fortunate that I'm not shouting from the balcony right now," he answered, and she blushed anew. "I'll be around tomorrow if you're free."

"I'll take that under advisement." He moved to kiss her on the cheek, but she deftly maneuvered away and turned for a half hug. "Merry Christmas, Ryan." Her stomach quaked at the touch of his hand upon her shoulder, and she found herself battling her own self-control.

He responded in kind, pulled away and walked across the room. "Liz," he said with a nod. She looked at him and rolled her eyes. "Good night, Ryan," she said, unable to muster any menace in her voice as she saw Maggie watching from the corner of her eye. She edged forward to hug him and spoke in a whisper "You had best know what you are doing, for her sake."

"I think we both do." He could feel her nod against his shoulder before turning away and he glanced toward Maggie, who was staring at him with a questioning look. Ryan raised his eyebrows in a shrug, said a few more goodbyes and hurried out the door while he still felt able to do so.

***

Ryan sat on the upper deck of his rental in sweatshirt and sweatpants, sipping spiked eggnog and watching the waves roll in. Several would come ashore in sequence, then came a lull as the next set worked its way forward and, with one spectacularly large crash against the sand, the cycle would repeat. Suddenly his monotony was broken by the sound of an angel coming up from below.

"'Twas the night before Christmas and all along the beach, only two creatures were stirring before frostbite did reach." He looked down and there was Maggie staring back up at him, her overcoat apparently covering her party dress from the way her calves peeked out from below the heavy fabric.

"How long did you work on that?"

"Most of the drive over here," she said, stopping in front of the stairs leading to his patio. "Are you going to invite a girl out of the cold?"

"Of course. Door's open."

Ryan heard the door open and close and, with a final sip of his drink, stood to come inside. His breath caught in his throat as he turned toward his bedroom. Maggie's coat was in a pile on the floor and she stood in the middle of his room wearing a midnight blue negligee, black lace running down the sides, additional lace revealing the top of her breasts and framing her tan legs from mid-thigh down. Her dark hair flowed over one shoulder as she stood, hands tucked behind her back and body arched forward.

"Wow," he said.

"You've been saying that a lot," she said with a smile. She moved her hands to reveal the letter he had left behind. "Though I have to admit that this was—"

"Sufficiently loquacious?" he interrupted, walking off the deck and closing the door behind him. His fingers tingled in the heat of the room and he felt himself quicken almost immediately.

"More than sufficient," she said huskily, stepping toward his embrace. "And enough to melt Santa's workshop, I dare say."

"Are you sure about this?" he asked.

She reached out her hand and grasped him firmly, and he let out an involuntary moan from deep within his chest. "I'm not sure I've been as certain of anything."

He leaned down, placed his hands on the small of her back, pulled her against him and kissed her, tentatively at first, but the building tide of desire soon swept over both of them. She loosened his pants as he pulled off his sweatshirt, her hands running along the contours of his now exposed chest as she kissed the matted black hair atop his sternum. Ryan's hands drifted up toward her shoulder blades, then out toward her arms before moving back to run the length of her side. He followed the lace until he reached the bottom of her negligee, and she involuntarily flinched at his touch on the outside of her bare upper thighs.

"Sorry," Maggie said with an embarrassed smile. "Your hands are cold."

"Should I keep them to myself?" She moved her hands on top of his and guided them to the tops of her legs. "Don't you dare," she whispered before kissing him anew, her own fingers drifting away toward his buttocks and sliding down as his pants followed. He shook his legs free then returned his focus to her, slowly slipping the shift upward. Maggie lifted her arms and he pulled the material over her head, then slid his hands slowly down the curve of her arms, past her shoulder and then lower, slowly tracing circles around the rose-tipped nipples of her pale breasts until they hardened, then pinching them gently between a thumb and forefinger. "Ryan," she moaned and he nuzzled her neck and shoulder, allowing her anticipation to build and then finally taking her breast in his mouth. She gasped loudly and seized him by the back of the head, clutching him close, not allowing him to move away. Ryan wrapped his arms around her buttocks and lifted, laying her down gently upon the sheets, but she sat up, took hold of him and pulled him down on top of her.

"Please," she whispered and he complied, driving inside of her. She arched her back and placed her foot behind him, moving him even deeper as he let out a low moan. Their lips met again, hungry, intense, and they fell into a rhythm, their bodies moving as one despite being new to each other. Ryan's breath grew shorter as the yearning boiled within him, and he buried his head in her shoulder, desperate to make the encounter last. Maggie's journey was ahead of his, her entire being compressed more and more tightly until exploding in waves of sensation that left her body weak. As the moment came upon her she leaned up and gently bit Ryan's shoulder, and his own resistance fell away in a wild, thrusting conclusion, his head light and body losing its rigidity.

Ryan propped himself up on his elbows and kissed Maggie deeply once again, then simply stared into her eyes. Neither wished to speak lest the words interrupt this space they had created together, but the silence was comfortable. Almost frighteningly so, if he were being honest. He felt his body slackening and started to move but she wrapped her legs around his hips and held him fast, shifting her weight to reposition them. "Not so fast," she said, smiling hungrily as she ran her hands through his hair.

Deep in his chest Ryan felt a palpitation, his heart seeming to skip a beat then recover. He dropped his head and took a deep breath and the smile dissolved into concern. "Are you okay?" His heartbeat pounded hard for a pair of counts then resumed its normal rhythm; when no pain followed, his newly tense muscles relaxed. "Don't worry," he said. "I'm not going anywhere now that I found you." Ryan leaned down to kiss her lips and they rolled onto their sides, bodies still intertwined, each unwilling to let the other go.

***

Gray sunlight streamed through the vertical blinds leading to the deck, illuminating Maggie's face. She opened her eyes slowly, looking through the narrow gaps in the slats to see waves the color of slate and the lighter shades of the thermal layer, still largely untouched by the rising sun. She felt disoriented for a moment, her sleep-befuddled mind unable to reconcile how close the water was until she remembered where she was. And why. Rolling onto her other side, she started to say good morning before noticing the space next to her was empty, the corner of the bedsheet tossed casually toward the footboard. Maggie traced a finger along the empty depression in the fitted sheet and, even as she felt a pleasant soreness between her thighs, the edges of her mouth turned into a satisfied smile.

The second time they came together had been slower, more deliberate. The white-hot passion fueled by mutual need had subsided into smoldering red embers of desire. For the first time in a very long time, she recalled just how intense a connection two people could create, surpassing the mere physical, leaving them almost as one.

Her thoughts were broken by the aroma of eggs wafting from below. She looked at the floor and recalled sheepishly that she had come to Ryan's house with only the barest of clothing, and the negligee was more appropriate for seduction than breakfast. Sitting up, she saw a walk-in closet to her left and padded over to look inside. It was mostly empty, which was expected for someone on vacation, extended or otherwise. Maggie shifted a couple of polo shirts to the side and saw a T-shirt with a half-clad woman riding what looked like a shark while holding out her margarita glass in salute. Her eyes rolled reflexively but, holding it up against her bare chest, she decided it was of sufficient length to suit her purpose. She slid the shirt over her arms and torso and turned to walk out of the closet when she saw the sweatshirt Ryan had worn earlier in the week, the day he had left the restaurant in an ambulance. She shivered at the memory. Everything was so impermanent, including his time on the coast. Renewing a lease was little more than an extension before his possible departure. *'I'm not going anywhere now that I found you,"* he had said the night before. All she could do was hope it was true.

"You're thinking too much," she said to herself. She glanced in the mirror over the dresser, ran her fingers through her hair until it sat just so, and went downstairs to find Ryan standing over the stove in a T-shirt and jogging shorts, moving side-to-side to a Jimmy Buffett song playing on the wireless speakers on the counter. She stepped behind him and wrapped her arms around his waist.

"It's not Monday," she said, "but things still seem all right."

He placed his hand on hers and lifted it to his lips, brushing the top with a kiss. "That," he said, "is an understatement." He reached back to the omelet pan, asked her to take a step back and flipped the eggs with a swift circle of his wrist. Maggie moved out from behind him and leaned against the counter to face him. She searched for any sign of the spell he'd had the night before but, under the recessed lighting of his kitchen and the additional burgeoning gold of the sunrise outside, she observed facial features more relaxed than she could recall seeing before.

Ryan caught her glance and smiled, and Maggie felt her stomach jolt with excitement. Whatever was happening between them, it had uncovered a need she had long set aside. She looked back at him through slanted lashes and his own desire began to stir. He turned off the burner on the range, slid the omelet onto a waiting plate and placed the pan onto a cold burner. Stepping boldly forward, Ryan wrapped his arms around her narrow waist and lifted her onto the counter's edge, pressing his lips against hers in a lingering kiss.

"What about the eggs?"

"I also have a microwave," he said. "Unless you're overwhelmingly hungry."

"I am," she said, "but not for breakfast."

***

An hour later they lay inside a comforter Ryan had taken from a linen closet and placed on the tiled dining-area floor close to the sliding door to the patio, sharing the reheated omelet and some fresh toast. The blinds were open a mere sliver, enough to see out while ensuring no one could see over the seawall and into the house, but the door itself was open and gusts of cool salt-tinged wind blew across the blankets. He lay behind her, resting his arm casually across her waist and reaching now and again for a forkful of food.

"I love the view from my home," Maggie said between bites of eggs mixed with mushrooms and red bell peppers. "I fell in love with it the first time I stepped onto my balcony. But I have to admit, this compares rather favorably."

"For what the houses here cost, I should hope so."

Maggie leaned back and looked over her shoulder at him. "You've looked?"

"I've glanced," he said. "Curiosity overtook me."

She rotated until she was facing him, propped herself on one elbow and pulled the sheet to her shoulders. "Curiosity," she said dubiously.

His expression turned serious. "I've got a few decisions to make in the very near future, Maggie. It doesn't hurt to know what options I really have."

"Regarding us?"

"Regarding everything." He watched as her expression fell, and his tone softened. "I know what I want to do," he said, running a finger gently across her cheek. "I need to make sure I'm not overlooking anything."

"I understand," she said without conviction, and he couldn't help but smile sympathetically.

"I'm not sure you do." He moved closer, rolled her onto her back and stared longingly into her eyes. "Everything I want is here in front of me, Maggie. But to make it so, I need to tie up more than a few loose ends. Now do you understand?"

Tears formed in her eyes and leaked down her cheeks as she said yes, pulling his head down until his lips met hers and allowing herself to dream of a future she had thought beyond her reach.

CHAPTER TWENTY-FIVE

M aggie walked from her studio to the lobby to discover a single red rose lying on the keyboard of her computer. This had become a daily ritual since Christmas Day, Ryan sneaking into the building and behind the front desk when she was otherwise busy teaching. Always a single rose, most often with a handwritten invitation to dinner.

There even had been a couple of days where he tiptoed into the back of the studio itself during class, rolled out his own mat and tried his level best to keep up with her regular students. She said nothing when he did, only acknowledging his presence with the occasional glance and smiling at his reflection in the mirror at the front of the room. To do more would have felt disrespectful. Better to let him become a part of her world in the manner in which he chose than to gush unabashedly and make him feel guilty for the times he didn't come to class. *This is his journey to take.*

Besides, they would be together later that day to talk, to eat and to fall asleep in each other's arms.

This time there was no invitation waiting with the rose because plans already had been made. It was New Year's Eve.

Maggie was teaching only a pair of morning classes before turning things over to the instructor she had hired. Where once she would work into the afternoon classes depending on her mood, these days she found herself departing happily, not because she didn't enjoy sharing the practice with others but from her desire to see Ryan. The mere thought of him and the attendant reactions—the nervous flip in her stomach, the warmth that filled her chest and the inevitable smile that spread across her face—left her shaking her head in surprise. There were times she felt less like a fully grown woman than a giddy Molly Ringwald in *Sixteen Candles*, staring across the street from the church to see Jake waiting for her.

Not that everything was perfect. There were moments when she would see him glancing at an alert on his phone and shaking his head in frustration, helpless to influence the events he was seeing, and there were nights where he muttered in his sleep about what she only could guess was related to politics. But those moods would pass and he would go back to being hyper-attentive, seemingly happy to set the rest of the world aside and spend time with her, leaving her giddy yet wary. At some point, his internal struggle was going to need to be addressed if they were to have a future.

"A future," she said, again shaking her head as she thought about all that came with that word, a lifetime of love and companionship and joy that she had thought all but impossible in the years since Bruce's death. It wasn't that she had stopped believing in the concept of love, but she had come to accept the notion that she already had experienced her one great love. To expect or simply hope for another would have been selfish, if not unreasonable. Yet that possibility was before her in the handsome, surprising, confused, unexpected form of Ryan.

This, she knew, was a relationship worth pursuing, worth fighting for, and not just because her subconscious had somehow allowed the remembered image of Bruce to tell her she could love again without guilt. That's what the admittedly smaller, logical side of her brain told her had taken place that night when she dreamed of her ex-husband in the fog, just before the less rational side chalked up the vision to an unexpected communique from the universe as a whole. Regardless of the source, the answer was the same—Ryan could be the man she had sought without knowing she had been seeking him out. Hopefully, the universe was leading him to the same conclusion about her and leaving him equally lovestruck.

***

An involuntary shiver ran through Ryan's body as he sat astride a paddleboard a few dozen feet from where the San Dieguito River met the Pacific Ocean at Del Mar's Dog Beach, the bright sun warm upon his soaked hair and wetsuit.

The ocean had invaded his dreams that early morning, the hypnotic rhythm of the waves merging with the remembered feel of the water's chill upon his skin as he had floated under the stars. Cup of coffee in hand after waking and leaving the morning rose for Maggie, his attention was drawn away from the usual knot of surfers looking for the rare rideable wave and toward a lone paddleboarder standing upon her board, working her way through the curling surf to the decidedly calmer water beyond the wave break. He soon was overwhelmed by the same siren song that had lured him into the water a week earlier, and he pulled out his tablet for one of the few times since, not to monitor the latest news from the political arena but to find a surf shop.

Joining Maggie's yoga classes had given him a measure of peace. But he wanted something separate from her here, something he could call his own. The call of the water had grown stronger with every day he spent along the beach.

"You ever done this before?" asked the owner, looking Ryan up and down with a bemused smile. Ryan's lack of experience

271

was betrayed by his lack of a tan and the dubious look he had given the wetsuit when it was handed to him from a shelf behind the counter.

"Can't say that I have," Ryan said as he continued to eye the neoprene skeptically. "But basically all I have to do is stand up, right?"

"Sure," the owner said dismissively. "Word of advice. Get down the beach and practice without the waves. But make sure you've got at least three to four feet of water under you."

"Why is that?"

"So when you fall on your ass, you don't jam your tailbone into the bottom. Hurts like hell."

True to the owner's word, Ryan had spent the better part of an hour trying and failing. Just as his feet found purchase on the indented center of the board and he attempted to firm his core muscles to strengthen his stance, one leg muscle or another would twitch and he would overcorrect in an effort to maintain his balance before flipping off the board, sometimes in spectacular fashion. He finally surrendered, straddling the board instead and gently paddling his way under the causeway separating the river from the ocean and into the slowly lapping surf of Dog Beach. True to its name, the beach was well occupied by dogs and their owners, all playing in the shallows built from the river's silty discharge.

A curious retriever waded through the water to sniff Ryan's leg and was rewarded with a scratch on the head before the dog jerked his head around at the sound of a squeaky ball.

Pavlov at his finest, he thought. *Just like me and my phone.* "Except this dog can unlearn some old tricks," he muttered to himself. The sound of a bird diving into the water to snare a fish a dozen yards distant caught his attention. Another smashed into the water before emerging triumphant with a small fish in its beak. Ryan slipped off his board, tucked it under his arm and started wading through the water until he was past the last of the unusually shallow area and standing on the edge of the ocean proper.

"Maybe it's time for a new trick." He climbed back aboard the board, lying prone with the long oar tucked under the right side of his body, and dog-paddled his way deeper. A cresting wave approached and Ryan paddled harder, lifting the front edge of the board as it reached the crest of the wave and then slid down the back side. He looked over his shoulder with a wide grin and, when he cut through a second wave in similar fashion, let loose with a celebratory whoop. The dogs, the river, everything was left behind and soon he was beyond the last wave break, resting upon placid waters broken up now and again by tame ripples of water. He kept the board oriented toward open water and carefully lifted himself by his arms and knees, pulling his legs under his torso and pushing off with his arms until he was kneeling, his weight on his heels. Ryan dipped the oar into the water and gave a quick pull on each side to test his balance then lifted his right knee, planting his foot on the board in its stead. He paused again, his focus narrowed to the few feet of fiberglass beneath him and the gentle rocking of the water. He took a deep breath, pushed up with his planted right leg and extended his left and stood up straight in the middle of the board, feet slightly apart, moving the oar in the air to help keep him upright. A small wave approached and rolled under his board and Ryan reflexively tightened his abdomen and envisioned his feet grounded into the board, one solid entity, inseparable.

Using the oar, he turned the board parallel to the beach and with tentative strokes started pulling himself through the water. The world faded away until there was nothing remaining but the water, the warming sun rising in the sky and himself. He continued paddling, pushing through the tops of the small crests until a larger wave caught him unaware and shoved him forcibly into the water. Unlike his earlier falls, there was no frustration. He had stood atop the ocean for a few minutes and it had been glorious.

As he climbed back atop his board, Ryan gave thought to standing a second time and riding into the beach on the foamy carpet of a breaking wave, but instead decided not to undermine his current high. He was sitting straighter on the board, unconsciously thrusting out his chest and arching back to allow the sun to further warm the thin layer of water trapped between suit and skin, practically basking like a seal on a rock. He wanted to share the moment, to exclaim his feelings and high-five someone and bring them into this bubble of satisfaction surrounding him. He swung the board until it was diagonal to the beach, and on seeing the now-small figures timidly inching into the surf and the dogs splashing around in pursuit of thrown objects, he realized what he had accomplished mattered far more to him than them, if they even noticed him at all.

Ryan's eye was drawn to a flash of color to his right, a cherry red hull topped with two tall sails chopping through the deep blue water near the horizon. He watched the sails flutter at a small change in the wind and wondered briefly where those on board might be headed, what adventure awaited them. Were they worrying at all about work or life or anything more than the direction in which their hull was pointed? Part of him wished he could stop them to ask. Then he heard Maggie's words echoing in his head—that's not your journey. "Then what is?" he asked himself.

A distant bark carried on the air, and he turned back toward the dogs and their owners. *Both splashing around the shallow water without a care.* A small wave lifted the back of his board while he was distracted and he nearly lost his balance, recovering just before ending up back in the water. He looked around to see the sailboat's masts sliding below the curved horizon and, though there were other people in and on the water, he felt incredibly small and alone, yet comfortable. For the second time in a week he was surrounded by the ever-changing Pacific Ocean, and this time he was able to go wherever he could paddle with no urgent need to return to the shore aside from the slight discomfort of his shriveling, water-logged feet. The freedom he subconsciously had sought was here for the taking, if he could muster the courage to claim it. He heard Janis Joplin singing in his head about freedom but had to disagree because he did have things still to lose—Maggie and his own health chief among them. But the best way not to lose those, he knew, would be to give himself over to the wishes of the universe.

"Easier said than done," he said to the water below. "But worth trying."

***

Ryan, Liz and Maggie watched a band warming up on the patio at Poseidon in advance of the restaurant's New Year's Eve event. They were seated comfortably inside, the ocean little more than a dark void beyond the windows. This had been where Maggie and Liz had welcomed the New Year for the past several years and, at Maggie's insistence and with only token resistance from Liz, Ryan was added to their plans. A just-opened bottle of champagne chilled in a copper bucket filled with ice to the right of the table as each contemplated the seafood-laden menu. Each had taken a flute but Ryan also had a club soda, determined to hold to just the one drink even on this night.

He reached out to take Maggie's hand after their orders were placed, and she felt a flicker of electricity shoot up her arm. Liz, catching the movement on the edges of her vision, rolled her eyes but couldn't stop a smile from forming. Maggie unquestionably was happy, likely happier than Liz had seen her for several years. Which left Liz feeling thrilled, but also concerned given that Ryan had no roots here, neither home nor family nor job. She watched Ryan as he watched Maggie, though, and got the sense he was in no hurry to move on.

"So what are your plans for our little lady here? You going to make an honest woman out of her?" Liz blurted out at random, causing Maggie to nearly shoot champagne out of her nose as she started laughing in embarrassment.

"Jesus, Liz," she said after she recovered. Ryan simply smiled and laid a comforting hand on her forearm.

"Since you're asking, Dad," he said, "I'm thinking maybe we get past the first month together before considering that step." Maggie glanced at him and he continued. "But, if I were a betting man, I'd say the odds were in favor of such an outcome if the lady was so inclined."

"You are a betting man from what I've been told."

"Then there you have it."

Maggie stared slack-jawed at Ryan for a moment, then looked across the table at Liz. "You two are both out of your minds. You know that, right?" Liz grinned and took a long drink of champagne while Ryan raised his eyebrows but said nothing. The truth, if Maggie were willing to admit it, was she wouldn't necessarily object to such a thing. Maybe not in the near future, given how new everything still was between her and Ryan—but somewhere down the line, why not? That mere thought gave her pause, considering the notion of ever marrying again had been entirely foreign to her until the past several weeks. Clearly, until the right man came along. She watched Ryan as he and Liz talked and joked naturally, and it felt they had known each other longer than they had, just like it often felt that she had known Ryan for years and not mere weeks. There would be work to be done, she knew, obstacles to overcome and deeper conversations to be had but, at least on the surface, it appeared he could fit easily into her life and she into his.

Their entrees arrived and the band started to play on the patio, the music easily audible inside but not overwhelmingly so, and their conversation faded as they turned their attention to the music and watched the first of the night's revelers arrive on the patio. Then dinner was over and they turned to watch the band. There was no hurry for them to depart, as the kitchen itself would be closing soon aside from a stream of appetizers and bottles of wine and champagne being delivered.

"Come dance with me," Maggie said suddenly to Ryan.

"I've not had nearly enough to drink," he said with a slight shake of his head. Maggie was about to say something more, but Liz stood up and took her by the hand. "Leave him here to watch our purses," she said. "Besides, I'm your New Year's Eve dance partner, remember?" Maggie took one more look at Ryan but he waved her off. "By all means, ladies," he said. "I'll be here watching...your purses, of course."

Watch he did as Liz and Maggie walked onto the patio, and he could see them talking the entire way, presumably about him. Which was fine, assuming Liz were to give him her stamp of approval. As they moved to the music, Maggie turned to wave Ryan outside. He shook his head no once, albeit with a smile, and she exaggeratedly pointed to a table under heat lamps just on the other side of the window where he already sat. This time he nodded in understanding, signaled to the server to say they were moving and grabbed the ladies' purses before heading outside. Maggie watched him settle into the new table and she and Liz danced a little bit closer, resting their drinks on the table and continuing their conversation.

Two songs later another man walked up to Liz and Maggie and asked if he could cut in. Maggie pointed toward Ryan, who subconsciously puffed out his chest, straightened in his chair and demurred, but Liz happily took the handsome stranger by the arm and pulled him away from the table with a pointed look at her friend, who returned to the table with Ryan.

"Someone you know?" Ryan asked as Maggie sat down and took a long sip of the water Ryan had requested while his companions danced.

"Vaguely," she said. "I think he's got some sort of shop in the Heights, other side of the freeway." Ryan nodded and watched Liz and the other man dance to one song then another. "Should I be worried about this territorial instinct?"

"Not territorial," he said. "Protective."

"Don't worry. Liz is a big girl. She can handle herself. Besides, it wasn't that long ago that you approached me like that."

Ryan's features melted into a small smile. "As I recall, you were the one who spoke first."

"Only because you looked entirely lost. I was doing my duty as a good citizen of this city."

"Now it finally comes out," he said with a laugh. "All of this is about you earning a merit badge."

"That's exactly it, Ryan. I couldn't cut it selling cookies, so I went for the 'help a lost soul cross the beach' badge."

"Glad I was the first to wander past that morning, then."

"Oh, you weren't," she said. "But you were by far the most handsome helpless fool I saw."

Liz came over just long enough to pick up her drink and move to her dance partner's table, winking at Maggie as she departed.

"I guess that leaves you as my dance partner for the evening," she said.

"I don't really dance," he said.

"Don't or can't?"

"All of the above."

"What if I were prepared to make it worth your while?" she asked, lifting her eyebrows and looking at him through downcast lids.

"One song," he said, pushing his chair back with his feet to stand. "We can discuss the cost back down the beach at my place."

CHAPTER TWENTY-SIX

Ryan and Maggie lay on their backs side by side in his rental's great room. He chivalrously had lent her his yoga mat and was going through the paces atop a beach towel.

"Believe it or not," she said, "you're getting better at this. The difference is obvious."

He followed her lead, stretching his arms above his head, palms together, then tilting to the side in a half-moon pose. "I can feel it. I never knew breathing was so complicated."

"It's simplicity itself," Maggie replied. "It's only our conscious selves that make it harder than it is. Besides, if you can control your core enough to paddleboard, you can do this."

"You should join me," he said through a tight smile.

She shook her head lightly. "I've tried once before. That was enough. I'm far more grounded on real ground."

She took his hand and led him to a sitting position on the floor to complete their flow. As they sat with legs crossed, they watched beachgoers walking past the patio on their way toward the main lifeguard station.

"I'm thinking it's time," he said.

"I think so, too."

***

"Are you going in?"

That was the question on the lips of most residents in the twenty-four hours leading up to Del Mar's Penguin Plunge. Ryan had seen the poster board signs up and down Camino del Mar and Coast Boulevard, and he had heard others discussing the event the day before when he was walking the beach before and after paddleboarding, and then again at dinner. Maggie and Liz had explained the basics to Ryan, who didn't understand the hoopla given there were people in the water every single day, rain or shine.

"The silliness of it all is what makes it memorable," Maggie said as Ryan shook his head. "And silly or not, it's the place to be tomorrow."

Despite his own skepticism about the event itself, he had no trouble deciding to jump into the water with everyone else, and he was wearing a T-shirt and swim trunks in anticipation of his own return to the water.

"You weren't kidding about this," he said, turning as Maggie walked up to him.

"It's something best seen to be believed."

"Then I guess we ought to make our way down."

As they walked along the sand they could see hundreds of swimsuit-clad people swarming over Del Mar Beach in front of the 17th Street lifeguard station, Poseidon and the Del Mar Motel where Ryan had first spoken to Maggie a month earlier. Firefighters and police laid out boxes of donuts and jugs of coffee on white plastic tables near the seawall while lifeguards scurried this way and that. Several lifeguards took to their red rubber zodiac boats and cruised a hundred or so yards into the ocean to form a floating barrier for those inclined to turn the plunge into a swim to Hawaii. Women sported tiaras and boas, men with enough chest and back hair to knit a sweater proudly strutted on the sand and a pair of high school seniors jumped around to avoid shivering in their matching hamburger and hot dog speedos. Someone in a cheap Santa suit and a couple of first responders stood in the shallow water with GoPro cameras, and a camera-carrying drone circled overhead to video the plunge to later upload to Facebook and YouTube.

Ryan surveyed the scene in wonder. "I can't imagine what this would be like someplace where it's actually cold."

"That's the beauty of it, Ryan. We don't even pretend to notice the irony of walking from fifty-eight-degree sun to fifty-six-degree water. It's the ritual of it all that matters."

"The ritual?"

"It's like what you said you experienced when you went into the water that night, that you felt like you had stepped into...what was the word?"

"A mikvah."

"A mikvah. All of these people are gathering here early on the first day of the year and yes, it's silly, but at the same time, at least deep in their subconscious, they are taking to the water to wash away last year and start anew. Maybe it doesn't have the outward trappings of religion, but it still serves as a sort of spiritual experience."

"Then they get a free donut."

"You explained that to me too, once," she said. "All of Jewish history can be summed up—"

"—they tried to kill us, we survived, let's eat," he finished with a wry smile. "Remind me to be careful what I tell you if you're going to parrot everything back at me like that."

Maggie stepped close, slipped her arms around his waist and tilted her head up to look into Ryan's eyes. "Is it such a terrible thing to be listened to?"

"Actually, it's a welcome change after this past year," he said, leaning down to kiss her.

Welcome messages were read through a bullhorn from the lifeguard station along with fifteen-, ten- and five-minute warnings ahead of the plunge. Finally, at 10:59 the final countdown started. Everyone on the beach yelled the numbers counting down from ten seconds just as they had the night before waiting for the ball to drop at Times Square and, with the count ended, the mass of people on the sand shuffled and jogged into the water. Some took only a couple of steps in the surf before turning around while others plunged forward, leaning into the crashing waves before turning to high-five those around them on another successful Penguin Plunge. Ryan paused for a moment to wrap Maggie in a close hug, lifting her out of the water as he kissed her. As he gently settled her back on her feet, he heard splashing over his right shoulder and saw a small group continuing further into the water, heading for one of the zodiacs.

"Go," she said simply, shaking her head and smiling, and, with a wide smile, he half dove to his right and followed the pack. A mix of kids and adults swam out to the zodiac just long enough to slap the hand of a lifeguard and turn back.

"Do you get the point now?" Maggie said as Ryan returned to her side in the shallow surf, slapping hands and yelling "Happy New Year" at anyone he saw near him in the water.

"It's making a lot more sense," he said. "But not caring what anyone else sees or thinks is a definite change."

"You'll adapt," she said, taking his hand in hers as they walked up the sand to get their coffee, donut and a baby blue cardboard certificate commemorating their participation in the Penguin Plunge.

They strolled leisurely back toward his house but, just before stepping onto the stairs to the deck, Maggie paused.

"It hasn't happened to you yet, has it?" She asked the question as a statement, and Ryan could only look blankly at her. "Your swim. Your time on the paddleboard. Today. You haven't heard her speaking to you yet."

"Her who?"

Maggie cocked her head back toward the water. "Her," she said. "The ocean. Spend enough time around her and it is bound to happen."

Ryan's skepticism kicked in anew. "What exactly is she going to say?"

"It's different for everyone," Maggie said. "Some hear it and never know it. Others, those who most need her message, do, and it changes everything."

"I'm not sure how much more change I'm ready to handle."

"You'd be surprised. But I really think you're going to hear her talk to you someday, Ryan," she said.

His cynicism melted away in the intensity of her earnestness. "How do you know that?" he asked softly.

"Ultimately, it's why you are here. It's why you didn't go back to Phoenix when your hotel reservation ended. It's why any of us come here."

"You make this sound like heaven's waiting room."

"Not quite," she said with a laugh. "But the very nature of the water does lend itself to an altered reality."

"Altered how?"

"Ryan, if you're living here, this close to the ocean for any length of time and you can't figure out what matters in life, you never will."

***

They drove back to Maggie's house, where Liz soon arrived with packages of hot dogs and hamburgers and boxes of wines. "Does your guy know how to operate a grill?" she asked Maggie.

"Her guy certainly can figure it out," he said with a smile, then retreated out the back door to familiarize himself with Maggie's four-burner propane grill.

"You don't have to cook," Maggie said when he came back in.

"It's fine," he said, shooting a humorous look at Liz. "At least once I realized I don't need a fire starter and tufts of dead twigs."

"You didn't seem like the spatula and apron type," Liz said.

"Someday I'll tell you about the weekly cookout when I was single," he said. "A quick trip to the warehouse club for discounted, heavily seasoned pork steaks and I was set up for a week."

"Suddenly the heart thing is making more sense," she said.

"Behave, you two," Maggie said finally. Turning to Liz, she said, "I wouldn't insult the man who's going to be cooking your food, dear."

"Fine," Liz said. She lifted a box of wine from the counter, opened the spout and poured herself a full glass of merlot. "I'll take my burger medium well." Ryan bowed. It was clear Liz viewed him with a healthy dose of skepticism, assuming him guilty of breaking Maggie's heart at some future moment until proven innocent. He couldn't blame her. He still was nothing more than an out-of-towner, albeit one with increasingly less desire to go home.

Others arrived soon after, some gathering in the living room and kitchen, others drifting outside to where Ryan stood guard over the grill. His clothes were saturated with the smell of smoke and he was sweating from the heat coming off the burners but he felt comfortable, at least as long as he didn't have to talk to anyone about anything more than how they wanted their burger cooked. Then all the food was done, and he found himself in much the same position he had been in on Christmas Eve. Some of the faces were now familiar, but he had little more to say today than he did then. Soon he was skirting the edges of the different groups in the house, eventually working his way toward the stairway to Maggie's bedroom.

Soon thereafter, Maggie started looking for him and, with a glance at the staircase, she knew where he had gone. She walked into her bedroom and saw Ryan sitting on the deck outside her room, gazing at the ocean with a bottled water in hand. Out in the distance she could just make out actual dolphins leaping in the water, enjoying a plunge of their own now that the humans had cleared out. She stepped onto the deck and draped her arms lightly around his neck, resting her hands just above his chest.

"Is this going to be a thing with you, hiding in my bedroom when there are people over?"

"Technically speaking, this isn't your bedroom," he said. "There are dolphins dancing out there."

"I noticed."

"That's more interesting than small talk with people." He tilted his head back toward her. "Present company excluded, of course."

"I should hope so."

"People ask annoying questions. What do you do for a living? How long are you going to be here? How did you meet Maggie?"

"That last doesn't sound like a terrible question."

"It isn't," he said. "But the first...I've got to be honest, it's been difficult at times to separate me the political consultant from me the person. They've been one and the same for as long as I can remember."

"Is that what you would prefer going forward?" She lifted her arms and moved to the chair next to him.

"Of course not," he said. "My eyes have been opened to things that had been little more than background noise to me, all to the good. But there's part of me that can't seem to figure out what the next step is for me. Paddleboarding and yoga and the rest are fine as diversions, but they're not the same as working toward something."

"Maybe the thing you should be working toward is continuing to discover yourself." Ryan gave her a sideways glance and shook his head. "I'm being serious, Ryan. It's okay to be selfish. You have earned the right to step away from everything. But you need to make that decision."

"I have," he said. "Or at least I've tried. The Arizona Legislature kicks off its session in a few days, and I've been at the capitol opening day for, well, damn near forever."

"So go."

"I don't have a place there, Maggie. My assistant Riley has all of that under control. It's to the point that if I ask what's happening, she tells me all is fine and to go back to walking the beach."

"If she works for you, then make her give you a more complete update."

Ryan shook his head sadly. "She's keeping me in the dark for my own sake. And it's not like I can't just jump online and see the basics of what is happening. It's just not the same."

"Maybe you ought to go back, see if you can find some closure or at least satisfaction with how things stand."

"Being with you should be satisfaction enough," he said.

"If this were a movie, maybe. But that's not how real life works. You don't meet someone and suddenly your life already in progress comes to an abrupt halt. My life hasn't. I've just rearranged things to allow us the time to be together. Maybe you ought to do the same."

"My job doesn't necessarily fit as easily into reality as yours."

"Then forget that aspect of it," she said. "Think of it as taking your girlfriend home to see where you grew up."

"You don't really want to see the state capitol, do you?"

"If it's where you've spent all these years, yes, I do. You've seen the site of my past—it's all along a three-mile stretch of beach. I'd like to see yours so I can understand you even better. It's only fair."

"The first day or two of the new session is hectic."

"Then we go a couple of days after, once the dust has settled," she said. "Your streak might end, but you'll still be there. Who knows? Maybe missing the opening will prove freeing in the long run."

He stood up, stepped in front of her chair and pulled her to her feet. "You really want to come check out Phoenix with me?"

"As long as you are there, then there's nowhere else I wish to be."

CHAPTER TWENTY-SEVEN

"Welcome to my humble abode."

Maggie followed Ryan into his central Phoenix penthouse loft and whistled softly at the view of the city's lights through the near-panoramic windows. "Humble isn't exactly the word I would use. Those views, Ryan..." she said, her voice trailing off.

They had enjoyed an uneventful drive across the desert, stopping once for lunch in Yuma and a second time for an obligatory date-infused milkshake at a wide spot in the highway known as Dateland, Arizona before arriving back in Phoenix.

He glanced casually at Camelback Mountain and nodded. "They're not bad."

She looked at him, dumbstruck. "Are you playing at being aloof, or do you really not see the beauty outside?"

Ryan turned toward her, then took a more studied glance. "I do," he said, "or I did once. You don't buy the penthouse without being aware of what's outside."

"Unless you're entirely pretentious and it's all about flaunting the money you apparently have and impressing whoever comes up here." She paused, then added with a wry smile, "Whatever gender they may happen to be."

He turned back to her and placed his hands on her hips. "I am wounded, m'lady," he said. "Are you impugning my honor and suggesting I would use the expanse of twinkling lights below as some sort of lure in an effort to woo women?"

"Women," she said. "Men from whom you are seeking some sort of political...what is the word you use...chit?"

He leaned in and kissed her on the forehead. "I think I should be concerned about how well you see through me."

"Sussing this out was not exactly solving the riddle of the Sphinx, Ryan. But you still didn't answer the question."

"Of course I am aware of the view," he said, "and when time allows I even enjoy it myself with a drink on the balcony. Back before Charlie told me I wasn't supposed to drink, that is."

"But..."

"But mine is not a career where there's a great deal of time for abstract reflection while staring at the moon. Besides, after thirty-odd years, the mountains lose their luster in a way the ocean never could."

She reached up and tapped him gently on the side of his head with her index finger. "It's all up here, Ryan. It's not a matter of what is around you. It's a matter of where you are up here while you are where you are."

"Such deep thoughts after such a long drive." Ryan kissed her softly and took her hand. "Let's see what the view is like from the balcony," he said, taking a step toward the arcadia door. Maggie didn't budge. "Later," she said with a coy smile and a nod toward the bedroom. "Let's give the moon some time to rise fully."

***

In the morning, they walked across the street from Ryan's building for breakfast. It was an unseasonably cold morning and their breath was visible in white puffs as they moved quickly to the front door of the restaurant.

"I thought this was the desert," Maggie said, blowing into her hands as they waited to be seated.

"San Diego hasn't exactly been a tropical paradise this year either."

Moments later they were in a coffee cup-shaped booth, warming their hands around a steaming cup of coffee before placing their orders. Ryan fell silent after the server walked away, staring thoughtfully into his cup as his left leg bounced energetically beneath the table.

"Ryan," Maggie started and, when he didn't react, she reached across the table and placed her hand on his. "Hey," she said, "where are you?"

He looked up and smiled sheepishly. "Let's just say I have a lot on my mind right now."

"About your last time at the capitol?"

"Among other things," he said with a nod. "Part of me wants to be back in the middle of the action. Part of me likes the idea of being able to walk in and walk back out without having to worry about anything more than parking."

She nodded as she studied his features. "But that's not all," she said after a moment.

"That's not all," he admitted. "I tried to renew my lease, but the owner already has the place rented back out."

"I see," she said, unable to mask her disappointment.

"I mean, it's not the end of the world," Ryan said. "It's more inconvenient than anything else."

"So you're still going to stay?"

Ryan tilted his head questioningly at the earnestness of the question before smiling. "Of course I'm going to stay, Maggie. Why would you even question such a thing?"

"It's silly," she said quietly.

"Try me."

She took a deep breath and began. "The whole reason we are here is because this is an unfinished chapter. I wasn't entirely sure whether coming back would cause you to want to turn the page, or go back to the world you know best."

Ryan paused as their breakfast was delivered and cups refilled. "I'm not going to deny that my ego wants me back here," he said. "But the rest of me wants to be where you are. I just need to find a place to stay. I'm sure something will turn up."

"I'm sure something will," she said before taking a bite of omelet and chewing thoughtfully.

***

They drove down 24th Street to Washington Street and turned west toward the state capitol. Soon they passed lower downtown and the copper of the capitol dome appeared in the distance. Washington ended at the edge of Wesley Bolin Plaza, named after the state's fifteenth governor, who had died in office of a heart attack in 1978. Dozens of monuments dotted the park and on the far eastern edge sat the eight-ton anchor salvaged from the USS Arizona, one of eight ships damaged or sunk at Pearl Harbor in 1941. Ryan drove around the park then looped back into the plaza's visitor parking. All his years downtown and he still parked in the park like everyone else. The better to keep himself humble, he supposed.

Maggie started walking north toward a memorial for veterans of the Battle of the Bulge. "How many monuments are here, Ryan?"

"To be honest," he said, "I've never taken the time to look."

She stopped and looked over her shoulder. "You must be kidding."

"I've always had somewhere else I've needed to be."

"And today?"

Ryan smiled and took her by the hand. "Today, Maggie, seems like a great day for a stroll."

They walked leisurely through the park, winding through monuments ranging from those for Arizona Pioneer Women to 9/11, the Vietnam War to the World War II Navajo Code Talkers. Sprinkled at different points were other pieces salvaged from Pearl Harbor—the signal mast and a fourteen-inch gun from the Arizona and a sixteen-inch gun from the neighboring USS Missouri.

"How is it possible I never looked at these?" Ryan said softly as they stood in front of a memorial to nineteen firefighters who lost their lives fighting a wildfire in Yarnell, Arizona, about ninety minutes northwest of Phoenix.

"Sometimes it seems you weren't doing a great deal of living while you were living," Maggie said.

"Apparently not." Ryan looked down as his phone vibrated in his pocket. He withdrew it from his khakis and glanced at the message on the screen. "Looks like it's time to head over."

"Are you ready for this?"

"Of course I am," he said. "It's home."

They turned toward the west and walked to the Old Capitol, topped with its copper dome and statue of Winged Victory carved from zinc, holding an upraised torch in her right hand and a laurel wreath in her left. On either side of the wide capitol plaza were the Arizona Legislature's two chambers. Ryan and Maggie turned to the right and walked through the metal detectors at the entrance to the Arizona House of Representatives. Ryan reflexively laughed after getting a secondary metal check with a handheld wand before they walked to the elevator to meet Dom Stephens in his third-floor office.

"What's so funny?" Maggie asked as the elevator doors closed.

"Only in Arizona," he said. "Visitors are put through the wringer for security's sake, and rightly so, but the legislators themselves can keep guns on the floor of the chamber."

"You aren't serious."

"Oh, but I am. A few years back, a House member was expelled because of a long line of accusations of sexual harassment. First thing the Capitol Police had to do was relieve him of the pistol he kept inside of his desk."

"Why in the world would someone need to have a gun in their desk?"

"Like I said, Maggie. Welcome to Arizona."

***

Stephens was waiting for them when they stepped off the elevator and directed them through the double doors, past the entrance to the balcony on the right and into his office on the west side of the third floor. Nearby palm trees and distant mountains were visible through the windows lining the right-hand wall of the minority leader's office. Stephens settled into one of the leather chairs in the front section of his office and gestured for Ryan and Maggie to join him.

"So this is the young lady you were telling me about, eh?"

"Yes, Dom, this is the one."

"Hmmmm." Dom leaned back as if to examine Maggie, cupping his chin and resting a thoughtful finger across his lower lip. "She seems far too normal for someone like you."

"Appearances can deceive," she said with a knowing grin.

Dom nodded and laughed heartily. "So can old politicians. Or at least we try." Looking back at Ryan, he added, "You just might have met your match in her, Willy."

"I certainly think I have," Ryan said.

"Whatever you do, Ms. Roberson, don't let Willy try and fool you. He's one of the good ones. Still adrift politically and hanging around with the wrong side of the aisle, but a good one nevertheless."

"Dom here has been trying to convert me for as long as I've known him," Ryan said. "But—"

"But," Dom interrupted, "he tends to find those of us languishing in the loyal opposition some decent partners sitting closer to the front of the room."

"And," Ryan said in well-rehearsed rhythm, "at the end of the day it's more about the work that gets done than who does it."

"See what I mean?" Dom said. "An idealist trapped in the guise of a common consultant."

"To think I never realized there were idealists in politics, only idealogues."

"I have been wounded," Dom exclaimed, his deep voice booming. "Or would be, if she weren't correct about so many of my colleagues."

"As much fun as this has been, Maggie here is a bit of an innocent," Ryan said, then, seeing her cutting glance, hastily added, "at least about this realm. I just wanted to give her the penny tour."

"If Maggie might interject," she said, "this entire conversation has been more enlightening than you might know." She extended her hand toward the minority leader and mockingly brushed her lips across his knuckles, earning another rumbling laugh. "Dom, I thank you for the insight into Willy here," she said, watching Ryan flinch at her use of a nickname no one but Stephens ever dared used. "I'll definitely keep my eyes peeled but for the moment I agree with you. He is a good guy, even if he doesn't always seem to realize it."

Dom looked first at Maggie and then back at Ryan. "You definitely have met your match, son. Come on," he said, turning toward the back, members-only stairwell leading to the second floor and the House chamber. "Let's get you in there while we're in recess."

The trio walked down the stairs, past the House Speaker's office on the immediate left and stopped in front of the chamber's heavy wood door. Dom paused with his hand on the handle. "I feel like Willy Wonka," he said with a grin.

"Are the theatrics entirely necessary?"

"Not at all, Willy. But they sure are fun." Dom opened the door, and they stepped onto the turquoise carpet of the House chamber. Most of the overhead lights were off, signaling the House stood in recess while most of its members sat below in the morning's slate of committee meetings.

"I assume," Ryan said, "the Speaker is aware that I'm here."

"Is there anything that happens around here that she doesn't know about? She has indicated you are to enjoy the privileges of the floor, as long as you don't break anything. Hell, she even told me to buy you two an ice cream sandwich in the cloakroom."

"I'll repay you the two dollars," Ryan said.

"Keep it, Willy. Your young lady here deserves the full show." Dom turned toward the door to return to his office. "Lock up when you leave. And don't worry about stopping back upstairs when you're done. I've got some actual work to do." He looked toward Maggie and nodded. "Ms. Roberson, it was a pleasure. Try and keep our boy upright, will you?"

"I'll do my level best, Representative Stephens."

"It's Dom to my friends," he said with a wink before slipping out the door to the corridor beyond.

***

Ryan took Maggie's hand and they stepped further into the chamber, pausing at the Arizona state seal embedded in the carpeting at the nexus of the center aisle and the area in front of the speaker's podium and turning toward the back of the chamber and the gallery above.

"There," he said, "is where I have spent years of my life, at least if you add all the time together."

"Close to the action yet so far away," she said.

"Only if you believe all of the action takes place here." Ryan turned 180 degrees to face the podium and the Speaker's offices. "Most of it takes place through that door to the left, or in the majority leader's office beyond that or, if the issue is insignificant enough, inside the caucus room out that door and down the hall."

"And yet, this is the place you opted to show me," she said, "so there must be some significance to what happens here."

Ryan tilted his head, then turned and sat down at the majority leader's desk in the front row next to the center aisle and motioned for Maggie to pull up a chair next to him. "Everything in this world is about power. Who has it. Who wants it. Who knows how to wield it and who's simply happy to be close to the action, even if they have next to nothing to do with the game."

"Then this is where all that power is on display—the place where the public comes to be awed by the spectacle of it all."

"Yes," he said, "and no. Rarely do issues come to the floor where the outcome is in doubt. All of those decisions take place off the floor in the real centers of power, where only members—at least some members—and a very rare few outsiders are permitted to go."

"Let me guess," Maggie said. "You are one of those rare few."

"I've earned some privileges, you can say," Ryan conceded. "I can walk from desk to desk in this room and tell you who my firm has helped get elected, who sat in those seats in the past, who came here for the pin that said they were a member of the House and had no further aspirations and those, like Flannery, who felt constrained by the smallness of serving in a state legislature. But it's more than just that. It's the rush of access."

"Explain."

"Have you ever gone to Las Vegas?"

"Of course."

"Then you've seen it in action," he said. "Everywhere you go, there's a line for the high rollers, for the frequent flyers and then for all the rest of the folks. Whether it's in line for the buffet or for show tickets or even just checking in, everything in that city is built around the concept of access. Either you have it or you don't."

"And you do."

"Of course I do, Maggie," Ryan said with a chuckle. "It comes with spending a lot of time at a lot of tables losing a lot of money, and still going back over and over again simply because I have the access every other piker there craves."

"I wasn't aware I was a mere...piker, was it?"

"You don't qualify," he said, earning an arched eyebrow. "You are one of the few people I've ever met who couldn't give two shits for that kind of thing."

"Nice recovery," she conceded. "Fortunately, you are correct."

Maggie stood and walked slowly down the arcing aisles, tracing fingers along the desks decorated with elephants and donkeys, depending on which side of the political divide the occupant fell. Ryan turned in his chair and watched her as she looked toward the gallery, then back at the desks and then the podium.

"What are you thinking?"

She looked at him and smiled wanly before walking back to where he sat and leaning against the desk.

"Maybe I see this all differently because this is not my realm," she said, "but I can't help but see the illusion and not the reality intended to be projected."

"How so?"

"I think if this is your reality, if this is where you live and breathe and work, it's easy to see the trappings as more than they really are. But, honestly, where does this supposed power come from? To what effect is it used? What impact does it really have? How can anything this ephemeral have any true meaning?"

"Decisions are made here every day that impact the people who live in this state," he said. "Look at the congressional level, where the lives of everyone in the country are in play, and that impact is orders of magnitude larger."

"It is," she said, "except it isn't. Yes, what happens here and in the back rooms does affect the general public but, if they only rarely acknowledge that fact and for the most part go through their days happily oblivious to those decisions, much less the inner workings of the system, does the power displayed here really exist?"

"If a tree falls in the forest," Ryan said.

"To some degree, yes," she said. Maggie looked closely at Ryan and saw conflicting emotions, his surprise battling against acceptance. "Ryan, I'm not diminishing who you are or what you do. I have total belief in your sincerity and your desire to help people's lives in the long run, and the exponential impact you can have helping many others get elected rather than only yourself. But what I see—from the other lobbyists hanging out in the lobby hoping for a moment of a member's attention, to the forced confidence with which everyone here carries themselves, to the peacocking of those members themselves— leads me to conclude that this is a self-contained bubble. Inside the bubble, this is the most important thing in the world. But outside, it's just not that important. Certainly not important enough to kill oneself in service to the bubble."

"That's essentially the reality for any business, isn't it?"

"I wouldn't know," she said. "I've never been in that type of business."

Ryan nodded slowly and looked around the room, trying to see things as Maggie did. Trying to see how someone could look at all the trappings and not the visions of power that came with them. This room, these buildings, had been the center of his existence since the first time he'd walked in the front doors. And yet he had seen for himself that there was a wider world than the one in which he had been living, and the one in which he had been working was becoming increasingly polarized, with the fringes overwhelming the middle in which he had tried to remain. In truth, Comstock's stars and bars-laden campaign was the logical extension of much of the insanity he had seen inside the Arizona Legislature and chosen to dismiss as the ill-informed policy of one or two doctrinaires.

How had he gone from scoffing at that kind of insular, paranoid lunacy to openly trying to help those ideas land in Washington? That was actually an easy question to answer—ego, the desire to move up the proverbial food chain. He had been exposed in Alabama for pursing power for power's sake in backing a hopelessly clueless, tactless candidate in hopes of moving steadily to the next step on the food chain. He knew he had forfeited his right to be sanctimonious the first time he shook hands with Rounds and Comstock.

Maggie watched the emotions swirl on Ryan's face as he worked through his recent decisions. "I've hurt you," she said matter-of-factly.

Before Ryan could answer, the door to the right of the dais opened and Ignacio Cruz Pérez, the Speaker of the Arizona House of Representatives, strode into the room.

CHAPTER TWENTY-EIGHT

"Mr. Speaker," Ryan said, extending his hand as Pérez approached with a grim expression on his face.

"I don't seem to recall granting you the privileges of the floor, Mr. Williams."

Maggie glanced up at Ryan and then at the doors, half expecting to see the Capitol Police storming the room. "Well, Nacho, you know I've never been one for the rules." Pérez stared at Ryan for an extra moment, then broke into a wide grin as he took firm hold of Ryan's hand with his own, then cuffed Ryan's shoulder with his free hand. "How did you know I was here?"

"Ryan, do you really think anything happens in my building without me knowing it?"

"Dom told you."

Pérez nodded. "Of course he did." The speaker turned toward Maggie. "He said a lowly lobbyist of mutual acquaintance had brought a lovely woman to see our humble chamber. One, I might add, who appears to be several levels above the lobbyist's lowly station." Pérez reached out with his right hand and introduced himself properly to Maggie, whose look of concern was just beginning to fade.

"No offense, Mr. Pérez—" she started, but Pérez quickly interrupted.

"Call me Nacho," he said. "Everyone else does."

"Okay then, Nacho," she said. "No offense, but I'm starting to think every one of you is a touch insane."

Pérez looked at Ryan and shook his head. "Did you not warn her what happens when you've spent too many years here?"

"It would be almost impossible to explain, my friend."

"Excellent point," Pérez said. "I suppose this also means that our Mr. Williams here didn't explain his role in helping me arrive here, did he?"

"He may have hinted that he had a hand in several careers here," she said easily if not entirely honestly.

"One or two, yes," Nacho said. "Now, Maggie, allow me to give you the tour not even Ryan here can provide." He swept a hand toward the open door leading back into his private office, and Ryan took hold of Maggie's hand and led the way. They walked into the Speaker's private office, a large walnut-paneled room separate from the foyer and administrative assistant's areas that completed the three-room suite. Pérez settled into a leather chair behind his heavy oak desk and gestured for Ryan and Maggie to take the seats across from him.

"So how do you like our home away from home, Maggie?" Pérez asked. The corner of Ryan's mouth tugged upward into a smirk, and he wondered whether she would tell her host what she really thought or what he wanted to hear.

She opted for diplomacy. "It's impressive," she said. "It's amazing to think of all that happens here that impacts citizens across the state, and yet I imagine few have ever seen the interior."

"Most people aren't that concerned with most of what we do," Pérez said. "Right or wrong, unless it's a case of NIMBY most of our constituents go on with their lives and trust that we know what we're doing."

"NIMBY?"

"Not In My Back Yard," Ryan explained. "What Nacho isn't saying is that there's an array of people here, some elected, some not, who try and keep an eye on what's happening in everyone's backyard."

"But," Pérez continued, "ultimately only a small percentage of views ever are heard. Such is the nature of the beast."

"Democracy at work," she said, her voice dripping with sarcasm.

"Representative government to be more precise," he said. "In any event, we do what we can. As does Mr. Williams here. Speaking of which, it looks like the time at the beach has done well by you."

"There certainly are worse places to spend a month," Ryan said. He sensed Maggie looking at him and quickly added, "Not to mention, they have the most beautiful welcoming committee I've ever seen." He looked in her direction in time to see Maggie roll her eyes, albeit with a smile.

"The bigger question is when you're coming back to work," Pérez said. Ryan saw Maggie's smile disappear.

"That," Ryan said, "has yet to be determined. A large part of me is inclined to take my various issues as a signal from the universe that it's time to enjoy life."

"If you could pull that off, I'd be the happiest person for you, Ryan," Pérez said with a knowing look.

"But..."

"No but," Nacho said. "If you can get all of this out of your blood, good for you. I'll be envious."

"Sure you will," Ryan said warily, sensing the trap within the Speaker's words. There was no doubt in Ryan's mind that this trip into the inner sanctum wasn't as much for Maggie as for him, Pérez's attempt to see if Ryan would feel the adrenaline start flowing simply from his proximity to the heart of the action. And in spite of himself he started thinking of the work still left to be done, not that there ever was a time when there wasn't work waiting. *Riley can handle it*, he thought. *But you still need it.* He wanted to ask Pérez more about the major bills that had been introduced, provide his input based on his experience. Being involved in the process was ingrained in his blood. Yet he was apart from it all, connected to this world only by Riley's daily two-sentence updates—"All is well. Enjoy the beach"— and the websites he had tried his best not to keep up with.

It would be so easy to jump back in with both feet, health be damned. But sitting next to him was the perfect reason not to risk it all again. Someone who knew him outside the career he had built and cared for him deeply anyway, someone who didn't view the cut of one's suit or the strength of one's handshake or the ability to maneuver unscathed through the shark-infested waters of politics as the definition of a person. He loved her. He knew it as certainly as he knew his own name. But the siren's song of the political world was calling. Part of him wanted to return. The rest loathed himself for giving the notion any thought.

Maggie watched him closely and could see Ryan's mind churning from the strained look on his face. As much as she could wish it away, she knew that walking away from this life would be difficult no matter his feelings for her. It was a fact she couldn't change, so she decided she had best learn to accept it. But acceptance didn't mean she couldn't fight. She reached across for Ryan's hand, pulling him out of his thoughts. "There's no need to be jealous, Nacho. You're welcome to come visit us on the coast whenever you like."

Pérez leaned back in his chair and looked at her appraisingly. "I just might take you up on that."

The trio chatted for another fifteen minutes until Pérez's assistant knocked on the door and reminded him of a meeting that Ryan was certain didn't actually exist. Which actually was fine. The pull to come back to work was stronger than he had anticipated. They all shook hands and Maggie repeated her invitation, as much to establish her territory as anything else, and Pérez thanked her.

Five minutes after they left, Pérez picked up his phone and made a call. "It's Nacho," he said when the call connected. "He may not know it yet, but he's back."

***

Maggie and Ryan sat low in Harrah's outdoor spa. Steam swirled in dense clouds as it rose off the bubbling water into the cold night sky. Ryan draped his arm across Maggie's shoulder and felt her tense unexpectedly. She had been quiet on the drive down and while they changed as well, but he hadn't thought much of it until now.

"Tell me what I've done wrong," he said. Her eyes darted toward him, and she opened her mouth to speak but closed it as quickly. He made a second attempt to engage. "I thought you would be happy about this."

"Is that why you did it, to make me happy?"

"Of course not," he said, withdrawing his arm and pushing off the wall to the center of the spa where he could face her. "It was what I needed to do for myself. That it was the right thing for us was a bonus."

"A bonus you didn't feel the need to discuss."

Ryan inched forward. "It's obvious I'm missing something here."

"How do men always miss the most basic things?"

"Probably because we are so blinded by the beauty of the women in front of us."

She shook her head but smiled nevertheless. "Flattery isn't always the answer," she said, the edges of her lips dropping as quickly as they rose.

"What is?"

"Communication, Ryan." Maggie sighed in exasperation and leaned forward. "How was it Riley knew your decision before I did? You can't tell me you decided on the spur of the moment."

"No," he conceded. "And yes. I don't think it was a secret that I'd been trying to decide what to do. Something about our conversation on the House floor today made up my mind for me. Then Pérez changed my mind. Then I changed it back."

"But you still said nothing."

Ryan took another step forward and placed his hands on the outside of her knees. He waited for her to tense again, to flinch, to pull away, but she didn't. "I wasn't sure I actually could say the words," he said. "Hell, Maggie, I wasn't certain I could tell Riley without changing my mind again halfway through. But the opportunity came."

"When I was stepping away."

"Entirely coincidental." Maggie raised a dubious eyebrow in challenge. "Okay. Somewhat coincidental. I didn't want you sitting there thinking I was making that decision solely for you. And why are we even debating this? You seemed happy with the decision. Unless that reaction wasn't genuine."

"Of course it was," she said. "But that's not the point."

"But it should be." Ryan lifted her off the plastered bench of the spa, spun around and sat down himself before settling her astride his lap, a move to which she offered no resistance. "I screwed up when I didn't tell you what I was thinking. I admit that, even if I wasn't sure what I was thinking myself. But look at the big picture here. I'm coming back to the coast with you. Granted, I'll be homeless in a week or so, but we are going to be together. Shouldn't that be what counts, Ms. Live in the Moment?"

Maggie started to respond but stopped. She knew Ryan was right. He also was wrong. The question was whether to continue making an issue of the latter. Unbidden, memories of calling her mother came to mind, specifically how her mother would spend the first two minutes of every phone call complaining that nobody ever called her which, naturally, left Maggie less inclined to pick up the phone to call instead of texting. So yes, she could continue this argument to an uncertain conclusion, or hope her point already had been made.

They returned to their room and she stepped into the bedroom to remove her swimsuit. Ryan moved behind her, lifted the straps off her shoulders from behind and slowly peeled her swimsuit off as he kissed the length of her spine. When he stood, she turned to face him and loosened the drawstring on his trunks then pushed them down until he was able to kick them off. He lifted her onto the countertop as he kissed her hungrily and started to move toward her when she flexed her thighs around his, locking him in a vise grip and stopping him an inch from entering her warmth. He looked at her, confusion and desire mixing on his face, and she took a deep breath.

"Next time," she said, "we decide these things together. You're either my partner or you're not. Understand?"

"Yes," he panted quickly, trying to return to what he had been doing, but she squeezed harder and he gasped at a sudden burst of pain. "Do you understand me?"

"I do, Maggie."

"Now, Ryan," she said seductively, loosening her hold, "do you want to be my partner?"

"More than words can say," he answered, finally driving deeply inside of her.

***

A few hours later, Maggie and Ryan sat a table overlooking the outdoor patio at Rustler's Rooste, a steakhouse sitting halfway up the eastern end of South Mountain, a series of mountains that formed the southern edge of the basin containing the so-called Valley of the Sun. They had returned to his penthouse long enough to grab their few bags then drove to Harrah's Ak-Chin Casino in Maricopa, twenty-plus miles south of Phoenix on the Ak-Chin Indian Reservation, where Ryan had booked a suite for the night atop the fifteen-story hotel tower. They showered and changed before Ryan called Riley and invited her and Nicholas to join him and Maggie for dinner.

Maggie found herself staring in wonder at the expansive view from the restaurant windows, encompassing the majority of the southern and central valley with Camelback Mountain prominent in the center of everything and Piestewa Peak rising further to the north and west. She already had engaged in a unique tradition at the restaurant, gliding down the polished steel slide that led from the entry level down to the main dining area. They then walked another few steps down to the level of the windows, as the restaurant's layout followed the contours of the mountain.

Their conversation since leaving the capitol had been stilted, with barely enough substance to count even as superficial. Maggie kept waiting for Ryan to say what she already knew. As much as he claimed that he was ready to walk away from politics, and as many steps as he had taken to try and distance himself from that world and commit to the nascent life they were creating in San Diego, the decision was nowhere near that easy. She could see it in the wistful way he had looked around the chamber, the sudden, subtle spring in his step when he was talking to Stevens and Pérez. There were moments when he clearly wanted to follow a line of thought through to an action plan, but he held himself back from actively engaging. The excitement and the following disappointment were clearly written on his face, and if she, who had known him only for a month, could see it then there was no question the two men she had met could see it as well.

There was going to come a time when he was given a choice to return or remain on the sidelines and, as much as she wanted it to be otherwise, she wasn't sure what his decision would be. She better than anyone knew life didn't deliver certainty, but that knowledge didn't stop her from wishing.

"You miss it," she said finally.

Ryan wanted to deny it but knew it would be a lie. "Of course. I've spent my life there."

"You want to return," she replied.

"Yes," he said, "and no. Yes because I know what I feel when I'm working, or at least what I felt until the last campaign. No because I'm not sure I'm prepared for what it might cost me."

"Your health?"

Ryan smiled sadly and shook his head. "You."

"That's not fair, placing the responsibility on my shoulders like that."

"I'm not, not really. I just know I'm stupid enough to keep charging into that arena, heart and health be damned, because I've never known how to do anything else. When I'm with you, though, I see options. The question is whether I have the strength to continue pursuing them."

"I hope you do," Maggie said. "Not for me, but for you."

Before he could reply, Riley and Nicholas stepped down the stairs and walked toward their table. Ryan shook Nicholas's hand and wrapped Riley in a heartfelt hug, then introduced Maggie to both.

"So you're the one who has turned Ryan into a human," Riley said as they sat down.

"Was he not human before?" Maggie asked.

"He was," Riley said, "but he wouldn't admit to it without grimacing."

"Riley," Ryan said to Maggie, "has styled herself as an expert on me."

"Because if I didn't understand why you're the way you are, there's no way I could have worked for you for more than five minutes." She turned toward Maggie and continued. "He always maintains this gruff, unemotional exterior. But beneath it all he actually does give a damn. Sometimes even more of a damn than the situation deserves."

"I know he does," Maggie said. "Though I haven't really seen that unemotional shell."

"Really?" Riley said. She turned back toward Ryan and studied his features, his posture, all the little aspects of him that she alone knew only from having worked so closely to him for so long. Riley cared for him, loved him even, at least as a father figure and friend, and what she saw on his face caused her eyes to widen in wonder. "I'll be damned," she said quietly. Ryan cocked his head to the side and looked at his protege. "You're happy." A corner of Ryan's mouth rose in a half smirk.

"Is that so unusual?" Maggie said.

"Actually, yes." Riley stood, walked around the table and wrapped her arms around Maggie. "Keep him this way," she whispered in Maggie's ear. "He needs it."

"I'll try."

Riley straightened up and Maggie stared in wonder as the other woman returned to her seat, unsure of what just took place. Riley's words felt like a parental blessing to date their first-born child.

***

The couples swapped stories during dinner, Ryan talking of his adventures in yoga and paddleboarding, Riley and Nicholas speaking of their ongoing wedding plans, all studiously avoiding the topic of politics. Maggie watched Ryan and saw a different mood than she had in Pérez's office, one she had become accustomed to the past couple of weeks as Ryan melted into the moment without attempting to drive toward any particular goal. She relaxed a little more. Hopefully, whatever spell Ryan had fallen under at the legislature was fading again.

After their plates were cleared and the server had brought them the Rooste's famous cotton candy for dessert, Maggie gently wiped her mouth and placed her napkin next to her plate, stood and excused herself to go to the restroom. Riley, following the age-old protocol only other women seemed to understand, removed her napkin from her lap and made to stand too, but Ryan stopped her with a slight lift of his hand. "Nicholas," he said. "Why don't you escort Maggie to the restrooms and then show her Horney." Riley stared at Ryan for a moment, then looked up at her suddenly slack-jawed fiancé.

"Horney?" Nicholas parroted back questioningly.

"Yeah, Horney. The bull out front."

"That's really not at all necessary," Maggie interrupted.

"It's fine," Ryan said. "Nicholas likes animals. Don't you?"

"I suppose I do," he mumbled in confusion.

Ryan took Maggie's hand and, faced with unexpected resistance, leaned forward to kiss her across her knuckles. "Trust me, Maggie." She pulled her hand away and pointedly looped her arm around Nicholas's as the two departed, leaving a dumbstruck and annoyed Riley staring at her boss.

"That's going to go over splendidly," Riley said evenly.

"For you or for me?"

"Both," she said. "But definitely worse for you."

"The cotton candy will make up for it," Ryan said, referring to the restaurant's signature dessert. "Besides, I needed to talk to you about something."

"It had best be worth it."

"You tell me," he said, pausing momentarily for effect. "I'm naming you president of the firm. No strings."

Riley said nothing as the words seeped in, then recovered. "Bullshit."

"Bullshit?"

"Bullshit," she said. "There is zero chance you're going to step away from the life."

313

"Jesus, Riley, you were fronting the parade pleading with me to do so and now that I do, you're telling me I shouldn't?"

"I'm not saying you shouldn't, Boss. I'm saying you can't."

"I can."

Riley shook her head and leaned forward. "How often have you emailed me so far this year checking on things?"

"I don't recall," he said with a wry smile.

"Every day. Every single day. And every day I've had to tell you everything's under control."

"So now I believe you."

"Bullshit you do. What's your title going to be?"

"Founding god. Or just founding partner. I'm undecided there. I need to see how it looks on the website."

Riley paused for a moment, searching Ryan's face for any hint of uncertainty or uneasiness, finding none. This really was happening, she thought. He wasn't a good enough actor to fool her, not after all these years.

"Jesus, Ryan," she said finally. "You're serious about this."

"I'm serious about this."

"Are you stepping away for her?"

"Not that it matters," Ryan said, "but no. But I will tell you she's opened my eyes to some things about the life that I probably always knew and wholeheartedly denied."

"She finally taught you perspective," Riley said. "I think I could kiss her."

"Don't let me stop you."

"President."

"Yes."

"Effective date?"

"As soon as the paperwork can be drawn up," he said. "I'm anticipating it will be ready in the morning."

"I suppose I should say thank you."

"Fuck the thank you. You earned this, Riley. And if I'm honest, you've been ready for a while. I'm the one who wasn't."

Riley's eyes brimmed with tears as she stood and wrapped her arms around Ryan. "Thank you nevertheless," she said.

She was just sitting down as Nicholas and Maggie returned, him still clearly confused and her still angry. Nicholas looked at the tears on Riley's face and exploded. "Holy shit," he said far too loudly, "you fired her, you son of a bitch."

Riley looked up at Nicholas, stunned, and then she and Ryan started laughing, further infuriating both him and Maggie. "Fired her? Christ, son, I just handed her the keys to the chocolate factory." Ryan stood and pulled out a chair for a now equally confused Maggie while Riley reached out a hand and guided Nicholas toward his seat. Diners who had glanced over at the raised voice slowly returned to their own meals.

"I'm not sure what's happening," Nicholas said.

"But I sure would like to know," Maggie said.

"Maggie, Nicholas, allow me to introduce you to the new president of Williams Consulting Associates."

Nicholas's eyes darted toward Riley, and he squeezed her hand. "President?"

"Yes," she said, leaning forward and kissing her fiancé fiercely.

Ryan turned to Maggie and saw her own expression soften. "What have you done, Ryan?"

"Only what the universe has showed me I should," he said. "My place isn't at the capitol, Maggie. It's with you."

She placed her palms on his cheeks and stared at him for a long moment, a confused look etched on her face, before pulling him close for a tender kiss. The server arrived to check on the couples, both of whom were staring at their mates, oblivious to all around them. "I'll um," he started, "I'll just go get some refills and come back."

CHAPTER TWENTY-NINE

Maggie looked around the small hotel room and smirked. "Weren't you the one telling me about privilege and access and such?"

"What was it you told me back at the Pillbox that one day? Sometimes a girl wants a burger and a beer."

Ryan had booked a couples massage at the casino's spa, and they left Maricopa after eating a late lunch and lounging around the nearly deserted pool for a couple hours, enjoying substantially warmer sunshine than the day before. Maggie had assumed they would be driving straight across Interstate 8 to get back to Del Mar but, a mile shy of the California border, Ryan turned off the freeway and drove into the entrance to an old-fashioned motel that sprawled across both sides of nearly two full city blocks. She glanced at Ryan, who merely winked, parked the car under an awning outside the lobby and walked inside to reserve a room. Their dwelling was almost the complete opposite of the strained opulence of the casino suite from the night before. The king-size bed, dresser and nightstand filled the room and an in-wall air conditioner/heater combo pumped dutifully and noisily away.

She had started to unpack but he stopped her almost immediately. "No need to worry about that," he said. "The clerk up front told me tonight's steak night next door!" Maggie shook her head at his inexplicable excitement but followed him out the door. They walked across the street hand-in-hand and into Yuma Landing, where Ryan guided them past the café on the right and the dark '50s-style full bar on the left and into the Hangar Sports Bar in the back. A four-piece band stood on a stage in the near corner, playing a mix of light rock and other oldies, and Ryan and Maggie had to maneuver past couples dancing in the wide aisle between the central bar and the black vinyl-coated booths along the far wall. The maroon and black walls and black ceiling outline giving way to white-gray tiles gave the room a secluded, forgotten feel despite a handful of flat-screen televisions and the band played Dwight Yoakam's "Guitars, Cadillacs."

"So how does someone who enjoys red-carpet treatment at the casino come to learn about a place like this?"

"Let's just say that after years working for candidates across the state, you create a full Rolodex of places where the food is good, the alcohol is cheap and no one much bothers you about anything," he said. "Bars like this are perfect for a local politician to meet some people in the café, do the whole hand-shaking thing, then drift into the back for an adult beverage without worrying about anyone judging them for it."

"Preserving the image at all times," she said, cynicism dripping.

"More to the point, being able to let the image slide a little bit. At least," he added, "as long as you're smart about it." Ryan jerked his head toward a booth on the opposite wall. "I was working with one guy years ago and we drifted back here after a tour around the historic district and such, just a quick stop for a drink or two to wind down. He didn't tell me he also had

318

popped a couple of sleeping pills to make sure he went under and stayed under."

"What happened?"

"He succeeded," Ryan answered with a grin. "He went right under that table, and it was all I could do to keep him from staying there."

Maggie stifled a giggle. "Did he drop out of the race?"

"Drop out? Hell, Maggie. It probably gained him some votes from the regulars who've done the same thing. But I wouldn't recommend it as a normal strategy."

The server came by and recited the food and drink specials. Maggie ordered a vodka with cranberry juice and, just before Ryan could pass on the happy hour specials, she jumped in. "He'll take that watermelon Hefeweizen thing," she said. Ryan looked at her, head tilted to the side, and she smiled. The server looked at Ryan and he nodded in confirmation. "Never say no to a beer when the woman says yes," he said.

"Good strategy," Maggie said.

"I'm learning. But you know I'm not supposed to be doing that."

Maggie reached across to take his hand and smiled widely. "I'll make sure you don't end up under the table," she said. "Besides, you've behaved yourself for what, a week or more? I'm sure your doctor would allow for this."

"I'll have him call you."

Their beer arrived and Ryan ordered steaks for both of them because, "it's steak night," he proclaimed happily. A second beer followed the first while they waited for their steaks and the band started playing the Temptations. Ryan slid sideways out of the booth, stood next to the table and presented a hand for Maggie. "Join me for a dance," he asked.

"I thought you said you didn't dance."

"Call this the exception for this year."

"How can I resist?"

319

Her arms around his neck, his around her waist, they spun in slow circles to the sounds of "My Girl," all but oblivious to everything around them including the arrival of their food halfway through the song.

"So, Mr. Williams," Maggie said. "How many women have you seduced with a dance here?"

"Honestly, not a single one. Until tonight, assuming you're feeling seduced."

"I find that hard to believe."

"I said my candidates enjoyed this place because they could relax. That doesn't mean I could let my own hair down. I had to be able to keep an eye on them, just in case."

"I'm really the first, then."

"You are," he said, "though you didn't say whether you were feeling properly seduced."

"You're off to a fine start...Willy."

Ryan tossed his head back and laughed, then dipped Maggie deeply as the song came to an end. "I'll keep working on it," he said, pressing his lips against hers as he pulled her back up to standing.

***

Later that evening, after some more dancing and dinner and intimate moments back in their motel room, Maggie lay on Ryan's bare chest listening to his heart beat as his chest rose and fell with the rhythm of his breath. "I've been thinking," she said softly.

Ryan reached down and ran his hand through her hair, then down past the nape of her neck before settling between her shoulder blades. "You still can think after all that? I must be doing something wrong."

"You," she said, pivoting to looking at him through drowsy lids, "did nothing wrong. But I have been thinking about what happens when we get back to Del Mar."

"In general, or just my being homeless in a few days?"

"The latter." Maggie shifted again and gently propped herself up on an elbow resting across his chest. "Perhaps you don't need to worry about finding yourself another rental." She took a deep breath and said what she had been thinking for some time. "Perhaps you come stay with me."

"Stay with you?" he asked as he worked hard to keep a straight face. "Do you have a guesthouse I haven't seen?"

She took a breath to answer, but then his body shook in a hearty laugh. He slid his hand down her back and pushed softly. She responded reflexively, lifting off her elbow and shimmying higher against him until their lips met. She pulled away and they stared at each other, an entire conversation of love and desire taking place in a silent instant.

"Say the words," she whispered.

"I love you," he said, "and I can't think of anything I want more than to wake up next to you every day."

She gazed at him in wonder. The swirling, confused, jumbled aura she had seen when they'd first met was gone completely for the first time. In its place was simple calm, warmth, trust. She reached our tentatively and placed her hand against his cheek, determined to say the three words she had not told anyone since her husband's passing. "I love you too, Ryan."

***

After breakfast at the café to the right of the main entrance in Yuma Landing, they loaded their luggage into the trunk of the car and started the short but largely barren two-hour drive past the Southern California dunes at the edge of the Mohave Desert, through the mountains separating the state's more arid eastern area from the inland and coastal cities in the west. Ryan's phone vibrated and a phone number flashed on the LED screen in the center console. He didn't recognize the number itself, but the 202 area code—Washington, DC—was hint enough that this was not a call he wanted to deal with. He pressed his left thumb on the call cancel button on the left side of the steering wheel and let the call roll to voice mail.

Maggie watched him with a raised eyebrow but said nothing. An hour later, a second call came from the same number, and a third followed as they were making the turn onto the 5 from Interstate 10. "Someone seems to be quite anxious to talk to you," she said.

Ryan nodded mutely and continued staring at the road ahead. Pieces of a puzzle fell into place. Pérez walking onto the House floor and the invitation back to his office was less than coincidental, and more than a test to see whether Ryan was ready to come back to working the local legislatures where he had made his name. Pérez wasn't asking Ryan how he felt for his own sake. He was asking for someone else, someone who wasn't going to spend the time picking up the phone themselves until they knew there was a reason to do so. Someone who wouldn't let his hand show even to the person who helped lead him into the position in which he now found himself. Ryan didn't recognize the number, but he knew George Flannery was on the other end of the phone, waiting to pounce.

"They've left you voice mail," Maggie continued, unaware of Ryan's realization. "Shouldn't you call them back?"

He turned toward her and shook his head. "If they're that persistent," he said, "whatever they need is more important to them than it is to me."

Ryan almost meant the words as he said them.

They stopped at Ryan's rental long enough for him to grab a fresh change of clothes. Everything else in his luggage he'd wash back at Maggie's place, where they headed straight from the beach. Ryan paused inside the garage after parking the car and stared at the door to the stairs that would lead to her house's main level.

"What's wrong?" she asked.

"It's a little overwhelming," he said.

"What is?" She crossed the front of the car to stand next to him, their luggage at their feet.

"The idea that I'm not just visiting you here," he said. "I'm coming home myself."

She leaned up and kissed him on the cheek. "Maybe move a few of your things in before you get entirely attached," she joked.

Ryan turned and lifted her in his arms. "My stuff doesn't matter," he said. "You're here. That's what makes this home." He dipped his head and kissed her passionately and started toward the door.

"What about our luggage?" she said with a laugh.

"It still will be here later."

***

Ryan turned on his phone and, in addition to the calls from Flannery he had ignored, he saw a voice mail from Riley.

"Shit," he muttered.

"What is it?"

"Riley called."

"It doesn't necessarily mean something bad."

Ryan shook his head and explained who had been calling him before. "As much as I wish this was coincidence, it's not. I've got to call her back," he told Maggie.

"What is it that Flannery wants from you?" Maggie asked, aware even as she formed the question what the answer would be and hoping Ryan would neither lie to nor patronize her.

"It's got to be something about the campaign," he said. "Hopefully, it's some minor flare-up and that will be the end of it."

"If it's not?"

Ryan looked at her but said nothing, not because he didn't want to ease the anxiety etched on her face but because he didn't have an answer for her. He kissed Maggie perfunctorily on the cheek, stood up, pulled on a T-shirt and a pair of sweatpants and walked outside to the balcony as his call connected. "What's up, Riley?"

"Flannery called," she said.

"He called you too?"

"Funny," she said humorlessly. "He told me, and I quote, to tell my 'goddamn boss to get off his ass and pick up the fucking phone.'"

"Did you tell him I'm not your boss anymore?"

"As a matter of fact, I did. He congratulated me and told me the promotion was overdue."

"And?" Ryan asked, knowing there had to be more.

"And then he said, and again I quote, 'now tell your fucking boss to return my call.' He doesn't sound happy about being ignored."

"Good," Ryan said. "I wasn't happy about being shunted to the side."

"Still... What if he wants you back?"

"Then," Ryan said, glancing quickly at Maggie, still laying in bed, "I've got some things to think about it, don't I?" He turned back toward the balcony's railing. "I need you to contact him, but not until I send you an e-mail with my conditions. He's going to have to crawl through shit before I talk to him."

"Is that really wise?" Riley asked.

"I don't care anymore," he replied. "Check your e-mail in the morning, okay?"

He disconnected the call and leaned heavily on the railing in front of him, scarcely noticing Maggie standing in the doorway.

"What's wrong?" she said, her brows furrowing in concern as she moved next to him and laid her hand gently on his arm.

"Nothing other than what I already knew."

"It wasn't coincidence."

"No."

She nodded and said, "What's next, then?"

"I imagine I'll sit down with him. I've known him too long not to."

Maggie shook her head. "That's not what I'm asking you, Ryan." He turned to her and was met with a steely gaze he'd never noticed before. "If he wants you to come work for him, what are you going to do?"

If only I knew. The smallest traces of adrenaline started churning through his system at the possibility of working on a presidential campaign. In spite of everything that had happened, he knew he still could contribute—no, fuck only contributing—he could dominate. If that was what Flannery needed, there was no question Ryan would return to the arena. Or it wouldn't be a question, if not for the woman standing in front of him. "It's complicated."

"Bullshit," she spat. He saw her eyes starting to glisten even as the vein on the side of her neck throbbed with anger. "It's a simple question. Would you go or would you stay? No essay required. Just one of two options. A coin flip."

"Because either option is so meaningless that I could leave it up to gravity," he said condescendingly.

"No. But if the choice isn't obvious, then one choice apparently doesn't have as much meaning attached as I thought."

"I need to think," he said softly. Ryan bent an index finger under her chin and she grudgingly met his eyes.

"So go think. But do it at your place," she said icily, turning on a heel and walking back into the bedroom. Ryan stared at her for a moment then followed her in, grabbed his wallet and his keys and headed out into the night.

Maggie rolled onto her back as the front door closed and stared at the ceiling through the dark. A tear slowly leaked from her right eye, and she angrily wiped it away with the back of her hand. What was she doing, crying like a lovesick teenager? Had he not already broken the one major rule she had established back in Arizona, to not surprise her like this? He didn't deserve tears, only anger, but even that felt wrong. Was this really who she was, what she had become after all this time? Petty? Overemotional? Out of balance?

She feared for Ryan's health if he returned to the political world, but that wasn't what she was upset about. Neither was it that she didn't want him to go because she would miss him. She was afraid that, given the choice between his prior life or this nascent one he had started to build with her, history would be too great a pull. And if she couldn't trust him to make the right choice now, what did they really have?

Maggie sat up in bed, crossed her legs, folded her hands in front of her and inhaled deeply. "Whatever he chooses he chooses," she said to herself. "It's out of my hands." Now if she could resist the urge to rest her hands around Ryan's throat.

CHAPTER THIRTY

F lannery acceded to Ryan's first demand when he agreed to fly to California rather than forcing Ryan to come across the country to meet in Washington or New Hampshire or wherever else he was speaking on his three-day weekends away from the Senate. The next would come when they met for dinner at Poseidon, when Ryan gave full vent to the accumulated fury he had worked so hard to bury only to have it bubble back to the surface the past two days. Ryan could feel it like a physical weight, pushing down upon him, leaving him snappish. It didn't help matters that he and Maggie had barely spoken since the night Riley called. He was prepared to give her whatever space she needed but didn't expect that she wouldn't have at least texted him. Ryan himself had picked up the phone and typed out a few words at least a dozen times before changing his mind and deleting the message.

He had thought of doing so again, asking Maggie to wish him luck without a thought about the irony, but then Flannery walked in. To say he and Flannery were off to an unusually rough start would have been an understatement. Flannery looked mockingly at Ryan as he took a drink off his iced tea after declining a round of scotch, pleading doctor's orders. "You weren't in the mood for milk?"

"Not in the mood to die today," Ryan responded smoothly. "Speaking of which, let's just cut to it. Tell me why the hell I should come work for you at this point?"

"Did I say that's what I wanted?"

"Remember who you're talking to, George. You don't fly anywhere for shits and giggles. So get to the point."

George smirked and shook his head. "You're pissed about Afolayan."

"Fuck Afolayan. I'm pissed about Comstock. You knew what I was walking into there."

George raised his hands in mock surrender. "Hey, I didn't realize he was going to try and make the South rise again." Ryan stared silently back, and Flannery tried a different approach. "The obvious lunacy aside, yeah, we knew he was a borderline nut, but I also thought you'd be able to pull it off and get a little more of a national profile."

"Then fuck you, too, for thinking it. I got exposure. Afolayan made sure of it."

"Like you weren't also trying to paint a new picture with a broad brush."

"Fuck you," Ryan said again.

"Fuck me. Fuck him. Fuck all of us. Whatever, Ryan. Seriously, though, do you want to sit here and do the whole who-blames-who routine for another hour, or start talking now?"

"Understand one thing, George," Ryan said. "You need me. We both know you wouldn't be sitting here unless you did. On top of that, you need me one hell of a lot more than I need you."

"You sure about that?" George asked. "I'm offering you a free pass back into the game at the highest levels, a pass you're not going to be able to get on your own for the near future."

Ryan laughed humorlessly. "Honestly, I could give a fuck less about that right now. So, again, you need me more than I need you."

Even as he said the words, Ryan knew he didn't mean them. He did care. He couldn't help himself, not after all these years led by his ego. Even worse, looking at Flannery, he could tell Flannery also knew Ryan didn't mean it. Rage surged through him—at Flannery, at Afolayan, at Comstock, at everyone he saw at a rally waving the stars and bars without any idea of what they were representing or, worse, knowing exactly they were representing. He realized he was even angrier at himself for allowing Flannery to goad him so easily. Emotions Ryan believed were resolved had been hiding just below the surface, waiting for the scab to be picked. Once Flannery did that—no, Ryan corrected himself with a deep breath, once he let Flannery do that—they all flowed freely, coating him in indignation and frustration anew. Ryan turned toward the window and watched a tall roller crash upon the sand, the sandpipers scuttling onto the fresh-washed surf to look for their dinner, then scurrying away ahead of the next wave.

Suddenly, the scene changed in his mind's eye. He was sitting a few dozen feet away at the bar, watching the sun slowly sink below the horizon. There on the beach was Maggie, just as he had seen her the first day in silhouette, except she turned toward him and smiled. "You know what to do," she said.

"Ryan?"

Sometimes people receive a message from the universe and accept it for what it is or, if the message isn't clear, they work to clarify. Other times, people receive that same message and bend it to fit whatever outcome they want. Ryan had spent the past two weeks attempting the former but here, with one foot back inside the political cocoon he knew so well, he couldn't help but take the message as affirmation regardless of whether that was the intent. Messages from the universe are only as good as the receptiveness of the receiver.

"Ryan!" Flannery barked, tired of the extended silence.

"Talk," Ryan said as the server delivered a wood board with pistachio-roasted brie lightly coated with jalapeno jelly, and an assortment of fruit and toasted bread. He reached for a small knife, sliced off a corner of the triangular cheese wedge and spread it on a slice of grilled sourdough. "You've got until the appetizer's gone to get my interest."

George waved at the retreating server and waggled his glass in the air for a refill. "As you have figured out, I want you to come work for me."

"Want's not going to cut it. Besides, you have your boy Seth to fetch your water."

"He's got things covered nationally," Flannery said. "I need local."

"Local?"

"Statewide, multiple states. Mostly out this way where you've already got the connections to get done what I need."

"Which is?"

"Down ballot organization." Ryan started to say something but George held up a hand. "Hear me out. You know what a clusterfuck the last election was below the main line on the ballot. The national campaign ignored the other races and paid the price on Capitol Hill."

"You've already lost one chamber, at least practically."

"You would know," Flannery said reflexively. Ryan tossed down his napkin and went to leave, but George grabbed him by the arm. "Sit, goddamn it. You know I don't mean it."

"You do."

"Yeah, well, I shouldn't," Flannery said. "The point is, the down ballot races are going to matter more than ever, and the last thing I need while taking on history's least popular incumbent since Ford is to have a bunch of alt-right yahoos eking through the primaries, then getting smashed in the general election."

"You wouldn't be the first president without his own party in charge on the hill," Ryan said.

"No, but I also don't want to be one-and-done. Only presidents who are viewed favorably either went two terms or got killed along the way."

"Always good to have a choice," Ryan said sarcastically.

"Right," George said, raising his newly refilled glass. "Anyway, you know the territory west of the Rockies. What I need is for you to put that to work, help guide those elections in the primary stages, do whatever is necessary to keep the nativists and the rest at bay and make sure we've got some electable candidates on the ballot in twenty months."

"I already turned this down once."

"Did you? I don't remember those words ever coming from you."

"The silence should have been a hint."

"I'm not much for guesswork. Besides, you and I both know the answer's never no until you hear the word. And even then, it's never final."

Their server returned for their dinner orders and Flannery lifted an eyebrow at Ryan, who nodded back. "You're good through the entree," he said, ordering the most expensive surf-and-turf combo from the menu as Flannery took a sip from his tumbler.

For the next twenty-odd minutes, Flannery outlined his plans for Ryan. As a nod to Ryan's recently cardiac troubles, he would have Ryan working out of a central hub with limited travel to meet with those chosen to lead the state-level organizations, and then to check back and make sure all was working as expected.

"I don't need you on the ground constantly," Flannery said. "Hell, I don't want you doing that. Not with what you've been through."

"I'm fine, George."

"Be that as it may," Flannery continued, "I'd just as soon see you live a while longer, whether you believe it or not. That's another reason why I want you doing this and not joining the national circus."

"Why not let the firm handle this? Riley's more than capable of doing what you're asking."

"She is," George conceded, "but she's got a lot on her plate as it is. I need total focus on this."

"In other words, the diva wants to feel like a diva."

"Divas don't become divas for nothing, my friend."

Ryan nodded, leaned back in his chair and stared at a spot just off Flannery's right shoulder. He ought to have known Flannery was going to push all his buttons, triggering Ryan's anger to flush it out of his system, then moving into the aw-shucks-you-know-I-can't-do-this faux humility routine he'd seen for decades, and then appealing to Ryan's undeniable ego. The worst part was, even as Ryan knew he was being played like a fiddle in the hands of Charlie Daniels, he couldn't help but see the logic in what Flannery was saying. Only then did he realize Flannery still was talking.

"For all I care, stay here and use this as your base," Flannery said.

"No," Ryan said, then added softly, almost to himself, "Some spaces need to be separate."

Flannery tilted his head and looked quizzically at Ryan. "I get it," he lied. "Set up shop wherever you want. Just set up shop for me."

Ryan looked up as their entrees arrived, picked up his fork and started pulling meat from his lobster tail without answering. He could feel Flannery glaring at him, waiting for an answer.

He knew how much Flannery hated silence when he expected acceptance. Ryan held his fork in the air in front of him, then dipped it in Flannery's direction with a wink.

Let him stew.

***

Ryan went straight to his bedroom after getting home from dinner with Flannery. He stripped out of his suit, tossing the jacket, shirt and slacks carelessly onto the floor before pulling a fresh fleece shirt and workout shorts from the dresser and heading out back to the beach. Clark Kent never changed that fast, he thought with a smirk. That ember of humor was extinguished almost immediately by the reality of the choice in front of him. Not that it felt like much of a choice.

What he had told Flannery was true—he would not let his political life enter the more peaceful existence he had carved out for himself once he let it go.

"I've got to tell you," Ryan had said eventually, "this retirement thing isn't so bad."

"No one retires from this," Flannery had scoffed, "at least not guys like us. No jab intended, but us old-timers basically will be doing this until our heart gives out. Unless you make it all the way to the top."

"President," Ryan said.

"That's the top," Flannery said as he nodded. "With some luck and a little skill, you get a full eight years to serve and you're off to do whatever you want. I mean, W. painting watercolors? Where did that come from?"

Ryan smiled as he thought about his own sudden interest in yoga and paddleboarding. "You never know what getting away will do to a brain. And I'll tell ya, it's a brain change for the better."

Flannery looked down at the freshly delivered check and his face for the first time showed the slightest hint of resignation. "You're not going to come back to the life," he glanced up and said, more statement than question. Ryan said nothing, instead looking again out the window. "Three months," he heard Flannery say in the background.

"Come again?"

"You heard me, kid. Come work for me for three months. Bust ass for ninety days, get the groundwork set and then do what you need to do at that point. You stay, you go at that point, it's your call."

"And when you win, I go back to my role as the forgotten one-time myth maker?"

"Only if you want to," Flannery said. "DC will be on the table regardless of whether you stay. Just give me the three months."

Ryan took a sip of his iced tea and suddenly wished it were scotch. "Three months isn't a lot of time to get this set."

"No," Flannery said, sounding sympathetic rather than forceful for the first time. Fully into deal-closer mode, he leaned forward, hands together, making himself seem smaller, less intimidating while actually increasing his presence through voice alone, a trick he'd used successfully for decades. "It's not a long time at all. But for you it's more than enough."

Ryan had seen this show countless times before, but it made him no less immune to the lure. "Give me a day," he said wearily.

"Just don't make it two." Flannery leaned back in his chair and grinned the grin of a man carving another notch in his belt.

Now, back at home a few hours later, Ryan shook his head and muttered expletives under his breath as he walked off his deck onto the beach. The gibbous moon hung high in the southeastern sky and cast faint shadows upon the sand in front of him as he headed north toward Dog Beach. The off-ocean breeze felt damp and cold on his exposed legs, but Ryan didn't care. What he needed most of all was the cool salt-tinged air in his lungs, pumped deeper into his system through constant motion. He searched for some sense of focus for his swirling thoughts, but to no avail. Ryan knew what he should do. He also knew instinctively what he was going to do. The only reason he hadn't already agreed to Flannery's offer was Maggie, but even his feelings for her would not override his ego's urging. Ryan knew it and he hated himself for it. So he walked, trying to put distance between himself and the decision he knew he was unable to stop himself from making—as if it were possible to run away from one's self.

He approached the northern edge of Del Mar Beach, where the sand abruptly ended in a wall of rock jutting into the surf. It usually was impossible to make the turn from this beach onto Dog Beach without wading into the water but tonight, with the tide only now starting to build back up, there was a narrow strip of sand leading north and then east onto the wide, flat sand and shallow water of the world's most dog-friendly beach. Ryan's ankles and calves were soaked by a leading wave, but he paid little mind to the discomfort as he made the turn. Ryan's heart pounded as he walked up the steep path—inclines had been giving him trouble since his episode in Birmingham—and he paused a few steps away from the top, leaning against a property wall just south of where the path converged with the main walkway.

Ryan pulled out his phone and, as had been the case since he'd left Poseidon, there were no messages, no texts. He had called Maggie from the parking lot at Poseidon, hoping to be able to talk to her about what Flannery had offered and the conflicting feelings he was fighting, but his call had rolled to voice mail. He called up his call history with two touches of the screen and was about to dial again but stopped. Not reaching her earlier probably was for the best, he admitted. This decision was entirely up to him. If he involved her, a part of him always would blame her for his not taking the chance. Even if he knew this was a chance that probably was best left untouched. He pressed the small x to close the history, then opened his photo app where the first several pictures were either of him and Maggie or her alone: standing on the floor of the Arizona House, outside Yuma Landing when they went back to the café for breakfast before returning to San Diego, a candid photo of her on his deck watching the ocean and pretending not to notice he had his camera out.

"I'm a moron," he said to no one. Then, with a long look at Maggie's image on his phone, he added, "Forgive me."

***

Maggie looked down when her phone started to vibrate. Ryan's name and picture appeared in the background and, with considerable effort, she pressed her thumb on the red icon to decline the call. Her need to punish him with silence overrode her own desire to talk to him. It was petty and small-minded and against virtually everything she had spent years preaching to her yoga students about allowing the universe to determine one's path and, whatever the path was, to walk it with a heart full of love and forgiveness. She loved him without a doubt. But forgiveness, especially for the path she knew he would be unable to surrender, was nowhere to be found. It would come in time, she knew. But there was a difference between forgiveness and continuing on as if nothing had happened. That was a bridge that might never be built.

She plugged her phone into a wall charger, poured herself a glass of wine and went into her yard. Maggie thought for a moment of calling Liz then decided against it. She had enough thoughts in her own head without needing Liz to come in and tell her to cut Ryan loose, just as she always had cut men loose at the first sign of trouble. Though that may be the eventual outcome, it wasn't one she was in the mood to consider quite yet. Not with this relationship, which had been the most significant she'd had since Bruce died. And not with Bruce telling me this was the man looking for me. The Bruce of her dreams still might turn out to be correct, but she couldn't figure out how. Which is the point of trusting in the universe.

"I get it," she said as she shot a sideways glance at the moon, as if that had been the source of her thought. "Just not tonight." Turning away from the moon, she flicked on the lights in her yard with a remote, set them for a cool blue, settled onto a lounge under a thick blanket and opened a book she had borrowed from the library earlier today. Romantic fiction of all things, she thought with a smirk before turning off her brain and starting to read, then falling into a dreamless sleep where she sat.

Maggie awoke a couple of hours later, wiped the dew off the cover of the book and retreated inside to a warm shower and the comfort of her bed. She was up again shortly before dawn and, realizing she couldn't fall back asleep, she dressed in her beach yoga attire and drove to the parking lot outside the 17th Street lifeguard station. The tide was up but there was room enough for her to set out her mat and start her basic flow about fifty yards east of Jake's—far enough from her normal location that there was virtually no possibility Ryan could chance upon her even if he tried. Then again, if he did appear at least it would prove he was making an effort, far more so than a phone call from someone only a couple miles away.

She returned home and took another shower before going downstairs and mixing yogurt and granola in a bowl for breakfast. Her phone vibrated on the counter next to her and, seeing Ryan's name, with effort she declined the call once again. Thirty seconds later the phone vibrated a single time as a voice mail alert. She slowly reached for her phone, opened the voice mail app and read the transcription provided. Words were garbled and missing as per normal, so she reluctantly picked up the phone and listened to his message. Ryan said he was going to work for Flannery. *Like I didn't know*, she thought bitterly. He loved her. He would miss her. He started to say he was sorry but caught himself, said it was something he needed to do for himself, and he hoped she'd understand. And finally he asked her to call him back whenever she was ready to do so.

Maggie listened to the message a second time and then saved it because, much as she hated to admit it, she wanted to have his voice on hand. However, she also knew she wasn't going to wait on him to figure things out. When you'd laid everything out to someone, held nothing back and told them they are your future, and they tell you the same and then decide to walk away anyway, even temporarily, there was no need to wait. Apparently whatever they had wasn't enough. "So be it," she said, not meaning it at all. She clicked to her favorites and called in a substitute instructor for her classes, then called Liz, who could tell from the sound of Maggie's voice something was wrong.

"Stay there," Liz said. "It sounds like you could use some mimosa therapy."

CHAPTER THIRTY-ONE

R yan sat on the couch inside his loft in Phoenix and stared at his tablet. He had been here the past several days, going over material sent to him by Flannery's assistants about the possible candidates and campaigns with which Ryan would need to coordinate and the assorted donors whom he would need to cajole. There were several familiar faces on the latter list, men and women he could call and be assured of a check following in the mail by the next day. But there were others who were unknown to him, those partial to one or two specific issues only, who might open their wallet for the right cause but would just as likely spend money to help defeat anyone of whom they did not approve.

The scope of Ryan's duties was overwhelming even for him. Ten Congressional districts in Arizona alone, seven in Colorado, five in Utah, four in Nevada and a whopping fifty-four in California. Not that Flannery would have chosen candidates in all of the eighty districts. Some seats were secured by the opposing party, others already held congressmen that Flannery could work with. The work would come in the districts that either were a toss-up or were held by remnants of the GOP's Tea Party past that Flannery would rather avoid. They may have been good people, but as a group they were more inclined to obstruct unless they received everything they wanted, rather than surrender to the perceived evil of negotiating.

Ryan's mind turned to Comstock, but he shunted the memory aside as quickly as it came. Instead he opened a spreadsheet and a map and started going over the travel itinerary he had been working on for the past two days. His goal was to get to as many locations as possible as quickly as was feasible, while at the same time not burning himself out or, more importantly, putting his health at risk. He'd found himself spending time online researching information he'd never considered before November—the risk of embolisms from spending too much time on airplanes or sitting in automobiles, for instance. Try as he might, the state of his health was never far from his mind.

All of which was making it imperative that he go somewhere else the next day to work, as he could feel the walls closing in on him. He had been avoiding alcohol but was falling into his old habit of taking a couple of Tylenol PM to help him get to sleep when he couldn't eject from his mind all the work that he had to do.

He picked up his phone, opened the messaging app and started typing a message to Maggie. Nothing deep, nothing complicated, just a simple hello and how are you. His thumb hovered over the send key, but he couldn't bring himself to press the button. He had tried calling her a couple of times since he'd arrived back in Phoenix, but his calls went to voice mail. Ryan actually had planned for voice mail the first time, phoning when he knew she would be in class and hoping she would see the missed call from him and call him back. It was a cowardly approach, trying to salve his own guilt with the knowledge that she wasn't so hurt or angry that she still would return his calls, and it backfired. His next two attempts were at different hours in the late afternoon and early evening when he assumed she would be near her phone and able to talk, but these calls also rolled to the recording.

If she's not going to answer your calls, she's not going to answer your texts. He held his thumb to the screen, chose "Select All" when options popped up, white letters on a black background, then clicked on "copy." Switching to his note-taking app, Ryan pasted the text below two other one-time text messages he had written and closed the file. When she was ready, she would call. He hoped.

***

Midway through the morning the following day, Ryan walked into his firm's Phoenix offices. "Good morning, Rosie," he said to the gob-smacked receptionist sitting at the front desk.

"Mr. Williams," she stammered. "We didn't expect to be seeing you...um...today."

"Relax," he said. "I've just got a few calls that I've got to make." He nodded a farewell and started walking down the long hall to the back offices as Rosie picked up the phone and hurriedly dialed Riley's extension. "He's here."

"Who's here?"

"Ryan."

"Shit," Riley said. "Thanks for the heads-up." She hadn't heard from Ryan since the night she told him Flannery was looking for him, which was surprising. Whether he signed up with Flannery or told him to pound sand, she was certain Ryan would let her know what he decided. Unless, of course, he was afraid she would try to talk him out of going back to work. Which she would have, though if Maggie was unable to do so, she had no idea what she could do or say to make him stay away.

Riley got up, walked around her desk and opened the door to his office just as Ryan stepped up to the doorway. He performed a double-take as he looked as the frosted glass to the side of the cherry-wood door that now read "RILEY EVANS, PRESIDENT." Barely a week and she already had taken his office for her own, not that he would have done any differently in her place. He suddenly felt foolish for thinking his office would be sitting vacant in case he returned even after the announcement that he had retired. Blood rushed to his face and he blushed as he looked up to see Riley standing in front of him, equal parts confusion and wariness on her face.

"Riley," Ryan said evenly.

"Boss," she replied. They stood an extra second or two in the doorway before she caught herself. "Sorry, come in. Take a seat."

"Just not the one behind the desk," he said with a nod as he walked in.

"It is your chair."

"No, it's not," he said as he settled into a chair. "It's yours, even if I hadn't considered the matter until just now."

"It seemed logical," Riley said defensively, and Ryan held up his hand.

"No need to explain," he said. "I did put you in charge."

"So, what's going on?" she asked. "When did you get to town?"

"A few days ago," Ryan said and, seeing the surprise on her face, he told her about his dinner with Flannery and the work he had been doing since. She noticed that he made no mention of Maggie or what had taken place with her before his departure, and she was gracious enough not to bring it up.

"That sounds like a hell of a lot to try and take on solo," Riley said when he was finished. "In fact, I can't imagine what made you think to try it without picking up the phone."

"With the legislative sessions underway, it seemed like you'd have enough work on your hands," he said.

"You know that's bullshit. There's no reason why I can't handle campaign work on top of everything else we have going when that's what you and I have done for years. So either you don't trust me, or you were avoiding telling me what you were doing."

"Jesus, Riley, of course I trust you."

She nodded in triumph, but her expression remained neutral. "I don't need to tell you that there was no logical reason for you to work for Flannery. You don't need to tell me how stupid it is given everything that's happened to you the past couple of months." She paused intentionally and added, "both good and bad," the lone allusion to what he'd left behind. "So I'm not going to do that."

"Gee, thanks."

"You're welcome. What I am going to do is tell you to send me your workups, and I'll get some people working on the logistics for you. Do what you need to do here in the state and we will get the rest calendared for you."

Ryan smiled with pride as he studied Riley behind the desk. Her demeanor and her posture said everything he had known for ages. She was long overdue for the opportunity.

"This wasn't supposed to be a firm-wide project," he said.

"But it necessarily has to be just from the sheer scope of it all. Even your insanely large ego should know that."

"Is this any way to speak to your boss?"

"As you mentioned the other night," she said, "you're not my boss anymore. But I'm going to help your dumb ass anyway." Riley stood and motioned to the door. "Come on."

"Where are we going?" he asked as he stood to join her.

"I can't get any work done with you sitting in my office," she said. "But I think I've got an extra office that the interns use when they're not running around the capitol."

Ryan started to say something but stopped himself. "The interns' office would be just fine."

***

The breeze off the ocean ruffled Maggie's bangs as she rested in lotus pose on a mat high on the sand near the seawall, not far from the lifeguard station. She kept her eyes closed, sealing herself off from the morning joggers and walkers and the muted shouts of the surfers and paddleboarders already on the water, and focused only on her breathing, unconsciously matching her inhale and exhale to the motion of the waves. This was familiar, and here she was safe. Safe from any doubts about having given her heart to Ryan, safe from the mixed anger and disappointment she continued to feel when she let down her guard, safe from her own self-recrimination. All of those could and would return later, sometime after dark when she was alone in her house with a glass of wine and she worked to turn her bitterness toward him into recognition that they at least had something special, albeit brief.

It was her way. It always had been her way, at least in the years since the night of her accident. Losing your husband and your unborn child, that was permanent. Surviving the same accident added the eternal unanswerable question...why? Why him and not her? Why not both? Or neither? The dual losses had been unfathomable to comprehend, all but impossible to accept. Except at some point, for the sake of your own sanity, you do learn to accept what had happened. Acceptance doesn't eliminate the pain, but it does compartmentalize it and allow for life to go on.

Compared to that, compartmentalizing another relationship—straining away the negative to leave positive memories interspersed with lessons learned—was simple. Breathe. Share her practice through the classes she taught at her studio. Rinse. Repeat. Simple. At least until now, with Ryan. She knew this pain wouldn't simply fade, not given the future she had seen for them. Maybe it never was him that she saw in the fog. Maybe that was something she subconsciously added to sell herself on the meaning of the dream. Such reason might come in time, but not yet.

Still, that didn't change how she had learned to deal with whatever the universe directed toward her. So she sat still on her mat, inhaling with the thunder of each wave, exhaling as the water receded, focusing all the while on anything other than her fracturing heart.

***

Ryan sat atop a stool and rested his elbows on the 140-year old Brunswick bar inside the Palace Saloon on Prescott's Whiskey Row, sipping now and again from a tumbler of whiskey. His Arizona tour had started a few days earlier with a series of easy meetings in Phoenix. Riley told him these would be a chance to stick his toe back in the water and get his feet set under him before the real work began. From there he had driven north on I-17 to Flagstaff, where he met with the campaign leads from Arizona's First Congressional District, the largest in the state geographically by a wide margin and the tenth largest in the country. District 1 covered all or part of eight of the state's fifteen counties in an arc reaching from the Utah border in the north, then south and east through Navajo and Apache Counties before turning back west and wrapping into Pinal County directly south of Phoenix. Though huge geographically, the district consisted of wide tracts of national forests and parks and was relatively lightly populated. Still, a seat in the House was a seat in the House, and Flannery wanted to secure his base in the state, so off Ryan went for a dinner meeting at a local steakhouse. Ryan was spared the usual nightcap only because the candidate's staff was relatively new, men and women he hadn't met before and who didn't strike him as even minimally experienced. The trouble with such green campaign staff was that as a whole they were overly doctrinaire, unable to connect the dots needed to turn their ideology into action. Explaining the wisdom of Reagan's half-a-loaf maxim—sometimes half a loaf was better than none—was tedious, if not pointless. Yet that's what Flannery wanted Ryan doing.

Things had been considerably different in Prescott, where Ryan had just met with a half-dozen familiar faces from the county and district level in the back corner of the main dining area, fewer than twenty feet from the spot where one-time town constable Virgil Earp and his brother Wyatt once had dined and Doc Holliday reportedly went on a lengthy winning streak at the poker tables. After the main meeting had broken up, Ryan found himself at the long bar with Colby Frank, the campaign manager for congresswoman Abigail Joyner and a longtime friend. Frank could get on a high horse as well as anyone Ryan had known, but he also knew when to dismount and find a way forward. Ryan's stool time at the bar was as much a part of the game as anything else he did, nursing a drink while letting old friends in on some strategic insights not commonly known to make each feel a little more special, all designed to frame Flannery's victory as inevitable assuming all his friends remained loyal. Those friends knew the game as well as their roles within it, so the next day Frank would make a few calls to drop hints at what Ryan had said without overtly sharing all of the information. In this game, knowledge was power.

Then Frank had departed and Ryan thought to follow, but a football playoff game on the television above caught his attention and he ordered an extra round. He could only just make out the players through the snow, not inside the stadium but in the television's reception, and he wondered if there were a pair of bunny ears hiding fallen behind the old television set. Flawless digital reception wouldn't have felt as in place here, he thought, not with staff in old-fashioned Western garb and a similarly attired piano player happily banging out tunes on an old upright near the entrance. Ryan listened to the old standards and watched the snowy screen and sipped his drink again and let his mind drift.

After a few more minutes and a final gulp, he left the Palace and stepped out into the brisk Prescott night. He turned left and headed down a couple of doors to the Hotel St. Michael, where he had taken a room. Riley originally had booked him for the night into some antiseptic chain hotel complete with a USA Today and a complimentary breakfast, but he changed his reservation himself.

Maybe it was the memory of his night with Maggie in the motel in Yuma. Maybe he just wanted to be within walking distance of his dinner meeting. Whatever it was, nothing sounded less appealing to him than waking up in a hotel room that could be in one of a million different cities and first having to remember where it was he'd fallen asleep. That was one aspect of past campaigns he could live without as long as possible.

He might make minor changes to his routine to accommodate some new desire for, if not adventure, then a wider awareness, but all of that ultimately was beside the point. Ryan was back in his element, guiding, directing, using his decades of experience on a far wider scale than he had at any time in the past. Why settle for impacting one campaign when he could have a hand in dozens? Imagine the gratefulness of a Pérez or a pre-Congress Flannery, writ on a national scale topped by the white marble of the US Capitol dome. Not to mention, he'd also have a friend in the White House. What more could he ask for at this point?

Ryan opened the door to his room, kicked off his shoes and stripped down to a T-shirt and boxers, then washed his face before sliding between the sheets of the king-sized bed. Within minutes he was asleep, and he dreamed of a Washington, DC awash in cherry blossoms.

CHAPTER THIRTY-TWO

M aggie found herself back in the now-familiar scene, standing barefoot on cool sand while fog swirled all around her. She waited, knowing within her dream that Bruce would be making an appearance. As if on cue, a small shadow appeared far in the distance and started walking toward her. At least she assumed it was far in the distance, given the short stature. A moment later, though, Maggie found herself staring at a little girl, her dark hair swept up in a ponytail not unlike Maggie's. Maggie looked left and right, searching for...what, exactly? The girl's parents? Or maybe just some clue as to what was going on in her mind right now.

"Hi," the girl said. She smiled and a dimple formed in her right cheek. Only her right cheek, Maggie noticed. She took a longer look and as realization dawned on her, she put her hand to her mouth as tears rushed to her eyes.

"Are you—" she started, unable to form the words "my daughter."

"I'm not who you think," the girl said as a larger shadow appeared in the fog, slowly taking shape as Bruce. He took the girl's hand in his, gave it a squeeze and nodded toward the left where Maggie just now heard the sound of the ocean.

"She's not ours," Bruce said once he and Maggie were alone.

"Who is she?"

"I told you he was looking for you," he said, ignoring Maggie's question.

She felt anger begin to surge even as she was entirely aware that this only was a dream. "He found me," she said. "And then he walked away."

"He has been lost."

"You told me that before," she said.

"Not quite," he said. "Happiness is in front of you, Maggie, if you allow it to happen."

"I told you. I tried that already."

Bruce looked up as if hearing something, and Maggie thought for a moment that she had heard the happy laughter of a little girl whose ankles have been surrounded by the surf. Bruce started to fade away into the fog once again and Maggie rushed forward, trying to keep pace with him as he receded only to find herself completely blanketed in mist.

He has been lost, she heard from the middle of the fog. What will you do when he finds his way?

She woke with a start and stared at the ceiling for a long minute before closing her eyes and falling back into a now-dreamless sleep.

***

"Ryan, why are you still doing this?"

Riley and Ryan sat inside a booth in Durant's, her nursing a martini while he sipped from a glass of whiskey and cola on the rocks. He was in town for a couple of days, just enough to turn over one set of clothing to the dry cleaner and pick up a new set to take back with him on the road as had been for the past five weeks. He had stopped into the office briefly near the end of business hours, hoping to slip in and out as inconspicuously as one can when their name is painted on the front window, but he had been caught in his escape by Riley. She had all but demanded that Ryan join her for dinner while Nicholas was busy at the state capitol meeting after-hours with staff.

Ryan's fatigue was apparent. Fatigue not just from his travel schedule, but from the constant effort to find candidates who actually would be worth supporting in the long run. Ryan's complexion was pallid and dark. Puffy half circles sagged beneath his eyes. His cheeks were drawn and his shoulders slumped even as he tried to present his usual robust visage. His suit hung on him awkwardly, seemingly too large in the shoulders and too tight around a middle bloated after many, many nights of mediocre chicken and beef and potatoes and pasta in the company of would-be candidates and their erstwhile promoters.

Riley's question hung in the air as Ryan stared down at his glass. Drops of condensation moved haltingly down the side of the tumbler in front of him and he thought of the rain running down the windows in his Del Mar rental, the ocean in the background surging and whipped to anger by the strong winds of yet another ocean-born storm. Suddenly his thoughts shifted to Maggie with him on his one-time patio, her lips warm against his in the otherwise cool twilight air. Ryan closed his eyes and shook his head, trying to shake the memory out of existence. Yes, Ryan, he thought, why are you still doing this?

Riley soon realized no answer was forthcoming. "Life on the road clearly isn't helping you," she continued. "You look like you've been beaten with a baseball bat in a cell filled with blinding light twenty-four hours a day. I mean, you are sleeping at some point, yes?"

"Yes," Ryan said testily. "Yes, I'm getting sleep. And yes, I'm still exhausted. And yes, the travel is getting to me."

"Then back to my first question. Why keep doing this?"

"Because, Riley, this is what I do. This is what we do. We work campaigns, doing whatever needs be done to help our candidate get into office. It's what I have done for the past two-plus decades, and I'm damn good at it. George asked. I accepted. Here I am."

"But at what cost? Are you honestly going to tell me there isn't someplace you would rather be than moving from city to city, hotel to hotel until the only thing helping you remember where you are is the weather app on your phone?"

"Of course there is," he snapped. "That doesn't mean that's where I should be."

Riley shook her head slowly. "That makes exactly zero sense."

No one retires from this. Flannery's words echoed in Ryan's head as he thought back to the ocean, to the cool salt-tinged breezes and the woman with whom he had fallen in love. Two worlds, impossible to reconcile. How could he be loving, thoughtful...emotional...present when on the campaign trail he had to do all he could to avoid any emotion? For his entire career, the only thing that had mattered had been the goal ahead.

Then there was the truth Ryan wasn't quite prepared to admit. Campaigns were simple. They started, they ended and another began. There were no long-term commitments, no lengthy need to impress and please. Relationships were infinitely more complex. And Ryan was afraid of what might happen if he failed to live up to someone's expectations over a period longer than a few months.

"Look," he said. "I made the commitment and I'm going to stand by it. I believe in what George wants to do."

"Does he believe in you, though? You're working in a position you already turned down when it was first mentioned."

"Technically I didn't say no."

"No," she said, "you didn't. You merely had a stress-induced panic attack at the thought of being involved in his campaign at any level other than the one you foresaw. You've been dreaming of Washington DC for so long, I'm not sure you even remember why you wanted to be there."

"Not true. I want to make a lasting impact. A positive impact. And the only way to do that is to work for the people who could best make that happen."

"Like Merrick Comstock?"

Ryan shot Riley a wilting look. "That's a little harsh."

"But absolutely true. I was there working with the asshole, too. We shouldn't have been within a thousand miles of that bullshit."

"He was a mistake I won't repeat."

"Really? Tell me about all of the wonderful prospective candidates you're glad-handing these days. Tell me all of the things they have in common with your views. Is there anything?"

Ryan shook his head slowly. "That's why George wanted me out here—to find some."

"Let me save you some time, Boss. There aren't any. It's an absolute fucking wasteland. Anyone worth your time has been swamped by the idiots on the fringes, and it's not going to change until some sort of catalyzing person starts sucking people back into the safety of the center, or at least away from the yawning abyss."

"Which is what Flannery is trying to do."

"In which he might utterly fail," Riley said. "You told me you told him not to announce this soon, right?"

"Yeah."

"You were right. He's going to get run over right now, and his only chance will be to drift toward the edges until you no longer recognize him. Maybe he'll come back to where he started. Maybe he'll stay there because that's where he needs to

353

be to be elected. But the only way anyone with an ounce of common sense is going to have a chance is to wait a while and hope the extremism burns out the bulk of the voters to the point they're willing to turn out for someone who is vanilla yet perfect."

"Flannery would blow a gasket if he heard you call him vanilla," Ryan said with a small grin.

"Compared to what's out there, he is vanilla. There are worse things to be these days."

"Like?"

"Extreme Double Nut Crunch with a side of Rocky Road."

Ryan laughed out loud in spite of himself. "Well played."

They both looked up as their steaks arrived, cutting the center of the beef to make sure it had been cooked to their instructions. Ryan nodded their combined approval, and the server departed as efficiently as she had arrived.

"You're right, you know," he conceded after taking a bite of a perfectly prepared rib eye.

"I usually am," she said. "But about what in particular?"

"It's thin out there right now. Some of these meetings, I'd rather have spent the evening chewing on tinfoil."

"So pack it in. Go back to the coast. Or don't go back. But get away from the road."

"It's not exactly that simple, Riley."

"Sure it is," she said. "Say I quit and drive away." Ryan said nothing and cut off another slice of steak. "Just do me a favor, Ryan." He glanced up to look at her. "Do it while you still can on your own two feet, not in a hospital bed."

Ryan held her gaze for an extra moment before nodding. "I'll do what I can."

***

What would Teddy Roosevelt do? Ryan thought. He was sitting at a table inside Duane's at the Mission Inn in Riverside, California, staring at The Charge Up San Juan Hill, an enormous oil painting painted by a Russian artist for Roosevelt himself almost 120 years earlier, purportedly picturing the Rough Rider-in-Chief as he led his troops up the famous hill during the Spanish-American War. Little matter that Roosevelt himself was on nearby Kettle Hill fighting at the time of the battle on San Juan Hill. The legend was too firmly imprinted into American history to be altered by small details at this stage.

Roosevelt was one of Ryan's political idols, someone who sought to do the right thing no matter how impolitic it might be. While reported as larger than life and often acting as if the world was too small for his personality, Roosevelt was, at his core, a real human—flawed, emotional, egotistical but always striving to be better. Ryan's admiration was shared by Flannery, one of the several things which had bound the two men together in friendship once upon a time.

Ryan couldn't help but cringe at the difference between Roosevelt who, at least before ego led him to abandon William Howard Taft and the Republican Party to form the Bull Moose Party and try unsuccessfully to be elected to a third term in office, stood on consistent principles, and the group of political wannabees surrounding him at the large dining table beneath the painting. Post-dinner conversation swirled around him but Ryan long since had tuned out the voices, deigning only to nod vacantly at this statement or that. More than a dozen women and men, and not a single actual idea between them more complex than blind dogma on whatever topic came up, from the second amendment to civil rights to the future of the environment. None had any concrete plans for anything more than getting elected so they, too, could spend their days voting no and pandering to the folks back home without accomplishing anything.

Two weeks earlier, Riley had asked Ryan why he kept doing the work on Flannery's behalf and now, sitting in the middle of California's Inland Empire with an admittedly delicious steak and utterly tasteless company, he found himself struggling for an answer. Every evening felt like another echo of the Comstock campaign, a constant slog through soul-sucking muck with no clear end in sight. Even worse, Ryan had been working without contact from the man himself. Ryan had been able to report to Flannery directly in the first two weeks back at work, but since that time had found himself trying to work around Afolayan and chief of staff O'Hanlon, both of whom were running interference for the candidate as if Ryan were a newcomer and not the person who'd helped launched Flannery into Washington in the first place.

"Knowing what's right doesn't mean much unless you do what's right," Ryan said softly as he looked at the blue-and-buff-clad soldiers climbing up the hill, the American flag prominent in the foreground. Roosevelt had said the words more than a century earlier and always had tried to match his own actions to the statement. Maybe what Flannery wanted to accomplish in the long run would be what was right, Ryan thought sadly. But in the short term, continuing to bring an air of credibility to the majority of erstwhile congressmen he had met so far was wrong, at least for him.

As he looked at the painting he realized this battle, this campaign, was no longer his, no more so than the journey those boats he had watched heading for open water was his either. Ryan made his decision in that instant. He had reached campaign's end for the final time.

He excused himself to go to the restroom but detoured when he saw the lead server for his dinner. "Close the tab," he said hurriedly, handing over his credit card.

"Is there anything wrong, sir?"

"Nothing that won't be remedied shortly. Just bring the slip up front and I'll sign it there."

"What should I tell your guests?"

Ryan's mouth tugged up at the corners as he thought of Maggie, the battle to win back her heart the only one worth waging. "Only that I had somewhere else I needed to be."

CHAPTER THIRTY-THREE

Ryan handed the surprised valet a twenty, lifted his suitcase into the trunk himself and hurried to settle into the driver's seat, then took a deep breath to calm his nerves. All he could think of was Maggie and the ocean. There was nothing he could do about her at eleven o'clock at night with Del Mar more than two hours away, but he could get to the water just by driving west. He did just that, skipping the interstate and the billion lanes of ever-present traffic and glowing billboards and congestion and everything else he was in no mood to handle and instead turning onto Highway 60 west toward Los Angeles. This highway was only a couple of lanes smaller but was different, at least to him, and that was enough.

Signs for obscure places named Rubidoux and Glen Cove and the better-known Chino and Diamond Bar went past Ryan in a blur, all adding up in his mind to little more than another step closer to the water. He stopped at a gas station in Whittier and for the first time opened the navigation app on his phone to find the nearest beach. Dockweiler Beach was at the top of his list and according to the map looked almost close enough to Los Angeles International Airport to reach up and touch a plane taking off. East of Los Angeles, his GPS told him to switch to the 710 Freeway heading south. Soon, darkness opened up on the horizon in front of him as he approached the beach itself while planes roared overhead at regular intervals. To his left was a water reclamation plant and to the right was a small, empty hill positioned just off the western corner of the runway with vacant land covered in scrub beyond to the north. He slowed as the traffic light turned amber and then red in front of him.

Ryan rolled down his window, but the wind carried a stronger scent of jet fuel than ocean spray, and he quickly rolled the window back up. Discouraged, he was about to look for another beach when he looked up at the street sign in front of him—Vista Del Mar. "No fucking way," he said. The light turned green and, as he turned left onto Vista Del Mar, Ryan laughed for what felt like the first time in weeks. He opened all the windows in his rental car and a combination of the strong, cold breeze off the water and the air being pulled into the car rushed through his hair, whipping his face and leaving his cheeks red and nose running from the chill. Driving south, the duality continued, the open ocean on the car's right side and an acres-large oil refining plant on his left. Ryan closed the windows and continued driving, wondering fancifully if Vista Del Mar—view of the sea—could carry him all the way back to Maggie.

Vista Del Mar turned into Highland Avenue near El Segundo and curved east away from the ocean for a block. Industrial gave way to residential and then retail housed in dozens of separate buildings spread on both sides of the road. He slowed as he the light turned red at the intersection of Manhattan Beach Boulevard and Highland and stopped next to a ubiquitous Starbucks. Across the street, diners huddled under heat lamps on the patio of a restaurant called The Kettle, whose neon sign proclaimed it would be open all night. Ryan felt the slightest rumble in his stomach after the drive, but food could wait. He eased into the intersection when the light changed and looked to his right. Manhattan Beach Pier glowed under paired globular street lamps, stretching out just less than a quarter-mile into the ocean. Ryan jerked the wheel to the right, crossing into the empty opposite lanes before moving quickly back onto the right side of the road. He turned left when he reached the Strand, away from the lights and lingering visitors to the pier itself, and parked in an empty metered spot located less than a foot before the asphalt street gave way to sand.

Ryan shut off the engine, opened the driver-side door and pivoted so he was sitting half out of the car. He kicked off his shoes, reached down to take off his socks as well, then got up and tossed them in the trunk. No sense ruining a $300 pair of dress shoes. He stood, locked the car, crossed the bike path separating the street from the beach and started walking across the sand. He had to maneuver around a handful of still-hanging volleyball nets as he drifted further away from the pier and toward a long line of three-story beach houses lining the sand. A few feet from the edge of the surf he paused, realizing that simply staring at the water wasn't going to be sufficient. Ryan glanced around to see if anyone was watching before unbuttoning his shirt and dropping it to the sand. He placed one foot on the shirt to make sure it wouldn't blow away, then unfastened his watch and slid it into a pocket of his slacks before unbuttoning and unzipping his pants and dropping them atop the shirt.

Down to only a plain white undershirt and navy blue boxer-briefs, Ryan walked the few feet to the water and stopped. He braced himself for the cold as he stepped onto the saturated sand ahead of a small breaker crashing home, and the Pacific Ocean rewarded him with an icy bath around his feet and calves. He let the cold register and moved forward again, progressing confidently into the surf. Only when he was waist deep did he turn back toward the shore and his abandoned wallet and watch, but the area around him was empty save for a handful of beach walkers moving closer to the bike path along the line of houses. Ryan turned to his right and stared southeast along the water line and thought of the beach house he had rented and that night in the water, looking back this direction toward Los Angeles. There was the faintest glow on the horizon and he imagined it was San Diego, though the light bleeding from that city toward the dark water was a fraction of what came from Los Angeles.

Ryan continued watching the horizon to the south and wondered, not for the first time, what Maggie was doing. She could be out enjoying cocktails with Liz. She could be out on a date with someone else, he grudgingly conceded, hoping it were not true. No, his mind's eye instead thought of her sitting on a lounge in her backyard. A glass of chardonnay sat on the small table next to her, and she sat under a light blanket with a book in her lap. Selfishly he imagined her thinking of him as she read and sipped her wine, though he knew he had no right to expect such a thing.

He had left her. Knowing full well that he was deeply in love with her, that in her own way she had helped piece his life back together and place it on a better, happier path. Knowing that leaving, the one thing she had feared most, would shatter her heart. And still believing that he would be able to waltz back to Del Mar after the few months working on Flannery's campaign and pick back up where they'd left off, as if he hadn't chosen politics over her in the first place. Stupid did not begin to do justice to what he'd done.

Ryan had more meetings scheduled the following day. Meetings with yet more potential backers and donors. Meetings washed down with a glass or two of scotch because the old ways never changed. Meetings that all would follow the exact same trajectory. Meetings that would be followed the next day by more of the same, over and over, with only the names and locations changing.

"Or I can just chuck it all," he said to himself, giving voice to the feeling that had been growing within him for the past two weeks. Doing so would be the end of his work with Flannery, if not his career itself. No one would hire a consultant who simply quit a campaign without notice. It was career suicide. But, he thought, it would give him his own life back in return. He would find a way to make amends with Maggie, no matter how long it took—and even if she never took him back, his penance would be seeing her and knowing he let the best thing that ever had happened to him walk away. No. That he had pushed away the best thing that ever happened to him. That decision was his to own.

He started walking out of the water, shivering from the water and the cool marine air on the beach, gathered up his clothes and walked back to his car. He popped the trunk, pulled dry clothes out of a suitcase and changed there in the parking lot, hoping no one noticed his bare ass as he quickly slid out of the wet boxers and into a warm, dry pair before slipping on a new white undershirt, the shorts he wore to lounge around his hotel room and a pair of flip-flops he had bought in Del Mar the day before he saw Maggie for the first time. He glanced to the side at his highly polished black dress shoes, the ones he was determined to save from the sand, and smiled. "I'm never going to wear you fuckers again," he said before closing the trunk and remote-starting the car. A few minutes later he was sitting inside The Kettle, ordering buffalo tenders and the apple walnut bleu cheese salad and wondering what he would say to Maggie tomorrow after driving the almost two hours south to Del Mar tonight.

Regaining her love and her trust. That was the only campaign Ryan had any interest in directing anymore.

Ryan opened up the text messages on his phone and typed out a pair of quick notes, one to Riley and the other to Flannery, then turned off his phone. No amount of huffing or puffing from the would-be presidential nominee was going to change Ryan's mind.

***

The next night, Maggie sat on the deck outside her bedroom, watching the last rays of the sun set below the horizon. She had taught two classes that day, only occasionally losing focus as memories of her dream came back unbidden. Liz had invited her to dinner but Maggie declined, instead wanting to return home and think more about what she had dreamed the night before. With luck, maybe she could find her way back to that beach of her mind once again to try and get more answers. She was imagining the wispy swirls of the fog on the horizon when a figure started walking up her street from her left, dressed in khaki slacks with a dark blue polo shirt tucked neatly in the waist. She stared dumbfounded as she watched Ryan approaching the stairs leading to her front door.

"That," he said, "is absolutely the most beautiful view I've seen in many weeks." When she didn't respond he added, "I was referring to you. Just in case the subtlety was too..."

"Subtle," she finished. "What are you doing here, Ryan?"

"At the moment? Looking up at you and wondering what kind of fool could walk away from a woman like this."

"If anyone would know, you would," she said reflexively. She was almost surprised by the iciness of her tone. "You didn't call."

"I did. You didn't answer."

"Not then," she said. "But that didn't mean to stop trying."

"I didn't think you wanted to be bothered."

"Not initially, but after a couple of weeks? A call would have been nice."

He nodded in admission of his error. "May I come up so we can talk?"

"No," she said quickly. What will you do when he finds his way?

"Oh," he said, suddenly looking at his feet as he debated his next step. Bruce's words echoing in her mind, she threw him a lifeline. "I prefer you do your explaining at a distance."

"Fair enough." Her driveway was at street level with the rest of the house and front yard above and to the left, and Ryan leaned against one of the driveway's side walls.

"Again, Ryan," she said, "what are you doing here?"

"This is where I belong," he said. "Those first couple of weeks away, I was happy to be back in the game. You can't understand how addicting the adrenaline rush of a campaign can be unless you've experienced it firsthand, and once I had that brief taste—"

"You were hooked once again."

"I was. Best of all, there was no negative feedback from my body, no cause to believe I couldn't operate in those conditions. It felt like all I had needed was a prolonged hiatus."

"I'm happy to hear you didn't have any heart issues, Ryan."

"Oh," he said, "but I did. That became apparent in the next two weeks, when I realized my heart wasn't in the work as it once had been. I mean, the adrenaline was addicting, but I had more and more trouble reconciling the dissonance between what is considered important inside that campaign bubble, and the real world that we theoretically were attempting to effect. It was like watching a really bad action movie."

"Explain."

"Years ago I went to see this one movie. It had all you could ask for—explosions, star power, chase scenes, the whole nine yards. Of course it was entirely over the top because over the top is a prerequisite of any action movie. Except I couldn't buy into it. For whatever reason, there wasn't a single moment

J.P. Dalton

where anything seemed even remotely plausible enough for me to give the movie a pass. So I spent two hours eating popcorn, shaking my head and rolling my eyes."

"Why didn't you just leave?"

"That should be obvious," Ryan said. "My date was smoking hot and she was enjoying the movie."

Maggie shook her head and laughed. "Typical."

"Like no man ever has done the same to remain in your company," he said. "Which reminds me, may I come up now?"

"Not yet. Tell me how you went from a bad action movie to my driveway."

"That's easy. The more I struggled to buy into the work, the more I found myself dreaming of the ocean. It started at night in my sleep but soon became a recurring daydream. I pictured myself standing in the surf, feeling the push and pull of the waves, the water crashing onto the sand and how insistent the withdrawing water would be depending on time and tide. Other times I would see myself sitting on the deck of that rental house, eyes closed, listening to the sound people try to imitate in their bedrooms through clock radios and the like."

"I see."

"No, you don't, Maggie. In truth, it was almost impossible to envision myself alone in these scenarios. I had spent a wonderful couple of months with the most remarkable woman I'd ever met before I left and, inevitably, she was with me in all of these thoughts. But as much as I wanted to do it, I knew I couldn't return if she was the sole reason."

Maggie stood for the first time and leaned on the balcony railing. "Why?" she asked quietly.

"Because," Ryan said, stepping forward until he was directly below her, "it wasn't enough that to me she was the song you hear that you neither can get out of your head nor truly wish to; the cinnamon aftertaste after the hard candy is gone."

"Pretty words," she said.

"But true. But the point is, she wouldn't want me to come back only for her."

"Why?" she asked a second time.

"One of the most remarkable gifts she gave me was the ability to live in and for the moment. I came to realize it was the key to finding some sense of inner peace without relying on external stimuli, whether it be the adrenaline rush or the butterflies felt at the touch of the right woman. I knew that if I returned before knowing for certain I was coming back to the coast for myself and only myself, some small part of me would resent her for my leaving, even knowing it was the right thing to do. And, knowing her, she would sense that small piece of my psyche no matter how well it was buried and feel guilty for it."

"How would this woman be able to do such a thing?"

"Because she sees everything about me," he said, his voice cracking. He took a deep breath to steady himself. "Not right through me like I was transparent, though I just might be. But, somehow, when she looks at me I feel almost naked before her, and I can't keep secrets from her any more than I could keep a secret from myself. The craziest thing is, despite all the work I've always done to shield myself behind a certain persona, I love her for it. She makes me mortal, flawed yet sufficient, naked yet clothed in love, undeserving yet grateful."

Maggie looked down at Ryan as tears ran down her cheeks. "Ryan," she said.

"Yes, my love?" he responded, his voice fully choked with emotion.

"Get upstairs. Now."

Ryan used his key to open the front door and rushed upstairs to her bedroom, where she met him halfway across and pressed herself against him as he enveloped her in his arms, reveling in the lavender scent of her shampoo. She shuddered once as she cried, but suddenly pushed herself away.

"You made me feel like I had no place in your life, Ryan," she said, suddenly angry. "Do you understand how that makes a person feel?"

"Maggie...baby...there always has been a place for you, even before I ever met you. But I needed to make sure there was no place in our life for my old life."

"And what happens if the phone rings again?"

"Then we decide what to do, together. And if an offer fits into the life we are building, it fits. If not, I say no."

"Let the universe decide."

He stepped back toward her and she placed her chin on his chest, looking up toward him. "It has worked well enough so far, when I let it."

"Do you know what the universe is suggesting now?" she asked, infusing her voice with a low purr. He responded by lifting her and gently placing her back on the bed. "I think I can figure it out," he said, reaching to his right to turn out the lamp on her nightstand before lying down next to her.

EPILOGUE

George Flannery strode confidently from the wings to the podium center stage at an auditorium in New Hampshire, backed by a trio of American flags—enough to look patriotic without appearing patronizing. Flannery smiled broadly as he soaked in the applause from supporters, his wife and two of his children behind him looking proud as they waved to familiar faces in the crowd of volunteers. Campaign signs rocked this way and that in front of the podium and balloons, recently dropped from the ceiling, flitted into and out of frame as they were propelled by the jubilant crowd. Not only had Flannery secured a victory that, at times, had seemed impossible, but he did so far earlier in the evening than anyone in the campaign could have hoped for. Now was the time for a victory lap, a show of that odd but necessary mix of swagger and humility and a call for focus since this was but one primary. That speech, undoubtedly, would have been written by Riley, who herself was on the fringes of the celebration on stage.

"Do you want to come see this?" Maggie asked.

"Maybe for a minute," Ryan said, walking from the mirror he had been standing in front of to his wife, who stood in front of a large flat-screen television turned to cable news. He instinctively placed his hand on her ever-widening stomach and was greeted with a kick from his soon-to-be-born daughter. "She seems to enjoy the show."

"Don't get too excited," Maggie said. "She does the same thing while I'm watching RuPaul."

"Point taken," he said.

There had been a time when Ryan would have done virtually anything to be standing where Riley now stood, waiting to hear Flannery read the words that Ryan had written for him. Even now, having trained Riley for all these years, he could predict what Flannery would say word for word. "Always know that there's a formula to this, Riley," he would tell her, then run down the essential elements, allowing for areas where the candidate could change the wording to fit their style and how best to reverse those changes as innocuously as possible. Manage the candidate, then the campaign.

This was one of the moments Ryan imagined as the pinnacle of his career, the first step in the journey to the marble-coated world of Washington, DC. Instead, he was standing in the music room at Del Mar Heights Elementary School ahead of a school board candidate meet-and-greet, nearly 2,700 miles away from the bright lights and signs and balloons and all the trappings of politics at the highest level. Within a month of his return to Del Mar, Maggie had decided to move into the house on the beach he had purchased, and two months later they were married in a small ceremony on the sand in front of Poseidon, Liz serving as Maggie's maid-of-honor and Riley as Ryan's best man. Or person.

Children had not been in the discussion but, as Ryan had come to learn, the universe has its own ways. Ryan had joked that he could set his watch by her time of the month so, when she was just a day late, he knew immediately what had happened. Maggie was less ready to embrace the change, having lost a child all those years ago in the accident. A second day passed, then a third. Ryan was buzzing around her like a hummingbird, not overtly referencing the unspoken reality but still hovering near to make sure she had all she needed. Now and then he would slip behind her, wrap his arms around her body and rest one hand just on her abdomen, and the warmth of his touch would seep into her. On day four she consented to purchasing a home pregnancy test which, of course, came up positive. She looked at him with a mix of happiness and fear, and he responded by playing Jimmy Cliff's "I Can See Clearly Now" on his phone, pulling her close and spinning her as they danced together and their tears flowed equally. Then he carried her upstairs and they made love slowly, tenderly, with him finishing and then sliding down her body and laying his head atop her navel as if listening for a heartbeat still too small to hear, but grinning widely as if he could.

A week later they were inside an obstetrician's office. Maggie lay on the bed covered with sterile paper and raised her shirt to her chest as the doctor squirted gooey aquamarine ultrasound on the mom-to-be's stomach. She gently pressed the transducer against Maggie's stomach and maneuvered right and left, the black and white images on the ultrasound monitor a blur until she found what she was looking for. Suddenly the jolting movement ceased and a large, dark void appeared in the center of the screen. Inside that void were two white spots, one the apparent size and shape of a peanut, and inside that peanut was a subtle rhythmic flicker.

"Say hello to your baby," the doctor said and tears flowed freely from both mother and father, hers a mix of joy for the moment and apprehension about everything that could happen over the next seven-plus months, his from the realization that love for another person he never had imagined possible now had helped create another peanut-sized human he already could not love more.

"Look at what we did," he said, leaning in to kiss Maggie on the forehead, and she could do no more than nod.

Knowing how anxious she was given the past, Ryan did everything he could to make her more comfortable and keep her widely varying emotions pointed more toward the positive. The roses still appeared daily at her studio, and soon he added a once-a-week ice cream run. She didn't finish the pints at first, causing a bit of a collection to grow within the freezer, but as the pregnancy advanced the ice cream disappeared in a flurry of cravings. Maggie continued teaching classes through her first trimester, then turned everything over to full-time backup she had hired after a three-minute interview. With yoga instructors, she explained to Ryan, either the aura and the energy was right or it wasn't.

That same concept applied to her locating a prenatal yoga class, a specialty unto itself and once she had studiously avoided after the accident. With the help of her instructor, she shifted from poses on the ground to those either leaning against a wall or with a chair in front for support. After all her years of practicing yoga, the assistance in keeping balance was a minor blow to the ego, but then the baby would kick her in the ribs as a reminder of why she had to take extra care. Not that she ever forgot. Before the pregnancy she would join Ryan for walks on the beach. Since that time, they moved to the sidewalks along Coast Boulevard where there was less chance of accidentally stepping in an unseen divot and losing her balance.

Maggie and Ryan debated whether to find out the sex of the baby, but logistics won—he wanted to be able to decorate the nursery in something other than neutral yellow or greens. They eschewed the huge gender-reveal party, instead hanging a single, pink mylar balloon on the door to her yoga studio and posting the photo on their shared social media.

Midway through Maggie's second trimester, one of the members of the Del Mar Union School District governing board announced her intention to retire ahead of the next election, opening a temporary seat to be filled in a special election. The announcement coincided with the governing board staging town hall meetings about the future of the district, including decisions on whether to close or expand existing schools. Ryan read the stories on the front page of the Del Mar Times with minimal interest until seeing a headline about a prospective candidate urging the schools to rethink their teaching of evolution versus creation.

Ryan wasn't anti-religious but believed science should be taught in science class, not religion. Something about that stance spurred his political mind. He dug further online and, with every successive article he found on every topic he could find, and as no other prospective candidates came forward, he found more and more to dislike about the only prospective candidate.

"They're all idiots," he grumbled one morning over a slice of avocado toast.

"If you're so unhappy about it," Maggie said finally, "run yourself."

"You know that's not what I do," he said.

"This is the governing board for a 4,500-student school district, Ryan," she said mockingly. "Nobody needs a consultant for this race. But if you don't think you have what it takes to be the man out front on a small campaign..."

He entered the race the next day and his schedule started to fill with small events—a school carnival here, a football game there. Through it all, he came to realize he was as content as he ever had felt, or at least would be if he could get his hands to stop shaking long enough to straighten his tie.

Maggie glanced over and saw a small line of sweat beading on Ryan's forehead. "Look at me," she directed and, as he turned to face her, she took his hands between hers and pressed them gently against his chest. "If you can handle that kind of madness," she said, gesturing toward the television, "you certainly can handle a hundred parents."

"I was the one hiding in the wings while that madness took place," he said.

"Physically, perhaps. Besides," she added with a smile, "what is it they always say about what is behind every successful man?"

Ryan gently pulled his hands free, placed them on her waist and kissed her forehead. "Well, I most certainly have the two best women standing behind me. So I should be fine."

"You will be more than fine. No one else running for a board seat has an iota of the experience that you do in the political realm and, though you are loath to admit such things, you have a warm and caring heart. You are everything we need looking out for our children."

"And if I fail?"

"Then you can look out for our children and spend the next two years making the board miserable when they do something you don't like."

Polite applause drifted in from down the hall, and a runner knocked on the door to retrieve Ryan from the wings. He thanked the teenager who was volunteering in that role for the evening, kissed Maggie on the forehead and took her hand to walk to the stage. Just before he stepped out from behind the curtain, he turned back toward his wife.

"How the hell did I get here, Maggie?"

She leaned up and kissed him gently. "Your heart, Ryan. It knew where you belonged. You just had to listen."

Author's Note

"Why don't you write a love story?"

My wife, Kathie, and I were sitting at lunch one day as I was lamenting my lack of progress on a different novel. Like every reporter I knew, I also felt there was a potential novelist buried deep within me. In truth, the transition from objective reporting to the unlimited universe of fiction is far more difficult than I imagined. It is one thing to write about something happening in front of you rather than creating scenes from whole cloth.

Since my other nascent book was going nowhere, I took her up on the challenge. The result is what you see here.

There are many people to thank for their support—friends and family who have provided nothing but encouragement as this process has gone on, those on social media who followed and put up with my updated word counts, the guidance I received from other authors in different social media groups who already have paved this path and shared their wisdom, even my youngest daughter who bought me an "Ask Me About My Book" coffee cup that I keep prominently displayed on my desk.

Additional thanks are due to those friends who read early versions of different chapters and eventually the whole and shared much needed feedback. I also want to thank Stephanie

Parent, whose wondrous editing helped bring this wild beast of a manuscript under control.

But most of my appreciation and thanks are to my mother, Shelly, who told a stubborn ninth grader to close his eyes and imagine the colors of the cars on the imaginary roller coaster that was the centerpiece of a homework assignment, and, again, Kathie. There would be no novel had she not pushed me in this direction, endured the moments I would take out my phone to write a few sentences when an idea struck and, most of all, kept telling me there was a good story here even when I doubted it. She has shown me love and brought me happiness I, frankly, never thought possible.

About the Author

J.P. Dalton has been writing professionally since he was 16 years old and has had bylines in more than two dozen newspapers, magazines and online outlets. He lives in the Phoenix area with his wife and a menagerie of dogs, though they all constantly dream of the ocean. This is his debut novel.